Steven Zeeland

Sailors and Sexual Identity: Crossing the Line Between "Straight" and "Gay" in the U.S. Navy

Pre-publication REVIEWS, COMMENTARIES, EVALUATIONS . . .

"**T**his new work by the author of *Barrack Buddies and Soldier Lovers* offers tantalizing vignettes and intriguing revelations. Zeeland describes the 'sea bitch,' homoerotic initiation rituals, Navy job specialties which are filled with gays, the eroticism of tattooing, and the rivalry between sailors and Marines which persists even when they get together in bed. . . . For all who want to understand the full story about gays in the military, this extremely well-written and scintillating book is an essential beginning."

William A. Percy, PhD
Professor of History,
University of Massachusetts

More pre-publication
REVIEWS, COMMENTARIES, EVALUATIONS . . .

"**A** startling and excellent book . . . . In the midst of all the debauchery there are glimpses of that sad, romantic quality that all sailors have–that otherness that comes because their calling makes them into distant objects of desire. They are the ones who go away."

Quentin Crisp

"**Z** eeland supplies what's been missing from the gays-in-the-military brouhaha. He states his primary theme with great lucidity: that 'gay' is not a relevant term when it comes to military life, and 'straight' is laughable."

Scott O'Hara
Editor & Publisher,
STEAM Magazine

"**A** remarkable achievement . . . the first piece of solid research to provide a coherent description of the sexually charged atmosphere aboard ships of the U.S. Navy. Sexual flexibility is a regular feature of naval life and Zeeland's sailors learned early in their careers that the aphorism 'It's only queer when you're tied to the pier' is more than a casual stab at nautical humor."

B.R. Burg, PhD
Author, *Sodomy and the Pirate Tradition*

The Harrington Park Press
An Imprint of The Haworth Press, Inc.

Sailors and Sexual Identity
Crossing the Line
Between "Straight" and "Gay"
in the U.S. Navy

HAWORTH Gay and Lesbian Studies
John P. De Cecco, PhD
Editor in Chief

Sailors and Sexual Identity
Crossing the Line
Between "Straight"and "Gay"
in the U.S. Navy

Steven Zeeland

Harrington Park Press
An Imprint of The Haworth Press, Inc.
New York • London • Norwood (Australia)

Published by

Harrington Park Press, an imprint of The Haworth Press, Inc., 10 Alice Street, Binghamton, NY 13904-1580

Library of Congress Cataloging-in-Publication Data

Zeeland, Steven.
    Sailors and sexual identity : crossing the line between "straight" and "gay" in the U.S. Navy / Steven Zeeland.
       p. cm.
    Includes bibliographical references.
    ISBN 1-56023-850-X (alk. paper).
    1. United States. Navy–Gays. 2. Gays–United States–Identity. I. Title
VB324.G38Z44   1994
359'.008'6642–dc20
                                                94-28996
                                                 CIP

For Troy

ABOUT THE AUTHOR

Steven Zeeland is the author of *Barrack Buddies and Soldier Lovers: Dialogues with Gay Young Men in the U.S. Military* (Harrington Park Press, 1993). He attended the University of Michigan at Ann Arbor and is a Research Associate at the Center for Research and Education in Sexuality (CERES) at San Francisco State University.

CONTENTS

The subtitle of this book contains a reference to the U.S. Navy "Crossing the Line" tradition, a time-honored, officially sanctioned initiation ceremony in which sailors traversing the equator for the first time may experience cross-dressing, sadomasochistic rituals, and simulated anal and oral sex. This is but one of the illustrations provided by the sailors in this book of the flexible boundary between what is "straight" and "gay" in navy life.

Foreword

The national debate over allowing homosexuals to serve in the nation's armed forces led to what the Clinton administration dubbed a "compromise," a policy that has been tagged as "don't ask, don't tell." There is hardly anything new about the policy except that the government is now forbidden from asking new recruits if they prefer or ever have had sex with someone of their own gender. Only a few brave souls already in the military had ever freely "told" about their same-gender preferences and, if they did, the revelation was usually followed by the firm (and astonishing) declaration that what they "desired" they still never "pursued" or, *horrible dictu*, actually tasted.

United States military policy past and present has been based on the tacit assumption that there are real *homosexuals*, a small minority species of the human race clearly distinguishable from *heterosexuals*, also very real, who, thank God, make up the vast majority of the human race and thereby guarantee its future survival. At another level, somewhere just below full consciousness (although it did get expressed occasionally during the recent national debate), there is the assumption that homosexuals are attracted to heterosexuals and will lust after and uncontrollably pursue them given the limitless opportunities provided by their showering, dressing, and sleeping together. This latter assumption rather awkwardly dovetails with a further belief, that homosexual men are really women equipped with penises and that homosexual women are men who have vaginas. Apparently, the homosexual male, despite the cross-sexed temperament and characteristics stereotypically assigned to him, retains the predatory sexual instinct of heterosexual males and therefore cannot be trusted with them in the barracks or the ship's hold. The possibility that heterosexuals might hanker after homosexuals, of course, is relegated to the deepest recesses of the unconscious. It is clear that military policy is hardly designed to protect homosexuals but it does intend to preserve what Steven Zeeland calls "heterosexual purity."

Anyone who watches movies that involve cross-dressing and observes the changing styles of female and male dress and adornment, must have learned by now that whatever may be the underlying female or male physical anatomy, it is the presentation of self with the endless feminine and masculine possibilities of emphasis and nuance that provide the basis for erotic attraction. We all wear the drag that we think best markets our bodies and promises the most rewarding erotic encounters. If the issue is one of gender rather than biological sex, then the question arises of who are the "homosexuals" for whom the policy was formulated to say nothing of the putative "heterosexuals" whom presumably it is designed to keep virginal, that is, free of homosexual taint.

Over the past 150 years the dichotomizing of sexual preferences into heterosexual and homosexual has been the result of political efforts to win recognition and acceptance of homosexuality by its practitioners and of their efforts to develop electorates that could win protection under the law and build communities where they could live free of the smugness and insensitivity of those who ignored them and the intolerance and rejection of those who were aware of them. The *gay* man was the person who made something of his homosexuality. Unwittingly it is that very dichotomy, which has been the basis for the gay liberation movement in its various avatars, that now provides the network of assumptions upon which military policy hostile to homosexuality has been and continues to be based.

Mr. Zeeland, in his frank and always compassionate interviews with sailors, reveals what military authorities and perhaps all of us know at some unacknowledged level of consciousness: that our erotic attractions to others can easily overflow the boundaries of gender. It should therefore not be surprising to discover that men, usually more straightjacketed by gender role than women, when they have the opportunity to live, work, and play together in intimate circumstance afforded by the military, should discover that erotic attraction and experience leads them to cross gender boundaries that they once considered sacred and inviolable and that they can enjoy having sex with other men.

John P. De Cecco, PhD
San Francisco, California

Prologue: "Are You in the Navy?"

I have never been in the military. My true qualification to author this book is the special attraction I feel toward military men, and the love, sex, and friendship I have known as a result.

I have several theories as to how this orientation came about. My current favorite involves an incident that occurred on my sixth birthday. My mother organized a party and invited other boys from my first grade class. One of the gifts I received was a GI Joe doll. This was during the Vietnam War, and my mother did not believe war toys were appropriate for children. The GI Joe doll was stowed in the closet. And it may be that I have been trying to get that little GI out of the closet ever since.

Twenty-five years later I am standing at the Pacific Ocean, having arrived in San Francisco yesterday from Frankfurt, Germany. I have ridden the bus from Castro to Haight and walked all the way through Golden Gate Park. It was sunny as I passed the Japanese Tea Garden, but by the time I got to the Dutch Windmill fog was blowing wildly overhead. I like the fog. I like the ocean. I stand a long time staring and shivering. A ship appears on the horizon. It's a U.S. Navy destroyer heading toward the Golden Gate. I feel excitement. I laugh at the idea: A sailor is about to step into my life.

Until now I have known only soldiers. While living in Germany I produced a manuscript on the subject that will become my first published book, *Barrack Buddies and Soldier Lovers.* I have returned to the United States expecting that I will be forced to eroticize civilians. San Francisco's Army base, The Presidio, is shutting down. Wandering among its weathered and empty wooden barracks I unexpectedly encounter a rare GI in camouflage pushing a broom over a sidewalk. We exchange timid smiles; I walk on. . . . Dusty silence. The Presidio is a place where men have been.

It is a feeling I encounter everywhere in the city. In a house off Folsom Street, once famous for its leather bars, my roommate, a person with AIDS, regales me with stories from the time before. I listen, again and again, until his monologues become a loop. I know he needs to talk but I close the door. He storms in, complaining that I have "moved in physically but not spiritually." I coldly demur that I still feel more German than Californian. He accuses me of being terrified of HIV. I am, but take up his challenge and get tested. Two weeks of torturous uncertainty, then: negative. I jump up and down on the street in front of the South of Market clinic and am actually so scurrilous as to yell, "I sucked all those GI dicks and got away with it!" But some of those soldiers did not. Some of them have it. And by the time I get home my joy is gone, and I wonder if my exclamation will come back to haunt me.

When my friend Bart picked me up at the airport, he carried a hand-lettered sign that said "Welcome to Homotown." We kissed, and he took me to his car, where a discarded jockstrap found on the street hung from his rearview mirror. His car stereo played Tony Bennett and the Revolting Cocks' "Beers, Steers, and Queers" while he drove me to the nightclubs End Up and Pulse, and to the sex club Night Gallery. But in San Francisco, queers don't need to seek out dirty dark spaces to find each other. We meet in the Muni, in the Safeway, anywhere we want.

I seek out a last surviving dirty dark space. The FBI has closed the Polk Street video arcades, so I zero in on a peep show on Kearny just around the corner from City Lights Books. (I divine its smutty presence when Bart takes me to North Beach for a Queer Nation protest of the movie *Basic Instinct*.) Faded Chinese letters on the building's exterior . . . a filthy indifferent European attendant watching a black and white TV . . . an Asian and an African American man I quickly identify as military chasers . . . a fading porn star who shows me his asshole through a glory hole. Two sailors tumble in for a few moments then back out onto Broadway. I follow, lose them, consider the Transamerica building and Coit Tower: What sort of life might I forge against this backdrop? I want to think up my own San Francisco and forget Armisted Maupin.

A parade is held to welcome returning Gulf War veterans. Protesters in black are almost as numerous as celebrants. Lumps in my throat mix; I identify with the soldiers but share a political sensibility with the mob. I take a snapshot of a woman who carries a sign:

"We love our gay and lesbian troops." She tells me, "I thought I was the only one!"

But I insist on being alone and straggle on to celebrate my 31st birthday in the North Beach peep show because it is the closest thing to the Frankfurt red light district and the farthest thing from my parent's Christian fundamentalist church in Grand Rapids, Michigan.

The sailor has a goofy scared smile and wears a black leather jacket with a hand-painted image on the back of a man blowing his brains out. We exchange dance steps around the perimeter of the peep show's museum 8 mm booths. An ancient grinning Chinese gestures to me conspiratorially: "He likes you!" I nod, circle, and invite the sailor to step into a booth. He balks. I smile. He asks: "Are you in the Navy?"

This book starts at that moment.

Thinking of Troy as a sailor excited me but very soon he became just Troy. He was probably the least military of all my military men. Troy did not even own a complete Navy dress uniform, and he once asked me to help square away his ribbons with the aid of the *Bluejackets* enlisted men's manual I bought to research this book. His hair was longer than Navy regulations allowed, and his speech, walk, and overall demeanor defied both military and gay stereotypes. (These of course were things I especially liked about him.)

When I first met Troy he was having an affair with a Navy chief petty officer's wife. They had had a fight, and he had gone out to look for trouble. He found me in a spot where he, having gone there first with a sailor buddy, on returning another time alone was somewhat forcibly subjected to the attentions of an aggressive cruiser who had burst open his locked video booth door and announced: "I'm here to give you a blowjob!" Troy had been frightened, but the experience did open other doors for him. When we met, Troy thought of himself as straight. I told him he could be bisexual, or just Troy. He now calls himself gay.

I climbed into his car and he drove me to the beach by the Dutch windmill.

Almost all of my year in San Francisco was spent with my sailor: careening over the Bay Bridge to Alameda and back in his little

Japanese car, eating at cheap Chinese restaurants, holding him in the loft bed of the house off Folsom Street. When the time came that he told me he was being transferred to a remote duty station on Whidbey Island, Washington, I told him I would follow.

* * *

I am again staring seaward by a windmill, this time in Oak Harbor, Washington. The town, I learn, was settled by Dutch immigrants arriving at the turn of the century, not directly from the Netherlands, but via Zeeland, Michigan. The windmill is a nonfunctional decoration. I muse grimly that my coming here is the fulfillment of some terrible destiny.

Oak Harbor is a foul pustule on the clean pretty face of Whidbey Island. Snowcapped mountains—Rainier, the Cascades, and the Olympics—ring the horizons; Douglas firs scent the fresh Northwest air; chill salmon waters of Puget Sound slap the belly of the Mukilteo ferry that brought us here . . . to the flat, tree-stripped lawns of City Beach in Oak Harbor thoughtfully adjoining the municipal sewage treatment center, astride a dull tidal basin resembling a stagnant inland lake, in a sterile, sober excised suburbia hell of 17,000 Navy dependent souls where the most meaningful expression of human activity is the Kmart. Troy had worried that I would not be happy here—but I had only waved away his concerns with a silencing hand and selected "Laura Palmer's Theme" from the *Twin Peaks* soundtrack on his CD car stereo. Now I almost wish I was wrapped in Laura's plastic death shroud, washed ashore beneath the 200-foot high Deception Pass bridge (a *must* for suicides from all over the Pacific Northwest), covered, perhaps, with the foot-long black slugs I have seen oozing about there after the rain. (The slugs, I learn, are not indigenous, but of a species introduced from the Netherlands.)

Desperate to identify some favorable omen that will keep me from turning right back around for San Francisco, I walk into 7-Eleven to appropriate some Red Hook ale and spy a magazine rack displaying *Navy Times.* On its cover is a handsome shorthaired sailor with a Dutch surname like mine and the headline FIGHTING THE GAY BAN. My spirits buoy. I buy this, my first copy of *Navy Times,* and install it as a declaration of purpose on the nightstand of

Troy's and my room at the Fat Trout Motel: I'm going to write a book about queer sailors.

But where will I find any? Certainly not through Troy who, lascivious grin and flashing eyes notwithstanding, is about as straight acting and looking as they come and never connects with anyone he works with. He bars me from attending any of his squadron barbecues, fearing I will compromise him, but, muttering vague warnings, does sometimes condescend to let me hang out at the base while he works. I prowl Naval Air Station Whidbey Island for a homosexual underground, in vain. Each time I end up sitting idly at the base McDonald's, watching pilots in flight suits eat, waiting for Troy's digital pager, set on vibrate, to go off in my pocket.

And so I give up on the base and adopt a daily routine whereby every morning I pack my lover's lunch, walk to the library to read the Seattle papers and to the post office to check our box, and then come here—to the windmill, the waterfront, and the City Beach men's room. It is the only gay meeting place for 50 miles.

Navy EA6B Prowler jets flange overhead. (This is, as a base entrance billboard reminds us all, "The Sound of Freedom.") I sit on a driftwood log that points cannon-like at the Seaplane base and watch ravens pick mussels from the shoal. They wheel skyward, let their prey fall and crack open onto the basketball court, and swoop down to eat the exposed meat.

I study their technique and look about me speculatively. But I see no one except the same to my eyes unattractive men "of a certain age" who camp out in their cars and pickup trucks every day at this time, now and again tromping over to the men's room in hopes that someone—anyone—will follow. I do not, and return my nose to Brian Pronger's *The Arena of Masculinity* (which contains a vignette about a Canadian football team ritual involving olives placed in foreskins), Martin Duberman's *About Time* (which tells the story of Chinook Indians who make their "olives" out of acorns soaked in urine), or any other of the 50 Sno-Isle Regional Library books I use as background reading for this book (which has an olive story of its own).

A month goes by before I even recognize Rainier a hundred miles distant on the horizon, previously lost among clouds, now assigned harbinger status: obscured, introspective day; visible, outward-looking day. I try but fail to find a job. I cook dinner in our one-bedroom apartment on my dwindling savings and Troy's meager E-4 pay-check. Soon we are reduced to macaroni and cheese, grilled cheese sandwiches, and ultimately what I black-humorously call Bosnia Salad—lawn clippings with vinaigrette (or close). Troy tells me his squadronmates call him "Stimpy," after the TV cartoon character (a dopey guileless cat). I worry that I am increasingly resembling Ren (a nerve-wracked "asthma-hound" chihuahua).

Seattle is two, Vancouver two and a half hours away. We drive there on day trips when Troy does not have duty, or we visit the gay bar in Bellingham, a town I do like, an hour to the north. Twice Troy goes on deployment and leaves me alone. I wander down to a straight bar that features "velcro wall jumping" and is popular with sailors, who I consider seducing at closing time. But this I cannot do to Troy. In a noble queer attempt at campy humor I buy the 1942 edition of *The Navy Wife,* for 50¢ at Island Thrift, and read:

> You, Nancy Lee, when you became a Navy wife, accepted a definite share of responsibility for the success of your hus-band's naval career. You cannot meet this responsibility solely by bestowing upon him your love and kisses. You must have married for love; no one could be so ignorant as to marry a naval officer for money. You may, of course, have been in-fluenced in your decision by the glamour that surrounds the Navy, or by a desire for a life of travel and adventure. . . .
>
> A Navy wife should be proud of the Navy and her connec-tion with it, and never by word or deed should she cast any discredit upon it. Times will be hard and separations may be long, but she should present to the world a cheerful agreeable-ness rather than a resigned stoicism. The Navy doesn't particu-larly care for a wife who is *too obviously* carrying her load. Take life as it comes in your stride, my dear, and you'll be loved all the more for it![1]

I know she is right. But it doesn't stop me from cursing Troy, the Navy, and my existence on this island, which, I ravingly point out to anyone who will listen, is named Possession at one end and Decep-tion at the other.

Things certainly would be easier if Troy and I were able to marry.

His lowly petty officer third-class pay would be increased substantially. As his spouse, I would enjoy preferential status in obtaining on-base employment, and failing that, at least an ID card to make better use of my food stamps at the base commissary. But we do not enjoy these heterosexual privileges, and life is tougher without them.

Eventually I do make some gay sailor friends, all at City Beach. I meet Trevor, a thin handsome yeoman from Missouri who had married a woman and joined the Navy in the belief this would make him masculine and heterosexual. (It does not.) I meet his friend Larry, a hospital corpsman and nascent drag queen from Oklahoma, whose bold, some say reckless, public appearances as "Destiny" at the Oak Harbor Safeway and 7-Eleven are a source of embarrassment and worry to Trevor. I meet Renaldo, a nervous uppity yeoman from La Jolla, California who told me he joined the Navy thinking it would "help him be gay" after reading an article about sailor sex in a porn magazine. And I meet Mark, an Aviation Electronics Technician from Montana who lives in nearby Coupeville with Michael, a social worker and AIDS activist who tells me about WIGs, "Whidbey Island Gays." This social organization he helped form had, in its heyday, a roster of 300 souls—until Naval Investigative Service agents infiltrated and launched an investigation that led to the discharge of several sailors. I learn that NIS and the Oak Harbor police had also cracked down on City Beach, explaining why cruisers there are so scarce and skittish.

I interview all of these men for my book, but the eight interviews conducted on Whidbey Island seem impossibly colored by my own sense of anomie. None of them are included here.

Troy and I decide I would be happier in Seattle, but before I can get there his father is diagnosed with a terminal illness. Troy elects to get out of the Navy and move back home. I decide that if I am going to write a book about sailors I had better go to San Diego and do it right.

* * *

On my way to Southern California I stop in San Francisco. I try to get some sleep in Bart's bed, but Navy Blue Angel jets have followed me—it is "Fleet Week." Before setting out to cruise the piers

I watch the videotape he has made for me of Kenneth Anger's "Fireworks." I talk to Melvin and James, the two military chasers I met here before. I hash over ideas with my editor, John P. De Cecco, and historian Allan Bérubé. For the next year, I will live only for this book.

* * *

It is one year later, almost. I am not standing on the beach but slouching before my word processor in Hillcrest, San Diego's gay ghetto, in my bedroom at the stylish Casa de las Pulgas, a 1920s Spanish-style apartment house with a cactus garden, cats, and a fading Bohemian charm. The vertical blinds are drawn. I don't like the sun. I refuse to drive a car. And yet I have come to feel surprisingly at home in Southern California.

I have met more than 200 sailors and Marines and taped conversations with 30. The transcripts of 13 are presented here. My goal has not been to collect as many interviews as possible, but to document the lives—both sexual and military—of men who I have connected with and learned from. To this end, I have relied largely on chance meetings in various settings. My San Diego stories are told in the introductions to the interviews and in the interviews themselves.

Some have criticized the interview format of my work, suggesting that I should filter, distill, and "synthesize" these stories into a nonfiction narrative. Like Stimpy, they say "Tell me a story, Ren."

But servicemen have their *own* voices. Over the past year there has been an almost sickening glut of public talk *about* gays in the military; here, they speak for themselves. It might seem anachronistic, in an age of highly publicized coming-outs by military persons, that these men are identified only by first names, sometimes fictitious. This is not so that they may hide, but to allow them the freedom to be open in ways that service members who face the bright lights of television cameras cannot. In this and my previous book I have worked to capture the lives of men whose stories would not otherwise be told, and provide information too complex and contradictory for propagandists to bother with.

I have had to overcome certain hindrances. One is the tendency of military gays, in the light of the public debate, to want to present themselves as favorably as possible. (Obviously, as a gay male I have an interest in combating negative stereotypes of "promiscuous and predatory homosexuals." I shudder to consider the vile ways in which bits of this book might be misappropriated by antigay demagogues to further their malignant lies. However, the veneer of tolerance generated by progay propaganda is thin; the truth, I believe, might actually be more useful. It is an unsurprising reality that *all* male sailors tend to be sexually adventuresome. It is one of many areas where a hard distinguishing line between "gay" and "straight" simply does not exist.)

Another problem has to do with whatever truth there might be behind the stereotype that Southern Californians are effusive and solicitous, beautiful empty husks. Even though most sailors and Marines come from other parts of the country, few remain uninfluenced by the local culture (as indeed I too feel myself becoming increasingly Californiaized).

It is hard for me to isolate differences between sailors and soldiers independent of the contrasting milieus of my two books. In Germany, the isolation from a foreign culture brought young Americans closer and mollified sharp personal differences that here—where most military men blend in with a very relaxed one million plus civilian population—often stand in the way. The warm, tightly knit sense of community I observed between and felt with GIs in Frankfurt does not exist in the same way among sailors in San Diego. Many do speak of a similar bond they have experienced while overseas, and some say they have felt the same bond aboard ship. But I have not gone to these places with them.

My first book was an outgrowth of my social life in Frankfurt. In many ways, my social life in San Diego was built around authoring this second book. To my friends in Germany I was just Steve. To the sailors I hung out with here I was sometimes that, but I was also a published author writing about them. Gay men in the military tell me that they avoid complications by maintaining a rigid separation between their professional and personal lives. For me, as I authored this book, both were one and the same. This was sometimes too much to handle, but I have tried to make my involvement the book's greatest strength. The best interviews here, as in my last book, are with the men I grew closest to.

And I did get close with sailors and Marines. I talked with and listened to them. I slept in barracks with them. I toured bases and ships and attended graduation ceremonies with them. I went shopping, made dinner, and killed time doing nothing with them. I danced with them, got drunk with them. I pulled one out of a police car, visited another in the brig. I watched them get tattoos. I was a loyal friend to some, somewhat cold to others. I became infatuated with several, loved two or three. And if it is true that I cultivated friendships in part for textual material, it is also true that these are mostly things I would have done anyway, even had I not been writing a book.

Some of these men had political motivations for agreeing to be interviewed. Others just thought it would be fun, were flattered by my interest in them, or agreed to do it because their friends had. A couple hoped it might get them into bed with me. But the primary reason for contributing for most of the men whose interviews are included here was friendship.

This friendship did not prevent me from asking them difficult and uncomfortable questions. In general, the interviews in this book delve deeper than those in my previous book. They are also on the average longer and, in some cases, are supplemented by follow-up conversations months later. Unless otherwise noted, all interviews were recorded in my room at Casa de las Pulgas. I have transcribed the conversations myself and have edited them for length and to focus on perspectives unique to each man.

In the two and a half years since I met Troy I can say with confidence that I have come to know sailors. I cannot yet say the same for Marines. This is due in part to Marines' smaller numbers and in part to their tendency to stick together in small Marine-only bands. Although organizationally a branch of the Navy, Marines are truly a different breed, more akin to Navy SEALS or Army Special Forces than regular sailors. Marines deserve their own book. . . . But maybe they deserve to keep their secrets.

Finally, I can tell you of one difference between soldiers and sailors. Army men are periodically transferred to different parts of the world, and they sometimes go on training maneuvers, or are sent to various schools and temporary assignments. But soldiers do not move around anywhere near as much as Navy men. This is part of a sailor's excuse for being a sexual adventurer with a girl, or guy, in every port. It is an important element of his appeal, but it is also the hardest part of Navy life. A sailor is always saying goodbye to buddies and lovers.

No, I have never been in the Navy. But as I sum up this book and think about the men I have known in San Diego, I think I feel something of what a sailor feels.

I wish to thank Phil Adams, Tom Adesko, Paul Aliferis, Chris Boadt and Dennis Caldwell, Trish Brown, Jeremy Buchman, my kind and generous publisher Bill Cohen, der ebenso grosszuegige Volker Corell, my wise and caring editor, John De Cecco, Troy Dixon, "Doc," Don, Heinz Kort, Major Luke, "Mark E. Mark," Peg Marr, Melvin, T. C. Merritt, Andy Miller, Morgan, Owen, Bill Palmer, Michael Patton, Michael Putnam, Rich, Eric L. Roland, Bart Snowfleet, Colin Tolly, Tony, Phillip Torrente, Trevor, Adrian Velazquez, Rick X, and Brian Younker. I owe a very special thanks to Allan Bérubé for taking the time to point me in the right direction.

Most of all I thank the sailors and Marines who so generously gave of their time and hearts.

Steven Zeeland
San Diego

Introduction:
The Myth of Heterosexual Purity

The writer from *Newsweek* sounded bored. He was calling me, he explained, in search of a new angle on the gays in the military issue. "If that's even possible," he added doubtfully.

Indeed, in the few intervening months since Bill Clinton had been elected President his pledge to overturn the Pentagon's ban on homosexuals had become the subject of impassioned national debate and saturation level media coverage. The Joint Chiefs of Staff and Members of Congress, led by Senator Sam Nunn of the President's own Democratic party, vociferously (some would say insubordinately) resisted the Commander in Chief, parroting existing policy regulations that decried homosexuality as a threat to military discipline, good order, and morale. Christian fundamentalists and Republican right-wingers fulminated against what they called the hidden "Gay Agenda," recruiting Marine Corps officers to distribute a videotape by that title containing "partly clad homosexuals writhing on floats in a parade" intercut with "children apparently crying at the sight of what are depicted as leering gays."[1] Gay activist groups countered by presenting wholesome, handsome, sexually unthreatening gay soldiers and sailors who had served with distinction. Gay journalist Randy Shilts published *Conduct Unbecoming,* a numbing account of lives ruined by Pentagon thought police persecution, offering thorough and horrifying documentation of the lengths to which military investigators have gone to eradicate queers. Army Major Melissa Wells-Petry published rationalizations for *Exclusion,* contending that to lift the ban would countenance criminal activity because homosexuals can be relied on to engage in bizarre, illegal sexual practices unknown to heterosexuals (anal and oral sex). She was echoed by retired military leaders who argued that it is not unreasonable to exclude homosexuals for their "lifestyle choice" because the military also discriminates against the blind, the deaf, the handicapped, paraplegics,[2] and murderers.[3] Gay rights activists put sighted, healthy, and nice gay veterans on a bus for middle America to see and hear singing "It's Not a Choice" and "Sexual Orientation Does Not Mean Sexual Misconduct."

The writer from *Newsweek* wondered: What more was there to be said? But there was, and remains, a gross disparity between the public perception of "gays in the military" and the sexual realities of military life.

The debate did accomplish some good. The gay soldier poster boys and girls helped to dispel public questions, if not privately held stereotypes, about whether gays are fit for military service. While a few people continued to doggedly insist that "gays should not be allowed in the military," most Americans came to understand that lesbians and gay men served in uniform already. Furthermore, attention given to the victimization of military gays perhaps engendered sympathy; polls suggested that most Americans, while split over lifting the ban outright, favored an end to Pentagon witch hunts designed to ferret out homosexuals quietly performing their military duties.

Unfortunately, publicity given to the victimization of military gays also helped further the justification of Pentagon officials that straight service members would never accept queers in the ranks, that attempts to force them to do so would result in violence, and that they, the Pentagon, could not control it.[4] Marine Corps Colonel Fred Peck appeared before Sam Nunn's carefully choreographed Senate Armed Services Committee inquisition to say that he would fear for his gay son's life were he to join the Marines. Military leaders extracted from the ranks a "We Don't Want No Fags In Here" party-line mandate worthy of an old-time Soviet election. A few brave GIs did speak up before TV cameras and senators to say they really didn't care whether their comrades were straight or gay as long as they did their jobs and did not molest them, but because of the existing policy, none could point to a well-integrated lesbian or gay in his or her unit without the queer being victimized and dis-integrated. Senator Nunn played on the prejudices and sexual fears of Americans by staging a loathesome and powerful photograph (see Figure 1) of himself and Senator John Warner ogling worried-looking sailors in the berthing of the attack submarine *Montpelier*.[5]

And so in the end, the reasonable arguments and earnest faces of gay model soldiers and sailors did not prevail. The Joint Chiefs, Sam Nunn, and a divided American public forced a weakened President Clinton to accede to the idea that lifting the ban would disrupt unit cohesion because straight service members would not tolerate the presence of avowed homosexuals living among them under conditions affording minimal privacy.

Certainly military gay bashers exist—at all ranks. However, it is an unacknowledged reality that expressions of hatred and intolerance are not the usual or even common result when gays come out to straight service members who they have already come to know and trust. The typical result is that the straight service member says, "It doesn't change anything. You're still the same person to me." The vague nameless dread of "some fag lookin' at me in the shower" is supplanted with, "Oh, that's just Johnson. He's a fag, but he's cool; don't worry about him." The conversations with sailors and Marines in this book show how known gay and straight men can and do get along in the sexually charged atmosphere of barracks and shipboard life.

The Pentagon knows, but does not *want* to know this truth. As Randy Shilts correctly observes, military leaders have long been less concerned with keeping out homosexuals than *appearing* to keep out homosexuals.[6] Clinton's proposed "compromise" policy, widely known as "Don't Ask, Don't Tell, Don't Pursue" was formulated to allow the Joint Chiefs to maintain this illusion. In announcing this policy, Clinton remarked, "It certainly will not please everyone—perhaps not anyone—and clearly not those who hold the most adamant opinions on either side of this issue." Truly, gay rights activists voiced bitter disappointment that he had reneged on his campaign promise, observing that the so-called "compromise" would merely codify how military gays were already being treated in practice. Antigay forces denounced any policy that would allow even closeted homosexual perverts to invade the armed forces and corrupt the morals of young service members. But paraded once again before Sam Nunn's cameras, the Joint Chiefs voiced more than mere grudging acceptance of the "compromise" and seemed pleased, even enthusiastic.

Why? If they recognize that homosexuals serve with distinction, why must the Chiefs insist that "homosexuality is incompatible with military service"? If the presence of self-identified gays is not threatening to the straight service members they come out to, why does the Pentagon demand that the presence of "avowed homosexuals" be understood as a threat to "unit cohesion"?[7]

The same day of the President's announcement, a new issue of *Newsweek* appeared on the stands with the cover headline, "HOMOEROTICISM: What the Military Won't Admit."[8] The article, by David Gelman, offered evidence, including testimony from my book *Barrack Buddies and Soldier Lovers,* of another unacknowledged truth: that "the male bonding so prized by military commanders . . . can engender another kind of closeness as well." It was the first suggestion in a mainstream national publication that a secret motivation for Pentagon remonstrations against the presence of "avowed" homosexuals might be a desire to protect homoerotic military rituals, homosocial lifestyles, and covert military male-male sex from the taint of sexual suspicion.

Hidden agenda indeed.

Consider Figure 3, a *Life* magazine photograph used in *Proceedings,* the naval officers' professional journal, in an issue devoted to impassioned, sometimes desperate pleas for the retention of the gay ban.[9] The picture shows a group of young Navy men—heads bent down, hands clutched before them—taking a very cold shower as part of SEALS endurance training. Photographed from behind in the soft misty otherworld of the unit shower room, they are not naked but wear white briefs. The caption: "For most active duty men the issue boils down to an uneasiness about potentially being regarded as sex objects. How will avowed homosexuals handle close proximity to men for whom they feel physical attraction?"

The question is offensive (it presupposes gay men to be incapable of controlling their sexual appetites—even in an ice-cold shower), but charmingly revealing. "How will?" disavows the possibility that any of the men in the picture might now be homosexually active, and so discounts the homoeroticism of the photograph by asserting the heterosexual purity of the huddling men. The word "avowed" *could* allow for the possibility that any of the men depicted might be *secretly* homosexual, and that is only an *illusion* of heterosexual virtue that must be maintained, but even this reality is denied. The elite, hypermasculine SEALS are cast in the feminine role; the question posed is not how they will handle the presence of a queer, but how the predatory pervert will handle them.

The tone of the caption is defensive, almost apologetic for the photo's disturbing erotic charge. Like Sam Nunn's *Boys' Life* pic, it says "Military life is not like civilian life. Here, embarrassingly intimate bonding is necessary to foster the unit cohesion necessary to win wars. You see now—don't you?—why a homosexual cannot be allowed among these vulnerable shivering boys."

It is of course possible that none of the dozen SEALS in this particular photograph identifies himself as gay. But it is a denial of sexual reality to assert that all but a small minority of military men are free of "homosexuality."

Boundaries between what is homo- and heterosexual, and what is sexual and nonsexual, are subject to disagreement. It is convenient to define a homosexual, as the U.S. Navy does, as "a person, regardless of sex, who engages in, desires to engage in, or intends to engage in homosexual acts." These are defined as "bodily contact, actively undertaken or passively permitted, between members of the same sex for the purpose of satisfying sexual desires."[10] (As we shall see, stratagems are in place for military men so that even genital contact may not be considered homosexual.) But homosexuality comes in many flavors, some known to the Joint Chiefs of Staff to be a natural part of military life.

A desire to be in close quarters with other military men in a tightly knit brotherhood might be homosexual. Navy initiation rituals involving cross-dressing, spanking, simulated oral and anal sex, simulated ejaculation, nipple piercing, and anal penetration with objects or fingers might be homosexual. An officer's love for his men might be homosexual. The intimate buddy relationships men form in barracks, aboard ship, and most especially in combat—often described as being a love greater than between man and woman—might be homosexual—whether or not penetration and ejaculation ever occur.

The U.S. military does not want these things called homosexual. To maintain the illusion that these aspects of military life are heterosexually pure it is necessary to maintain the illusion that there is no homosexuality in the military. This is the function of "Don't Ask,

Don't Tell": for boys to play with boys—and not get called queers, and not get called girls.

*   *   *

Throughout this book, buddy love and military homoeroticism are revealed to offer the possibility of homosexual expression to men who, had they not joined the military, would presumably not have ventured from the straight and narrow. Men who already had strong homosexual feelings before joining tell how they found that the military, despite its antihomosexual stance, actually helped them to shape a gay identity. This idea—that the military could "make someone gay"—might not appear politically expedient. Gay rights activists prefer to market same-sex attraction as an innate, immutable, biologically predetermined condition, a "sexual orientation" making homosexuals a discrete social minority deserving of civil rights protection.

In a *New York Times* Op-Ed piece critical of efforts by scientists to discover "the gay gene," Ruth Hubbard, professor emeritus of biology at Harvard, wrote

> Many people believe that homosexuality would be more so- cially accepted if it were shown to be inborn. The gay journal- ist Randy Shilts has said that a biological explanation "would reduce being gay to something like being left-handed, which is in fact all that it is." This argument is not very convincing. Until the latter half of this century, left-handed people were often forced to switch over and were punished if they contin- ued to favor their "bad" hand. Grounding difference in biol- ogy does not stem bigotry. African-Americans, Jews, people with disabilities as well as homosexuals have been persecuted for biological "flaws." The Nazis exterminated such people precisely to prevent them from "contaminating" the Aryan gene pool. . . .
>
> Studies of human biology cannot explain the wide range of human behavior. Such efforts fail to acknowledge that sexual attraction depends on personal experience and cultural values and that desire is too complex, varied and interesting to be reduced to genes.[11]

The debate over "what makes people gay" is not likely to be resolved any time soon. But why should the question matter? When gay people plaintively cry, "We didn't choose to be this way!" we reveal our endorsement of the idea that heterosexuality is the natural human condition, the cause of which need not be questioned, and that homosexuality must be accounted for and explained.

I have not undertaken this book with any simplistic political agenda. I do not incline to dogmatism, and I seek neither debasement of the military nor anyone's approval of my own sexuality or beliefs. I do however hope that an improved understanding of the sexual realities of military life will contribute to the discrediting of falsehoods and lies used to justify oppression of persons who self-identify as gay, lesbian, or bisexual, and anyone who participates in consensual sexual activity with others of the same sex.

If homoeroticism and covert homosexuality are natural and perhaps even necessary components of military life, I would suggest that it is hypocritical of the military to persecute "avowed homosexuals."

* * *

Interestingly, many self-identified gays do not want the homoerotic aspects of military life termed homosexual either. As ironic as officially sanctioned manifestations of homosexuality in the antigay U.S. military may be, there is further irony in how gays act as willing supporters of the myth of heterosexual purity.

In Randy Shilts' *Conduct Unbecoming,* "genuine" homosexuality is the sole property of "The Family," women and men for whom gayness constitutes a quasi-ethnic identity. Only two types of human sexuality are recognized: under the rubric "The Dangerous Difference" 1,100 stories are distilled and filtered down into a dichotomized homosexual minority (Us) sought out and hunted down by a heterosexual majority (Them).

Overlooked by almost all of the parties to the gays-in-the-military debate is the reality that gay and straight service members do not comprise two species. They are not necessarily different at all, perhaps not even in their sexual desires. More accurately, they are all different, embodying a multiplicity of variegated and highly complex individual sexualities that are only crudely consigned to polari-

ties of Us and Them. Humans do not fit into neat, convenient cate-
gories. The demarcation line between gay and straight is a ragged
boundary subject to sudden and unpredictable shifts. It is often
breached and occasionally vanishes altogether, only to reappear on a
different spot on the map. It sometimes follows, but more often
skirts or messily tangles with the barrier between "feminine" and
"masculine." Nations, religions, eras, and persons hold variant
views of what various kinds of same-sex attraction mean. (In this
book, when I refer to people as "gay" or "straight" I mean people
who call themselves gay or straight. While I dispute the polarity
these words suggest, I ask you to forgive this usage as a necessary
shorthand—and to take note of the differing meanings assigned to
these terms by the different sailors interviewed.)

Nuances and subtleties of human sexuality are largely absent
from *Conduct Unbecoming*. Only one of its 784 pages is devoted to
homosexuality involving men who do not call themselves gay.
These are limited to Vietnam.

> Straight guys had a hundred reasons why [sex with other men]
> did not make them queer. They were just horny. . . . As long as
> they were not having sex with a woman, they were staying
> faithful to their wives. Getting a blowjob from a guy wasn't
> real sex, anyway.[12]

Yet Shilts and the gay soldiers he interviewed accept these excuses in
maintaining the polarity between "genuinely homosexual" soldiers
and men for whom "Male-male sex was just something they thought
of when they found themselves in a strange country without any
Caucasian women. Psychologists call it 'facultative homosexuality.'"

Three hundred pages later, Shilts identifies the Navy as the service with the most "pervasive homosexual subtext" and, in a pas-
sage describing a Navy initiation ceremony, has one of his subjects
marveling "at how utterly unconscious heterosexuals could be
about that part of their psyches that responded with such enthusiasm
to this sexually charged contact among them. . . . Heterosexuals
denied the rights and humanity of homosexuals, even as they partic-
ipated in rituals designed to release their own homoerotic energies
during the periods in which there was no possibility of heterosexual
activity."[13] Shilts, like his gay sailor subjects (and mine, and indeed

perhaps most people), feels that homosexuality in straight men must be accounted for and explained. Unvoiced is the truth that homosexual expression is a natural possibility for men who identify themselves as heterosexual, and that the unavailability of women is often not so much a cause of, but an excuse for, sexual feelings for other males.

Excuses, endorsed by queer and straight alike, are in place so that sexual contact between two males might not be called "gay," providing certain agreed upon conventions are observed.

But this is nothing new. In 1919 the U.S. Navy conducted an investigation into homosexuality at the Newport, Rhode Island Naval Training Center, entrapping "queers" by recruiting straight sailors to have sex with them. In an analysis of the investigation, historian George Chauncey Jr. describes how neither the Navy, the queers, nor the straight men believed "that the sailors' willingness to allow such acts 'to be performed upon them' in any way implicated their sexual character as homosexual." In 1919 Newport, "The determining criterion in labeling a man as 'straight' . . . or 'queer' was not the extent of his homosexual activity, but the gender role he assumed. The only men who sharply differentiated themselves from other men, labeling themselves as 'queer,' were those who assumed the sexual and other cultural roles ascribed to women."[14]

Ultimately, the Navy was charged with having used "immoral methods in its investigation," but only after investigators made the mistake of targeting Episcopal clergyman Samuel Kent, citing as evidence of perversion his "sissyfied" and "effeminate" manner and his pleasure in the company of young men. In so doing, "the Navy defined certain relationships as homosexual and perverted which [the clergymen on Newport] claimed were merely brotherly and Christian.[15] Feeling threatened, the Newport Ministerial Union and the Episcopal Bishop of Rhode Island successfully rallied to Kent's defense—to protect the idea of Christian brotherhood, and themselves, from sexual suspicion.

*   *   *

Enough gay-straight sex was happening in 1919 Newport for one excited queen to exclaim, "Half the world is queer and the other half trade!" Some of the stories in this book of 1993 San Diego might prompt a similar observation and underpin a long historical tradition of sexual freedom among sailors grounding the sometimes exaggerated position sailors occupy in gay folklore.[16] Quentin Crisp, writing of his experiences with the "fabulous generosity" of the preconscription British Navy of the 1930s, speculates that "perhaps the act of running away to sea was an abandonment of accepted convention and, after a sojourn in strange ports, they returned with their outlook and possibly their anus broadened."[17] Historian Allan Bérubé writes that in this country during World War II gay men on the prowl for men in uniform "believed sailors to be the most available and Marines the least. Sailors acquired this reputation because they were out at sea without women for long stretches of time, they were younger than men in the other branches, and their tight uniforms looked boyish, revealing, and sexy."[18] The Village People's 1970s disco song "In the Navy," the art of Tom of Finland, Charles Demuth, and Paul Cadmus, and literature from classic Melville to pulp *Horndog Squids and Cherry Marines* all celebrate the sailor as homoerotic icon.

As David, one of the sailors interviewed in this book, observes, "A lot of it is not based on any fact. OK?"

Do not conclude that all sailors are studly bisexual adventurers who, when not ravaging prostitutes in foreign ports, are precumming under the lash of pirate-clad flagellators or blowing each other on the fantail. (Only some of them.) However, there is considerable evidence that young male sailors are more inclined to exercise sexual fluidity than their civilian counterparts. The conversations in this book show that sailors of the 1990s have ways of organizing and understanding homosexuality that in some ways resemble the Newport model and sometimes appear to almost invert it, but often these ways of life represent a surprising departure from the conventions of contemporary urban U.S. gay culture.

In his interview, Eddy describes toying with the Navy "sea bitch" tradition, which allows straight men to flirt with designated "pretty boys" who may or may not provide sexual release to shipmates who only "receive" oral sex. Trent tells how he played the receptor role in anal intercourse to straight sailors who came to his rack in the berthing at night. And Jack details sustained relationships with straight men for whom sex with him was the only "gay" aspect of their lives. In all three stories straight sailors are shown employing strategies to keep their heterosexual identity intact by imposing ritual limitations on their homosexual activity, e.g., reciprocating in only limited ways or not at all, refusing to kiss, and especially by playing only the top role in anal intercourse. But each of these gay sailors has a different opinion of the straight sailors' "true nature." Trent calls them bisexual; Jack suspects them to be closet gays. Eddy, who equates homosexuality with effeminacy and passive anal intercourse, is happy to allow such men their straightness—as long as they stick to the rules.

Ten of the 12 gay men interviewed here have had sex with straight men; seven have had sex with women. The meanings assigned by these men to their heterosexual experiences are also variant, but usually after coming out the episodes are dismissed as youthful foolishness or denial of gay identity. Growing up, all of Anthony's sexual fantasies were about females, but now, like Gregg and Ray, he is repulsed by the very idea. Jack insists that he never enjoyed sex with his ex-wife and mother of his two children. But Joey has had enjoyable sex with women and feels a potential for heterosexual relationships that puzzles him.

Definitions of what is gay and what is straight are revealed to be as likely to determine, as be determined by, sexual behavior. A straight man who experiences homosexual desire knows he cannot speak of it without his heterosexual identity being questioned. (I encountered numerous straight sailors in San Diego who have sex with other men, but none were willing to be interviewed for this book.) A gay man who feels a heterosexual desire must wonder if he is not denying the gay identity he has worked so hard to feel good about. (In military, as in civilian gay culture, declarations of bisexuality are regarded with suspicion, even contempt, as they are thought to almost always be a ruse to win social acceptance from straights. "True bisexuals" are believed rare.) But, as Kevin points out, human sexuality is not defined by orientations or genitalia, but by individual human personalities.

Different kinds of sex are described in this book: anonymous sex at sea; drunken sex in port; group masturbation at Camp David; sailor-Marine sex; officer-enlisted sex; military-civilian sex; sex with romance, sex with love, etc. Sex itself holds different meanings and serves different purposes to the men interviewed. Gregg wants to meld with his partners; he seeks enduring union. David compares sex to eating and likes truck stop food. Nonsexual homosexualities —loving intimacy between men that does not require genital expression—are also described. Lieutenant Tim feels intimacy for the sailors under his command; Joey feels it for his shipmates. Anthony yearns for but does not find it with his fellow sailors and envies the brotherhood of Marines, which he eroticizes and dreams of.

For all of the men in this book, sexual feelings and yearnings for nonsexual intimacy interpenetrate sexual identity, military gay "family" identity, male identity, and sailor identity in complex and often confusing ways.

As for the homoeroticism of military life, what is homoerotic is subject to at least as much disagreement as what is homosexual. Some sailors feel an erotic excitement (often mixed with pride and patriotism) about their own and other men's uniforms (especially Marines'), but to others the uniforms are merely clothing. Anthony and Joey describe life aboard ship as a charged and cruisey atmosphere of continual teasing, penetrating looks, innuendo, and homoerotic horseplay. But Sonny and Gregg dismiss outright the possibility that there could be homosexual overtones to the behavior of men they consider straight.

Nine of the 13 sailors interviewed here have gone through the "crossing the line" ceremony. In this Navy ritual sailors crossing the equator for the first time ("pollywogs" or more frequently simply "wogs") are initiated (as "shellbacks") by undergoing acts of ritual humiliation, some perhaps sexual—but only for some men. Sonny does not see anything homosexual or erotic about having another male sailor apply Crisco to his anus. Gregg recounts ordering wogs to feign copulation and admits that the "wog queen" contest on his ship (through which the winning drag escapes the unpleasantries of the rest of the ceremony) was won by a rubber-glove-happy physician known as "Doc Finger," but is angered by the suggestion that the ceremony is anything but an innocent tradition. Eddy, however, saw plenty of sexual meaning in being mounted and aggressively humped by his shipmates, and Joey experienced something akin to ecstasy through the attentions accorded him by half-naked shellbacks in pirate garb. None of the gay sailors in this book won the "wog queen" contest; Sonny competed but lost. And Trent, mortally offended when his division mates tried to force him to dress in drag, boycotted the entire ceremony. He may have played the sea bitch to straight sailors in a lifejacket closet, but he was not about to dress up as a woman, thank you.[19]

Sailors believe that a separate sexuality exists for Marines. All of the gay sailors interviewed here were familiar with the gay military stereotype that "all Marines are bottoms," reflected in such jokes as "How do you tell a butch Marine? He holds his own legs up." To what extent this folklore is rooted in truth (or whether it is only the seeming contradiction of muscular macho Marines *sometimes* playing the "woman's" role in anal intercourse that demands explanation) is beyond the scope of this book. Certainly, considerable anecdotal evidence and some personal experience do nothing to refute the stereotype, but more to the point are sailors' differing explanations for it.

Both Gregg and Ray had sex with Marines who said, "I'm not gay, I just want you to fuck me." Gregg recites the most common sailor explanation for this: Because Marines work so hard to always be macho and in control, in bed they compensate by being passive and feminine. But Ray (who, like other Navy corpsmen both gay and straight, has had his nipples pierced to prove that he is "hard" enough to serve with Marines) confirms what some Marines have told me: that they do not see getting fucked as feminizing, but on the contrary view it as a test of manly endurance. Another common sailor view also cited by Gregg holds that since men come into the Marine Corps to remedy a deficient sense of masculinity they might be expected to remain "naturally" sexually passive. But another Marine told me that it is Marine Corps recruit training that instills Marines with a need to take orders and be dominated, and leads some to eroticize the drill instructors' humiliations. This might explain why one Marine begs sailor Anthony to "fuck me like the dog I am."[20]

Chaplain Phil describes how the protection of masculine brotherhood allows Marines to engage in group and mutual masturbation without thinking of it as gay. He articulates his belief, based on the confessions of recruits he has counseled, that the bonding process of Marine Corps training releases an innate potential in many men for homosexual expression. He cites another gay military joke: "What's the difference between a straight Marine and a gay Marine?" Answer: "A six-pack." "Three beers."

Or, "A shot."

And sometimes not even that. I once had sex with a Marine who, as his excuse for "facultative homosexuality," throughout the act kept repeating his *intention* to get drunk, at some later time.

* * *

Ironically, once self-identified gays are finally allowed to serve openly, homosexuality in the armed forces might actually decrease. Discussion of military sex and gender issues, while hopefully leading to policy changes that result in better treatment of service members who call themselves lesbian or gay, has a dampening effect on the homoerotic charge of military life. In the wake of the Tailhook sex harassment scandal the U.S. Navy has outlawed much of the crossing the line ceremony; gay and straight sailors alike mourn the passing of the wog queen competition and the spankings. Anecdotal evidence suggests that increased awareness that gays serve in the military now is already inhibiting covert homosexual expression; the excuse that "It's only queer when you're tied to the pier" simply no longer works when "out" gay sailors are present to equate any male-male sex with gay identity (especially when in most men's eyes gayness is equated with effeminacy). Once it is known that there are gay Marines, it becomes considerably more difficult for straight Marines to engage in sexual "Marine stuff" without questioning whether it might be queer. As Phil observes, "If you have all the gay people out being gay, the things that are more homosexual are going to be labeled as homosexual. A lot of the free sex environment, or the fantasies and occasions for a quick whatever in the military, will fundamentally change. Some of the things they claim are time-honored traditions are just amazing in how far they cross the line of what would be proper."

A parallel might be made with the effect a growing awareness of lesbianism had on women of the 1930s. Writes historian Lilian Faderman: "No one could pretend any longer that it did not exist. Knowledge of sexual potentials . . . necessarily had complex effects on female same-sex love: for example, it made love between women 'lesbian'; it challenged women to explore feelings that they would have repressed in other eras; it frightened many women away from any expression of love for other women."[21]

In this I worry that maybe the Joint Chiefs are half right, that new uncertainties about their own sexual identities might for some men stand in the way of military buddy love. But this need not be the case, as the gay-straight buddy relationships described in this book attest. In these instances, gay and straight military men found that they were able to be close friends once they realized that the imagined barrier of sexual identity is, as Ray says, "not a hard line."

Myths serve a purpose. I don't want to ruin anyone's secret kick. The thrill of the illicit is intoxicating. Some of the best sex I have had has been with straight men who hated the idea of gayness. But the thrill can be self-destructive, as it was for the eight sailors discovered by a Marine sentry engaged in a "daisy chain" high atop the bridge on an aircraft carrier over the moonlit Indian Ocean, begging for capture, dishonor, and imprisonment.[22] And the thrill can be evil; just consider Phil's story of the chaplain who publicly tells troubled young men that homosexuality is an abomination then goes home to his homosexual lover.

In the naval officer's magazine, a few pages beyond the hot/cold SEALS photo, a former lieutenant offers his own compromise: that the avowal of *any* sexuality be grounds for discharge from the military. "[Enacting] this ban would send the refreshing message that there is room in our society for a sense of decorum—perhaps even good taste. A nice reminder that sexuality, like the other bodily functions, is only a fit subject for public discussion by the depraved or the puerile."[23]

One wonders what sex is like for this man, for whom the act of making love is equated with a trip to the toilet. But gay sex, too, enjoys a long toilet tradition. Good sex thrives on repression. One thinks of film director John Waters, "I kneel on the floor beside my bed, thanking God I was raised Catholic since sex will always be better because it will always be dirty."[24]

Raised a Christian fundamentalist, I could never see why love, or even lust, between two—or more—persons of the same—or different—sex(es) should be immoral. Killing seemed to me immoral. Lying seemed to me immoral. Only a small percentage of women and men in the military who experience homosexual feelings are ever investigated and discharged, but all of them are asked to be dishonest. This, I believe, is a more insidious and larger burden than the threat of dismissal.

There is a thrill to illicit pleasures, but there is something to be said for telling the truth.

Anthony: The Boot Camp Dream

San Diego is an excellent place for sex and Mexican food. And of course the beaches, but that may be the same thing as sex.

"L.A. has the most beautiful men in the world," opined Edmund White in *States of Desire*.[1] He was quite close. San Diego offers the same brand of too perfect white-toothed surfblond brown-smooth gym-buffed melanoma aspirants, but does its smazey neighbor to the north one better with a massive, ever-renewing infusion of 140,000+ sailors and Marines enlivening the beaches and strip malls and taquerias of this dessicate, slow motion sub-la-la-land with the unstoppable pounding young blood of virile tattooed love boys, flown in fresh from every region of that wholesome milk-drinking Wonderbread *real* America existing somewhere beyond the Sierras.

San Diego has the most beautiful men in the world.

In this sperm pool of servicemen, every ethnicity, every body type is represented (within the strict Marine Corps and laxer Navy physical standards). Some are able to mesh effortlessly with the locals, adopting a surfer dude lingo and pacific pose, while others are conspicuous for their provincial Midwestern/Southern attire, a consistent two years out of LA/NY fashion. I will confess to often finding these men the most attractive of all, as my taste runs not to Ken doll perfection but rejoices in foibles and flaws and rough unpolished edges. The challenge, for men with a "military chaser" predilection, is in distinguishing between the genuine article and those civilians for whom the dog tag wearer represents an ideal they (we) perhaps seek to emulate. Haircuts are, for this reason, an unreliable clue. Base windshield stickers (red for enlisted men, blue for officers) are better. Military tattoos are a dead giveaway. Even the most ardent military chaser is unlikely to get a U.S.N. or U.S.M.C. logo permanently emblazoned on his hide.

I had been in town less than a week when I met Seaman Anthony at a Hillcrest video bar popular with gay sailors. He had just come off a cruise on the USS *Ranger*, and I was attracted to his Marine-style "high and tight" haircut and air of corrupted innocence. Engaging the 23-year-old in conversation I thought first he must be European; his accent, I later learned, was the product of speech therapy undertaken to lose a burdensome Brooklyn patois. This soft careful emphasis of consonants does not come across as an affectation, however, and serves to complement the Sicilian-American's poise and bearing. Anthony, a former go-go boy, exudes a continental masculinity—manly but less wooden and gruff than the American brand. He purports to enjoy opera. But while he admits to being more refined than what he calls "Navy white trash," he takes pride in being able to spit, belch, and curse as well as any other sailor.

Like so many other young military men I interviewed, when asked why he had joined the service Anthony first told me that it was for money for schooling and other practical reasons. Only later did he confess that he had another reason for enlisting: to bolster his image of himself as a man. He imagined that by becoming a sailor he could masculinize himself. Little did he know what other possibilities for gender and sex image enhancement lay in store for him.

Part one of this interview begins after our return from a downtown tattoo parlor, an appropriate a setting as any to begin a book about sailors in San Diego.

Anthony: Going into a gay bar in San Diego is just like going into an enlisted club. A lot of the people in there are in the military. Almost everyone in the San Diego gay community that I have come in contact with is either active duty or formerly in the Navy. And you can just walk up to someone and say, "Hi, where are you stationed? Do you like it?" and that will be your opening line, rather than "What's your sign?" [Laughs.]

Zeeland: Of course there is still the danger that some of those people could be in the Navy and working for NIS [Naval Investigative Service].

A: My job requires me to have a top secret clearance. During basic training, I had to go through a variety of interviews with different NIS agents to be granted my clearance. This one particular agent, the last agent I spoke to right before I graduated from basic, was a very effeminate guy. He had bleached blond hair and wore makeup—foundation and eyeliner, whatever. One of the last questions he asked me was, "Do you consider yourself to be a homosexual?" Of course I wanted my clearance, so I said "No." That was all well and good; I graduated and went on to go through [Class] "A" school, and the time came when I eventually discovered the gay scene in San Diego and started going out.

So I'm in one of the bars, and I walk around the corner, and there he is—this same NIS agent. I was so scared and frightened. I was going to run out, but he had already seen me. So I just sat there and pretended like I didn't see him. He came over to me and said, "So. Do you consider yourself to be a homosexual now?" And I just shrugged and walked away. I wasn't even going to talk to him.

Z: This morning you invited me to watch you pay seventy-five dollars, plus a five dollar tip, to endure forty-five minutes of pain. What was your motivation for getting tattooed?

A: I was always interested in tattoos. The only person in my family who has a tattoo is my dad. And it's not like he has a lot of them; he only has one. It had always been a masculine thing to me, I guess because you're putting yourself through pain to make yourself look good. This particular tattoo that I got caught my eye, and I just felt that the time was right for me to get it.

Z: It's a Mohawk Indian in profile?

A: Yeah.

Z: I believe it was the only male figure available at that shop.

A: You brought that up. I didn't even think of the fact that it was another male, a guy putting another guy on his arm. I didn't think of it as being a gay tattoo. The only other males that they have are cowboys. Or Indians. So I think it's more a cultural thing. But for me it was just cool.

Z: Your other tattoo also has sort of a secondary gay meaning, doesn't it?

A: Well, that was also unintentional. It's a heart with a rainbow inside. It caught my eye just because it was bright and very colorful. I got it on my hip in my . . . groinage area. [Laughs.] After I got it, someone pointed out to me that it looked like the gay pride flag. That was when I first realized it. Maybe subconsciously I got it for that reason, but I don't think so.

Z: What was the reaction of the other sailors you work and live with when you showed them this new tattoo?

A: They all really really liked it. Everyone in the barracks. They even called some of their friends to come see it. But that's basically the way everyone is when someone gets a new tattoo. It's a big thing.

Traditionally, sailors get tattooed the second they get out of basic training. Or during "A" school. I got my first tattoo about a month after I graduated from "A" school. I kept putting it off because I was under the impression that it was going to be absolutely painful. So I made excuses.

Actually, the pain becomes numbing after a while, and you don't even realize that you're doing it. I fell asleep my first time.

Z: You mentioned that some of the other sailors you know found the experience of getting tattooed sexual.

A: Yeah. Some people actually thrive on the pain of getting the tattoo. Because they think—and I believe also—that there's a fine line between pain and pleasure. And tattooing is right on that line. It's a very sharp stinging pain. I suppose that if you're so inclined to enjoy pain it would be an enjoyable experience.

Z: What did they say to make you think that it was a sexual pleasure for them?

A: 'Cause they would get hard-ons. They would say, "I got so hard while he was giving me this tattoo. I wish I had someone to suck my dick while I was getting it." They'd say, "As soon as I got back to the barracks I went and jerked off." A lot of the straight sailors would go with their girlfriends and get a hotel room after getting a tattoo, and go fuck or whatever.

I think that tattoos are very sexy. I like it when a man has a tattoo. It turns me on to see it, and I like to . . . lick it. [Laughs.] I don't know if some people think that's sick, but that's what I enjoy doing.

Z: How do your sex partners react to your tattoos?

A: They like them. They also think it's sexy, or manly. Some people are surprised to see the one on my hip. Everyone who's gay perceives it to be a gay-themed tattoo in a place where no one else would see it.

Z: Have you had anyone call you "fag" in the shower?

A: No, because everywhere I shower, we have private showers. It's not a community shower. And I'm not exactly going to walk around and strip down past my underwear and say, "See my new tattoo?"

Z: What is your job in the Navy?

A: I am a radioman. Basically I help in the handling of communications between my ship and the rest of the ships within the Navy, and with land bases and other navies. My job is very cushy compared to other jobs in the Navy where you're really physically working all day, carrying things, or working in boiler rooms where it's extremely hot. My space is air conditioned. I work in an office-type atmosphere.

Z: Have you found that gay Navy men tend to hold certain jobs?

A: I'm sure that there are lots of gay machinist's mates and gunner's mates and boatswain's mates, but most commonly they're either radiomen, yeomen, or hospital corpsmen.

Z: Can you speculate why that might be?

A: Because they're cushy jobs and I guess we don't want to get dirt under our fingernails. [Laughs.]

Z: Why did you join the Navy?

A: After I quit my modeling career I had an excellent opportunity to become an investment banker. I was in a test program where they were taking people who were in college and giving them positions that were customarily given to people who had already graduated. So I had a very good job, I was making a good living. I was living in my own apartment in Manhattan. Then the rug was sort of pulled out from under me. The stock market crashed and the company went under—they couldn't survive. I tried for a while to get a new job. I did get one, but I wasn't really happy there. I was approached one day by an Army recruiter. I considered it, because I really had nothing going for me at the time and I wanted to continue my education. I decided to look into all the other branches, and the Navy had the best education package of them all. So that's why.

Z: You told me that you love the Navy.

A: Yeah. I like the camaraderie, the whole brotherhood thing. I like the fact that, even though I really love my family, I'm away from them. I have my sense of independence now. I've been to foreign countries where I would otherwise never have gone. And I like the regimented lifestyle. I'm proud to be in the Navy and I'm proud of my ship. I love my ship. I have several of these shirts that have my ship's name on it.

Z: You feel a sense of camaraderie with other sailors?

A: Oh yeah. When you're traveling and you're in an airport and you have a connecting flight and a two-hour wait, there's always a USO you can go and stay in. You've already established that you've got something in common with these people, so it's really easy to talk to them. Especially in the Navy, and especially if you're on the same ship with them. On my ship, although there are people that I personally don't like, if it came down to risking my own life to save them, I would do it. That's how strong the sense of camaraderie is. And I like that.

There is a strong sexual overtone to this camaraderie. You're all in close quarters and your beds are on top of one another. You're all getting undressed in front of each other. There's an incredible lack of privacy on a ship, unlike on a shore command where you have your own room. There's a lot of joking around, patting the butts, "Look who has a hard-on!" And they'll go and try to grab it or whatever. Sort of similar to a football team in a locker room. But I tend to shy away from that kind of stuff, as probably would most homosexuals, because of the fear that straight people have of homosexuals. I don't even acknowledge or give any sort of answer to anything like that.

Z: Tell me again about your company commander at boot camp.

A: I was a pretty good recruit. I never really got in trouble. The way they punish you in basic training, as most people know, is by making you do pushups. I never really did anything all that bad, so eventually the company commander made me do pushups for the people who would do bad things. So let's say Joe Recruit did something wrong; he would also get me down on the floor. I don't know if he liked me in that position or whether it was because he was frustrated that he couldn't get something on me the right way. He would stand right over me. And the proper way to do pushups in boot camp is to look up, not down, at the floor. And his—his crotch would be just inches from my face . . . and rather bulging, and would get even more bulgier. I guess he was turned on by the fact that I was in this position.

He was a chief. He was somewhat attractive. A little heavy, but not all that bad. He talked continuously about his Filipino wife. All the time. How we were all stinking, disgusting recruits, and while we were lying in bed dreaming about our girlfriends back home, he would be fucking his wife. That was just to make us all feel bad. And I guess to make us admire him, although I had no admiration for him at all.

A: My roommate at "A" school became my closest friend for the four months that I was there. He was very different from anyone that I had ever met. He was exactly opposite from what I am. Not so much physically, but personally he was very different. He had a different value system and was more of a nickel and dime type of guy, where money meant an incredible lot to him. Whereas I, growing up somewhat spoiled, didn't have a high regard for money, and if something cost a little more, oh well. He became my closest friend. If I hadn't been in the military, I probably wouldn't even have looked at him, much less sought out a friendship with him.

One night that sticks out in my mind is. . . . We were both in the same class. We had gone through this grueling week of tests. In a five-day week we had taken four very major tests, basically to determine whether we were fit to graduate or not. And we both got hundreds on all four tests. We were in a celebrating mood, and decided to go out, as sailors do, and get absolutely shit-faced drunk. So we went to an enlisted club on base and got as drunk as two guys can get without dying. [Laughs.] You never saw such a funny sight, where two drunk guys were trying to help each other walk. As soon as one would get done falling on the floor, the other guy would help him up and then that guy would fall down. It was a ten-minute walk, and it took us a good thirty-five minutes to get back to our barracks. After we got there we were talking about home, and how excited we were to go back there before we went to the fleet, and how nervous we were. Then there was the famous lull in the conversation. There had been a certain sense of sexual tension because I found him attractive. And I assume that he did the same. It was sort of like a mutual thing. I don't know who was the aggressor. I mean, I made the first move, but it was something we both wanted. If he didn't want it he could have really beaten me up, and I don't know whether it was the fact that he was drunk that he let me come on to him or—I honestly don't believe that if he was sober he would have let me. But we did have sex, and—

Z: Sex by your definition?

A: No. Sex by my definition is actual penetration. This was oral sex. I consider that to be fooling around. So we fooled around. [Laughs.] He gave me oral sex, I gave him oral sex. It was great; it was something that I wanted for a long time and I finally got it. And it was good.

The next day we sort of glossed over the whole issue. We didn't really talk about it. I wasn't going to ask him, "Do you regret what we did?" But we still keep in touch. I get a letter from him at least once a month. He's engaged to marry this girl he's been dating a while. He was really surprised to find out that I got married. I told him—and this is true—that I married a girl that I dated in high school. Right now he's on the East Coast, so we're kind of far away from each other.

I found that in our friendship I was sort of the father figure and he was like the child. Because he was younger than me. I was constantly looking after him. He was very bad with his money. As much as he valued it, he didn't save, and he would make poor decisions about what to buy. So I was always managing his money. I was always looking after his uniform to make sure that—I wouldn't iron his uniform for him, but I would say, "Your military creases are crooked," making sure that he did well in inspection.

And I'm like that with Eddy, my best friend on the ship. Eddy has absolutely no regard for money. He'll spend his entire paycheck in one day and then borrow off of everyone else or send a letter home to have his mother wire him money. I'm like a father figure to him, too. I don't know what it is. Maybe it's that I'm older, and I feel I have to care after these guys, but I seem to—my friendships, at least in the military, have always been like a father-son type of thing.

Z: You're twenty-three. How old are these guys?

A: Eddy's twenty-one. There's really not that much of an age difference, but I guess mentally there is.

A: There are definite cliques at sea. All the single guys who are into country [music] stay in one group, all the gay guys sort of stay together, and all the married guys stay together. Although I'm gay, I did get married for convenience reasons. And because of this, I was sort of pulled into the married man clique. It was unwilling. They said, "Now that you're married you gotta hang out with us." And I kind of felt bad saying, "No, I'm not going to hang out with you." When we were in Vancouver, we would go to these horrible tit bars and see girls with blond hair and big tits bouncing in front of us. I would have to pretend to be turned on and go, "Oh yeah, oh. Look at her." It was horrible; I hated it. I knew that my friends were dancing their asses off, having a great time, and maybe meeting someone.

One night in particular they [the married men] invited me to go out. I said, "Oh no, I feel tired, I'm going to hit my rack." It was our last night in Vancouver. They were going to party it up, and go to *two* tit bars! Oh boy. The ecstacy of that thought just made me more tired. So they said, "Oh well, OK. You sure?" I made sure that they left, and I hurried up and put on my clothes and ran out to meet my friends at some of the gay clubs. One of my friends came back the next day, and they asked him where he went. There is an assumption on the ship that this person is gay. And he said, "Oh, me and Anthony went to some of the clubs around town, really cool places." So he sort of ratted on me, exposed my sneaking out to escape. They never asked me to go out that much anymore, which I was kind of glad about.

Z: Tell me a little about your social life at sea.
A: The bigger boats, like I've been on, have a twelve-hour working shift. So if you're out on a six-month deployment like I was, and you're traveling twenty-three days before you hit your next liberty port, there really isn't a lot of time for social activity. There are no bars or clubs on the ships anymore. There used to be in the old days. Now social activity is just basically working out. What I would do with my spare time when I was out to sea was just go to the gym or sleep. Basically that's all you really have time for.
Z: Were there times when you could have had sex?
A: All the time. Very rarely did a day go by when I didn't get at least one offer from someone. A look, a wink, or a snap as I walked down the passageways. I would just ignore it because—because sex on the ship is so forbidden. And I just steered away from it. That's a really good way to get kicked out of the Navy.
Z: Someone who snaps his fingers at you probably identifies himself as gay. Were some of these advances made by men who consider themselves straight, do you think?
A: Yeah. A guy would be talking about his wife one minute, then the next

minute would start rubbing his crotch and say, "I'm really lonely." I consider that to be an advance. But I would just say, "Well, the shower's over there," and just get up and leave.

Z: Have you gone through the shellback initiation?

A: No, I haven't. Unfortunately. I was really looking forward to that, because occasionally I do need to be beaten. [Laughs.] A slap on the ass is good every once in a while!

A: My being gay, or the first time I had sex with a male, it was sort of thrust upon me. I was raped when I was twelve. He was in his thirties. It's left a lot of mental scars, and I think that contributes to my theory that all men are pigs. I've noticed—because I've been told, not because of anything I've seen myself—that I'll never get into a submissive role sexually, ever. Absolutely not. I will never get on my knees and give someone head. Never. I consider myself to be a top. Occasionally I do enjoy receiving anal sex, but I will never be physically on the bottom with my legs up, because that's how I was raped. The one time that I did do it that way, which is when I noticed that I can't have sex in that position, it brought back all these flashbacks and I saw this man's face in front of my eyes. It's not like I have nightmares every day about it. I've sort of put it on a back shelf and gone on with my life, but there was a time when I was really kind of messed up.

Z: Had you had any feelings of sexual attraction for other males before that age?

A: Not really.

Z: Have you sometimes wondered whether that experience made you gay?

A: Yeah. For awhile I blamed it on that. I'm not so sure if I still hold that belief now. I think—I really don't think about why I'm gay. I just know that I am and I'm happy this way. But this person took advantage of me, and, from what I understand, many other people.

What had happened was—this girl I was dating back in junior high school—we were at her house. This man was there, he was a friend of her mother's. Physically a very big man. He was at least three hundred pounds. Not that tall, just huge. I had homework to do before my mother got home, and I had certain chores to do. So I decided to leave this girl's house. I only lived two or three blocks away, so it really wasn't that far to walk, but he offered to drive me home. I said, "No thanks." He said, "No, that's all right, I'll drive you." And again I turned him down. I left. I took a short cut, which was an alley, and he was driving toward me in the alley. He said, "I'm going your way, why don't you just let me give you a ride?" So I figured, what the hell. I got in the car, and we started driving in the opposite direction from where I lived. I said, "This isn't the way back to my house." He said, "I have to go get something from my apartment before I drive you home." So, being young and naive, I trusted anyone who was older. We got to the apartment and I said, "I'll wait here." He said, "No, why don't you come up, because I'm going to be a while." Eventually he got me in his apartment, and then he locked the door, and then I realized what was going on. I ran for the door. I almost made it. He just overpowered me, because he was just physically such a big man. I wasn't frail by any means, but there was no way. . . . And that was it. After it all happened, I felt that if I could have fought better—that maybe it was my fault. That came after the anger and the feeling of dirtiness. Now I realize that there was really nothing I could have done.

Z: Did you ever see him later?

A: Yeah. I've seen him. I haven't seen him lately. I assume he either died, is in jail, or moved away. I wish he is dead.

Z: Did you consider telling anyone?

A: He told me that if I told anyone he'd kill my family; he knew where I lived. I had reason to believe him, because he told me things about my family no one else without knowing my family would know.

Z: You told me that you would like for your interview to be titled "All Men Are Pigs."

A: They really are. I guess what we were talking about the other day is: Is it possible for two men to have a soulful loving monogamous relationship like a man and woman can when they get married and have children? I really don't think so. I mean, it's very rare, because basically all men are pigs. Myself excluded. Men want to have sex all the time, and I find most men to be very anti-monogamous. I think that it would be almost impossible for a man to have a marriage-type relationship with another man because of that.

Z: Do you know any gay men who are in long-term monogamous relationships?

A: No. I think that it's very hard to find two men who are completely compatible personally.

Z: Is that because you think they've been socialized to be aggressive and competitive to the point where they can't properly give of themselves?

A: Sounds good. I don't know. I really haven't delved into deep psychological reasoning. I just blow it off with "men are pigs" and that's it.

Z: You did tell me you feel love for Eddy [see "The Sea Bitch"].

A: Yes, I do. I care very much for him. I was sexually attracted to him when I first met him, but we're just close friends. As close as two people can get without having sex. I care about what he thinks; I care about his opinions; I care about what he does. I don't want him to make bad choices. So I think it's more of a fatherly type love.

Z: Is he still a pig?

A: Yeah. He is a pig. Because he's just easy. He reminds me a lot of me when I was seventeen. And he's twenty-one.

Z: You mentioned that you dated girls in school.

A: Yeah. I can remember being as little as five or six having strong feelings for girls and wanting to play doctor and explore girls' bodies. I never really had any sort of attraction for other boys. So I dated a lot of girls. And when I was going through my denial stage that I might be gay, I was dating girls and guys, and I considered myself bisexual.

Z: You got married after you joined the Navy?

A: Yes. I married for the money.

Z: Do you ever talk about your wife to your shipmates?

A: Sometimes I pepper my conversations with little anecdotes about my wife, and they're true, because we did grow up together. She's a lesbian, though. I wear a wedding ring I guess just to alleviate suspicions. There was one person on the ship however who is also from New York and is very streetwise and worldly, and I think he's a real jerk. He said, "I know you got married for the money. I'm from New York, and I can see right through you." I said, "I don't know what the hell you're talking about," and just blew it off. But after I left the room, I was really afraid, because he has a pretty big mouth and could blab that I'm gay and really ruin everything. But he really hasn't said anything, except to me, that I know of. When I first got on the ship, almost every word out of his mouth was how queer I seemed. Every time I'd talk he'd mimick me in a conventional gay voice, even though I really don't talk like that. I'd get really aggressive with him, almost to the point of fighting him. He stopped doing that; he's become more personable. I guess the fact that I did get married blew his line of attack.

Z: You were going to tell me about the guy you wrestled with.

A: It was this guy! It was this particular guy, Petty Officer Columbus. When you're at sea and you're working twelve long hours, you get kind of restless. So we were all sitting around doing nothing, waiting for something to happen, because it was a relatively slow day. He had said something rude to me, and I told him off. We were arguing back and forth; he pushed me and I pushed him back. Then he grabbed me from behind and started wrestling with me. In my effort to wiggle out of the hold that he had on me, I sort of rubbed my ass up against his crotch, which produced a hard-on for him. And I just found that intriguing. Here's this straight guy who has fucked hundreds of girls and is engaged to this one but dates that one, got a hard-on over me rubbing against him. So I turned around and said, "What's that?" He got all embarrassed and flustered and left the room. I just found it funny. No one else noticed, but I thought it was absolutely hysterical.

Z: I'm trying to make the transition here to Marines. I asked you to remember what you told me before. . . .
A: Marines are a curious bunch. They seem to be in a world of their own. I think out of all the services, they tend to stick together the most, because they're taught that in their basic training. Marine boot camp is twice as long as Navy boot camp. It's really more a mental workup than anything else. In Navy basic training they break you down and build you back up, and that's it. Whereas in the Marine basic training, they break you down, build you back up, and drum it into your head that you'll never make it without the other Marines. There's definitely a strong brotherhood thing. You'll never find a Marine talking to a sailor.

They always seem to be on the ground level of everywhere I've ever been, as far as where they live and work. Where I'm staying now in the barracks, they're at the ground level of the building. On my ships that I've been on, they were always on the ground level. Sort of on the bottom, and me on the top. Which is where they belong. [Laughs.]

My best friend back home, her cousin was a Marine. She knows that I'm gay, but she hadn't told him because it's really none of his business. And he just naturally assumed that I was gay because I was in the Navy. That's the mentality of the Marines, that everyone in the Navy is gay, and everyone in the Marines is straight. She was getting dressed in the other room, and it was just me and him. We were talking about different experiences, and he was telling me about working out in the field, and all this stuff that I just find so interesting. There was again that lull in the conversation, and he said, "So you wanna give me a blowjob sometime?" I was just amazed at the gall that he could actually say something like that to me without even knowing me. And that is the mentality I've found in the Marines. After I got out of "A" school, I didn't really understand why there was such friction between the Marines and the Navy. More so than let's say between the Army and the Navy or the Navy and the Air Force. We all are there for one purpose, and that is to protect and serve, but I think that the Marines are so proud, and they can't accept the fact that they are just basically a branch of the Navy.
Z: They can't accept that they're subservient to you?
A: Exactly. We're on top and they're on the bottom and that's how it should be.

Part Two, Four Months Later

Seaman Anthony became my best friend in San Diego. One Sunday morning just prior to part two of his interview I went with him to watch as his former ship, the USS *Ranger*, pulled into port.

On the Coronado waterfront the master-at-arms struggled to re-strain a bulging erection and several thousand boisterous screaming wives and children who had come to greet their returning husbands and daddies, who were visible high above us like parade-rest paper dolls manning the rails of the ten-story tall aircraft carrier while heroic music blared and banners waved. As the 5,000 officers and crew began to stream over the brow—lugging heavy sea bags, sweating in their dungarees and dress blues under the punishing San Diego sun—I stared at their faces and bodies, determined to form some composite picture by inspecting every last one of them. All around us little family reunions played out, sailors kissing girl-friends, wives, babies, and a few hugging other men. Anthony pointed out a gay Navy clique assembled before us, but it was not his own, and we did not find his best friend Eddy in the chaos. Hours passed and still the men kept coming and I kept staring until old salt, young squid, fat chief, skinny Marine, ethnic, white, ugly, studly—all became a blue-black blur of *men.*

A few days later Anthony escorted me on a private tour of the ship. He showed me the fantail, the galleys, the officer's staterooms, and of course the enlisted berthing, including the "rack" he had slept in directly beneath the wheels of fighter jets screaming down onto the flight deck less than five feet above him.

As it happens, this was the same carrier that David, a chaplain's assistant I interviewed (see " 'Hard' Not 'Tough' ") had served on. Feeling a sense of history, I asked Anthony to escort me to the Chaplain's office "head." True to David's description I found the stall partitions riddled as with machine gun fire by holes drilled to facilitate contact. But this was not a part of Anthony's sex life, and as I returned from the men's room I noticed his habitual look of annoyed concern for me—not so much disapproval at the seaminess of tearoom sex as fear that I would be bashed by sailors.

It was with a very different facial expression when Anthony pointed out the hatch to the Marines' quarters below, to which sailors and tagalong civilians have no entrance. Looking down we could see them strutting about in their camouflage utility uniforms. He smiled. Marines, to Anthony, mean sex.

Almost by accident—after he was ordered to shave off a long Navy haircut and opted for a "high and tight"—Anthony discovered he could easily meet butch, buff Marines, and that many seemed to ache for him to play the rough dominant sailor top. This was a different brand of masculine validation than he had anticipated finding in the Navy.

Z: You've had a recurring dream these past few months.
A: I dreamt that I was sent to the Marine Corps. I don't remember if it was by my own free will, but I had arrived at Marine Corps Recruit Depot. I went there with an attitude of: I've been through all this before. There's no need to cut my hair, because I know it's a mental thing to demean me. For some reason these drill instructors didn't want to hear anything from me. They were sort of nightmarish. I'd wake up in a cold sweat. I've had the dream three or four times within the past two months. The same dream. Showing up there with everyone else, knowing that it was all a mindfuck. I don't know whether it's because I've been staying with a lot of Marines lately. Maybe I have a desire to be a Marine.

Some of the best sex I've had has been with Marines. Some of it has been absolutely incredible. Some Marines that I've been with are insatiable and are not afraid to try anything and do everything.

The first Marine I had was in Yokosuka, Japan. I met him in Roppongi in a club called Java Jive. The first night I had gone there was with a friend of mine from the ship who's straight. We went there to dance and have a good time and just hang out. He knows I'm gay. I saw such an influx of Marines there. At that time I thought that I was totally out of their league because I always saw Marines hang out with Marines, and I was very obviously a sailor because my hair was long.

I went back there alone the next night. My friend had duty and there was no one to go with me. I got a little drunk and worked up some courage to go over and talk to this Marine who was just standing in a corner by himself. We were talking, and he was telling me cool places to go in Tokyo. He was staying in a hotel in Roppongi because he had some liberty; he invited me back just to hang out. I thought, well cool. I honestly didn't think that we were going to have sex because he seemed pretty straight.

We got back to his hotel. He had some beer in his refrigerator. We started drinking and he got really drunk. He went to the bathroom, and when he came back he had taken his pants off. He said that he had spilled some water on them. I noticed—which was really funny—that his name, his last name, was written across his crotch. I thought this was really strange, because in the Navy we put our name in the right-hand corner on the back. But he had his name handwritten sort of diagonally across where his cock is. So I made a comment: "That's a pretty long name you have." [Laughs.] He grabbed his dick and said, "Yeah, it's pretty long." I guess that was the icebreaker—we had all kinds of sex. That was the first Marine that I fucked. It was great.

I actually didn't expect that; I expected that Marines were tops. They seem so masculine when you see them, you think that would translate when they go to bed. But I've found—not only in that experience, but in all the other experiences I've had—Marines to be quite the opposite. Every single solitary time with no exception at all. Marines, although they are quite masculine and butch during their everyday goings on in life, are absolutely total bottom men when they get in bed, which is fine with me.

I did let him fuck me too. I found that pretty enjoyable, because it had been a couple years—and it was just great. Slapping, and spanking, which I like. Rough sex. He was very good looking—built, and blue eyes, and dark hair. He had sort of a Southern accent.

Z: But if he fucked you also you really can't call him a bottom.

A: But he didn't initiate the fucking of me. I jumped up and sat down on him. I was on top the whole time. So it's not like he threw me down and bent me over.

Z: What actually happened after he said, "It's pretty long"?

A: I was sitting on the bed and he was standing up. He walked over to me, and he was like, two feet in front of me. He was grabbing his dick. So I stood up and took off my shirt. We started licking each other and biting and stuff.

We didn't really talk much the next morning. I got up, took a shower again, got dressed, and left. I'm sure that he considered himself straight but he was drunk and just let it happen. It was fine with me. It was good sex, and it sort of opened up Pandora's box for me. Now I couldn't close it if I wanted to!

Like I said before, Marines sort of stick to themselves, and they wouldn't even give me the time of day if I walked over to them with the long hair I had before I went on WESTPAC [Western Pacific Cruise]. It was way over the Navy regulations, which is four inches on top; mine was seven and three-quarters inches. I was getting pressure from the Navy master chiefs to get it cut or else I wouldn't be allowed to leave the ship.

So while I was in Saudi Arabia I got it all cut off. Really short. Not as short as it is now. It got progressively more Marine-like as time went on. Now it's absolutely without a doubt Marine, and it does allow me to meet more Marines this way. They'll come over and just rub my head and that will be sort of an opening line. I had one Marine come over to me and rub my head and not even say a word to me. He just kissed me and stuck his tongue in my mouth.

Z: This happened in the galley?

A: [Laughs.] This happened at the club.

When I met Danny, he came over to me, and we sort of looked at each other. He was sizing me up, looking at my body, trying to determine whether I was Navy or Marine. I was looking at his face, and I thought he was really good looking and very butch looking. There really wasn't very much conversation. He rubbed my head; I rubbed his head. I asked him if he danced, and he said, "Yeah, but not to this music." He likes fast-paced techno music, which is the music most Marines like, because it's more macho than house music. So we waited until some techno came on. We danced for awhile. I was drunk so I was bold. I said, "So, do you have a place? I think we should go there." He agreed.

Again, incredible sex with a Marine. And that really leads me—I've made a mental Top Four list of the best sex I've ever had. And number four just happens to be Danny. His was the most versatile of sex that I've ever had. He's an aggressive top and a loud aggressive bottom. Like a wild dog. "Fuck me harder! Turn me over! Split my legs and slap my ass and pull my hair! You like fucking me!" He was very vocal. He was totally insatiable. We've had sex four times.

Number three on my list is my current boyfriend, Keith. Keith is very loving and very good in bed also. The first time we had sex was of course in your apartment, while you were in your room with his straight roommate. The second time was at Camp Pendleton, where he's stationed. He had been working all day. He was all hot and sweaty. We had gone to his PX and gotten some Marine cadence tapes. We listened to them while we were driving around Camp Pendleton. In the beginning they were kind of stupid and anti-Navy. Calling out that the Navy are a bunch of faggots and they can't run. Of course Navy cadences are the same way, kind of anti-Marine. But there were a couple of these cadence calls that were so masculine they turned me on. We got back to his room, and I just tore off his uniform and went down on him and had incredible sex. I had this dog collar that someone gave me for Christmas. Well, that you had given me for Christmas! He went to the mirror and it turned him on to see himself looking like that. Looking like a dog. It turned me on also, I thought that it fit him. He got on his hands and knees and started barking, and just kept on barking. He's a true bottom—very submissive, very childlike. Even out of bed. In bed he's even more so. He needs to be held and caressed—and spanked. These Marines need to be disciplined!

Number two on my list: Three weeks ago I was at one of the bars. I saw this tall beautiful built guy with a military haircut who I thought for sure was a Marine. So of course I went over and talked to him. He told me that he was in the Navy. He was visiting from Bremerton with one of his shipmates. They were very nice guys, real down to earth, unlike a lot of the other sailors I've met or been stationed with. One was taller than me, about six-foot-four. Lean but very muscular. Great butt. Dark hair, green eyes, real nice teeth. The second sailor had a little bit longer hair and was short and stocky. He was about five-foot-eleven. We got pretty drunk. They didn't have a hotel room, so they suggested that we go to a bath-house. I had heard about Club San Diego and had been real intrigued about going there. So I agreed, and they paid for me to get in. We just went right to the room. It seemed like it was a hotel, except there was this music blaring through a really bad sound system.

That was really fulfilling sex. There was a lot of roughness and raw sexuality. They were into total pleasure. There wasn't anything that either of them had any reservations about. They were into fucking and getting fucked, licking and punching and slapping and biting. It went on for four hours. I didn't think you could have sex that long. I was totally drained the next day, good for nothing.

Z: What was their relationship with each other?

A: I think they were just basically fuck buddies. One of them would suck my dick while getting fucked in the ass by the other. I turned in a good performance. It's not just a job, it's an adventure. [Laughs.]

I really like group sex. My number one best ever sexual experience is group sex I had with four Marines in a whirlpool. I had met one of these Marines before. Bill. The next time I saw him he had four friends with him. One of them was not a Marine, he was much older, forty or fifty. Bill said, "He's just one of our good friends." He introduced me to his three other Marine friends. I suppose they were impressed with me, and thought I was cute. Maybe Bill had given them some sort of idea about our previous sexual experience. They all just kept patting my butt and rubbing my crotch in the club. Bill said, "Why don't we go back to our hotel room? We have a hot tub there." All the other guys were coaxing me to come along.

This older guy, I don't know if he was their Sugar Daddy, but he evidently paid for their room and stayed in a smaller adjoining room and watched. It all started off pretty casual. We sat around, watched TV, had some beer. There was a lot of kissing necks and rubbing. We all undressed and got into the hot tub. There was a bowl of condoms, sort of like pretzels. We spent a few minutes in the whirlpool just relaxing. Then we all started playing around and massaging each other. Biting and licking. Then they were like, "We really want you to fuck all four of us." I was amazed. It was totally unexpected. I thought maybe I would fuck one or two of them, and the other two would go off on their own, but I had no idea that I was going to have to play top man for all four of these boys. But I didn't turn it down. They were practically begging. Because I was like, "Well, I don't know." "Oh, you know you want to!"

It was such a sight to see them all lined up. Marines just have the most perfect butts. So I went and I got the bowl of condoms and laid a condom on each butt, sort of like a mint on a pillow. Opened each condom, and fucked all four of them. A couple of them were really tight, and I got the impression they hadn't done this sort of thing a whole lot. They were really apprehensive. So I had to go easy for awhile, but then they started being really rambunctious and screaming and yelling, "Fuck me harder! You like this Marine ass!" and shit like that. They'd play around with each other while I fucked their buddies. A lot of kissing and groping, all that kind of stuff. After I'd get done fucking one, I'd take the condom off, put a new condom on and fuck the other one, then the two I'd just got finished fucking would then fuck each other. It was just a real raw scene.

That is without question so far the best sex that I have ever had. And Marines, without a doubt, out of all the people that I have had sex with, and there are many, are just the most pleasurable lovers. Putting aside the fact that they really don't talk to you much the next morning.

A: I wanted to talk about the stupidity that's been going on the last week over the military ban. Just the notion of people in the military that homosexuals don't exist. There are homosexuals in the Navy *now*. And nothing's ever happened, the heterosexuals have never had advances put toward them, they've never felt uncomfortable before. But now because we're asking for the right to stand up, they feel they have to be scared to be in the shower and scared because there might be a homosexual working with them. That's just totally asinine. I had this one first class petty officer who's been in eighteen years tell me that he was going to write to his congressman and say what a terrible breach of his rights it is to have openly gay people in the Navy. Just going on and on and on about it. And I said to him—which is kind of bold, I'm normally not like this at work—I said, "How do you know there aren't homosexuals working with you now?" And he said, "Why, do you accept homosexuals being in the

Navy?" I said, "It doesn't matter one way or the other. They've served in the Navy and they'll continue to serve." I think we just have to be acknowledged. That's all we're asking for. We're not asking for any special treatment or anything.

I do however think that once this executive order has been made there will be people who will join the military for the wrong reason. I think that some people are going to think of it as their sexual dream come true: "Now we can join the military and be right alongside hot Marines or hot sailors and go to sea and have wild crazy sex." And I think that's really the wrong reason to join the military.

Z: Reading your interview might inspire someone to do just that!

A: Joining the military just to be alongside sailors or Marines is really the wrong reason. You really have to have a strong love for your country. It may sound stupid, but I really am ready at any time to die for my country. I'm not scared to die. I'm not wishing for it, I don't have a great penchant for death, but if it came down to it I'm prepared to die. It may sound corny, it may be inappropriate for this interview, but that's how I feel.

Z: And anyway, one doesn't have to join the military to have sex with military men.

A: That's true.

Z: Are all men still pigs?

A: I still do think that, but I no longer think it's impossible for two men to have a soulful monogamous relationship, because I'm in one now.

Part Three, Five Months Later

Anthony and I remained special friends. He gave me a CD player for my birthday, I gave him the keys to my apartment at Casa de las Pulgas and allowed him to entertain Marines there in my absence. We ate dinner and almost always hit the bars together. People often assumed that we were a couple.

Anthony played a special role in the authorship of this book, introducing me to many sailors and Marines and acting as a sounding board for my ideas. I gave Anthony unusual control over his interview, allowing him, in the parts you have read so far, to tell his stories with the help of carefully prepared notes. But for this third and final install-ment I decided it was the interviewer's turn to be on top.

In reflecting on the foregoing interviews Anthony voiced concern that the sex stories he had recounted would present a negative public image for gay sailors. "Only for people who think sex is bad," I told him, pointing out again what I wrote in my Prologue: that all male sailors tend to be sexually adventuresome.

In placing Anthony's interview first I do call immediate attention to one sailor's thirst for sensory threshold experience, a taste that some will say is not typical or *wholesome*. But, as later interviews remind us, spanking is a Navy tradition.

Z: Tell me about the dream you had last night.

A: The final dream starts where the last dream left off. I'm in Marine Corps boot camp. They're yelling at me because I'm being disrespectful and not a good recruit. I'm looking around at my fellow recruits, and they all look pretty familiar, but I just can't place them. I remember feeling very uneasy. I go to the drill sergeant and say, "Listen Sarge, why don't you just teach me how to use a rifle, because I've already been through all this." And he says, "That's it! You're going to the pit!" Now, there was a military themed club in New York called The Pit—it was kind of trashy and I think they wound up closing it—but there also really is something called the pit—a sand pit—in Marine Corps basic training. I get there, and it isn't a sand pit at all. It's this big room decorated with camouflage and netting, and in it is every single Marine that I've ever met in San Diego. They're not wearing uniforms, they're just in briefs and underwear, and some of them are naked. They're holding and fondling each other. I begin to back away, but the drill sergeant is behind me, and he shoves me in there and closes the door. One of the Marines is Danny, from my Top Four list. He grabs me, and says "Now that you are so close to graduation it's time to act like a Marine." [Laughs.] There had to be twenty Marines in the room. And they all . . . you know.

Z: No, I don't know. It's not my dream.

A: They all fucked me really, really terribly. I'm sure that I must have been screaming while I was dreaming this. It was terrible, but exciting at the same time.

Z: Was this a wet dream?

A: No. But I woke up with a raging hard-on.

Z: Did you tell me that you had just had sex with some other nameless Marine a few hours before you went to bed?

A: Yeah. Which is what may have inspired me to conclude the recurring Marine Corps dream.

Z: What makes you think that this is the conclusion?

A: Because in the dream I finally become a Marine and serve as a bottom to all these other Marines. There was a final feeling about the dream. That this was the end, and there's nothing else to be said.

Z: Why did you have these dreams?

A: I don't know.

Z: One would think that the final dream might offer some clue.

A: I think that probably deep down subconsciously I really wanted to be a Marine and wanted the camaraderie that goes along with it, because there's really a close brotherhood there. It exists in the Navy in a different way, but not on such close terms as it does with the Marine Corps. I miss that; that's one thing I regret I don't have in the Navy, so I think I look for that in other ways. Such as my attraction to them.

Z: The first time I interviewed you you told me that you joined the Navy largely for pragmatic reasons. You couldn't find a good job, et cetera. Later, during a dinner conversation with my editor, Dr. De Cecco, you told him, not me, that you had joined the Navy with the idea of hetero-sexualizing yourself.

A: There are multiple reasons why I joined the Navy. I really was at a dead end. I was at a crossroad in my life and I needed a change. I needed money for college. I refused to accept money from my parents . . . I needed a sense of independence, and I wasn't going to find that anywhere in New York. But the additional reason is, I was very confused. I didn't know if I was straight, bisexual, or gay. I was having sex with men and women. What I was feeling inside bothered me, because I was walking around not knowing who or what I was. The military back then was perceived by me to be a very male and masculine environment, and I thought that joining the military and being around all these men would in some way "straighten me out." And give me some sort of positive answer as to what I am.

When I first joined the military I was terrified. I didn't have sexual contact with anyone for the first six months of my enlistment. I didn't masturbate at all during boot camp: the first time I even touched myself was when I was home on leave. I was more concerned with getting through training than any sexual thoughts or feelings. I wasn't sexually attracted to anyone in my company. I did have sex with my roommate, but that was the day before we left. It wasn't until I got to the *Ranger* and become reacquainted with my sense of independence that I began experimenting in the gay world again, and realized that this is really where I belong. I tried dating girls. Eddy, me, and another shipmate of ours went out right before WESTPAC to a couple straight clubs downtown. We met these Korean girls. We danced and we kissed, but it just wasn't there for me. The night before Eddy and I had gone to gay clubs and had a great time. The straight club was fun, but we were bored after about an hour.

Z: When I first met you, I asked you if you considered yourself masculine, and you didn't have an answer for me. We talked about this again more recently, and you told me that you didn't think it was an issue; that you don't worry about whether you are masculine or feminine. But I pointed out that all the guys you date conform to an image of, at the very least, conventional masculinity, and in some cases—including all but one of the guys you've dated for any length of time at all—an exaggerated hypermasculinity.

A: I don't go around pretending to be butch. I don't go around practicing my walk, so that when I'm walking down the street I have it down perfect. For me it's not a big deal. I just am myself. It doesn't even cross my mind to wonder: am I a queen or am I butch? I just enjoy being me. Why do I enjoy butch men? Something just clicks in my head. I like being with a *man*; a big guy who makes me feel good.

Z: A big guy who makes you feel good. *Why* does that click for you?

A: [Sighs.] There's just—when you get together with a guy who is masculine, there's just—there's just something. You just have a total feeling that this is right; this is what gay sex is supposed to be like. It's not supposed to be drag queens and go-go boys, it's supposed to be rough sex with slapping and spanking and—

Z: You talked before about what you enjoy and when sex is good for you. It's tempting to conclude that you seek out bigger, more masculine men to dominate and thereby build up your own sense of power.

A: [Smiles.] Mmm-hmm.

Z: But recently you started complaining that you don't like to be called a top. Why?

A: Because I'm not a total top. I do occasionally, when I feel the time is right—and only when *I* feel the time is right—like to get fucked. I don't see anything wrong with it and I don't think it's a departure from my "true self." There is no true self to me. I like to have all kinds of sex.

Z: The other night I showed you a porno video of four Marines together with a woman. I find it sort of quasi-homosexual-erotic, but you were utterly nauseated by it, although you were laughing at the fact that the woman was spanked. You called that "demeaning to women."

A: I was laughing at that and also that she was moaning every second. I hate it when women do that.

I live with this roommate. He's straight. And he's usually never around. He's just gotten back from a three month deployment with the USS *Constellation*. "The Connie."

I came back from your apartment after watching that—atrocity video; I went to my room, I was tired, I got in bed. I'm sleeping, and all of a sudden he comes in with this girl. They're giggling, they're talking for awhile. I slowly begin to fall back asleep. Then I'm awakened again by creaking in the bed and her moaning every second, just like the girl in the video. She's saying, "Deeper! Right there! Oh, oh, *you hit it!*" They both come. And then they do it again.

Z: The lights were off when this was happening?

A: The lights were off. He does this all the time. I really don't have a problem with it, because I happen to like his girlfriend. But this wasn't his girlfriend, this was just some cheap one-night thing. Usually when he does it I put my Walkman on and listen to Martha Wash or something to drown out the sounds, but I had run out of batteries, so I had to listen. It disturbed me. The next day I was very uneasy.

Z: Are you attracted to your roommate?

A: Not at all.

Z: By my calculation you have had sex with five people in the book. Does that make you a slut?

A: Five? That's it? [Laughs.] There's a stigma attached to that word. I don't consider being a slut a bad thing. I look at it as: I'm young, and if I can go into a club or a bar and make a friend and have a relationship or just have sex then that's fine. There will come a time one day when it will be difficult for me to do that. I think that some of my so-called friends who call me a slut in a joking manner really aren't joking at all, and that it's really jealousy.

Z: You mean Ray [see "The Navy Corpsman Nipple Piercing Ritual"]. You think the reason he calls you that is because he's jealous of your sexual exploits?

A: Very much so. I think that he's very jealous. I think that he is cold and really lonely and that he doesn't feel confident with himself, and so when he sees someone like Kevin [see "The Network"] or me who is sexually free, he very vindictively calls us sluts but disguises it with humor and laughter. But he really does mean it.

Z: What makes you certain of that?

A: Because I can just see how he says it, and that he really does look down on Kevin and me.

Z: Since our last interview you and I became part of a small group that had about seven core members, a few fringe personalities, and occasional special guests. Do you think that there was anything special about this group of people, or was it just a bunch of friends meeting for parties and picnics?

A: I think it was special. I think that we found something in common within the whole group. It felt like we belonged with each other. The "love-ins," as you called them, were just exactly that, like love-ins of the sixties, where everyone would get together and drink and lay all over and on top of each other and just have lots of fun. Until—I noticed that things started deteriorating after the third or fourth one. People started getting hooked up with other people; people started deciding that they didn't like this one and didn't like that one. After a while they became very forced sessions, where people would do it just for the fact that, "Oh, we've done it before so we've got to do it again." When Kevin and I started seeing each other and dating, people became very jealous of us, for whatever reasons they had.

Z: You've heard my analysis that Kevin was the center of the love-ins. You disputed that idea, didn't you?

A: [Pause.] Not really, now that I look back on it. While it was going on I didn't think so. But retrospectively, yeah, he was pretty much the center of attraction.

Z: How would you describe Ray's role?

A: His role was basically monetary. He paid for a lot. [Laughs.]

Z: What I mean is, to someone who had never seen Ray in action, how would you describe his behavior at these events?

A: Ray basically just flails about from person to person, giving them hugs and kisses and saying "hello, dear," sometimes getting a little intoxicated, wavering about like Morrissey does in some of his videos, and trying to be the social butterfly—trying to be the net that holds the whole thing together. I think he was jealous that Kevin was the center of attraction.

Z: Were you jealous of Kevin being the center of attention?

A: No. Not at all. I was very happy that he was, because I very definitely didn't want to be. I have been the center of attention of other groups, and it's fun and nice for a while, but then it gets trying, because you have people talking about you all the time.

Z: As the love-ins deteriorated, Gregg [see "The Unmaking of an Activist"] seemed to alienate himself from the group faster than anyone else. How?

A: It was mainly that he acted aloof, and maybe above us all, toward the end. In the beginning, like the first and second love-ins, he was participating in a lot of the different activities going on, the spanking, the licking—

Z: The chocolate dripping *everywhere*.

A: —and all that. But then I think that maybe he thought that this was getting a little too carried away and boring and old, and he just didn't want to take part in it anymore. It became a chore for him. And people had a problem with that. People saw him as being a spoilsport, or like a grandma not wanting to participate in anything, coming to a party and leaving five minutes later, not even saying goodbye to anyone. I think that's how he alienated himself.

Z: And Russell [see "Strong Friendship"]? What did you think about his presence there?

A: I thought it was good. I thought that—I don't want to say that I respect him for it, because that's sort of not the right thing to say—"How wonderful of this straight person to be around us." But I mean, most heterosexuals wouldn't hang around a bunch of homosexuals, not to mention a bunch like us, acting wild and ripping off clothes and biting people's nipple rings and everything else that we've done. But it was fun to have him around.

Z: You and Kevin started a clandestine sexual relationship behind the backs of the other members of the love-in crowd until it became impossible to conceal it any longer. You told me that it was a very special relationship.

A: Kevin and I are cut from the same cloth. I didn't notice it until other people told me that they saw a great similarity between us. Kevin and I both had a lot of the same experiences growing up. We both enjoy the same things out of life, and we both enjoy the same things out of sex. We don't have any sexual hang-ups. We're not afraid to try anything. When I first met Kevin, the sex was great, but it wasn't really what I was accustomed to. I sort of introduced him to the world of pain. I don't know if he's continued on in that world or if he's gone back to his world of vanilla nothingness, but after I introduced him to it he really got into it. The whole spanking and pulling hair and biting—

Z: But of course pain can be taken to further extremes than that. Some people would consider that to be beginner stuff—

A: While having sex, pain is a very necessary thing for me. I need to either inflict pain on someone else by spanking them or hitting them in some way, or have it done to me, depending on my mood. I think that everyone deserves a good slap on the ass.

Z: Well, you said that before—

A: And I'll say it again. Because it's true and I mean it; it's what I feel, and it's my philosophy. For someone who isn't expecting it, it startles them, it might wake something up inside. And because that's taboo, it might make them feel dirty—and make them feel good at the same time. Then they'll moan and they'll say, "Oh do that again." Which is usually what happens.

Z: What is the furthest you've pushed those limits? I haven't seen you with any broken bones or bruises.

A: None that you can see! No, I'm not into torture, but it's not just a slap on the ass and that's it. It's slapping hard and very frequently. It's not just licking and maybe a little bite, it's gnawing, almost to the point where. . . . Like I said before, there's a fine line between pain and pleasure. I like to just cross the line and then come back. Inflict pain, and then as soon as it starts to hurt, stop, then make it feel good, then inflict pain, go a little bit further, and then when it starts to hurt, stop and make it feel good. And people love that. I don't have any shackles in my barracks hanging above my rack. But I could never go back to having mutual oral sex and then maybe getting fucked without any slapping or biting and then coming and rolling over and going to sleep. I just can't do that anymore.

Z: At one of the love-ins, Russell, who is straight, took off his belt and—playfully at first but then more and more violently—whipped both you and Ray. Did you enjoy that?

A: No, because I knew that he didn't mean it. He was just doing it for the crowd.

Z: Something else you didn't tell me until that dinner with Dr. De Cecco was how Eddy played the "sea bitch" role on the *Ranger.* You said it was sort of a contest to see who would take that title, him or you. How did it get to be him? Was it just because you left the ship?

A: Probably. They were betting on who was going to be the wog queen or the sea bitch. The guys were saying, "Anthony would look better in makeup, but we really can't find any clothes in his size, so it's gonna have to be Eddy." They were teasing the both of us. We were looking at each other like, "You're gonna do it! I can see you in heels!" No, *you're* gonna do it! You've been in heels before!" We would play along.

Z: But weren't there other elements to this sea bitch role apart from competing in the wog queen contest?

A: When you're out to sea for sixty or ninety days or whatever, and you're the sea bitch, or what some guys also called the sea pussy, it's expected of you to perform sexual favors. People come to your rack, and it doesn't matter whether you feel like it or not, you're going to get them off. You're going to suck their dick or jerk them off or do whatever. People would come back to me and tell me what other people were saying behind my back, that they're gonna "tag my ass," or they're gonna "get that" by the time WESTPAC was over. Straight guys, married guys. There was this one guy, he's married and he had a newborn and another one on the way, and he was always hanging around my rack, wanting to go to the gym at three o'clock in the morning. And there was my bunk-mate who lived below me—I was on top of course—and he was always saying that he was gonna jump up there in the middle of the night. I would just play along and say, "Well come on. It's here." There was all that teasing going on, and there was always looking, and people would know who the candidate for the sea bitch was. . . .

A: I mentioned before that I found myself to be a father figure to Eddy, and that I was the one on the ship who watched over him and made sure that things went right for him. I find that still to be the case now. I really worry about him. Sometimes he makes the wrong decisions when I'm not around. He comes from a troubled background, and I feel that if he stays with the wrong people he might begin to slip back. But for someone who has gone through what he has, he's really turned out pretty great. And I love him very much.

I know that the time is going to come when he's going to be stationed in Virginia or somewhere, and I'm going to be sent to Japan. Then he's going to be out of the Navy and go back to Missouri and I'm going to continue on. I'll probably never see him again, and that's going to hurt. Just like my old roommate in "A" school; I still get letters from him about once a month. He wrote me a letter finally making a reference to that one night. He said that he had a really great time with me, and he can't wait to come back to San Diego and see me and drink some Jack Daniels and "have fun again." But the chances of me seeing him again are slim. When he left, I cried; I was miserable for a couple of days. When Kevin left, I was depressed. And when the time comes for Eddy to leave, or when I leave, I'm going to be very upset. That's the thing about Navy love, is that it's very—matter of fact? It's just for the moment, because you don't know if you're gonna be here next month. You could get orders to go to Okinawa or Virginia or San Diego. You've started a relationship, and all of a sudden you have to leave. I think that had Kevin not gone off to Okinawa, we would have continued on in our relationship, because it was going well until it was time for him to get his orders. When he realized he was going to Japan, he backed off. I think we could have had something great.

Z: It's kind of hard for me to picture either of you really settling down. You're both such adventurers, and Kevin has a way of running away from other people while pretending not to. You even asked me to "keep you from getting into a relationship."

A: No more relationships for me. The last two relationships have been tumultuous and terrible and I don't ever want to experience anything like that ever again.

Z: You concluded part two of your interview by saying that, while you still felt that all men were pigs, you no longer thought it was impossible to have a "soulful monogamous relationship" because you were in one at the time. For the record, your relationship with Keith ended when you heard him calling out someone else's name in his sleep.

A: He was going on a three and a half week deployment in the mountains of California. It was a month-long Marine Corps cold weather training extravaganza. He had told me that he really wanted us to keep what we had going, because I had reservations about not having any companionship for a month. He convinced me that this was the right thing to do, to be monogamous, that he loved me and everything. And I loved him; I'm not going to lie and deny it. So I remained monogamous, as hard as it was. About a week or two before he left, I introduced him to the corpsman who was going to go with the group. Ben was very interested in meeting him. His eyes lit up when he met Keith, and he slipped Keith his number— which I saw happen and Keith didn't mention. But to make a very long and boring story shorter, he left, he went on his deployment, he had a great time, he came back. The day after, we're together and he's calling out "Ben baby, Ben baby!" in his sleep. I woke him up and confronted him with this. He was very defensive, and then arrogant about it. First he said, "I don't know who Ben is. I never met a Ben in my life." And I said, "I introduced you to one; he was your corpsman." And he said, "Well I talk in my sleep, excuse me." I said, "Well! You're excused." He slept on the couch and I slept on the bed and a week later we broke up.

Z: As much as I hate to call you on it, you did just say something that isn't really true. You said as hard as it was, you were monogamous for the three and a half weeks that he was gone. And you weren't.

A: You don't know that.

Z: Well, I do. Because you were seeing Kevin during that time; that became apparent.

A: Kevin and I were very good friends.

Z: You were sleeping in the same bed and—

A: Two men can sleep in the same bed and not have sex, Steve.

Z: But you forget that I interviewed Jack [see "Don't Kiss Me, I'm Straight"], who gave me an explicit account of your meeting, which happened while Keith was still gone. I don't think that Jack is creative enough to have fabricated the story. [Pause.] So how can you say that all men are pigs except you, when you're cheating on a man who you agreed to be faithful to?

A: [Pause.] I have no answer.

Z: Last week we got together and we went out for coffee and you looked very morose and said that you were unhappy with your life.

A: I'm tired of having sex all the time, and it not leading to something more than a trick in the night. But I definitely don't want a relationship, because first of all, I haven't had luck with my recent relationships, and secondly, I don't really have time for a relationship. My orders are going to come soon and I'm going to be leaving, possibly going to another country. It would be unfair to myself and another person to be in a relationship. But I really would like to develop more friendships out of all these people that I meet, rather than them just being tricks.

Out of all the people that I've met in San Diego, there are only two people that I've fallen very hard for. The first person is Kevin. And I still love him. I never got over him. It was hard to see him with other people. I've tried the best I could to get over it, to just convince myself that this is the best thing, he's going to Japan, I'm going wherever, maybe one day we'll see each other again. But I love him and I think I always will. I don't know whether he feels the same way or not. I honestly don't think that he does. But I do care a great deal for him. I'm gonna miss him a lot. The second person that I fell for was Eddy. The love that I feel for him is much different than any kind of regular love. I love him as a friend and a brother and I would do anything for him, and I hope that he knows that.

Eddy: The Sea Bitch

At 22, Eddy is still just a kid. In moments of boredom his daz-zling smile warps into some silly face. He loses his keys, his money, his ID card—his friends joke that he forgets his last name. Yet Eddy seems incapable of much anguish. Like the sad story of his child-hood, any crisis is shrugged off like a cloudy day at the beach. It is easy to see how Anthony has come to play "father figure" to this attractive Navy radioman of Pacific Island ancestry.

Eddy lost his biological father and mother at age nine, when he and his identical triplet brothers (the other two are straight), were taken from their child- and substance-abusing parents and put in custody of the state. Soon after, both parents committed suicide.

Eddy told me that as an orphan he was sexually abused by three men, two social workers and a cook, who exploited his and other boys' hunger for love and affection. He described his molestation by the first man as having initially been physically and emotionally pleasurable. "I wanted him to lay with me. I asked him to. It was just oral sex with me. He didn't want me to do anything. It was more or less like he was comforting me. For a while I did enjoy it, until I got older and realized that it wasn't right." He first felt that it was not right when he saw the man get into another boy's bed. Eddy told me that all of his adolescent sexual fantasies, as well as some recur-ring dreams and nightmares, involved this social worker.

At 14, Eddy was adopted by a white schoolteacher couple, and at 16 he had sex with a girl for the first time. It happened in the back seat of a Toyota Tercel, with male friends in the front seat watching. Although he says he only did it to prove something to his friends, Eddy says he enjoyed the experience and continued having sex with various girls until a year later, when he ran into another boy from the orphanage whom he knew to be gay. Eddy initiated sex with him, and the two had a "major relationship" lasting three years until, at

20, Eddy enlisted in the U.S. Navy and was sent to the fleet. He came on board the USS *Ranger.*

Zeeland: What led you to join the military?

Eddy: The gay issue really made me join. I lived in a small town in Missouri, and I felt like if I got away I could be gay, and be happy, without my family realizing. So I joined the Navy. I was twenty. I waited one year after high school. I graduated a year late, because of dropping out and stuff.

Z: You joined the Navy to be gay knowing that it was prohibited to be gay in the Navy. What did you think about that at the time?

E: I just figured that no one would ever know. Back then I was so straight acting. When I joined the Navy no one in the world could ever tell. Now, I still don't think I act like a flamer, but you could probably pick up on it.

Z: Why did you choose the Navy and not some other service branch?

E: Because my brother was in the Navy. He seemed to like it and have fun.

Z: What was boot camp like for you?

E: I had fun in boot camp! I loved it. I got along with everybody. Everybody liked me. I was really like a class clown. You know how some people hide out and remain quiet just so they can get through boot camp? Not me. If there was something that needed to be said, I said it, to anybody. And my chief and my company commanders respected that, too.

Z: It was probably relatively easy for you to adapt to, having grown up in an institutional environment.

E: Yeah. I grew up with eighty kids living with me every day, so it was no big deal.

Z: What was your first awareness of gay men in the Navy?

E: Of course in boot camp. You take group showers with everybody. They haven't had any kind of sexual contact in so long, and you can just see who's looking at you as you dress and shower. So I knew who was gay instantly. I guess people knew I was, too. I didn't actually talk to anybody about it, but I had my eyes roaming.

Z: But when was the first time you met someone who you were sure was gay and had some real interaction with?

E: I was at North Island, stationed on the *Ranger,* and one day I decided to go to Balboa Park. No one told me [that it was a gay meeting place]. I was just sitting by my truck, and a group of people came up to me. They were pretty much hitting on me, and I told them my name and what I did. "No way! We're on the *Ranger* too!" That's how it started. And all of a sudden—boom!—I started goin' out and meetin' everybody.

Z: When was the first time you had sex with somebody in the Navy?

E: I never slept with anybody in the Navy.

Z: Are you sure? Stop and think.

E: [Pause.] On WESTPAC. That was the first time, and that was just a couple months ago. I usually stay away from people in the military, period. But it wasn't available anywhere else. I was horny, and I was on the boat—it happened on the boat, in fact. I was laying in my rack, and this guy, Jonny, came up to me and started talking. He physically stuck his head in my rack. [Laughs.] He closed my curtains and he—he did it, while everyone's walking around. He gave me head. I was sort of freaking out because if I got caught, then I'd be in trouble. But I wanted it so much that I didn't care, and we never got caught.

Z: Was he just one of the gay guys you knew from the scene?

E: No, he wasn't. He never even told me he was gay. I guess I knew though, because he always went out of his way to say hi to me. When he came to my rack I wasn't really surprised.

Z: Are there also straight men who have sex with other men at sea?

E: Well, I think there's a lot of straight men who will be glad to *receive* it, just because in their mind they're justifying it by saying, "I don't have to do anything; I never slept with a guy, he slept with me." I think a lot of my straight friends had contact with other men.

Z: What do you base that on?

E: Well, I know. I know, because—I have some what I call straight friends, and they consider themselves straight—they had sexual action with other men, yet they're totally straight.

Z: They told you that, or the gay guys told you that?

E: No, they just—it happened where everyone knew. One instance that I know of for sure was with one of my good friends who is married and has children, and who is totally straight. In fact he looks down on gay people; he's always got something negative to say about them. We went to a port in Australia, and he didn't want to sleep with a girl, because he thought it would be cheating on his wife. So he had sex with another man. Two of my other friends were with me, and we all saw it happen.

Z: You didn't actually watch them have sex, though.

E: Yeah! Well, we watched this guy give him head. It was in a bar downtown in Australia. He didn't think twice about it.

Z: A gay guy gave him head right in the bar?

E: Uh-huh. Oh yeah. Australia is a wild place. And he justified it by saying, "He gave me head and I'm not gay."

Z: You had a good time in Australia yourself.

E: I had a blast in Australia! I met a guy and fell head over heels, and that was it. We were there for a week, and every second of my port visit I was with the same guy. He took me everywhere. Usually I feel guilty after I sleep with a guy. I don't know why. But with him I didn't at all. He cried when I left. I cried, too, because he was just really special.

Z: Do you still stay in touch with him?

E: Yeah. He writes me. And I have a big phone bill!

Z: Tell me about the concept of the "sea bitch."

E: The sea bitch? You mean as in—What do you mean?

Z: You tell me. What does that term mean?

E: Well, I was the sea bitch. [Laughs.] Mainly because of how I acted. I don't think anyone actually thought I was gay. Toward the end my whole compartment found out, because of the fact that Tony, the person I met in Australia, was writing me letters, and people found them. But before then they called me the sea bitch because—not that I'm extra good looking or anything, but I'd always be taking care of myself, and a lot of people called me "pretty boy," just because I was younger than most of them. Maybe they did know I was gay . . . to this day I don't know. But I was called the sea bitch. That's just someone who—I think it's just a way for straight men who have gay tendencies to let some of their frustration out. Because if they're saying stuff toward me, it's nothing serious, 'cause I'm the sea bitch, right? And if there was no sea bitch then they couldn't say it.

Z: What exactly would these guys say?

E: People would come up to me and say, "I'm gonna fuck you tonight. I'll pay a visit to your rack." They'd joke around about it, and yet I think a lot of them were dead serious. A lot of them would have.

I played a big role on WESTPAC as the sea bitch. I think I played a dangerous role. I mean, I just teased a lot of guys. I flirted with them a lot.

Z: Someone reading this might wonder whether you're being completely honest, and whether you might not actually have performed the role sexually for these straight men.

E: Uh-uh.

Z: I interviewed another sailor [see Trent: "The Boatswain's Locker"] who said that straight guys would come to his rack at night, and he would go with them into a lifejacket closet.

E: I slept with people on the ship, but the people I slept with were gay. There's no doubt about it. I did have guys come to my rack and hit on me, in their nonchalant way, saying things like, "You're tense, let me give you a body rub," or, "I'm gonna hop in there with you," but I never actually engaged in it with them.

Z: What was your reason for not taking full advantage of that sea bitch role?

E: Because at that time there were a lot of witch-hunts going on, and to this day that scares the shit out of me. You don't know if someone's just doing that to find out if you are gay.

Z: Were you a part of a gay clique aboard the *Ranger?*

E: Well, yeah. I knew almost all the gay people on the ship. We knew when to talk, when not to talk; where to meet and where not to meet. We knew. No one sat down and explained the rules of the clique, but yeah. Ed and Anthony and all of us, we knew where to go.

Z: How many of you were there?

E: As a clique, I'd say twenty; as good friends, I'd say about four. Then of course we knew tons of other gay people that weren't in the clique who were just too scared to come out.

Z: Did some of your friends have lots of sex aboard ship?

E: Oh yeah. Definitely. [Laughs.] I had gay friends who would have sex in the showers. It was so dangerous, but I guess the need for sexual contact was stronger than the danger of getting caught.

There are so many places on a ship that you can have any kind of contact. The fan rooms, just because they lock. I was involved in some-one's work space. He was a first class, and he was the only one who had the combination to the lock, so it was a hundred percent safe. If anyone knocked on the door, all we'd have to do is put our clothes on and leave. And then there's the fantail, which is the very end of the ship where we throw our trash off. It was so dark back there . . . I mean, at night, out on the ocean, you couldn't see anybody. And you could literally go back there and have sexual contact with people you didn't even see. You didn't see their faces, you didn't care what they looked like. I knew lots of friends who would go down there every night. It was just something they did. It was like going to the clubs; they'd go down to the fantail. I can honestly say I never went down to the fantail because I found that—I have to see a person. If I'm gonna have contact with them I have to see them. I can't just go walking in the dark.

Z: This man you had sex with in his work space—was he somebody you met aboard ship, or did you know him from before?

E: I didn't even know him. I was in a smoking area. And his look was so intense. . . . At first I thought, well maybe he just thinks I'm gay and he's mad at me or something, but I just knew. He looked at me so long and so hard. We didn't say a word to each other. Not a word. He walked straight to the fan room, and I followed him. And then it happened and that was it.

Z: And was it good?

E: Yeah! Just oral sex. Of course when you don't get it and you think about it all the time, that just makes it even better. I don't know if my standards were lower or what, but I hadn't had it for three months.

Z: What is your feeling about men having sex aboard ship? Is there anything wrong with it? Should it be allowed?

E: I don't think there's anything wrong with it. It's gonna happen. I don't see where they should have it in front of people: in public it's just not right. But when you can find spaces to do it where no one's gonna find out, yeah, I think it's great.

Z: That's refreshing to hear. A lot of gay sailors—even ones who have sex aboard ship—are so anxious to sell people on the idea of gays in the military that they would not be that straightforward. But what exactly should the official policy for sex at sea be?

E: If I was the one to decide? Actually, it's really contradictory, because I think it should be stated that it's not allowed, but when it happens I don't think that anything should be done. I mean, when guys and girls are on the ship, they're not supposed to be having sex: it's illegal. Yet when they do, nothing really happens. It's not like they go to captain's mast for it. But if you're smart—there's so many spaces, and so many times that you can do it, that you don't need to get caught.

Z: How did you meet Anthony?

E: I can honestly say that Anthony is my only friend on the ship. I have other acquaintances.

I was on the ship a year before Anthony even got there and I never had a friend. Anthony just showed up one day. I had no idea he was gay. I mean, a week later I knew! But at first I had no idea. There was some kind of chemistry between us. Not as gay people, but as friends. He was unpacking his stuff, and I was leaving the ship and I simply said hi to him, which I usually don't do. People come and go and I never say hi to them. Me and Anthony started talking. He said, "Well, do you wanna go see a movie sometime?" And I said, "Great." I blew him off for about a week, and he's like, "Well, when are we going to see a movie?" I said, "Oh, let's go see one now." And for two weeks we played this game of "I'm straight." We both said we were straight.

I wanted to take him to Rich's [a dance club] so bad. I said, "Let's go dancing." Anthony said, "Okay. Where do you want to go?" I said, "Let's go to this place my friend Coco knows about." I said, "But I think there's some gay people there." Anthony said, "Oh, that doesn't matter. I'm from New York." So we went.

Then afterwards we went to Coronado, and before we went to the ship I went driving around to the beach. We went walking, and Anthony said,

"Can I tell you something?" "What?" "Will you promise you're gonna like me as a friend just the same no matter what I say?" And I said, "Anthony, I already know." "What?" "You're gay." And Anthony said, "Well, I'm *bisexual.*" Then he asked about me. At first I said I was straight. And then I go, "Well, I'm bisexual too." And then it just went from there. We became best friends. We started slowly to admit that we were gay.

Z: I showed you the part in his interview where he talks about you.

E: Y-yeah.

Z: And he says that he was almost like a—

E: Father figure. [Laughs.]

Z: What do you say to that?

E: As much as I hate to say it, it's true. He's the only person I have to really look after me. I mean, I've met a lot of people in San Diego/Hillcrest who want to be friends with me, but none of them are as good as Anthony is. They're just fake. There's nothing Anthony wouldn't do for me. I don't think there's anything I wouldn't do for Anthony.

Z: You know when the *Ranger* came back in that day—when I went down and watched everybody coming in, and Anthony was looking for you but he didn't have his contacts in, and you whizzed by us somewhere in that huge crowd—he was actually scared that you would just walk past him and say "hi" and not even stop and talk to him.

E: Oh he's ridiculous! [Laughs.] That's so ridiculous. Me and Anthony, we were inseparable. People thought me and Anthony were together on the ship. That really surprises me to hear that. I don't blame him, because of the fact that I've had so many relationships with friends that I question it too, sometimes, but I didn't question it with Anthony. I knew he'd be there.

Z: Still, there is this element of military buddy relationships where guys get real close, and yet there is a recognition that that closeness is transitory, because you could be sent to some different station at any moment. Or in wartime, which is also kind of a reference point even when you're not in war, the other guy could die at any moment. So it's like, maybe you're real close now, but then in five minutes you could not be close.

E: Anthony could feel that way, and that's fine, but as far as my side—no matter what—Anthony's the kind of person that I will never ever desert. He just is. No matter where I move, Anthony will always be my best friend. He's closer than any friend I ever had back home.

Z: Would you say that you love Anthony?

E: Yeah! Yeah. I love Anthony. Don't tell him that, but. . . . Definitely don't tell him that! But yeah, I love Anthony.

Z: Have you found love in any of your gay sexual relationships so far?

E: No. No. I think I probably could have somewhere along the line, but people who know me know that I don't give it a chance. And sometimes I go on these straight kicks. Right now I would consider myself more gay than straight. Just because of the fact that I have chosen to stay more with gay people. But if you had asked me five months ago when I was seeing Christine, I would have considered myself more straight than gay. I believe in bisexuality totally, because I think I am. Some people say, "When I have sex with a girl I have to think of a guy." I didn't think of a guy when I had sex with Christine; I thought of her. And it worked out fine. Only when she dumped me did I totally depend on guys. . . .

With a woman I want an emotional kind of relationship. If I could have a mental relationship with a woman and a physical relationship with a man, I'd be a hundred percent happy.

With a girl you just go through the motions, you're just having sex with them. A guy always wants to try new things. At least the ones I've been with. Even though they know I don't want certain things, they'll push me, and I like it. I don't let anyone have anal sex with me, but a lot of guys will push it, and they'll get so far that I'll consider it. But at the last moment I'll be like, "I don't think so." When it happens one day I'll know that's the person for me.

Z: You never let guys fuck you?

E: I let one. Two years ago when I first came out, I met this guy and I fell head over heels for him, and he had anal sex with me. It hurt so much. And he was very, very small. To be blunt. So from this day on, there's just no way!

Z: Anthony believes that anal sex is the only sex, anything else is just foreplay. Is that also what you think?

E: No, because I know I get a lot of pleasure out of the other things.

Z: That's still sex for you?

E: That's still sex for me. Otherwise I would run around saying, "I had sex once in my life," and people would be laughing at me, going, "Yeah, right."

Z: But you told me you were a top in a teenage relationship you had with another boy back in Missouri.

E: Yeah, I was a top with him.

Z: So why would you say that? Sex isn't only being on the receiving end, or is it?

E: I guess that's what I always considered sex was—being on the receiving end.

Z: Why?

E: That's a good question. I don't know. I just always considered sex being the one who receives. I think basically if you're a bottom you're more feminine and if you're a top you're more masculine. And I am so worried about my masculinity that I feel if someone does have sex anally with me, enters me, then I'm going to turn into this big [snaps finger] queen and just be going "Hey girl."

Z: Why would you think that?

E: Because most of the bottoms I know are just really feminine. I don't want that to happen to me. I consider myself masculine, especially when I'm with a girl. Not because of the fact that I'm with a girl, but I think. . . . Every once in a while I go through these relapses. I'm with the guys, then all of a sudden one day—boom!—I have to go sleep with a girl. I'll ask myself why, and the reason will be that I have to prove that I can still be masculine.

Z: What do you look for in another guy?

E: Straight acting. I love queens for friends. They're awesome. The ones that snap their fingers and do the walk and just totally act like girls. But when it comes to sexual contact I like someone who acts straight. Someone built. Very handsome, but more boyish than anything . . . I don't want someone who looks like they're really manly.

Z: Unlike Anthony you don't have any special attraction to Marines.

E: Not at all. Even the non-attractive Marines think they're *all that,* and to me—I'm not saying I couldn't find a nice Marine with a nice personality, but I've never run into one. They're all these people with boxhead [sic. He means "jarhead."] haircuts who are just manly wannabes.

A lot of people think, oh Marines, they've got to be the biggest men in the world. But the ones I've met are really fake. It's just acting. I wish Marines would just let themselves go. I could see if you're with a lot of straight people at work and you're a Marine, then you should act manly. That's what duty calls for. But when you're at a gay party, then that should drop. You shouldn't be walking around like you're Jesus.

Z: You once went to an all-Marine party where you were one of only several sailors.

E: Yeah! That was hilarious. I went there just because my friends were going. It was all Marines, and five of us. It was not that we were especially attractive or anything, but I guess it was the fact that they were Marines and we were sailors. They wanted us, and most of us wanted them, besides me. It was a blast, because it was a straight-gay party, and at twelve o'clock they kicked all the straight people out. They just said, "Party's over." As soon as the last straight person left, the guy said, "OK, strip." One by one everyone started taking off their clothes and jumping in the pool. Everyone was paired off, but there were a lot of extra Marines left over. There was one who was acting too manly for me. Too straight, too stuckup, and only when he came up to me—because I wasn't about to go up to him—only when he asked me to come to his bedroom did I go in there with him.

Z: What did you do?

E: Just basically touched, and gave each other head. Again, nothing anal. He wanted to.

Z: What did he want?

E: He wanted to fuck me. I was trashed, but there was no way.

Z: What do you think is up with Anthony? Why is he cutting his hair so short and working all these Marines?

E: I have no idea. I think Anthony looks a lot better with longer hair.

Z: But why do you think he does that? You must have some ideas.

E: Because I think he. . . he just likes Marines. I think for him they're sexually better than either civilians or sailors or any other kind of military person. They've got better bodies. I think they're rougher.

Z: Anthony of course believes that pain is a necessary part of good sex.

E: Oh! [Covers his face.] No no no no no. Well, that's what Anthony has said to me, "You've never had sex until you've had a Marine." The way he talks about it is like it's sexually rougher, more pain involved. That's just where me and Anthony differ. If someone puts even a slight bit of pain on me, they're out the door. See you later. There's no way.

Z: Like a lot of sailors Anthony has tattoos. Do you?

E: No.

Z: Why did you decide not to get any?

E: It's like a song: you listen to it so many times you're gonna get sick of it. People are gonna see that tattoo forever, and you're just gonna wanna get rid of it some day.

Z: Do you think you look sexy in your uniform?

E: In my blues, yeah. I don't know why. Sometimes when I've seen movies—when I go to the store and one of my friends is renting a porno, the ones I've picked out have guys in Navy uniforms. Just 'cause it's something close to my heart. It's just sort of sexy. You're different. You're not this average civilian. It's like, pride. But as a whole I just don't like sailors.

Z: Why would you rent a sailor porno but not want to have sex with sailors?

E: Well, I know how I am; I'm not going to go so far as to say I'm a big slut, but I've had my share of men. When you're out there looking for a guy, you would like to think that you're gonna get someone who hasn't slept with so many people. And the Navy motto is sex sex sex, sleep with who you can get. Even though sometimes I've been like that, it's not what I want.

Z: Do you think that, in the Navy, gay men are more promiscuous than straight men?

E: No. Straight guys, especially in the Navy, are more promiscuous than gay people. I had my friends come back and brag about how many women they slept with. Whereas I think gay people are more particular. Like myself and a lot of my friends, we have standards; we have to find "the best looking guy in the bar." But a lot of straight guys are out to just get laid, period. It's just sex. It doesn't matter what the woman looks like.

Z: Tell me about the crossing the line ceremony.

E: I was really surprised, because I thought I was going to hate it, but I had fun. Some people quit, the people who couldn't take it anymore, men who were crying . . . it's really degrading. I had food all over me. I had Crisco oil poured on my face. I couldn't breathe, I got all this stuff in my lungs and in my eyes. The reason I think I liked it so much is because I went through a lot of summer camps. Being in a children's home they sent you to summer camp; that's what you did. And so I just had a blast. Everyone thought I was going to break down. Everyone. All the straight people. "We're going to break you." I never did, and they just kept walking me through it again and again. I mean, you can be there all day. Everyone else just went straight through and was done with it. But me, they kept on sending me through it, and I never got upset about it. The only time I got agitated was. . . . What are those things called, where you stick your hands and your head in, and they lock it?

Z: Stocks? The pillory?

E: Stocks or whatever. The only time I got really upset—not upset, but mad—I was in there on my hands, and my head was locked in there, and I was bent over, and someone was behind me pretending they were having sex with me. And another guy was pouring three-week-old food on top of my head, and it was dripping all over my mouth. I couldn't breathe, I couldn't wipe my face.

Z: What do you mean, pretending to have sex with you?

E: He was behind me going like this [gets up and demonstrates], humping me. And this supposedly is a straight guy, who I know isn't so straight.

Z: How do you know that?

E: Well, I don't know; it's just a feeling that I have.

Z: Could you actually feel his dick?

E: Yeah. Oh yeah. But that wasn't unusual, because everyone was doing that that day. Wog day is a day for everyone to just have fun, and if anyone ever had a thought about any kind of homosexual tendency, they could do what they wanted to do without anyone even thinking about it.

Z: Was his dick hard?

E: No, but another guy's was. I know it was. And I think he thinks I probably just thought it was big.

Z: He was humping you, too?

E: They would give you orders. You are a slave—someone with no authority whatsoever. So I would get behind this guy and I'd be like this, having sex with him, and everyone would be laughing and stuff. You know straight people were gettin' off on it. I could just tell.

Z: In what way?

E: Because they wouldn't just do it once. All of a sudden I'd look over and I'd have this straight person on top of me, riding me. You knew that it was more than just a thought, because they did it for so long.

Z: I thought that that stuff was now supposedly illegal.

E: We didn't have the wog queen ceremony and we didn't have the spanking, but a lot of the stuff that was supposed to be out, like touch-ing—it don't matter who said you can't do it; it was still done. The higher-ups didn't watch it, it was just us. Some people were getting hit; the people who weren't liked very much were getting hit a lot. It got really disgusting. People were peeing in jars and saving it for weeks and pouring it on top of us. The whole time I just kept on saying, "Live through this and you'll be fine. After this day is over you can go to bed and you'll be a shellback."

Z: Why would straight guys want to hump you? What does it mean that this is done in an organized, ritual way?

E: I don't know. Even though they say they're straight—I'm sure they are straight—sexuality and what gay people do is still on straight people's minds, no matter if they think it's wrong or right. So that was a day for someone just to say, "Hey, you go have sex with him," and get away with it. It wasn't like they were just pretending. I was on all fours, like a dog, and someone would be behind me actually hitting me with their dick like they were having sex with me. It wouldn't be a light thing, it would be, boom boom boom! And you could tell that that's what they were curious about.

Z: What did you think about that while it was happening?

E: I was laughing. Because for some people who I thought were really attractive, that was the only day they were going to get to do that, to get away with it, even with me.

E: I was totally straight acting on the ship and played off being gay very well. No one even had a clue. Then one day I went to a bar in Australia and I got these coasters, and some guy wrote his name on them. "Call me for a good time." Someone was nosy and went through my jeans and found them. They made a photocopy of it and passed it around my division. It didn't say my name or anything, but everyone knew where they got it from. So that blew over, right? Then I started getting letters from this guy from Perth. Of course everyone else is getting letters from Jenny and Margaret and Mary, and here I am getting letters from Tony. One of my dickhead so-called friends actually opened the letter and read it. It was very emotional, one of those "I really like you a lot and I wish you lived in Australia and things would be great for us" letters. It was just totally incriminating, so once again they made photocopies of it and distributed it throughout my division.

I was wrecked. There was no way I could deny it. Every time I tried to deny it someone would just show me the letter. So finally I was not admitting it, just not saying a word.

I got back off WESTPAC and I was amazed, because I found that people were OK with it. Even the straight people were coming up to me and saying, "You do what you want. I don't hold it against you; I still think you're a nice guy." I only had maybe one or two people who gave me shit about it. It shocked me, because the ones I thought would give me the most stuff about it—the married ones, the masculine and musclebound men—were the ones coming up to me and going, "That guy had no right to open up your mail. Fuck him. You're a good guy. It doesn't matter what you do, I still like you." It turned out really great, because the ones who were giving me shit were the ones I didn't care about.

One guy to this day does bother me about it, and the thing is, I know he's gay. Fred. I would party with him overseas, and he would hit on me. And people were walking around saying he was gay because he acted it and he looked it. His way of getting the topic off him was to say stuff about me. If I wanted to be a dickhead, I could have been like, "Look at you, I think you're gay," and people would have started talking about him, but I'm not like that. I just said, "Whatever, Fred," and went about my business.

Z: How were you affected by the public discussion of the idea of gays in the military? People you work with must have started talking about that after Clinton got elected.
E: Yeah, that was a real bad time for people to find out about me. Because it would be on the news out at sea, and people would be looking at me saying, "Eddy's kind's coming in the Navy." But a lot of it was just out of friendly joking. I think they respected me, I really do. A couple times we were with a whole bunch of people and we did get in a heated discussion,

and I said, "Look, there are so many gays working here. Half you guys who say you're straight are gay." I looked at a few people, and they knew who I was talking about. I said, "Don't tell me that's gonna start affecting you. There's gays in the military and there's always gonna be gays in the military. So get used to it." And a lot of 'em saw my point.

Z: The guys you worked with, including the ones who knew you were gay and accepted you—how do you think they would respond if some TV reporter came up with a camera and a microphone and asked them what they thought about gays in the military?

E: They'd say, "No way." I think even a lot of gay people would say, "No way." Because that's something that could endanger your career. If it didn't get you kicked out of the Navy, it still could make it impossible for you to work inside your division. No one wants extra work, no one wants extra ridicule. So a lot of people are going to say, "I don't want 'em in the Navy," even if they're gay themselves.

Z: Do you still have friendships with straight sailors?

E: Oh yeah. Only one close friend knows I'm gay. He's married and has a child. He's great. As far as friends go—I think Anthony's my best friend, of course, but this other guy's my second best friend. In fact, the reason he became my good friend is because he would talk me through a lot of this stuff. Even though he knew I was gay he would still come to my rack and risk everyone talking about him. And people did. People said, "Eddy and that guy, they're together." But he didn't care. He'd come to my rack and say, "You'll get over it. Don't worry about it. It's no big deal."

Lieutenant Tim: The Uniform

Christmas usually depresses me. Any organized simulation of goodwill does. Rather than degrade myself by participating in some ritual display of forced, artificial cheer I prefer to spend the day wallowing in sadness and honest resignation—listening to depressing music or watching movies about the Holocaust. It is my way of purging a year's accumulation of disappointment and despair in safe advance of January 1—the day statistics show Americans most favor for suicide.

It was easier when I lived in the former West Germany. There I could ride the U.S. Army train to West Berlin and spend Christmas mornings walking along The Wall, staring down East German guards and flirting with American MPs but eschewing any closer, more dangerous human contact. The Wall helped make certain truths clearer to me and I always returned to Frankfurt ready to start a new year.

In San Diego I foolishly imagined the sun and the palm trees would make it possible for me to simply ignore Christmas—as if Christ had been born in a Midwestern blizzard. Friends called, pressuring me to partake in some ersatz dysfunctional family display. To escape them I took the bus to "The Library"—queer slang for a cruisey video arcade down the street from the Naval Training Center. Surely, I reasoned, only the most desperate lost souls would be in evidence. Leaning against a booth door jingling my tokens in brazen challenge of the surveillance cameras I could savor the cold empty feeling of Christmas alone, a time when people try to come together but cannot. Who would save me?

I had only been jingling a few minutes when He appeared: my Savior with a U.S. Navy haircut, boyishly handsome face, and buff massive chest. He threw me a cautious but ready smile. I half nodded, looked away, and prayed that one of three "mini theater" booths with lockable doors (large enough to accommodate a wedding party but perpetually occupied by lone marathon masturbators) would soon open.

Miraculously one did. I stepped in. Closing the door behind me I imagined His ears outside straining to hear the lock click and shared His heightened anticipation when it of course did not. I dropped in a token and idly flicked past channels, barely registering the screen.

The door opened. My Redeemer asked me, ever so politely, would I mind if He watched pornography with me. Pulse racing, I shrugged and returned my unbeliever eyes to the monitor.

In a moment I had dropped all pretense of resistance and let His huge arms embrace me. Some men are so tender at impersonal sex. Halfway through He stopped to ask me one question: "Are you in the Navy?" "No. Are you?" He was. I used the moment to surrender all of my remaining tokens and felt a warm Christmasy glow take hold of me.

As we made ready to leave Tim told me his real name and shook my hand. I presented him with a card identifying me as a writer. I asked him where he was headed. The beaches, he said, but offered that he would call. I knew I would believe him and walked to the bus stop humming a carol in spite of myself.

A car pulled up. Tim beckoned me to climb in. Complying, I commented on the blue Navy decal on his windshield identifying him as an officer. "So you noticed that," he remarked, looking uncomfortable. Then, "So I want to ask you: What do you write about?"

I soon found myself with a crush on this handsome, charming, and smart man, son of a suburban New York City shopkeeper, who fascinated me with his butch chumminess (pummeling me in the ribs whenever I saw him in the bars, or with constrictor approach from behind purging my lungs of stale air) and exasperated me with his numinous tortured Jesus aspect. I do not mean to be blasphemous, but Tim—a secular Jew—did aspire to impossible spiritual ideals: The bond he had felt as a leader for his sailors was the only love he permitted himself. The lingering pain of a failed relationship seven years earlier and his always being at sea had caused the 30-year-old lieutenant to erect a wall between himself and anyone who came too close. (Talking to him on the phone I could almost see an outstretched palm.) Circumstantially prohibited from attaining an enduring spiritual union with a life partner, Tim aspired to monastic abstinence, but when this was not possible he found "sailor sex" the simplest solution.

I later learned I had caught Tim after his ending six months of self-enforced celibacy while on deployment. He had taken me on appearances as a "youthfully masculine" sailor available to provide him sexual release without fraudulent pretense of feeling or any closer, more dangerous involvement (unless it be for him to play counselor to a lost sailor, which is why he asked if I was in the Navy).

We got together for this interview one month later. Tim was not himself. After 12 years in the Navy he was getting out, and said he felt without any sense of direction. I was able to cheer him up over dinner and Chianti, but afterwards he grew pensive again. Tim did not want to go to my place and suggested we instead drive to Oceanside. He would show me spots to cruise Marines, and I could interview him on the drive up.

Northbound on Interstate 5 to Oceanside

Zeeland: Since we're on our way to Oceanside . . . I told you that I'm interested in the sexually charged rivalry between sailors and Marines, and you said "Every sailor wants a Marine, every Marine wants a sailor." Tim: That's just an old saying. I don't know if there's anything much to it.
Z: Have you had much involvement with Marines?
T: I've had my share.
Z: How are they different from sailors?
T: I think it's self-image more than anything. Every kid that goes into the military goes into it for his own reasons. A lot of kids join just to get away from home, to try and better themselves in some way, or escape from some bad situation. But every kid who joins the military joins in part to fulfill an image. The Marine Corps is the one branch that really markets itself for that. There's a whole machismo thing. The idea of proving or sanctifying your manliness by joining the Marines. A lot of times you'll see little wiry kids, who don't have much threat to them anyway, join the Marine Corps because it's going to make them something they want to be.
Z: Do you think having survived boot camp—which is so much more rigorous in the Marine Corps than in the Navy—that afterwards Marines have less to prove?
T: I don't think so. I don't think that's how the mind of an eighteen-year-

old kid works. I think an eighteen-year-old kid thinks he's never gonna die and he's big and he's bad and he can work anything that comes against him. It's a constant pissing contest trying to prove how good you are, how strong you are, how brave you are. I don't think that it ends at boot camp.

Z: What were your reasons for going into the military?

T: There were some good reasons and some not so good reasons. I was really patriotic. At school I was at the point where I had to consider what I wanted to do with my life. I figured that the greatest thing I could do with my life was to sanctify it through service to something greater than myself. That was during the Carter years when we lost the helicopters in Iran, and American hostages were still being held by a foreign country. It was a time when the U.S. military was really being mocked. In conjunction with my view of life, the military seemed like the natural thing to do.

But there was also another part of it, and these are the bad reasons. It was because of being gay. That was a large driving force for me to join the military, because just as I described my view of an eighteen-year-old kid now, when I was seventeen, eighteen years old I had the same view. I wanted to go and prove myself. It wasn't necessarily to prove myself through machismo so much, though I guess that was part of it, but it was more to prove my self-worth—that I could go and serve where I'm not wanted. I had this obscene fantasy of going off to war and getting killed and being a war hero. And that was a way to sanctify my life. By being gay I wasn't accepted, and when you're seventeen that seems insurmountable. I guess it's probably why the suicide rate among adolescent gays is so high. The whole idea of rejection on that scale for a seventeen-year-old kid—they see it as an obstacle that can't be overcome. For myself it was definitely the view that, "I've got to do something to prove my life is worthwhile." Going off and fighting battles and getting killed and having people weep at my funeral and say how patriotic I was—that was one way to do it.

A little further down the scale in importance, I think there was also a definite attraction to being in a masculine-dominated environment. Especially going to Annapolis. That to me was the ultimate in what I could set out to do, to survive in that type of environment. It was not only an attraction to the masculinity of it, which definitely existed—I don't necessarily mean anything in a sexual sense, because my whole time in Annapolis I was far too scared to think about doing anything sexual there, but more in the sense of—I don't know, I guess an unrequited attraction. Just being in that masculine-dominated environment and proving myself there.

I enlisted in the Navy for a year before I went to the Academy. That was my first time in an all-male environment.

Z: I'm finding evidence that that kind of environment fosters a homoeroticism that makes some men more inclined to—not necessarily come out, but to become aware of homosexual feelings.

T: I think that's very true. One thing I learned from being a really well-respected officer on-board ship is that there is a part of good military leadership that is inherently homosexual in nature. And that is love for your fellow man. Just being an incredibly strong paternalistic figure for a group of guys who are searching for what to do next. I think the Spartans understood that. It's only in our twentieth century conservative Judeo-Christian mindset that we find it so incompatible with military service when in actual practice today—we don't call it homosexuality, but I think every good leader feels something of that. A yearning for his men. Not that it's consecrated physically, but it's everything just short of that, and the feelings are just as intense.

I've always been extremely—effective is too antiseptic a word—I've always been a *revered* leader on every ship I've ever been on. Just really sought out by the troops. And I'm certain my disposition has a large part to do with it. *I know* that my being gay does a lot to make me a better Naval officer.

On my last ship I was the ship's first lieutenant, which is a job that is normally hated by officers because it's one of the toughest. You're responsible for all the external areas of the ship. Just real basic, hard-work kinds of jobs. Chipping and painting, and keeping the ship looking good. A lot of intensive physical labor that you're responsible for making sure your men accomplish. And the type of troops you're given are the most junior guys on the ship, or they're guys who, because of problems elsewhere on the ship, have been kind of washed out to you. Guys that have gotten into trouble with drugs or something else where they've lost their security clearances. They send them to deck division. Well, that was my job. It's probably the thing I'm most proud of in my life.

When I first walked on-board the ship, it was a typical deck division fraught with problems. There was fistfighting going on down in the berthing area. There was a lot of drug use. The ship looked like hell, rust all over the place. Despite the complaints of the captain, no one was ever able to get things to change. Morale was at an all time low because the guys were getting worked to death. They were just being absolutely bloodied; working—while in port—fifteen-hour days. There was no sense of reward for them.

I walked down into the berthing area for the crew, and it was a hellhole. These guys were living in a shit pit. A berthing area on a ship—in this case it's sixty guys living in an area about the size of most people's living room at home. Bunks stacked three high, one on top of another. So when you have a bunch of guys that are just pigs, and they're infringing on each other's space, it's a serious demoralizing force.

I figured that was one of the areas where I could make a positive difference right away, do a lot of good things, and establish my authority. So I told my troops that I was going to guarantee them certain things: a clean place to live and sleep; that they'd be taken care of; that they would see the output of their work in some meaningful way rather than just an endless job that never got completed because they were always being sidetracked to other jobs. I promised them that they would see a ship they could be proud of. And—we had a deployment coming up where we were going to spend two weeks in Hawaii. I promised them that if they stuck by me, when we got to Hawaii I'd make sure that I took care of them.

So the first thing I attacked was the berthing area. I was relentless. I was down there every morning, just hammering on my senior leadership. So now when the guys got off work after working an incredible number of hours they had a place to go where they could live and be a little bit more comfortable. And then I was always out on deck, making sure that what had to happen was happening. That guys weren't just painting over rust. When I saw things weren't happening right, I'd get the most senior man who was in charge of the junior guy who was setting a poor work standard, and I'd take them to task.

Gradually things started changing. After a couple weeks, I told them to take a look around and see what they'd accomplished. When we deployed, the ship looked outstanding. When we got to Hawaii, I ended up making sure that they were the first guys off the brow every day.

So I established a lot of credibility with my troops. They knew I would take care of them whatever the problem was, whether it was personal or professional. I stood in the pay line more times than I could count to take care of guys' pay problems. I was the only officer doing that. I had guys who came into my room in the middle of the night, crying to me. This one kid came to my room because he was having nightmares about when he was a little kid and his mother used to lock him in the oven when he was bad. When I did my job right, I was everything to my guys. I was boss, I was father, teacher, preacher, disciplinarian, best friend—I was everything to them. You serve in a position like that and you're larger than life.

A year and a half later I left the ship. My guys were trying to make it a real tear-jerking affair for me, which wasn't too hard to do. One of my best sailors came up to me and described life in terms of movies that he'd seen on the ship. He said that I was a cross between Sydney Poitier in *To Sir with Love* and Henry Fonda in *Mr. Roberts*. That was about the most flattering thing I could have thought of anyone saying. It was the best way he knew how to express something.

A couple days before I left the ship the captain came down to quarters—quarters is my time in front of my troops where they stand in formation—and awarded me the Navy Achievement Medal. And my guys broke out singing "For He's a Jolly Good Fellow."

I wanted to throw a party for them when I left, but we were in an Arab country, and it's difficult to find places that serve alcohol. I found this one place—a merchant seaman's club in Dhubai. Place was real seedy, but it served alcohol and I knew my guys could go out and have a good time without getting into trouble. It was about half a step above the Intergalactic Saloon in *Star Wars*. You walk into the head and there was about two inches of urine on the floor. It was disgusting. Fistfights breaking out all over the place. Just incredible. Amid all this chaos my guys were having a good time.

We're kind of segregated off from the general crowd in the place, and all of a sudden my guys get real quiet. "Hey Lieutenant, come here!" I walk over there, and they hand me this wrapped up thing. It was an engraved plate. "To Lieutenant Tim; Good Luck from Deck Division!" I was just about in tears. Then they handed me this small little package. I opened it up and—my guys knew I believed in what I did. I've always loved ships, and I loved the ship I was on, and I loved my men. They didn't know I was gay, but they knew I loved 'em. And they gave me a gold necklace. It's a chain with an anchor on it. I've never taken it off since. It's my prize possession, and I can't think of having anything that will ever mean more to me.

In the military, my experience has been that if you're gay, regardless of rank, you know other people that are gay. It's one of the most incredible network schemes going. That's why it's kind of a laugh now, all the hubbub about allowing gays in the military. I used to think that people looked the other way to pretend that there weren't so many gays around. But as more and more people talk about gays in the military, I'm convinced that people are really ignorant and just don't realize how many there are. I mean, I know admirals who are gay.

Anyway, there was this one enlisted guy on my ship. I'd seen him on the few occasions I went out when we were in our homeport. We developed a rapport; we'd just talk and stuff. Never in my mind did it ever occur to me to do anything unseemly, or anything that would ever compromise my authority or my position on the ship. Like I said earlier, guys were constantly coming to me—I probably had more people coming to me than the chaplain did. So I told this one kid if there was anyone he knew who was gay and having a tough time dealing with it, it was okay for him to tell them to come talk to me.

This guy was pretty open about being gay, and a lot of guys on the ship knew he was. So when I left the ship, he used what I told him—he misinterpreted it to his liking. He went and told people that once I left the ship I wanted him to let people know that I was gay. He went telling people in my division.

I went back and visited the ship a couple months later. She pulled into what became my new homeport. Got some odd looks from people, but after that it was the same as it always was. Bunch of guys came over to my home that weekend, and only one guy would talk to me about it. He said that this kid kept bringing up the fact that I'm gay and basically everyone refused to believe it. I guess you have to refuse to believe a negative stereotype if you really like a guy.

Z: But what did you say to your men in response to that?

T: [Pause.] I definitely did not tell them I was gay, but to what extent I denied it, I don't remember. But that's another complaint I have about this discussion about gays in the military. If you're in a unit, a tight unit, and it comes out that you're gay, people will go to incredible lengths to cover for you. There was just a case out in Japan where some poor kid was beaten to death because he was gay. Unfortunately I'm afraid that type of stuff is going to happen also, but that happens where you're not in a tight military unit. He was on a ship where there probably wasn't that type of camaraderie.

My first ship was homeported in Hawaii. Oahu is a fairly small place, and if you're going to go out to any gay places you're going to be known. I was always incredibly paranoid, but I can only assume that after being stationed there a year and a half people saw me going out. I am certain that there were many guys in my division then who knew I was gay, but again, I had the same type of rapport with my troops where I was really well respected and highly regarded. There was one guy who lived down in my berthing area who was gay, who didn't work for me, and I would talk to him from time to time when I saw him out. He would always fill me in on what was happening—from time to time someone would joke about me being gay and would get slapped down immediately by everyone around him. "Just shut up. You don't know what the hell you're talking about."

Z: Why did you choose the Navy over the other service branches?

T: From the time I was a little kid I've just always loved ships, and had this fascination with the ocean. I've wanted to go to sea since I was seven or eight years old. Finally one day I had the opportunity to do it.

After graduating from Annapolis you could go into the Marine Corps. They allow fourteen and a half percent of every class to go Marines. I was kind of attracted to that idea. A lot of it was probably to fulfill the more negative motivations I had for going to Annapolis—get a chestful of medals, be a revered dead hero. There was also the masculine appeal of it all. And the Marine Corps professionally has a great appeal to me. But the thing that made me go Navy instead of Marines was that I've loved ships. I don't think there's anything man can build more beautiful than a ship. I've always loved going to sea. Now that I'm getting out I'm going to miss the hell out of it.

Z: What can you tell me about life at the Academy?

T: Besides just talking about the daily toils of life and daily challenges everyone goes through, being gay at the Academy was an incredibly repressive experience. In spite of the fact that there are women there, it is very much still a masculine-dominated environment. Even more so than on-board ship, because on-board ship you have a cross section of the Navy. At the Academy it's guys who are eighteen to twenty-three or twenty-four. That's that point in life where most guys are spending a lot of time pissing into the wind and trying to prove how great they are physically and how much more of a man they are than the guy next to them. So going through that place—it was very repressive. I don't mean only sexually repressive, it was emotionally repressive. My greatest regret now of having gone through Annapolis is that—you develop these incredibly close relationships with a lot of guys, and I had to lie to so many of them by pretending to be something I wasn't. Even now, to this day, seven years after I graduated, I bump into classmates that were close friends of mine, and I still feel these pangs of guilt because I was dishonest with them. While I was at the Academy it caused me to be very guarded around even my close friends, and after I graduated it caused me to be very distant from them. Most people at the Academy developed close friendships that last a lifetime. For me they were guarded relationships that I couldn't wait to make distant so I wouldn't have to deal with the dishonesty.

And it was definitely sexually repressive because it was a point in life where libido was definitely up there and you couldn't do much about it. Kind of like being a eunuch in a harem I guess.

Z: How did you deal with that aspect of it?

T: I don't want to talk about that crap.

[We arrive in Oceanside and I shut off my tape recorder. We drive down Hill Street, the main drag, where even late on Sunday evening there are Marines hanging around on almost every corner, easily identifiable by their "high and tight" haircuts and muscular rounded buttocks. Tim points out the pier, the adult bookstore, and the park where men meet each other. In the dark we see a few lone Marines, one smoking, another just standing staring at our passing car. He remarks on them in a tone I comment rings of sadness. "No," he says, "not sadness." "Weariness?" "That maybe comes closer."

Tim tells me he had been tempted to drive up here recently, but can't feel good about picking up Marines. They are all so young, and he has just turned 30. They are enlisted men, he is an officer. He worries he could corrupt them. And anyway, cruising is something he only does after coming off of deployment, providing him what his straight sailors obtain from female prostitutes: sexual release and an ersatz intimacy that he believes corrodes the soul. "Sport fishing," he calls it; "I blame it on being a sailor." I click on my tape recorder.]

Z: Sport fishing?
T: I'm not going to answer that. Nope.
Z: Does it have to be bad?
T: No, it doesn't. It's just something private. I believe it should be private.
Z: [Pause.] Okay.

[Tape off. There is an awkward silence. We drive around some more, then go to Denny's for coffee. Ineffectually groping for a way to bring up my own feelings for Tim I remark that I will always be grateful to him for cheating me of my Christmas depression. Tim is puzzled. "What happened on Christmas?" "That's when we met." He looks pained. "It was Christmas? I didn't remember that."

Ouch.]

Southbound on I-5 to San Diego

Z: Some gay men have sex while they're at sea. Do you think it also goes on among straight men?
T: I imagine it does, but I really don't know. I was always very far removed from that, and I never minded being removed from it either. What I didn't know couldn't hurt me.
Z: Sailors have a reputation: a girl in every port, or maybe a guy in every port.

T: My roommate on my first ship was an old guy by Navy standards. He was probably in his mid-forties, early fifties. He'd been deploying to the Philippines for years and years. When the guy was at home you would never think of him as being anything other than a family man. Devoted to his wife and his kids, churchgoing, good family man. But when we pulled into the Philippines he was always getting dolled up to go out every night to visit Mamasan, a prostitute he'd been seeing since the time he was in Vietnam and passing through the Philippines. They'd maintained this relationship over years and years. Finally our last night in port—he knew he was retiring from the Navy, so he figured he was leaving the Philippines for the last time—he was taking Mamasan out for a real romantic dinner and night out on the town.

That type of relationship is not unusual for sailors. It's one of the things I always found distressing about the job. Guys develop these very transient relationships, develop a lot of them for different places and different times. I attribute that to be one of the reasons why the Navy has such a high divorce rate.

It's kind of hysterical whenever you hear the military talk about morality and maintaining a standard, especially when they talk about gays being promiscuous. Well, I'll tell you. Everyone from the captain on down, on most ships, is going out when they get into port to carry on and get laid. And it's well known. The captain on my first ship—and this was the captain himself doing it, not doing it by proxy—would get up and remind us going into port how many days we had until we got home and what the incubation period was for various venereal diseases.

The Navy is an organization of whoremongers and other types of deviants. I don't make excuses for it; I'm not proud of the service in that way. I've just completed a six-month tour in the Philippines, and I've never seen a more promiscuous group than the thirty-odd guys that were assigned to me. It was absolutely disgusting. Guys having contests, bragging about who got more venereal diseases. I was trying to quash that as much as I possibly could by withholding guys' liberty when I thought they were getting out of hand. I had the doctors coming from Preventive Medicine to give the lectures and show all the gory slides. And these guys still were absolutely without shame, unabashed.

There was something on-board ship—and this was explained to me by the executive officer of my ship who was number two in command. It was explained in front of the whole wardroom, and it was for my benefit because I was the new guy on-board at that time. They called it the One-eighty Rule. And the rule is: we're on the other side of the world, one hundred and eighty degrees away from home, and what happens here stays here, we don't talk about it back home. So all these guys who are supposedly loyal husbands could go and screw around. It's situational ethics; the same rules don't apply. What is bad and unethical and immoral back home is OK here because we're someplace different. And generally that's how the Navy works. You see it in the Tailhook scandal. Unfortunately, that's the depth of the moral ethos of the Navy.

Z: Are gay sailors equally promiscuous?

T: I don't think so, at least not on cruise, because I think it's much more difficult. The ship pulls into port, and there are women all over the place, and guys are going after them. Whenever I pulled into port and wanted to go and relieve months' worth of pent-up frustration and tension—there were places to go, but it was just too difficult having to watch your tracks, and guard yourself.

Z: Is there a certain brand of Navy masculinity that is expected of sailors?

T: I don't really think there is. I think the Marine Corps would be much more on that type of image. I don't think it exists in the Navy to the same extent.

Z: What is your own definition of what's masculine?

T: How do you mean? Masculine physically or masculine emotionally or . . .

Z: What comes to mind when you think of the word?

T: It would be too easy to answer that question with a stereotype—the big brawny guy—but I don't think that is necessarily what is masculine. I don't know, I—I don't know. That's tough.

Z: You mentioned that someone had told you that you were unusually masculine for a gay man.

T: Yeah. In most people's eyes it's physical stature somewhat. But that's not necessarily true, because I've known a lot of guys who were masculine and didn't have a lot of stature to them. I think it's courage. Moral courage, as well as courage just to go do what has to get done. I think there's a certain amount of boyishness to it. That mischievous type thing that gets you into trouble every once in a while where you're caught doing something that you shouldn't. Someone who has some unrequited boyish goal and he keeps trying to fulfill it. A certain sense of adventure, I guess.

Z: You told me one reason you want to get out of the Navy now is because you have lost your boyish idealism.

T: Yeah, that's true to some extent. I was one of the guys in charge of the honor system at the Academy. At the end of my year I was given the award for the guy who did the most for the honor concept. I did my damnedest and was very successful in getting guys thrown out of the

Academy for. . . . A daily requirement when you're a plebe is to read two front page newspaper articles and one sports page article. I got a guy thrown out because he said that he'd read a newspaper article when in fact he hadn't and was just trying to lie his way through it. The way I looked at it then was, I was upholding an ideal. I was ridding the Academy and the Navy of someone who did not have the moral turpitude to do his job, and who would be a general blemish on the officers' corps.

When you get out to the fleet you realize that that mark is so out of touch and unrealistic. The Navy is made up of a bunch of guys who are legitimized pirates. Especially on surface ships in the Navy, regular combatant ships. Very often how well you steal from the government is a mark of how well you do your job. How well you lie is often a measure of how well you do your job. Your captain never wants you to lie to him, but your captain always wants you to lie for him. I always thought a hallmark of being a good officer was how much of a good leader you were and how much people would be willing to follow you—and all too often I've seen officers fall short of that mark. I've seen officers treat people totally without regard for their well-being or without any regard whatsoever for decency. If you're successful in that type of bureaucratic amoral institution, you have to start questioning your means of success. If I do well among a group of thieves and whores, what does that say about me? And that's the question I started asking myself. Being that the Navy hasn't ended up being what I had hoped it would be, and what they taught me it would be back at boat school, and being that I've done well at it, I have to start to question: Am I starting to lose something here? And I'm afraid that I might.

Z: You said that loving men made you a superior officer. What did you love about your men?
T: One of the great things about sailors—there's no greater piece of Americana than a cross section of sailors. From the kid growing up on the farm in Oklahoma who has never known anything but planting corn and feeding cattle, to the kid who was raised in a ghetto and is finally able to eat three square meals a day. There's a certain part of it which definitely appeals to my idea of patriotism. Wow, this is a picture of America right here. Part of it is the boyishness of it. No matter how old a group of sailors are, because of the retarded type of lifestyle it is, they're a very boyish group. But beyond boyishness there's just an incredible vulnerability about them. You realize how much these guys need to be led. How much they need to be taken care of. They've all got their good points, they've all got their foibles and their weaknesses.

Once you establish yourself with those guys, there's just an undying loyalty that you have with them that is unequaled by anything I have ever experienced.

Z: Do you feel a special camaraderie with all sailors, as opposed to Marines or other servicemen?

T: You feel for the guys you've served with. Beyond that, I don't know how much further it goes because the experiences are just too varied and different. In the Navy you could be talking to a guy who's been out to sea and has done a lot of things you've done and experienced the hardships and trials that you have, or you could be speaking to a guy who's been sitting on shore duty for his whole career. Same thing in the Marine Corps. I could be speaking to a guy who's seen combat, as I have seen combat, or I could be speaking to a Marine who hasn't really done anything other than shine shoes or stand guard at an embassy. The camaraderie comes from the commonality of experience. And that doesn't necessarily come from wearing the same uniform.

Z: Some men tell me they feel a sexual attraction to other military men they say is rooted in those common experiences.

T: There's definitely an attraction. I don't know that it's common interests. There is an attraction for the youthful masculinity of it. I think that's a larger part of it.

Z: Have you encountered civilians who were attracted to you for your being in the military?

T: Oh yeah. Yeah. A lot of guys are—I call them military chasers. I think for a lot of guys sexual conquest is almost a way of consecrating their own shortcomings. "If I could conquer this, then surely I must be that good." So for the guy who has questions about his own—whatever it might be, however he perceives someone who's in the military, whether it might be strong, whether it be masculine, whether it be domineering— whatever the positive attributes might be that that guy assigns in his mind to someone in the military, he feels by conquest of that, "truly I must have those attributes myself."

Z: Do you have an attraction to men in uniform?

T: Yeah, I do.

Z: Any particular uniforms that you like?

T: [Annoyed.] Ah geez. The attraction for the uniform just comes from having worn it for so many years. And because of having worn it, there's definitely a pride you feel in the uniform, particularly when you're really young. When I first enlisted in the Navy, it was hard to get me on liberty out of uniform. Buddies of mine used to laugh at me, but I was just so proud of it. It was an identity, it was being part of this greater organization, with all these great traditions. I guess the attraction for the uniform, or finding guys in the uniform attractive, still stems from that.

I think the greatest uniform, because it is just so traditional, is Navy crackerjacks. That's not to say I hang around Navy bases waiting to grab a guy wearing crackerjacks. That's not the way it is. I'm not even talking sexual appeal. But just attractiveness, I think it's the greatest uniform.

Z: Officers don't get tattoos, I guess, but probably a majority of the Navy enlisted men do.

T: A lot of guys do, yeah. It's not considered a proper thing for an officer. There are officers with tattoos—usually they have them in places that aren't readily obvious—but generally speaking they don't get them. Or at least not with the frequency and flamboyance and exposure that enlisted guys do. I've never been attracted to them, never thought they looked good, and I've never gotten them.

Z: Tell me about the class distinction between officers and enlisted men.

T: It's incredible. Huge class difference. The military is a very stratified society. In terms of pay scale, enlisted pay doesn't compare even minutely with officers' pay. In terms of prestige, in terms of how you're treated. . . . Under the Uniform Code of Military Justice, the justice that can be doled out to an enlisted man is much stiffer than the justice that can be doled out to an officer. On-board ship officers live in a place called Officers' Country. Officers' Country is where the staterooms are, and enlisted men aren't allowed to enter Officers' Country unless they're on official business. They can't just walk through it. Officers eat in a wardroom; enlisted guys eat in a galley and they eat different food. Even living ashore—for an officer to live on base in the bachelor officers' quarters, which is the officers' equivalent of a barracks, is almost unheard of. For an enlisted guy to live on base, it is standard. So the difference is just huge.

Z: It's been suggested that gay relationships tend to bridge class, racial, and other differences more often than straight relationships. Some people theorize that it's almost a way of creating the kind of friction that exists between men and women. Do you think that makes for a special attraction between gay officers and enlisted men?

T: No. I can't imagine that. I think fraternization is wrong, at least within the same command. It happens on ship when there are women serving on-board. It's not good. If it happens with officers with enlisted men on their ships, I don't really know.

Z: Would your attraction to other military men just as easily find as its object other officers as enlisted men?

T: I don't know, I've never quantified it. I wouldn't go after an enlisted guy in my command.

Z: Let's say outside your command. Would there be a special attraction
that—
T: No. It's not a factor.

Z: What do you look for in a man? What is your ideal?
T: I don't know. I don't know. Someone who's going to make me see stars
and make my heart go pitter patter.
Z: Over the top of my notes I made after our first conversation I wrote
"Distant Hero," because of your being larger than life to your men and
your aspirations for glory. You told me that was kind of how you perceived yourself. And you also talked about the distance you needed to
keep from people and wanting to be seen that way. I wonder if you've
cultivated this, kind of, in your persona.
T: It's not wanting to be seen that way. I think I have been seen that way.
It is the way I am, I recognize that. I don't—I don't like being close to
just—I don't believe in having close superficial relationships. So it means
that I can be a nice guy, and certainly be there for my troops, but it doesn't
mean I have to be an open book for them. I'm generally that way in my
personal life as well. I think being personal and maintaining a certain
distance for your own privacy to protect your own uniqueness—I think
that's a good thing to do. It's not trying to cultivate an image. It's just the
way I am.

Part Two, Five Months Later

The day Tim got out of the Navy a party was thrown for him by
his good friend Holger. Tim wore his dress white uniform. Holger
decorated his apartment with Navy recruitment posters and other
materials, and scolded me when I picked up a carefully positioned
brochure (which another interviewee had modeled for).

Picturing Tim as somewhat of a loner, I was surprised at the large
and spirited crowd that came to fete him, including numerous other
gay Navy and Marine Corps officers, and a woman who explained
that she had been Tim's "beard"—his date at Naval social functions. At the party's climax Tim was made to sit in a chair in the
center of the living room and submit to the attentions of a male
stripper commissioned by Holger to embarrass him. I felt a vicarious discomfort for my friend as the stripper stood before his face,
and through some contrivance set the crotch of his leopard skin
loincloth aflame, and ordered, "Blow me, Tim."

Tim has confessed to me that he reddens even at saying the word "sex." He bought a copy of *Barrack Buddies and Soldier Lovers,* but had no comment for me about it. At my prodding, he confided that he "had a problem" with its frank discussion of sex (not to mention its "tawdry" title), which he said "went beyond what is necessary" to educate the public about the plight of gays in the military. He said it reminded him of tabloid journalism. I told Tim that I would be including even more sex stories in this book, but only ones that illustrated connections between military life and sexuality. "Why is that important?" he asked, and warned me against assigning relevance where none exists. Somewhat defensively, I explained that my editor and other gay writer friends had told me of the value my work will have to historians and other scholars. But Tim only smiled and said, "Your editor wants to sell books."

My decision to describe here the circumstances of our meeting was a difficult one. Anxious for Tim's approval, I told him exactly what I would write about him, and my reasons for doing so. He told me to write what I must, and said he trusted me to be truthful—and added with a smile that he might never speak to me again after the book comes out.

Part Two of this interview finds Tim in an upbeat mood. He had just accepted an executive job at a private corporation. Tim took me to see a Walt Disney movie, then to a cafe in Hillcrest, where I again turned on my tape recorder. A few days before, Clinton had just announced his "compromise" policy on the gays in the military issue.

Z: Tell me your reaction to the President's policy announcement. "Don't Ask, Don't Tell, Don't Pursue"—is that what they're calling it?
T: Yeah. That's kind of a misnomer, because they can still investigate. I think it's a real crying shame.

He's been forced to compromise and that's sad, because the compromise policy will not serve the real purpose. It will not change much substantively for very many gays in the military. There's so much politics being thrown back and forth, by both the arch conservatives and the people involved in gay rights. And that's what's been forgotten: What does it take to serve justice, to treat people fairly? I don't blame the President. I think it's real unfortunate he was forced to back down. Maybe he's a coward; he's been called that. I don't believe so. I think he's maybe a pragmatic idealist. He couldn't have happen what he wanted to have happen. He's acknowledged that. Unfortunately, it's going to bring years more of injustice for thousands and thousands of men and women. It's cause for great personal sacrifice, for no reason, to people in the service who happen to be gay.

Being out of the Navy for three months now, the effect for me—of course my identity after twelve years is still so closely aligned with the Navy, but it bothers me as an American, the same way that it would bother me if I was alive in the Jim Crow South. It bothers me because I love my country; I believe in what we're supposed to stand for. And we're falling short.

Z: Under "Don't Ask, Don't Tell" military homosexuals are asked to remain celibate. That would have been the case even if Clinton had lifted the ban, because only Congress can rescind the prohibition of sodomy in the Uniform Code of Military Justice. Is it honest to expect that gay people would remain celibate? Is it fair to ask that of them?

T: No, it's not honest, it's not fair. To say, "Okay, throw out gays: unless they don't [admit to being gay], don't have any relationships, and don't have sex. . ."

There are so many words in our language we think of as dirty, sex being one of them. Maybe I'm somewhat guilty of that mindset, preferring to keep private things private, for my personal taste. But the fact of the matter is, it's part of the human experience. And to say to a young man or woman who enters the military at eighteen years of age, "If you want to [have] a career in here, never have sex, be celibate, be alone—" If we are to do that we are asking someone to sacrifice a large part of the human experience, the want of intimacy with another human being. It's very unrealistic. It's very unfair. But then again, the whole policy of not allowing gays in the service is a policy that's rooted in unfairness.

Personally, who really cares if I'm gay? How does my being gay affect someone else's life?—other than someone who I choose to be with, where there's a mutual decision to be together. It's so easy for people who aren't gay to sit around and pass judgment on "those people. They're obscene; I hear they're all child molesters and necrophiliacs as well." All sorts of ridiculous assumptions made on ignorance that breed hatred.

Z: It's been suggested that what clinched the doom of the President's pledge was the photograph of Sam Nunn and John Warner touring a submarine, shown leaning their heads down in the berthing. The implication is that these young sailors are innocent uncorrupted boys and introducing homosexual perverts into the military would—

T: Anyone who would think that lifting the ban on gays in the military can be done with no problems whatsoever is mistaken. It will be a difficult policy to enact when it does happen. It is a very emotional thing [for a straight service member to consider]: "Gee, I'm gonna be doing all the most personal things from showering and shaving to getting dressed in the morning inches from the face of someone who's gay." And usually it's said with much more pejorative terms.

Z: "I don't want no fag lookin' at my butt and/or dick."

T: Certainly that's the way it's normally put, which should be reason to question the judgment of whoever's saying it, being so willing to pass prejudicial aspersions. But let's detach ourselves from it a bit: it's happening right now. Right now today, this night, I can guarantee you someplace out on the big blue there's a ship bouncing around; there's some gay sailor taking a shower in front of his straight shipmates and he's managing to do it without getting aroused, and there's some straight guy getting undressed next to the bunk of a gay guy and he's managing to do it without getting grabbed. It's happening now. I've been on submarines. I've been on ships, both in enlisted status and as an officer. I managed to shower without getting aroused or making some untoward come-on. It was a conduct I knew was demanded of me.

Z: They argue that "sexual misconduct" will increase once gays are allowed to serve openly. What would you do if you were a commander and you were faced with adjudicating a case involving a man caught having sex aboard the ship? You could sentence him to five years in the brig. Do you think that would be appropriate?

T: I think five years in the brig is inappropriate, but I think discipline is incredibly important. I think it would be vital to discipline a guy.

Z: But how? Would you discharge him?

T: It might well be. It would depend on the circumstances. There are different aspects to discipline. Part of discipline is deterrence; part of discipline is punishment. Part of discipline, though, is to set a standard, and I think it's very important that the standard be maintained. Your conduct is expected to be professional.

My first deployment I was on a destroyer on the North Arabian Sea. We pulled up alongside a destroyer tender. Destroyers, being combatant ships, don't have women on-board. Destroyer tenders, being auxiliary ships, do. I remember walking on-board the tender and going into the ship's store and seeing condoms stocked on the shelf. Who's buying condoms at sea? I was shocked. Not that men and women have sex; but that it was happening at sea, and that the attitude of the command was, "If you can't beat 'em, join 'em." I'm not saying selling condoms is wrong, but to allow things like that to go on to such a degree, where women are getting pregnant at sea and there is no disciplinary action taken, was appalling to me.

Z: Beyond that it's a violation of law and in your judgment unprofessional, what actual harm is there in such infractions?

T: Now here's something that's going to sound a bit inconsistent from things I said earlier: If no one knows about it, there probably is no harm, but once people do know about it you have problems. It breaks down discipline. And I hate saying that phrase, because it's one used so readily against gays.

One thing my troops could always be assured of in dealing with me was that I was a sonofabitch to everyone. I took care of all my guys really well and I was well respected for it, but if anyone stepped out of line, no matter who they were, they got hammered. They got hammered hard. My guys knew—no matter who they were, no matter how much I liked 'em—that I hung all people equally. "You step out of line you're gonna walk the plank. And I don't care who you are." I think it is very difficult to maintain that objectivity if you're sleeping with someone. But more than being difficult, I can't imagine any way you're going to be able to maintain the *appearance* of being evenhanded if you're sleeping with someone.

Z: I told you before about a conversation I had with [historian] Allan Bérubé about how the military is itself a sexual culture, and you responded affirmatively to the idea. In what ways is that true?

T: You take a group of guys, you put 'em out on a ship for up to six months at a time, remove them from all things that are familiar to them— family, friends, girlfriends—whatever intimacies they have back home . . . when a ship goes to sea, and you're out of sight of land, it is its own world. It's a microcosm of the larger world around it floating out in the middle of nowhere. All common references are lost. It doesn't matter that you're lonely, because everyone's lonely. In that type of environment, I think there is something in good leadership and in being a good sailor, and being a good shipmate, and taking care of your buddy—and "unit cohesion" or in whatever military terms you want to couch this thing—I think there is something about it that is inherently . . . intimate, on an emotional level.

Z: You said that last time, only you called it "inherently homosexual" then. But whether it's necessarily homosexual or not, I've since come to understand that this is really what the Joint Chiefs mean when they talk about "unit cohesion"—that the presence of avowed homosexuals would taint military buddy love, which is supposed to be heterosexually pure.

T: I've heard more stories about guys who are straight who have had homosexual experiences based upon that bond. On submarines they have a joke that "it's only queer if you're tied to the pier." In other words, out at sea sex is okay, but once you're in port, you can't talk about that, or they'll throw you out for it.

Z: How could they ever find room on a submarine?

T: I'm not sure.

Z: Unless there was group complicity—

T: That's very possible. But part of that whole fear I believe is, "If I'm out at sea and I have sex with a guy, I'm not gay, I'm only having sex with a guy." Where if you have gays out there, then "that risks redefining what I am." I think that is on a very personal level part of the paranoia and absolute hatred people have for the idea of having gays serve with them. Something that happens though, is, once you put a face on it, people's attitudes change.

A friend of mine back East just died of AIDS. . . . Six or seven years before, [his lover] died. Al's father went with Al to his lover's funeral. Al was totally distraught, ripped apart. And Al's father, who served in the Marine Corps in World War Two, embraced his son, and said, "I understand what you're feeling. When I was on Okinawa, one of my buddies was killed. And he was the only person I ever really loved." When he told me this story, Al just kind of looked at me and smiled and said, "I didn't ask my father anything more about that." It was probably a very deep and secret thing for his father, that he was only admitting because of the extreme grief that Al was feeling, trying to comfort Al. I guess that's what I always think of when I think about intimacy bringing men close. I could only suppose that in circumstances like that there is a possibility that something can happen. I don't understand it. For myself, I'm gay, I always have been. I can't imagine being physically intimate with a woman as being anything at all satisfying or anything I would want.

Z: You never had any sexual feelings toward a woman ever?

T: No. I never did. Regardless of what my feelings for her would be emotionally. So I'm trying to be fair at looking at it from the other end. I can't understand how a guy who doesn't have that attraction could want to be physically intimate. If in fact that's what Al's father was talking about, it's something outside my realm of experience.

Z: The guys I'm interviewing, so many of their stories suggest that male sexuality is much more fluid than is generally understood. But like you I've never been conscious of any sexual arousal contemplating a girl or a woman. I remember the first time, though, that I ever had a one-night stand; the lights were off, and it was the first time I'd been with another person in that way. And I thought: *I could do this with anyone.* Because the experience of physical closeness with another body was so different from my fantasies. And a few years ago I had a German teacher, a stern and icy woman who was not especially beautiful, but there was a strong sexual tension between us. We would get very bitchy with each other for no apparent reason in class; the other students were always looking at us and smiling. I was very confused by it. And I later had dreams about her, and—

T: [Turns tape recorder to face Z.]

Z: [Laughs.] That's just my reverse reference point for the unexpected attraction some straight guys feel for men.

Z: In your first interview you talked about "military chasers." It's not a phenomenon unique to San Diego, but I suspect it's more developed here than in any other U.S. city. It varies among the different personalities, but some of them cut their hair like military guys, some of them have fake dog tags, some of them even manage to get base stickers for their cars so they can cruise the bases. I don't know who exactly you were thinking of, but you explained how in your view these guys operate from some deficient sense of masculinity. And—I guess I felt affronted, because I thought you might have been talking about me.

T: No, I wasn't.

Z: OK. But then I had to wonder, here we were driving around Oceanside admiring Marines. You had talked about your attraction to other military men, and you said it was rooted in an attraction to masculinity. So—

T: What's the distinction? The distinction is [between] what we pretend to be and what we are. There's a difference between saying, "Generally I'm really attracted to guys in the military," and having that as a pursuit because you need to have the image fulfilled.

A friend of mine [pretends] like he's in the military. Big, muscular, short haircut, wears fake dog tags. Now, I enjoyed the military. I loved the identity. But it was mine; it was my life; it was what I was living. I like short hair. When I was a little kid I always got crew cuts. However, in the time I've gotten out, my hair has grown out—

Z: [With regret.] It has.

T: —it's as long as it's ever been in twelve years. I have my own dog tags, I don't walk around wearing them. I haven't worn my uniform—none of those things that guys who want to live for the image do. It has nothing to do even with being gay, I don't think. I think the issue is more . . . living life with integrity, being true to yourself. If I think being a fireman is the absolute best thing I can do in life because it fulfills my sense of masculinity, I'm not going to dress up as a fireman, I'm going to go be one.

Z: But for me I wonder if it's not almost the complete opposite. I have a strong attraction to military men, and sometimes only to military men, but I don't have any desire to be a military man. It seems like I eroticized what I could not accept as viable in the soldier I followed to Germany. I was a pacifist; when he joined the military I was very distraught over the image of him in uniform. And all of sudden I found myself turned on by it. I think that was kind of a solution for me.

T: There are a thousand reasons to have an attraction. For whatever it is, straight or gay, or even for totally nonsexual things—I think that's okay, if you know what it is and you can acknowledge it. I don't like being judgmental, but now I'm going to be: for me, the distinction comes in how honest you are in living that. Do I want to dress up and play house, or do I want to go out and live it? I think that's the crux of it.

Z: You've told me before that you resent the "trivialization" of the military uniform by nonmilitary men for whom it's a turnon.

T: Yeah.

Z: When I first met my ex, Troy, I was excited by the fact that he was in the Navy. "This is a sailor that I'm with." Soon that image of him gave way to my feelings for him as just Troy. So I think I transcended that attraction to image. But I still wanted to see him dress up in his uniform, and undress him out of his uniform. I had to beg and plead for months to get my little fantasy fulfilled, and when I finally did it caused the first major argument in our relationship. Not because he had any special respect for the uniform, but I think he felt it was a cheap objectification of him for my kicks.

T: I can't comment on his motivations, but for myself— I obviously had a lot of problems with the Navy because I got out. But I had problems with the Navy, the system; I've never had problems with the Navy, the substance. And by the substance I mean ships, I mean sailors, I mean God and country. I loved that. Part of that for me was the tradition of it. I loved and cherished Navy tradition. . . . To me [the uniform] represents an object of reverence. Kind of like the flag. I revere the flag, I revere the uniform. I don't want to get too mom and apple pie right now—

Z: Although you could.

T: Although I could. [Laughs.] That certainly is something that appeals to me.

Three weeks after I got out of the Navy was when the big gay march on Washington occurred. I traveled back east to go to it. Reluctantly. I didn't want to go, because I didn't think it would be anything special. As it turned out, it was a catharsis for me. The whole issue of lifting the gay ban was coming up, and it's obviously an issue that I do feel very passionately about. So I was thinking about bringing my uniform and wearing it, to make a statement. Navy lieutenant, twelve years of honorable service, Annapolis graduate. I think I represent myself well, and I'm proud of my service. [Pause.] I decided not to wear it because my military upbringing [taught me] that it is inappropriate to wear your uniform to a political rally. Of course, when I was told that in boot camp, they weren't talking about gay marches; it could have been a rally for Jesse Helms and it [still] would be inappropriate to wear, because it implies service [endorsement] of a certain political stance and it's necessary for the military to be apolitical. So, I have a certain reverence for the uniform because of what it represents.

Z: Of course had you worn that uniform you would have had thousands of men lusting after you in it.

T: I would have been a lot more comfortable with that than I am with talking about it. I've got no problems with being found attractive.

Z: But they would have been lusting after you *in uniform*, as an officer.

T: I really couldn't care less.

Z: I went to the *Ranger* decommissioning ceremony, and it was the first time I'd seen a lot of sailors together in their whites. I found myself eagerly ogling and objectifying them. In fact, I took my video camera, and I got some footage of them climbing the steps to the brow. And as I did it I thought to myself, "Lieutenant Tim would be really disgusted with me for this."

T: Yeah, I probably would have been.

Z: Tell me about the march on D.C.

T: I didn't expect it to be anything special. But every step along the way I was drawn further into the happenings there. Like I said, I didn't think I was going to go. Then I figured, I'll go, but I'll just stand by the sidelines and watch. But then I found out that there was a group of gay service academy graduates—alumni from all of the service academies—that was marching. I wanted to be part of that; marching with people who had a shared experience with me from what was a very repressive lifestyle. The next step was, I heard about a rally at the Pentagon the following morning, and I wasn't going to go to that because, hell, I was just recently out of the Navy, that was too close to home; there are too many people I know who work at the Pentagon. I wasn't ready to out myself to former commanding officers I had. But then after the march I was so inspired, that I ended up going there.

The thing I walked away from [the march] with, is— I got out of the Navy and nothing in my life substantially changed. I just woke up one morning and I didn't have to get up and put on a uniform. Nothing changes in your life just by virtue of being out; nothing changes in your mindset. So I was still living as I had always lived. Same outlook, same fears, doing the same things that I had always done. Covering my tracks just enough when I went out, being just a little bit on guard meeting new people, being sure not to divulge too much of myself. When I went to the march—and I'm not sure what it was that brought it out—I realized that we, as gays, consent to our discrimination. People say "What you are is dirty. Be ashamed." So publicly we respond with the requisite amount of shame. We hide our heads, we don't divulge ourselves in the workplace or to family and friends. People crack fag jokes around us and we either sit by passively like a beaten child, or maybe we even join in because we don't want to arouse suspicion. Society gives us this little shoebox that says: "Fit your life inside this and keep it there and maybe we won't bother you." And we say, "OK." Historically, prior to Stonewall, police would go into bars and beat gays and arrest them, and finally people started to fight back. We've allowed society to define us in a very negative way, and we've never challenged it. Those people who are stereotypical can't challenge it, so people are always pointing the finger and telling jokes about them and laughing, and those people who aren't stereotypical realize it's a lot easier just to live and be part of the mainstream, at least in appearance. "Why make waves? Why give myself a hard time by coming out? I'm just gonna go with the flow." I went to the march and I realized: I no longer consent. Dammit, I'm mad! I spent twelve years of my life being in the military to defend a principle that I believed in with all my heart and soul. Not only am I not gonna hide, but it is very important to me that people who I am close with who don't already know, do know.

One of the things that being in the military did for me, in a very negative way, was give me a very segmented life. My professional life was very separate from my personal life. You couldn't mix the two. The conversations I could have with close friends of mine from the ship were different from conversations I could have with close friends of mine who weren't in the Navy, straight or gay. Looking back at myself when I first enlisted in the Navy, looking back at myself in Annapolis, looking back at myself on my first and then on my second ship, it's very—It's almost as if those experiences had been had by people other than myself who told me about it. That's how divorced and separate each chapter of my life was. And I want integrity in my life. I want to be able to have the pride I had in my service and not have to lie about it. I want to be able to shake the yoke of feeling so much guilt from lying to people who I was close with. I want to claim my past as rightfully mine. So the catharsis from going to the march was, not only am I not going to allow society to define me—I've got nothing to prove, I'm not going to be an in-your-face Queer Nation type homosexual; being gay is only a small part of what I am. It's an important part, but it's only one of many facets of my life. I'm not going to just go with the flow and allow other people to point fingers at me. I've started telling people who I served with, who I was close with, that I'm gay. Overall they've been incredibly supportive.

I feel I'm starting to claim what's rightfully mine: my past. It's not something experienced by different people, it's stuff experienced by me. That is the catharsis that broke me out of my shell of living in this little defined world that being in the Navy had created for me, and finally living life on my own. And that's been incredibly important.

Z: Your first interview ended with me calling you a distant hero. The officers that I've met here in San Diego all seem to be a little bit lonesome. Socially, whenever I see you, you're almost always by yourself. Whereas the enlisted guys run around in bands, a lot of them. We talked [off the record] about reasons why you might have been distanced from people in the past. Has that changed in connection with this catharsis?

T: Well you know it's difficult. You don't change what you are overnight. It's something I've given a lot of thought to. I'm not sure how my being an officer differentiates me in that regard from an enlisted man. It was a very very lonely experience. I was naturally reluctant to open myself up to meeting people, to establish friendships or relationships, because of fear of being found out. How has it changed for me? It's a good question. [Pause.] It's funny, because there's a certain aspect of it that I think has nothing to do with me being an officer, it just has to do with me being who I am. I'm a very private person; I'm a very introspective person. And— this is going to sound arrogant, but what the hell—I don't like wasting my time with people who don't exist any deeper than what's on the surface. It's very easy for me to get very bored with people when I go out. My natural inclination is to be very familiar, "Hey, how's it going, nice to see you," and become quickly bored and move on. So I'm often alone when I go out. Ironically, since I've gotten out of the Navy, my social life has plummeted. By choice. I've just gotten tired of the whole social scene. And that's not because the gay social scene is awful or predatory—no more so than going out to a straight bar would be—but just because I got tired of the superficiality of it all. So there's a certain part in me that has chosen—I don't want to say "be alone," because that sounds too final and certainly I don't want to condemn myself to eternal loneliness. But even though I now have no reason to live being paranoid, there has been no compelling reason for me to behave any differently than I have in the past. Now whether the way I behave is the way of conditioned training from years of necessity, I don't know. I'm not sure if I can dig that deep. But certainly it's something I think a lot about, because I don't want to spend my life like that. However I do know that if I stayed in the Navy, I would have. Now I don't think that that is a necessary consequence of my life, that I be forever alone.

Z: Anything else you want to add?
T: Not that I can think of. Yeah, did I ever tell you about the time when I had sex with someone out on the . . .

I'm only joking.

Trent: The Boatswain's Locker

Overseas, the gay American soldiers I met often adopted a European civilian look for their forays into town. They did this in part for aesthetic reasons, and in part to avoid being shot in the neck by terrorists. Conversely, some of the German gays in Frankfurt cultivated a faux-GI look, getting military-style haircuts, and commissioning soldier lovers to procure them PX clothing. The trick was to tell who was what. I usually could, by their shoes.

Here in San Diego, gay servicemen have forged a kind of queer-military chic that boldly celebrates both sexual and military identities. It is not uncommon to see sailors in gay bars wearing ball caps and T-shirts emblazoned with the names of their ships. One Navy petty officer I interviewed intertwines his dog tags with rainbow freedom rings. A Marine I know has a tattoo of the Marine Corps globe, anchor, and eagle superimposed over a rainbow "gay triangle" (see Figure 2). And although gay military men often have ambivalent and complex feelings about the sex appeal of their uniforms, some occasionally experiment with the effect their uniforms have in gay meeting places.

Trent is a 22-year-old African-American Navy personnelman from a small town in Georgia. We met at a Hillcrest dance club. It was "military night" and patrons were encouraged to come in uniform. Only a few active duty military personnel did, and some of them had received astonishing promotions: one Navy seaman from the *Ranger* donned the camouflage fatigues of an Army colonel and gyrated on a go-go boy platform beside his shipmate, a petty officer third class packaged in the dress uniform of a lieutenant junior grade. Ray (see "The Navy Corpsman Nipple Piercing Ritual") came as himself, in his dress blues. Ditto Gregg (see "The Unmaking of an Activist") who, though now out of the military, arrived in his crackerjack jumper top, complete with ribbons and medals (albeit wearing grievously mismatched khaki shorts). And there was

Trent, drunkenly sashaying about the club in the same snugly fitting dungarees he would soon be sporting in the Navy Consolidated Brig.

Trent was in trouble—UA (Unauthorized Absence) from the Navy after receiving death threats for being gay. He did not, he told me, want to end up like Allen Schindler, the gay sailor so viciously beaten to death by shipmates that his mother could only identify his corpse by his tattoos. But Trent failed to contact the gay veterans organizations, which might have helped him with his case, or a lawyer. A few weeks after this interview he turned himself in. He served 20 days in the brig, and then was discharged under Other Than Honorable conditions.

The photo of Senator Sam Nunn of Trent's home state (Figure 1) was staged to suggest that gay men can be counted on to prey upon vulnerable and innocent straight boys who sleep on their stomachs in the berthing of submarines. But Trent's unapologetic account here of the sexual realities of life for men at sea reveals how the reverse sometimes happens: as a known gay, he was harassed by straight sailors who came to his rack at night demanding sex. Trent freely admits to servicing some of these men in a life jacket closet, for kicks, but rejected those who he heard by day making homophobic remarks.

Trent: In 1991 we was on WESTPAC. We was over in Australia. This girl knew I was gay, because the first night I went out was to a gay bar, and she was in there. Then the last night my ship was in port I went out to this straight bar, and she was there.

Over in Australia they don't care if you're gay. I told her, "Look. All these guys here are off my ship, so don't go saying anything about where you met me." She was like, "I already know." We was going to go back to the gay club, but they wouldn't let her in. 'Cause on certain nights they have male only. So we ended up going to this other straight club. Guys off my ship was there. We went to this after-hours bar—me, her, and this other guy from my ship. He was straight. Totally straight.

In the after-hours bar we was getting pretty toasted. We started kissing in the bar, and started dancing on the dance floor.
Zeeland: All three of you?
T: No. I would be out there with her, then he would go dance with her. We had to be on the ship at six-thirty in the morning, so I was like, "Let's buy

a twelve-pack and go back to my motel room." And I guess you could say
we had a three-way. We was back there, and we was already taking off all
our clothes, and I started kissing her, and he was sucking on her titties and
stuff. While one was making out with her, she was giving the other one a
blowjob. Then we swapped.

Z: Did you and the guy do anything?

T: No. We never touched each other.

Z: Was it exciting for you to look at him, or just that he was there?

T: No, not really, because I didn't think he was attractive at all.

Z: So your excitement was more with her?

T: No, I wouldn't say that either, because I had to think about my ex-boy-
friend to even get aroused. It was different. It was very awkward. I
wouldn't say I was forced into it, but it was like I was in a predicament to
where if I didn't do this with this guy that was on my ship that was
straight, when we got back it would be all over the ship that I was a faggot
or something.

Z: Did you ever come out to this guy?

T: No.

Z: Did you become closer to him as a result of this experience?

T: A little. We became just a little closer friends. But he left the ship not
too long after that.

Z: Why did you join the military?

T: Me and my best friend at the time, we had a painting business together.
Then we got a condo. His girlfriend moved in, and then she just became
third partner without even consulting me. Everything went haywire. I left
and went to Alabama for two weeks with a friend of mine that's in the
Army. I thought about it and thought about it. I was going to go into the
Navy before, so when I got back I just went ahead and joined.

Z: Why did you pick the Navy?

T: 'Cause I knew about the Air Force, how they live and everything.
Knew about the Army, 'cause I was there for two weeks. I definitely
wasn't going to think about the Marine Corps—too gung ho. I picked the
Navy because they go out to sea. Just being on the ocean, having that
breeze, that fresh air. And going to different places. And those cool
commercials. Those nice uniforms—the officer's uniforms, especially.

Going through boot camp, it was what I imagined. Then when I got to
my command I started seeing a lot of racial stuff. When I first checked
on-board, there was this incident where three white guys had wrote on
this guy's truck "Nigger we're gonna get you." I didn't expect this. I
mean, I'm from Georgia. I did not see that much racism [back home]. You
would expect I would, but I didn't.

Z: Do you come from a big city or a small town?

T: A small town. Basically everyone knew me or knew who I was. That's the reason I wasn't even thinking about being gay back then. I knew too many people.

Z: When were you first aware of your sexual feelings for other males?

T: High school. Actually one of my teachers. We seen each other for two weeks. It was during spring break. We went down to Tampa Bay. Just me and him.

Z: Who made the first move?

T: I think I did. 'Cause I talked to him one day after school, and I told him—He could tell I wanted to talk about something serious. He closed the door. He asked me if my step-dad beat me. I said, "No. It has nothing to do with my family." It took me about an hour to say what I had to say. "I think I'm gay, because I have feelings toward other guys that I shouldn't have. But I still like girls." He said, "Well, maybe you're bisexual." The next thing I know I was at his apartment.

Z: Why did you pick him to tell? Did you suspect him of being gay?

T: Yeah. Just the way he carried himself. I guess it's like the saying, "Family can spot family." He was a new teacher there, and I just thought he was. . . . He taught me the ropes. "Watch out for this type of person," and that kind of stuff.

Z: You said that you still liked girls. Did you think of yourself as gay when you joined the Navy?

T: No. Because I was still looking at females like, "Oh, she's hot." It's just that I wasn't sleeping around with anyone. Actually the only person I slept with in high school was my teacher. But I didn't find out—I mean, I knew I had these feelings, but until I finally went ahead and acted on how I really felt. . . .

I was twenty-two. I was hanging out with two guys from my ship that were very immature. At first I thought they was cool guys. Well, they are, but they were just childish. I didn't like hanging out with them. There was this other guy that was sleeping in the berthing with me, and I kept thinking, "God he's hot." Then finally one day I got on the bus and went downtown, and walked on this one street in Long Beach. I was going, "Should I go in here? What if somebody sees me?"

Z: How did you find out about this street?

T: My ship. When you first go somewhere, for some reason, the Navy always tell you, "Don't go to this area because they have drugs. Don't go to this area because it has fags. Don't go to this area because it has prostitutes." They tell you all the places where you may wanna go! They tell a person where to go to get anything he or she wants.

So I knew about this spot. The bus that we took to go over to this mall, it went straight down this one street. I got off on it and just kept walking back and forth. And finally I was like, "OK, I'm gonna do this." Finally I got up the nerve and I went in there . . . it was a learning experience. Then I started going out there every weekend.

Z: When did you decide that you were gay, that that was what you would call yourself?

T: It was maybe a month, two months down the road. I was like, "I've been coming to these bars now, having these guys buy me drinks." Then I met my best friend. He's in the Navy also. He wanted to have a relationship but I didn't. Over time we just became real good friends, we became best friends. My policy is, I don't do my friends, even though we had slept together once before. After we had been friends for a certain time, I don't know, I felt like I just wanted to be his friend.

Z: Was it especially important to be friends with another gay sailor? Or could he just as well have been a civilian?

T: No, I think at the time it had to be another squid, because he was teaching me how to watch myself and how to act when I was at work. And as he say, "You can let your hair down once you leave work." He had been in for four years already, so I valued his opinion about things.

Z: Are you still close friends today?

T: Yeah. Since everything that's happened, I don't talk to him as much as I used to. He's stationed up in L.A. When my ship moved down here for homeport I used to go to Long Beach every weekend I had off. When I went on leave, I would be with him and his lover. I just felt real close with them. It was like a close-knit family.

Z: Are most of the people you hang out with now sailors?

T: Yeah. Guys and girls. It's wild, because it's like, every ship, there's somebody that is family on there, and they're doing the exact same thing that you are in some way. Either you're going to run into them in the club, or you're going to see them in the known gay areas in town, or you're going to think that they are gay and throw lingo, and see if they catch it. That's how I found a couple guys on my ship that was. I used the term "family," and that's when I seen this one guy's head turn. My best friend told me, "Just start using terms and see what kind of reactions you get." That was a big reaction, because this guy was in a conversation with someone else, and when I started saying "family"—it was very noticeable. Then I seen him out in the club that weekend, and I was like, "I knew you were!" He's like, "I knew *you* were!" And we became to this day real good friends.

On my ship, we used the fantail as our little get together. When we was on the fantail, if you came back there we would all look at you like, "Do you know where you're at? I hope you know we're having a tea party back here!" It was like that. The entire time we was on the fantail no one else ever really came out there, unless they was trying to work us.

Z: Would men have sex back there?

T: No, we'd just hang out. There was about seven or eight of us. It was quite festive.

Z: How many people were on this ship?

T: About four hundred and fifty, five hundred. Only men. It was a cruiser.

I had my own little spot where I had a couple rendezvous. It was where we kept our life jackets. You could dog it all the way down, and you'd have to be pretty strong to bring it back up, and by the time you got it open. . . . But the only thing was, if you were to get caught in there with another guy, it would be too obvious what was going on. There was no light in there, and it's only so big.

Z: Like a walk-in closet?

T: Smaller.

Z: A broom closet?

T: Yeah. If someone came in, you would be caught. But my friends, they had their own little spots. One of my friends had this fan room he used to go into. This one guy, he was an SH [ship's serviceman], and he used his laundry room, because he could lock it up. I've used my office before. I used the boatswain's locker before, too. Where first division—where they keep the outside of the ship looking good. That was their space. I wasn't even supposed to be up there.

Z: They're like, real rough guys?

T: Yeah. First division, the boatswain's mates, they have to have this image of being macho. After work, they're laid back. A lot of people think that boatswain's mates don't have brains, 'cause anybody can be a boatswain's mate. But a lot of those guys, they know what they want, and they pick the boatswain's mate rating so they don't have to sweat over little stupid stuff. Even though they work extra hours than normal. They put up with it because they get a lot of leeway. First division is a division on its own. They do a lot of work with hardly no tools. You'd be amazed at what they accomplish. It was very exciting, it was a lot of fun. When I first checked into my ship, that's where I was. So if I would have gotten caught in there, it wouldn't have been nothing 'cause I hung out there a lot, too. Even though I was in a different division, I got along with the chief. The chief knew I was gay, because I told him back in '90 that I was.

We was over in Hawaii. We made a pit stop for a day and a half. We was going to the Gulf. We had to be back to the ship at 23:45, and I was late. I was pretty drunk. When I got to the ship I knew I was going to be in trouble. Then the taxi driver was trying to gyp me, 'cause I had fell asleep in the taxi. He was trying to say it was thirty-five dollars. And I guess because he knew I was going to the base and that ships was going to the Gulf and just making pit stops for a day and a half, he thought I didn't know. But I'd been to Hawaii for two months straight so I knew the price of a taxi from downtown. I was like, "I'm not paying you thirty-five dollars because I know the price!" He was like, "I'm going to get the shore patrol!" I was like, "You get the shore patrol! I'll tell them you're trying to gyp me! It should be twenty-five at the most, thank you." So we had the gate guard come up. I had only twenty dollars on me. I said, "Look, I got money in my rack." So I went to my rack and got my money and threw it at the taxi driver. I said, "You can keep the change. It means nothing to me."

On the quarterdeck they was going to take my ID away from me 'cause I was late, and plus on top of it I was drunk. My chief goes, "Why were you late?" And I was going off about the taxi. I said, "I'm getting ready to go over to the Gulf to defend this country, and you all are gonna believe some taxi driver over me? This is not what I thought the Navy would be like." I said, "I'm gay anyway. Go start sending out my paperwork. I'm gay. I just want out!" He's like, "You sure this is what you're saying?" "I'm positive!" "No, I think I'm gonna let you sleep it off." "No! Why don't you fuckin' listen to me?" And I punched the mirror. "No, you go to bed right now." I started screaming. "I'm gay! Let me out of here!" "No, you go get in your rack and I will talk to you in the morning. If you still feel the same way—But I don't want you to go. I think you're a good guy."

The next morning he asked me and I was like, "Well, I am gay, but the alcohol had a lot to do with it. Plus, you guys didn't listen to me over a taxi driver. That really hurt. That hit home." He was like, "You know how the system works." "That's why I want out." "No, I know you can handle it. You're pretty tough." He talked me into staying in, and we became real real good friends. He never made an advance toward me or anything, we just became good friends. Chiefs are not supposed to hang out with junior guys, but we hung out.

Z: He was straight?

T: Yeah.

Z: Did you ever talk about your being gay, or was that something that just wasn't discussed?

T: We used to kid around about it a lot. Sometimes, if he knew I was down, he would come around and say, "Girl, let me tell you somethin'."

He just made me feel good. It was awesome. Chief was a trip! Then he would walk down the passageway like, "Girl, let's work the boys on this ship." I said, "If only you knew!" He helped me through a lot of stuff on the ship, because there was a time when some word had got out about me being gay. A couple guys had bumped me in the P-way and said, "Faggot!" So I went to the captain about it, and he asked me, "Are you gay?" I told him "No" because at the time I still wasn't too sure that this is what I wanted to be. The captain talked to the command master chief, and the command master chief talked to everyone in my division. He told them "I think he's a pretty good guy, and the captain has said 'If he comes up and files a report against anyone for saying he's gay or a faggot, you're gonna fry.'" So after that everybody was cool with me again.

Z: You said that you don't have sex with your friends. So I guess you did work the boys on the ship. How would you do that?

T: There was family friends, then there was my so-called straight friends. The guys that I didn't hang out with I didn't call family friends, and those are the ones I basically messed around with. There's a lot of drinking involved. Then going on ship. A lot of times you'd go out, party, go back to your motel room, and—I didn't have no intentions of sleeping with some of the guys off my ship. I mean, I thought they looked good or whatever, but it was just—

For some reason, if you're suspected of being gay, all these guys still want to hang out with you, go get drunk, and get a motel room with you. Either they want you to give them a blowjob, or have anal sex with you, or something. I could talk to numerous friends, and they would tell me "Oh, this is how I got with this one guy." And the stories all sound the same. It's incredible that you know this one guy and he had this other guy off the ship and you had no idea that he even thought about being with another guy.

Z: You think a lot of these guys you had sex with were straight?

T: Yeah. Or bi. There's a great deal of them that are bi. A lot of married guys. Then you got your old timers that have been in the Navy for a while. They try to work you, too. They patted me on the butt, and said these things like, "Oh, you know you want it." I'm like, [Sarcastically:] "OK, I guess you know what I want." Right on the ship. During working hours.

After working hours they're like, "Where you goin'?" "I'm gonna go out to the movies." You always find yourself lyin'. Because you can't straight up and say just where you're going. Especially if they didn't really know that you were, but they suspect that you were. You always had to cover your tracks—go out with a couple straight guys every now and then. What I would do, I would lose them. We would go out, start drinking, and I would say, "Oh I gotta use the phone to call home" or "I gotta go use the restroom." And I would never come back. They would always ask me, "Where did you go?" "Oh, I met this chick and we got to talking. She took me here and there." And they always believed it! It was so easy to get over on these people.

Z: You said a lot of these experiences had to do with drinking. Then you'd come back to the ship, and go to your life jacket room?

T: Yeah. That happened a lot. Especially over in the Gulf when we pulled in, 'cause we was out for sixty-two days straight. I was out with this friend of mine, which was family, and we had no intentions of getting with anyone or doing anything, except for going out and having a good time. We went back to the ship. This other guy comes to my rack and wakes me up, talking this trash. He said, "You couldn't handle this." His private part. I'm drunk and I'm going, "Hold up, hold up. Wait a minute. What did you just say to me?" "You heard me." "Child, you ain't got enough down there to be talking that trash to me. Don't make me get out of my rack to do something you goin' regret in the morning." He grabbed my hand and put it on it. I'm like, "See, now you gettin' me all upset."

He's like, "Where we gonna go?" "I got a spot. We'll go one at a time." I told him where it was at. I said, "If you're not there within two minutes after I get there I'm getting out. Even if you're comin' in when I'm gettin' out, I'm just goin' to hit my rack." Most of the time they came within the two minutes. They would follow me, and I was like, "Look, wait until after I get in. Then look around just to see if they seen me come in. Then you dash in there real quick, and we'll dog it all the way down!" We have a rover that roves around the ship to make sure everything's locked up.

Z: These straight guys picked up on the fact that you're gay and tried to work you?

T: Totally. There was a lot of them I had to say no to 'cause I was like, "What do you all take me for?" Just because I knew their attitude toward gays, or fags, or whatever they'd say. Then when they get drunk they want to come back and get their dick sucked. "I don't think so. No."

Z: Were these both black and white guys?

T: A mixture. A lot of black guys talked to me but they kind of knew that I wouldn't go to bed with them. I guess you could tell that I was into white guys and Mexicans. They were like, asking me, but they wouldn't say "guys." They would say, "So what do you see in white girls?" "I just think they're petite. Got the nice little whatever." And I think they kind of knew. I told 'em, "I grew up around white girls. A couple of my friends are black, but the majority are white."

Z: A lot of the gay people that are coming out publicly declare that they keep their professional and private lives totally separate. The lieutenant I interviewed last night [Tim] told me that he never had sex at sea, or even on liberty during his six-month deployments. Some people will read your story and say that it's bad that you had sex aboard ship. What do you think about that, and what would you say to those people?

T: I would say, wake up, open your eyes, you know that it's happening and it's true. There's people gonna do what they have to do to keep themselves sane. And if you had the opportunity you would probably do it too.

Z: Do you think there's any potential harm in it?

T: Not as long as you keep it discreet and not be very flamboyant about it. It was fun. It was like a chase or some kind of game—a challenge.

Z: Do you think that the Navy expects a certain masculinity of sailors?

T: No. Because I've seen some guys that you could spot a mile away. Just by the way they walk. Then when you hear them talk you're like, "You're in the Navy girl? You better butch it up a little bit!" So I would definitely say no.

Z: Do you consider yourself masculine?

T: Now I do. But that's after I started hanging out with the crowd I do now. When I first came out I was getting pretty much on the fem side, getting close to being flamboyant. Being on a ship, a small ship, you don't want that. Everyone knows who everyone is, because you work around them all the time. The guys that I hang out with now, we don't try to act real sissyfied. I don't think it looks real good for a guy to act like a woman. If you're a man, have a little masculinity about you.

Z: Do you think the Marine Corps does have a standard of masculinity?

T: Yeah. Definitely. Marines—a lot of 'em are gung ho. And they're into physical fitness. You can tell the difference with Navy guys and Marine guys because Marine guys are all buff and looking very macho. But a lot of Navy guys look very fem. You can spot a Navy guy very quick, just like you can spot a Marine.

Z: Have you noticed any differences sexually between Marines and sailors?

T: Yeah. Marines are bottoms, to be blunt. When we think of jarheads we think of bottoms. Most of the ones I've encountered are bottoms.

Z: Why do you think that would be?

T: I guess 'cause they have to play this macho role all the time. It's like you get tired of trying to be so butch, constantly, and when you finally let your hair down. . . . It's weird. Even the ones my friends have encountered, most of them have been bottoms. So when we go home with a Marine we end up having to be a top.

Z: How do you feel about having these big butch men throw their legs up in the air for you?

T: It's a big turnoff for me. If I go home with someone that's bigger than me—that's awkward. Most of the guys I pick are normally pretty big, and I can't see me pumpin' their kitty.

Z: You're a PN?

T: Personnelman.

Z: There's a stereotype that gay men in the Navy tend to be in certain fields. Yeomen, hospital corpsmen, chaplain's assistants. . . .

T: You got your gunner's mates. Your airedales. You got a lot of ETs [electronics technicians] and stuff. But normally everyone picks, like you said, the PNs, the YNs [yeomen], the HMs [hospital corpsmen]. The admin side. But I've learned you got a little of everything in all the different ratings. And don't forget the biggest ones, the OSs [operations specialists]. Oh God. On my ship we called them the Beverly Hills Girl Scouts 'cause they were so Miss Prissies.

Z: You're UA now. Tell me how that came about.

T: [. . .] We went up to Canada. I met this guy at a bar in Vancouver. He gave me his phone number. Normally I don't give out my right phone number, but I gave it to him. We called each other. He picked up everything and came here to San Diego. I was like, "God, it's gotta be something if this guy's picking up his whole life and moving here for me." We ended up getting an apartment together. Everything was going great at first. But me having to go out to sea—it played a big role in the relationship, because he started having doubts about me. He thought I was cheating on him. We'd go out to sea for two weeks at a time and I'd come back—even though I hadn't seen him, I wanted to be by myself, because I didn't have any privacy on the ship. He didn't understand that. He thought I was just messing around. He started making me feel like I was the guilty party. And the whole time he was guilty of something, but I didn't know it.

I was in San Francisco one weekend, which is where my ex lives. I got back and things were not the same. I kind of sensed something was up. We had a fight one night, and I confronted him about sleeping with my friend, and he didn't say anything. I called up one of my lesbian friends and said, "I'm gonna spend the night at your house, because it's over between me and Jim." She and her lover talked me into giving it another try.

We were out at sea doing training exercises with other ships. That's when he left me. Someone had told him they had seen me in town with some other white guy. We pull back in, and my real good close lesbian friends, they're on the pier waiting for me. And I didn't see him. I just dropped my head because I knew he had left. And they told me, "Well, we got a little more to tell you. He took your TV and your VCR and your clothes. . . ."

It messed me up. I never had anything like that happen. To this day it bothers me, but I try to block it out. It had a lot to do with the situation with me now and the Navy because when it happened I was just wantin' to get out. I thought he had gave me some kind of disease because a couple times times the rubber popped. I went and got tested, and luckily everything came back negative. At the time I was telling my ship, they knew I was going through something, but they didn't know to what extent. I couldn't work, I couldn't perform like I normally would. I was sitting there crying at my desk. They was like, "Just go to the fantail and take a smoke break or something." I moved out of that apartment 'cause I just couldn't stand being in the same place.

It's made me take a look at myself and what was wrong with me for all this to happen to me. "God, am I that messed up?" I had a lot of doubts about myself. But it was not me, it was him.

Z: You told the Navy that you're gay?

T: Yeah. I told a lot of guys in my division. The guys in my division was real supportive. They was wanting me to find Jim and everything. After I told my captain, that's when things started gettin' very bad—all of the higher-ups kind of started turnin' on me. I started gettin' a rough time. After I came out to my captain—about two weeks after that I answered the phone in the berthing. "We're gonna get you faggot. We're gonna beat you." I felt like I had no support with the command at all. So I left. I just up and left. I felt like my life was in danger.

Z: You mentioned that you knew Allen Schindler. How did you hear about what happened to him?

T: A friend of mine, John, told me. He goes, "You knew Allen, right? He used to bring [his pet] lizard in the bar?" I was like, "Knew him? You're talking past tense." "Yeah, some guys beat him to death." And right after that I left. I just couldn't think of me getting beat to death all because of my sexual orientation. Now, I just want out. So I can piece my life back together.

Z: Tell me about your straight friends. These are guys from your ship?

T: Yeah. We used to wrestle in the berthing. I guess I was handling myself pretty well to where they felt comfortable. These guys are black. I told them, "I don't act like no sissy when I go out. I don't act like no flaming faggot." One day they was like, "Hey, why don't we go out and do something?" At first I was a little hesitant, because I didn't know what their intentions were. But as it turned out they just wanted to be my friend. Plus they wanted to know about me being gay and being black and their being straight and being black, how the two act, or how I would act around girls or whatever. So we went out and went to parties and stuff. I'm straightforward about what I do. They see I'm secure with who I am, and I guess they're pretty secure with themselves to be hanging out with me.

Z: Did they know any other gay men before they met you?

T: No, I don't think these guys did. We've talked a great deal about gay. The typical image of someone being gay was that all gay men sleep with every man, and that you walk around puttin' on women's clothes.

Z: You refused to participate in the crossing the line ceremony because your division told you that you were going to [compete for] wog queen.

T: Yeah. I thought that was a disgrace. I don't ever see me putting on a dress. I think that would be a low point. I have a couple friends that do drag shows. And that's fine with me, that's them. But it's not for me.

Z: What do you look for in a man?

T: My taste varies. You have to be attractive, intelligent, know who you are, and definitely know your culture. Know where you came from. Have a little masculinity about yourself and a military style haircut. I hate long hair. That's one of the biggest turnoffs for me.

Z: So you do have a special attraction to military men?

T: Yeah, somewhat. There was a time I wouldn't do nothing but military guys. For one, I knew that we get checkups—get tested. And I guess I was just into the crewcut hairstyle. And a lot of them have a nice physique because you go work out when you have nothing else to do.

Z: Do you have any special attraction to uniforms?

T: Mmm. Marines, their dress uniform.

Z: What does that do for you?

T: Ooooff. If I could, I'd just go rip off their clothes right there!

Z: How about the sailor uniforms? Do you like any of them?

T: I like their working blues or their dress blues. I like the dark uniforms on a sailor. And oh, I like the officer uniforms. And I like cop uniforms.

Z: Have you experienced civilians being attracted to you just for the fact of your being in the military?

T: Yeah.

Z: How does that make you feel when that happens?

T: Like a number. 'Cause a lot of them guys I wanted to have a relationship with, but they just wanted me 'cause I was in the Navy. Like around this area in San Diego—"Oh, you slept with a military guy"—it seems like a big deal here, and personally, I don't think it's *all that.*

Z: You mentioned AIDS and the idea that military men are tested annually. But even if they test negative, it only means they haven't been exposed to the virus six months or longer previous. They could have gotten infected a year and a half back and they wouldn't know. So isn't that a false sense of security?

T: Yeah, but most of the people that I run into we normally get tested once or twice a year by the military, and then a lot of us get tested once every three months. I try to get tested every three months just so I know.

Z: Do you try to practice safer sex? You mentioned some condom breakage with your ex-lover.

T: I definitely believe in safe sex. If I were to go home with someone and I see that they're not willing to have safe sex, I'm out the door.

Z: Has that happened?

T: Yeah. That's happened quite a few times. I have nothing to say to them guys, 'cause I feel, if you want to kill yourself, don't try to take my life with it. I'll find someone that will practice safe sex.

Z: I've met very few guys who regularly use condoms for oral sex.

T: Oooff. [Pause.] Oooff. That's a definite, I think definite, no matter what you should use a condom.

Z: You use condoms for oral sex? The taste of rubber doesn't deter you?

T: Um, yeah. The taste of a condom, especially if they have that dry kind—it's nasty. But I've sucked without a condom and I don't like that precum. Oooff. I personally never really liked sucking anyway. Recently my friends got me into it. "It ain't nasty. You like to get yours sucked, so." But, I think you should use a condom. Because there's no definite study saying that you can't get AIDS from sucking. I've talked to a lot of my friends about this stuff. We go out, maybe to a bar, and then we all go somewhere to eat, and sit around and talk. We talk about sex a lot of times. Talk about, what do you like to do? 'Cause we already know we're not gonna sleep with each other. So we feel comfortable talking about what we do.

Z: Did the Navy fulfill that desire you had originally of going to sea?

T: Yeah. You can do a lot of things on the ship. You're for sure learning how to play cards. You learn how to play all these different games. You learn all these different customs. All these different nationalities. How they live and what kind of card games they play or what kind of foods they eat. You learn a whole lot on a WESTPAC.

I would sometimes go up on the fo'c'sle and just stand there. We'd be doing fifteen, eighteen knots and you could just feel the wind—oh, that was awesome. It gives you that exhilarating feeling. I loved it. Even when it was real cold. There was just something about being on the open seas for me. It just felt great. It was something that I have never experienced before.

Z: Is there anything else you want to add?

T: [Pause.] How one minute if your peers don't know that you're gay, when they find out how they treat you. You'll find that some are gonna treat you the same. 'Cause they're like, "Well, you're the same person that I've always known. Just as long as you don't try to push yourself off on me." But then you got your ones that try to be all homophobic about being around you. And a lot of times they're either in the closet or bi. I've encountered a lot of bisexuals on my ship. Married guys especially, whose wives come on the boat and say hey to you. I'm goin': if only you knew. But yeah, you can see the difference, before and after. You'll lose some friends, but a lot of people in the military are open-minded. The ones that accept you and don't care that you are, they're goin' to be your friends. I think definitely the ones that don't care if you're gay, straight, or whatever, it outweighs the ones that are not secure with themselves.

David: "Hard," Not "Tough"

I am standing on the beach in San Diego's Mission Bay with Anthony and some other friends, talking with Alex, an almost unbearably cute 21-year-old of German, Jewish, and Native American ancestry from rural Wisconsin. Alex is just coming out and has a lot of questions. Because he is a Marine, I have some questions for him, too. He pretends to be more innocent than he is, but that's okay with me. I enjoy—no, *require*—a modicum of wile in men I am attracted to. We drift off from the others and enjoy a spirited conversation.

I tell Alex about this book and how I had originally set out to document the sexual charge to the famous rivalry that exists between sailors and Marines. Elite, hypermasculine, tightly disciplined Marines look down on "squids" as sloppy and unprofessional; they tell jokes about sailors giving Marines blowjobs. Sailors have their own oneliners about dog-like "dumb jarheads" and jeer that the Marine Corps is merely a subservient branch of the Navy. I tell Alex I see this as a struggle of sexual power—about who's on top.

"Well, you have to refute that stereotype," says Alex, who is not dumb. "What stereotype?" I ask, more innocently than I am. "That Marines are, you know, passive." I look at him sharply. "They're not?" He frowns. "Well no. I mean, not always." Alex would like for me to tell the world that, if it is true that Marines do more often play the receptor role in anal intercourse, it is because they have been instilled with a need to serve. "There are times when I like to play the bottom, and there is a naturalness to it that I attribute to being in the Marine Corps. In the breakdown phase of recruit training they totally debase you. The drill instructors talk down to you, call you 'maggot'—they make you feel worthless, subhuman. They totally strip you of your identity, so as to build you back up as a Marine. Even outside of basic training, the Marine Corps still debases you. As a Marine, you always strive to please your higher ups.

There is a craving to serve, to win approval, or even love. . . . When I play bottom I get no physical enjoyment out of it; I go through the abasement and pain out of a sense of duty. So you could almost say," he laughs, "that being the bottom is mission oriented."

Alex agrees that Marines deserve a volume of their own. I threaten I may yet write one. He answers flatly, "You'd have to coauthor it with a psychologist." I repeat to Alex what Lieutenant Tim said, "Every sailor wants a Marine, every Marine wants a sailor," but tell him I have concluded that it often seems to be a one-way street: Gay sailors like Marines. Gay Marines like Marines. "Yeah, we do. I would prefer, in all honesty"—we both throw a glance to be sure Anthony, Alex's date, is out of earshot—"to be with a Marine over a sailor.

"Marines tend to be more honor and duty bound, and more serious. Sailors tend to be slimy and nasty and just do whatever they want. Although that's not totally true. There are some good sailors. Corpsmen." Alex and I talk about the stereotypes of "hard" Marines and "soft" Navy hospital corpsmen and how interesting it is that the only sailors to work with Marines serve in nurturing, "feminine" capacities: corpsmen, doctors, chaplains, and chaplain's assistants. Alex confirms that Marines hold these men to a laxer standard of masculinity, but says that, while they are joked about, they are not necessarily looked down upon for being that way. I tell him about a Navy RP (religious program specialist) I have interviewed for this book who thinks of himself as somewhat of a queen but has found greater acceptance from Marines than from other sailors. Alex nods. "There's an RP where I'm stationed who's kind of like that. Everyone thinks he probably is gay. And he's really well respected, it's true."

It is the same chaplain's assistant.

David, the subject of this interview, is a 33-year-old of German and Welsh ancestry from a middle-class Kansas family. I met him through Renaldo, a sailor friend from Whidbey Island. Both men belonged to a close-knit friendship network formed at sea aboard the USS *Ranger.*

Like many other gay sailors I spoke with, David described feeling a sense of "family" with other military people that extended beyond his individual clique. But did not include me. We met only twice, one week apart, soon after Clinton's election. While eager to talk, David voiced concern that he was using up his 15 minutes of fame on this interview, then promptly vanished from my social world and did not return my phone messages.

(But Alex and I became buddies. Alone, later, he asks me which service branch I like best. He says he realizes it's a personal question and tells me I don't have to answer. I consider and tell him that each branch, with its own haircut, uniform, and traditions, has a distinct image and even a culture and range of physical types that holds a different erotic appeal for me. He waits expectantly. I tell him that, because I like short hair, Marines *are* especially attractive. "Do you?" "Mmm." I touch his bristles. "And, Marines really do seem to have the nicest butts." "For real?" "Yes, yes. It's a generalization, but any amount of casual observation around Oceanside confirms that it's true. It must be all that running they make you do, or something." He pauses, then asks, "Do you think I have a nice butt?" I cannot lie to Alex.)

Zeeland: The subject of gays in the military has been a big news topic this last week [in the wake of the November 1992 presidential election]. What are the people you work with saying?

David: There's been a lot of derogatory talk, of course. Most of them don't want fags in the military; they don't want to serve with them. But there are also a lot of people who are coming to the defense, saying "It's no big deal. They're already here." I can't say it's split half and half, because there are a lot of people who just don't have a comment on it. The people who talk about it in loudmouthed voices are the people who talk about anything in loudmouthed voices.

Z: Does all this attention to the topic make you feel uncomfortable?

D: It does. Because I'm hearing some derogatory comments from people I'd least expected it from. People who treat me with respect and are likeable. It's kind of surprising that it's coming from them. It's kind of distressing. But what's really odd is that it's never directed toward me. Nobody's ever trying to get me to make a comment or a statement about it. They never insinuate that they're talking about me. In fact, nobody's ever asked my opinion about it, which kind of tells me that they're saying, "Hey, we know. We like you and respect you, and out of respect we're not going to confront you with this."

I'm in the U.S. Navy, but right now I'm stationed with a Marine Corps unit at Camp Pendleton, and they just don't care what you do on your off time. As long as you are professional at work, in the office, or out in the field, that's what counts. And there they want you to give a hundred and ten percent, because that's the way the Marine Corps is. As long as you're willing to do that and abide by their standards of professional behavior, they could care less what you do on your own time.

If the policy does change I'm sure I will have some of the people I'm closer to come up and ask me. I'm kind of expecting that. But I'm certainly not going to stand out in company formation and announce it because most people don't need to know. They didn't need to know before, they're not going to need to know now.

The only person I might voluntarily come out to would be my commanding officer. Only because he's such a neat guy, and a good leader, that out of respect for him I think I would like to tell him. Lord knows what he would say. He's a Marine colonel. He's a hard liner on Marine Corps honor and standards. He may want me out of his unit. Even if it is legal, he could still have me transferred. I would have to risk that.

Z: I'm not sure I understand your motivation for taking that risk.

D: The motivation would be out of respect for him. He's already been really supportive of me personally in his command. I've had some private talks with him about other things related to my job. He's just been wonderful.

Z: So you'd just like to have that feeling of him knowing?

D: Yeah. Just having him know. Even if he doesn't like it. He probably would suspect it anyway. Just because of the way I talk, and of course the way I walk. The way I carry myself is kind of effeminate. Not all the time; I can act campier than I do at work. And I did, when I was on the ship. I wouldn't do that where I'm at now, because hell, they don't even expect a girl to act like that! It would be frowned upon.

But what they want me to be is myself. I learned that a long time ago. Anybody I've ever worked with has wanted me to be myself. I had a really rough time when I first got in the Navy and was on a ship, because I was pretending I wasn't gay, when everybody could see that I was. I talked about girlfriends I had back home. I just gave the attitude that I was straight. People didn't believe it. Then when I started acting like myself, the big queen that I sometimes am, I got along famously with everybody. It took a while for *me* to be myself. But once I did, I decided: never again am I going to put on some act.

Z: Have you ever received unfavorable comments from people?

D: Oh yeah, I've had people call me "fag" in the passageway or in the mess decks. But again, most of the time that happened when I was trying to act butch. As soon as I stopped doing that, and people got to know me, and I let people be around me—it didn't stop, but it got a whole lot more infrequent. Mainly because I knew a lot of people by that time, and people liked me enough that they weren't going to do it. It would be the new people that would come on the ship that would say it. And I never saw anybody do it but I'm sure my friends told them, "Hey, lay off. This guy's alright. We don't care if he's a fag. We like him."

Z: Today I read a letter in the *Navy Times* from a distraught sailor who pleads, "Please don't make us bathe and berth with homosexuals!" I know the answer is he doubtless already has, but . . . are you hearing Marines express those kinds of fears?

D: At first I did hear a lot of that. "I don't want no fag watching me take a shower!" Now, as people realize it's inevitable, I'm hearing more jokes about it. Like, "Hey, I see you looking at my butt! You can't do that, it's not legal yet!" That kind of thing. Yes, there are still some people that talk about it in a hateful way, but these are the people who years ago made the same kinds of comments about blacks in the military.

Z: But then there is this special element of sexual fear. Do you take communal showers with the men you live with?

D: Not where I live now. I live in a barracks with one roommate. He's straight. His wife's in Okinawa. We get along great. We're going to spend Thanksgiving Day together.

Z: Are you out to him?

D: No, but I probably could be. He's another one of the people that if and when the policy changes, I would probably come out to. Just because he's a friend and my roommate. And he probably knows anyway. I've got to live with him seven days a week. He's exhibited no fear of me. He takes off his clothes in front of me. Obviously he's not too afraid.

I have lived in open bay barracks where there was a communal shower. It's never been any big deal. I always walked into the place with the idea that I was there to take a shower. Of course, yes, you do look, but you don't touch.

On a ship, when I'd go into the shower there would be guys who, if you asked them, would say they didn't want any fags looking at them. But as soon as I walked in they started showing off. Not just to me, but to several of my gay friends. The guys with good bodies or good equipment—they would flaunt it. Their egos took over. Now, I never made a pass at them, because it's too public a place. That's just the wrong place to do it.

Z: You think these guys had some awareness that your friends and you were gay and wanted to tease you?

D: Oh yeah. But that's just it, it was looked at as a game. I'm not going to make a pass at them if they're giving me every indication that they're not available. Now if I see someone at a gay bar, yeah, I might come up and ask you to dance or ask you to go to bed. But I'm not going to do it at work! Even if it's out in the field or when I was stationed on the ship—I'm not going to go up to someone and proposition them.

Z: When you have met men aboard ship, how did it happen?

D: There are ways to meet. You get talking with people. And—what can I say?—I have met guys in the head.

Z: Who were there—

D: Cruising, yeah. The straight guys come in, go to the bathroom and leave. The ones who want to play come in there and cruise.

Z: In accordance with the classic rules: tapping feet or looking through peepholes?

D: Right. And I assume, if they're in there to play, then they must be willing. But there's only going to be a certain amount of people that go in there and do that.

Over a period of months, as you get to know people on your ship, you know who the people are it's just a game to, and then you find out the ones that might be available. They give you signals that are more than just teasing. They'd like to get something on with you. That's generally how you meet people. But usually—when you're on a ship you're working most of the time. You just don't have a lot of free time. And most of it, when I was there, I spent in my own bed. Asleep.

D: Mike was a guy I worked with in my office. I came out to him when one of my gay friends who worked in the legal department let several of us in the gay community on my ship know there was an NIS witch hunt going on. They supposedly had a list of names of people they suspected of being gay, and of course I was on it. Nobody else ever saw the list, so we don't know whether it was true or not, but it freaked enough of us out that we kind of laid low for a while.

I was just all shook up about it, and I confided in Mike one day. When I told him I was gay he said, "I knew already." It didn't matter to him. He liked working with me, and I was fun to be around. He ended up being real supportive. We partied together pretty frequently. Nothing sexual ever happened, we were just real good friends. He was straight, and I was gay.

And—Mike used to go out with the ugliest girls. He was a nice-looking guy, but he'd get shitfaced drunk and go to bed with these—*dogs*. I used to give him a lot of grief about that.

One night we were on the ship, and I picked somebody up in one of the heads. It was one of the few times I actually had sex on the ship. Anyway, the guy I had sex with wanted to come down and see me again after a couple hours. We worked the midnight shift, and we were going to mid rats [midnight rations] together. By that time [laughs] I didn't want to see this guy again. So I told Mike to head him off at the pass. He goes, "You go out and pretend you're doing something. I'll stall him and tell him you'll be back later."

When I came back, he said, "I don't *ever* want to hear you make fun of the girls I sleep with again. I can't believe you did anything with a guy *that ugly.*" He said, "I thought you had more taste!"

Z: Is there a rigid kind of masculinity expected of Navy men?
D: Yes, even more so than with the Marine Corps, which is surprising. The Marine Corps—to society at large they present themselves as the most macho people on earth. But they're only exhibiting their professional face. When you are with them and get to know them on a personal level, they don't expect you to act macho all the time. It's almost like they realize that it's the individuals and whatever unique capabilities they have that make the Marine Corps successful. Yes, there are standards of behavior for your professional life, but whatever abilities you have they want you to apply toward that contribution. Whereas with the Navy, I felt much more pressure to act a certain way in my personal life.

To give you an example, I don't care much for sports. I got a lot more harassment about not being a football or baseball fan in the Navy than I did from the Marine Corps. The Marine Corps doesn't care that you aren't the jock. The Navy did. The other sailors were like, "You don't like football? You're un-American!" I never get that attitude from the Marine Corps. I thought they were going to be worse. I was actually really scared to go with them. But no, they're the most accepting people I've met. At least my unit. Maybe I'm lucky.

When I first got assigned to them there was probably some aspect of me that was afraid—I hate to say of being a man, but there was always some part of me that was afraid I didn't measure up as a man according to society's rules. I get with my Marine Corps unit, and they're going, "Look, you do!" They helped me be free of all my fears of that. "Be whatever kind of man you want to be." Because it's when you are accepting of yourself that you're going to give your hundred and ten percent. The Marine Corps helped me become a man—not according to their standards, but according to my own standards.
Z: What is your own standard of what is masculine?
D: Actually, it does kind of correspond with their ideals: honor to yourself, personal integrity, respect for yourself. They want all their people to have those feelings about themselves because when they do, then they're going to be good Marines.

We went on a fifteen-mile hike Thursday. We camped out and hiked again fifteen miles Friday. My legs are really sore today! To them, it's not a sign of masculinity that you can hike thirty miles. There are a number of women in my command who hiked thirty miles. It doesn't make them masculine because they can hike. It makes them Marines. That's very different. When I first got there, somebody told me, "Never refer to yourself as 'tough.' Anybody can be tough. If you're a Marine, you're 'hard.'"

I think the ideas that most sailors have about masculinity are much more subject to the pressures of the traditional macho image. I know that sounds so strange! This is of course my impression. But I've been in almost nine years, and I've seen how guys act with each other in the Navy, and I've seen how guys act with each other in the Marine Corps. And it's different! Sailors reinforce the ideas of masculinity by what they do. And with the Marines, it seems to be more like how you *are,* and less of what you *do.*

There are sailors who don't care what anybody thinks of them. I've met lots of straight guys who like flowers, and all the nontraditional stuff, and they didn't give a damn what anybody else thought of them. But to give you another example: I like the color pink. I have a pink bathrobe; I have pink shirts. I got more grief about that from the Navy than I did from the Marines.

Even though I'm in the Navy, I go out there and do all the things they do and they think that's great. They treat me like I'm a Marine. They even tease me by calling me sergeant sometimes. One of the guys at work gave me a Marine Corps emblem to stick on the back of my truck. I said, "Wouldn't this piss Marines off? I'm not a Marine, I'm a sailor." He said, "What? You're as good a Marine as half the people we've got in our command. We'd think of it as a *compliment!*" I haven't put it on there yet, but I'm going to.

Z: I'm wondering if you're becoming more like the Marines in other ways. I notice that your haircut—

D: I do the haircut because I had a corpsman friend tell me that if you get a high and tight and go out and do all the hikes, it lets them know you want to be a part of their unit. They will warm up to you that much quicker. It will kind of grease the wheels. They hate it when they get Navy people who won't take part in their activities. In my own command we had Navy corpsmen who, when it came time for a hike, would ride in a truck. The Marines don't like that. They'll still respect the guys as corpsmen, but they respect them more when the corpsmen get out of the truck and hike with them. So, they like the fact that I wear a high and tight. They go, "We don't even wear our hair that short!"

Z: How long have you been gay?

D: I was twelve when I first realized there was a sexual attraction to guys.

Z: How did you realize it?

D: My dick got hard when I saw another guy. That's a pretty good clue. Straight friends ask me the same thing. I tell them, "What did you do when you were twelve years old and you thought about a naked girl? Your dick got hard, right? Well, duh." And that's just the reality. You realize, hey, this is what it is.

Z: You mentioned that you are grateful to—

D: Dr. David Rubins, author of *Everything You Always Wanted to Know About Sex But Were Afraid to Ask.* He said some of the most hateful things about gay and lesbian people, but he gave me great cruising tips. I would never have thought to go to a public restroom and cruise somebody if I hadn't read his book. I think I was fifteen. "Oh. Great! Now I know where to go!"

Z: Did you go out and do that right away?

D: Yeah, actually. I went to the nearest—I think he mentioned a bowling alley. I went to our local bowling alley and of course there was nothing there. So I went to a mall that had peepholes, and I realized that it could be any bathroom, not just a bowling alley.

Z: Had you had any sexual experiences before then?

D: No.

Z: What did you feel about joining the Navy, knowing being gay was prohibited, and I guess having to lie about it?

D: I did have to lie about it, yeah. It's awful that you have to lie, but common sense tells you, if you want to be in the Navy, you have to mark "no" on this question.

I wondered how I was going to really fit in. I was twenty-one at the time. I figured I couldn't be the only one. In my boot camp company I met two other guys. You really don't have a lot of time to do anything in boot camp other than go through training, but you know, you get stationed on the midnight to four watch with somebody. It's not like we have radar or anything and can spot each other, but I kind of figured that there were these two that might be. In fact, one of the other guys was thinking about me. He finagled it so we got put on watch together. And since we were the only two up at one in the morning: whisper whisper whisper talk. Which of course you're not supposed to do at all at boot camp. But you do it, and you get away with it.

It was just nice knowing that there was somebody else. I remember that feeling of comfort, to know there were other gay people in boot camp with me. Then to realize that our sister company next to us in the same building—there were five or six guys there who were gay. We didn't know it until after boot camp was over with and we'd come to the bars here in San Diego and see them.

It was the same kind of thing on the ship. There were people you saw around and kind of suspected. You very cautiously got to know them, and then you'd talk about it. Of course then there are some people so blatant they came right up and approached you, "Look, I know you're a fag! Let me introduce you to these people."

We had one guy on our ship who was a cook and a screaming queen. All the people he worked with knew he was gay. He told them he was. They didn't care, because he was the perfect person to go party with. He'd go out and get drunk, and just party party party. Of course there were all these people who liked that. "Hey, the guy's queer, but he can party. We'll go out and have fun with him." He introduced me to several people. He was like a welcoming committee. We'd keep track of new people on the ship. Kind of like screen them, feel them out.

There was like a little gay—I hate to call it a clique. It was kind of loosely organized, there were no boundaries. It's just that after a while we had kind of identified each other. There was a core group—five or six of us—who ended up becoming friends and staying friends. We still maintain contact, even though myself and one other person are the only ones still in the military. There were other people that we knew who were on the fringe of the community. We didn't really want to be close to them, because they were backstabbers, two-faced. It was real important when things got really bad, in whatever aspect, that you had somebody who understood, somebody else who was gay and was going through the same kind of thing. A shoulder to cry on. And people you could be queens with!

One of my friends was a barber. When we were on WESTPAC, we used to gang up in the barber shop after hours and watch *Dynasty*. Close the door, lock it, put a piece of paper over the window, sit in there and just snap fingers with Alexis and Crystal. All over their gowns, or how vicious they were being with each other that week. We just couldn't do that openly; we got together so we could be that way with each other.

Z: Gay men and lesbians in the military use the word "family." Have you had relationships that resemble family relationships?

D: Oh yeah. My friends Dean and Alan are like my brothers. We get together; we celebrate Christmas. I don't know what we're going to do this year, because this couple has now broken up, and their house was always the center of things. I think that people are going to take sides. I hope not.

Z: Why did you join the military?
D: [Pause.] It's so far back, I couldn't even tell you now. Honestly. There was a certain amount of patriotism involved, there was a certain amount of—I didn't want to go to school, I didn't want to live at home anymore. I wanted to get out on my own but I couldn't afford to do it.
Z: Why did you choose the Navy?
D: I chose the Navy because three of my uncles were in the Navy. And I liked the uniforms. [Laughs.] I thought the Navy would be an adventure. I know that sounds really cliché. All the services go to foreign countries, but the Navy goes to more.
Z: Compared to the Army, Navy people do tend to move around more. What effect does that have on sailors' relationships, and their attitudes toward relationships?
D: I think they're much more volatile. Not just gay relationships, but straight relationships too. They're at a bigger risk of breaking up. With the straight people I've met—the Navy sanctions their marriages, so when it comes time for the sailor to get moved they'll move the family too. But even then it takes its toll. A lot of dependent wives and husbands won't put up with it, so they get divorced.
Z: Do you know of any long-term gay Navy relationships?
D: Dean and Alan. They met while we were all stationed together; they were together on the ship. They worked for two completely different work sections, but everybody they worked with knew they were involved with each other. My God, how could you not know? They were always going to visit each other. They always went to lunch together, they always did things together, they shared an apartment off base together. Everybody they worked with knew that. Duh. I think only the stupidest people didn't consider it. It didn't bother anybody in the least.
Z: You've never been in any relationships like that yourself?
D: No. No. I'm still looking.

Z: It's a stereotype that gay men in the Navy tend to be yeomen, corpsmen—
D: And chaplain's assistants. There are certain ratings that people don't expect you to be really butch. Even in the Marine Corps admin types aren't expected to be as gung-ho rugged as infantry guys. But there are a lot more straight people in those ratings than people think. And there are a lot more gay people in the nontraditional jobs, like Navy machinist mates, boiler techs, the guys who work down in the heat and do the rough

physical work. In the Marine Corps there's a lot of gay guys in the field in infantry who do all the really rough stuff.

Z: When we met last week, you weren't sure you wanted to talk about your job.

D: For a long time the only Navy people with the Marines were corpsmen. I've worked for the chaplain's office, which is a unique situation. I've worked for a variety of ministers—Catholic priests, a Lutheran, a Nazarene, and several Southern Baptists. I've had a few I would never say anything about my homosexuality to, and was actually very on my guard around, but then there were quite a number who pretty much knew I was gay, and said so by the way they treated me. It didn't bother them. I was a good sailor, I was a good assistant to them, and they didn't want to lose me. If I had actually come out to them they would have been bound by duty to turn me in and get me kicked out. That would have—not broken their hearts, but it would have upset them, that they would have been forced to do that. They didn't want to get put in that situation. So we didn't talk about it.

Yeah, they kidded me about various things. One of them even paged me one time when I was on the ship cruising the head. He knew that's where I went. So he came back there looking for me one day, which really pissed me off. I thought I was being cool about it! Now everybody there in the head knew who it was because he said my name, and I was foolish enough to answer up. The only reason I did was because if he came back there looking for me, that must mean I should have been back at work. I didn't want to get into trouble.

In the Navy and the Marine Corps—and I can only assume that it's the same thing for the Army and the Air Force—chaplains are the fix-it people. When people have personal or emotional problems, they come to the chaplain to help them get it straightened out. That's part of the chaplain's job. My job is to assist them. I set up for weddings, set up for baptisms—whatever religious denomination needs something, I'm there to provide it for them. I don't have to believe a word of their dogma.

I like what I do. I'm having fun dealing with people who are Catholic, people who are Jewish, people who are Muslim. I like that smorgasbord. It's important to me, because I do have a firm belief in God in my own life.

Z: You know I want to hear more about sexual tension at sea.

D: No matter who you are, whether you're straight or gay, when you get away from your normal sexual outlet, there's sexual tension. "Do I or don't I try to satisfy my need in this situation?" That's where it's really risky. There are a lot of straight guys who are willing to play, and I can only say: you have to use your own common sense. Like right now, at the command I'm with, I wouldn't do it. OK? Only from the fact that it could cause problems. If I were to get into a sexual relationship with somebody in my unit that I work so closely with—Say we break up; unit integrity could be brought down a little bit, because this person and me hate each other now. That's detrimental. If I was caught up in a relationship with somebody I work with, maybe I would play favorites even though I knew it was wrong. But the Navy is not so unit-focused on that small a level. There's a big distinction. So what was allowable activity to me in the Navy is not allowable activity with the Marines.

Z: Were the men you had sex with aboard ship typically not men you worked closely with?

D: I would never have slept around with anybody I worked with in my office. I think that's bad form. I'm not talking about people in another work section; I'm not working with them twenty-four hours a day so I can have a boyfriend from that place.

Z: You told me that you have had sex aboard ship, enjoyed it, but still feel somehow that it is the wrong thing to do.

D: Only for that reason. I didn't— The potential that it could be detrimental was there. Or that I could get caught. It's against the rules. It really— [Sigh.] If you're just gay, they can kick you out for that. But they have to give you a discharge that's up there with your level of performance. If you're a good worker, they're going to give you an honorable discharge. But if you get caught doing something on a ship—

Z: Your career might end in a military prison.

D: Right. So, it was risky that way too.

Z: Did you feel bad about breaking the rules?

D: At that time I knew I was breaking the rules and I was kind of sorry the situation was there where I was tempted to do it. We were out at sea, and it just happened. But I didn't go out looking for it all the time.

Z: No?

D: Sometimes I did, yeah. There were certain heads on the ship known to be cruisy. Mostly it was mutual masturbation; you know, reaching under the stalls. You really never even got a good look at the person you were cruising anyway, so it really couldn't cause problems in the workplace.

Z: Were these mostly gay guys, do you think?

D: Oh no. There were a lot of married guys.

Z: Do you have any preference between the two?

D: No, not really. Whoever's willing to play. And really, most of the sexual activity I engaged in was that. There were really only two other instances. One was a one-time thing with that really ugly guy. I was desperate!

We went to some storeroom. Lord knows I couldn't tell you how to get there again. We went through so many hatches I got lost. And the other guy was a guy I met and we went back to my office when there was nobody in it. I kind of had repeat episodes, but it was with him only.

Z: Always in the office?

D: Yeah. He was a machinist's mate and worked in the machinist's room. We couldn't go down there. I happened to work in an office that was lockable. So I had a place.

Z: Why shouldn't men be permitted to have sex at sea?

D: I don't think there is any harm if they don't work together.

Z: It's hard to imagine the American public condoning gay sex or sex between unmarried heterosexuals aboard ship. But that doesn't mean that it's wrong.

D: The thing is, the rules are on the books for both gay people and straight people that you don't have sex aboard ship or on military bases. Yet they conveniently look the other way in some situations. It's not condoned, it's just that the officials realize—I'm not talking about the senior officials in Washington, who apparently never have sex—but the reality is people are going to have sex, whether it's between men and men, men and women, or women and women. It goes on. And some rules do need to be in place so it doesn't become an abuse of power.

Z: When you've had sex with Marines, did you notice any different attitudes about role playing?

D: No. The Marines I met never had any weird attitudes about they're only going to do this because that's the guy's role. Never. And I can't say I've met Navy guys who were into role playing either.

Sailors are easier to pick up in uniform. If you're cruising a head someplace, a sailor wouldn't see a problem going in wearing his uniform and cruising, but the Marines won't do that. They would change into civilian clothes first. One Marine, he was getting kicked out, for reasons other than being gay. He wanted to get it on with me while he was wearing his dress blues. But at the last minute he backed out; he just couldn't bring himself to do it. The Marine Corps instills that much pride in their being Marines that you don't do anything that would discredit the uniform.

Z: Were you looking forward to seeing him in his dress blues?

D: I was. It was a fantasy, but. But he was a fantasy out of his uniform too, so.

Z: Is there a special excitement you get from men in uniform?

D: Really kind of not anymore. It's still there, but then it's like: I am too. Because of the fact that I'm a sailor, I realize that people have fantasies about me. So I can get into that role playing, too.

I had somebody I met at home one time, a civilian, who was obviously having this fantasy about making it with a sailor, so I played the role. "Yeah, I can get into this! I'll be the sailor boy. Arrgggh!" It kind of caught me by surprise. I was new to the Navy, so of course it was kind of a turn-on for me. I was thinking, "Yeah, I *am* a sailor now." It was fun; he wasn't getting somebody who was an imitation, who just went out and got a uniform, he was getting the real thing. But most of the people I meet in the military, because we're both in, we're not fulfilling each other's fantasies.

Z: Your uniforms are just the clothes you happen to be wearing?

D: Right. That's all it is. It's kind of lost its mystique. Most of the people I've met have wanted me to deal with them as a person. Not because they're a Marine or a sailor, but because I think they're cute or something.

Z: Do you still feel sexy in uniform?

D: Oh, I do. But patriotic, too. When I put on my dress blues with the thirteen buttons and the neckerchief, I'm thinking, "This is the uniform of somebody serving their country. That's me." Maybe that's a little overly patriotic, but I'm not going to apologize for my patriotism. I like being an American. I'm proud of my country, and to me it's a real privilege and an honor to serve it. I want people to understand that.

Z: Do you have any tattoos?

D: Yes.

Z: Part of the Navy tradition?

D: No. Believe it or not, I got a tattoo because it was the gay thing to do. I was reading an article on tattoos in the gay community, and how a lot of gay people were getting tattoos because I guess it was some kind of masculine fantasy thing. I got one before I joined the military. And once I was in the Navy I fit right in because I had a tattoo! It's a little heart and a cross. I wanted a tattoo that was me. I am going to get a tattoo of an anchor with the USN on it. I'm waiting until I become a first class petty officer. I'm a second class now. I'm an E-5, so I'm kind of in the middle of the enlisted ranks. But when I make E-6 I'll get a Navy tattoo. [David was out of the Navy for several years before enlisting a second time.]

Z: I asked you before about the shellback initiation, and you told me you didn't see anything homoerotic about it.

D: No, when I was getting spanked it was not erotic! Pain is not a turn-on for me. Wearing my clothes inside out and backwards is not a turn-on. Or having sour milk put in my hair. Or being made to crawl around on my knees. It didn't become a turn-on until the very end, after we climbed through the trash chute. Your clothes are so filthy, you take them off and you throw them off the end of the ship. So on the ship I was on there were four thousand naked men. Then it got to be, "Hmmm. This is kind of nice!"

But I've thought about it some more and I guess there is kind of a sexual aspect about it because it is men doing S&M type things with other guys, beating them with—they call them shillelaghs, but it's a section of firehose you swat them on the butt with. I can see that it's there. And they have the wog queen competition.

Z: Were any of your gay friends involved in that?

D: Only one. And believe it or not she didn't make wog queen, she was only a wog princess! He was really slim and effeminate, dressed up in a bathing suit with makeup. It was his own hair that he did. He looked amazingly like a woman. There's a picture of him sitting on the command master chief's lap, and the master chief has this evil lecherous grin on his face. It was just really funny.

The whole event is a morale booster. It's a sailor thing to do, so everybody takes part. In fact, the people who don't take part—because you're not required to do it, you can refuse to do it—are looked down upon. If you don't take part, you're kind of telling everybody you don't like being a sailor.

I actually did kind of have fun, in a sense. Because it was just so bizarre. Of course it would be much more fun to go through it on the other end, now that I'm a shellback. And I get to beat people. Maybe it will be erotic!

Z: What is erotic to you?

D: Eroticism is in your head. I have no particular . . . [Pause.]

Z: Well, you did tell me that you—

D: I have a thing for truckers. That's where I can see where people could have an eroticism about sailors and Marines or guys in uniform. There are certain types of people where there's a fantasy element about the job they do. Truckers are by themselves on the road for long periods of time without contact with women. Sailors and Marines and soldiers are like that too. So a mystique develops. A lot of it is not based on any fact! [Laughs.] OK?

There was a magazine called *18 Wheeler* devoted entirely to sexual experiences with truck drivers. The stories were hot and erotic, and I was thinking: these people are actually cruising truckers and only truckers. There was a method to do it. I thought: that might be kind of fun! I tried it one time, and I snagged somebody. It was a really hot erotic experience. It's not the only sexual activity I engage in, but it's one aspect.

Z: You mentioned that you arrange to make at least one cross-country trip every year.

D: Every year. I go home more than once a year, but at least once a year I drive. Part of the fun is that I can cruise truckers. It gives me an opportunity. It's real hard to do here in the city. When you only have one or two days off a week you can only travel so far.

Z: Truckers are thought of as being rugged and masculine. Is that part of your attraction?

D: That's part of it, yeah. And to a certain extent with the military. If I'm cruising and being successful with other military guys, that's real hot, because these are really masculine guys. And if I can do this, I'm a masculine guy, too.

Z: Do you ever have sex with men who are less butch than yourself?

D: Oh yeah. Some of my hottest sexual experiences have been with guys who were bigger queens than me. We sat there and talked about chandeliers and fabric. But when the opportunity presented itself I had a really good time with them in bed. They were really fun. And what was surprising was, when we were in bed, there was no femininity about them. Not at all. It was just as hot, and just as erotic, as it was with men who were overtly macho. It was the same. I was in bed with another guy.

Z: When sex is really good for you, what's it like?

D: Mmmm. Hot and sweaty. Raunchy. You want me to get into my preferences? No, I won't tell those. I told you personally. It's not a matter of public record.

Z: We were talking about HIV, and you said—

D: What all of a sudden became safe sex was what I enjoyed doing anyway. Mutual masturbation, lots of touching and hugging. I've always liked that. Before, it was almost a specialty if you enjoyed that. And now it's the way you're supposed to play.

Z: You did however say that you engage in oral sex without a condom.

D: Yes, I do.

Z: To include swallowing?

D: No. I don't swallow anymore.

Z: You spit?

D: Yeah. Unfortunately. I remember when it used to be that if you spit it out, it was almost a slap in the face. And nowadays you're looked on as crazy if you don't. So I don't swallow anymore, but I do engage in oral sex without a condom. I don't think they've concluded overwhelmingly that it's a means of transmission. It's one of those iffy behaviors, and I guess I'll just take my chances on it. I haven't become infected yet. I don't engage in anal sex. I never really liked it anyway. Maybe that's why I'm not HIV positive right now.

Z: Have you had friends in the Navy test HIV positive?

D: Yes, I have. Four. One I've lost contact with. One recently passed away. Two of my friends now have it. They're out of the Navy now. One's retired, medically, and the other got discharged.

Z: Another sailor I interviewed has a policy of avoiding sex with sailors who have been out at sea for fear they may have had sex in foreign ports with HIV infected prostitutes.

D: If I'm on a ship for four years, I know when that ship has been in port. Six months after we've been back, yeah I might play. But if we're over there in the Philippines, I'm not going to mess with anybody on the ship. If you saw the clap lines on the ship you wouldn't either! They're long— hundreds of people in them. Me and my gay friends, we didn't go out cruising right after the ship was either in port in a foreign country, or right after it left. It helped when we had a friend who was a corpsman. He would give us the heads up on who to avoid.

Z: Since you don't have lover relationships, do you find that you are able to get some of the same physical and emotional benefits through alternate means?

D: There are people that I've had that are like fuck buddies, but we were friends, too; I could go out, go drinking with them. Then there were the people in my close circle of friends. I've never had sex with any of them, but that's not what we came together for. We came together because there was a bond of love. It's like circles—the circle of close friends, then the outer circle of people who are pretty close to you. And it overlaps the working relationships, too. Because you work with them so closely, they are closer than somebody else you meet. There are people that you go party with, but you would never invite them over to your house for dinner. Yeah, so the friendships were there. That's where I got my sense of security. This is my family, because this is where I get my love.

I'm from Kansas. The heartland values. I was raised with them, I still kind of abide by them. Loyalty to your family and your family as a place of nurturing. I've extended that into the nontraditional aspect, my friends are now family too. What's so wonderful about my circle of friends is the way the members are enriched by our love for each other. That's a heartland value! That the members of the family feel love and can grow.

I was born and raised a Catholic. And even though I'm not aligned with the Catholic church anymore, to throw it away would be to throw away my history. I can't do that. Whether it's bad or good, I value what happened. Take the good, keep it, take the bad, and grow from it. And I think that's what a lot of people need to do. Your childhood and your past isn't all bad. There were good aspects of it. You take those and you keep that.

Z: Maybe you do have a calling, David.

D: I think that's what the function of a really good minister is. To make people realize: there is hope. Life isn't totally evil.

Z: You believe in good and evil. Do you believe in hell?

D: Yes, but not in the way religion or the media tells you. The most convincing vision of hell I've ever seen was in *The Devil in Miss Jones*. At the end of the movie Miss Jones was sent to hell. Not because she was a slut, but she went to hell, and for eternity she was put into a room with a guy where she was enticing him into screwing her and he wouldn't do it. So she was bound for eternity to have unfulfilled desire.

Z: But isn't that much like life here?

D: We do make our own hell on earth. When we're offered love daily throughout our lives; people make overtures of love to us, and we refuse them.

Z: Is it bad to be a slut?

D: Maybe it is if it's hurtful to you. If it's causing you not to grow as a person. It's like being an overeater; if it's causing you not to fulfill yourself as a human being, then overeating is bad for you. To me, sex and food and the pleasures of the world are meant to be enjoyed, but they shouldn't become an obsession for you, to where that's your reason for living. The reason for living is to be in contact with other human beings and love them. To reach out and connect, in however many varied ways there are of connecting with other human beings.

I've found acceptance in places I've never looked for it. I've learned to accept other people, people I normally would never have associated with before. I always hated the jocks in high school and I would never become friends with them. What a loss for me! These people could have been good friends, but I was too scared of myself, and too selfish with what was inside of me, to allow them into my life. That's wrong. If I wanted understanding from them for my difference, I need to extend that to other people too. I think when I learned that I needed to do that, that's when I found acceptance.

I just think, for the record, that most of the fears that are being expressed by the supposedly straight guys and girls about gays in the military really for the most part are unfounded. We've always been there. We're gonna be there. If we haven't molested you by now we're not going to. That's not what we're there for. Even if we do engage in sexual behavior, or might think to ourselves "this guy's pretty cute," or "this girl's pretty cute," that's not why we're there. We're there to serve our country. If that's not their motive for being there, then maybe they need to question why they're in the military. We're not going to go away. Fortunately, it's been my experience that the majority of people in the military are willing to get along.

There are people in the forefront of gay liberation who are out in the public eye, coming out on national television. There's a need for that. But for most of us, our way of liberating ourselves is to just get in there and blend in. And just be good sailors, and be good Marines, and be good soldiers. That's how we're going to get the acceptance. So that when the rules get changed, people will say, "It's not such a big deal."

I've already marched in the San Diego gay pride parade. I marched with the Institute for Feminist Thought, because one of our lesbian friends was in the organization. My friend helped do the banner for them. So we got to march with them. My mom would have been proud of me! She was a big feminist. She's been dead for five or six years, but she would have been proud of me.

I go to the parade every year. And yes, I would like to march with the gay veterans association. I would love to march in my uniform, I really would. I'm not going to do it now until the rules change, but I would like to do it. So that once it's OK I don't have to be invisible anymore.

Ray: The Navy Corpsman Nipple Piercing Ritual

In the Navy, no job specialty is more often stereotyped as likely to be occupied by gays than the hospital corpsman rating. Ray, an elfin white 22-year-old from a Methodist, middle-class, Michigan family, unapologetically embodies certain gay and corpsman stereotypes.

For my first visit to Balboa Naval Hospital, Ray treated me to lunch in the galley, then gave me a tour of "The Starship of Navy Medicine." In the corridors I noticed other sailors sashaying in the manner of Ray, enjoying the special freedom the Navy has long granted its gay medical personnel. Ray commented on the adjacent, old Navy hospital, a Spanish Mission kind of castle, which he explained has been known to generations of corpsman queens as "The Pink Palace." He also pointed out several men's rooms known to be cruisy, including two with operating glory holes. (I later returned to the hospital alone and enjoyed illegal public sex with a uniformed corpsman "A" school student, who told me of a Navy woman friend at the hospital who since Clinton's election had taken to calling any sailor she thought might be gay "One of Bill's.")

Part one of this interview took place in Ray's barracks room. Compared to the Spartan austerity of Marine Corps' quarters I visited at Camp Pendleton, and the crowded and raucous Army infantry barracks I knew in West Germany, Ray's home is a casual and relaxed environment similar to a coed college dorm, civilian in flavor except for the presence of uniformed sailors at the quarterdeck and signs identifying restrooms as "MALE HEAD" and "FEMALE HEAD." Ray has a small room to himself with a private telephone line and an answering machine that plays a bitchy, disdainful message. His small window affords a pretty view of Coronado Bay. Taped to his door is a poster of the singer Morrissey.

The first time Ray flashed me his nipple rings I assumed that he, like legions of modern primitives I saw in San Francisco, had visited a piercing parlor for the kink/kick of feeling metal through his tits. From this interview I learned that the truth was otherwise, and was delighted to discover another dimension to the special relationship Navy hospital corpsmen enjoy with Marines.

Zeeland: A lot of sailors have tattoos, don't they?

Ray: I've met more Marines with tattoos than I have sailors.

Z: Do they attract you?

R: Tattoos? They don't attract me and they don't push me away either. As long as their body is not covered with them. I can handle a tattoo here and there. I don't have any tattoos.

Z: But you do have your nipples pierced.

R: Yes, I had them done when I was over in Okinawa. It was a tradition for the corpsmen who were stationed at Camp Hansen with the 3rd Medical Battalion to have their nipples pierced. I did it for the tradition and also because it was something that I just wanted done. I thought it was interesting. Another corpsman would do it. It was supposed to show that you were hard and you could handle being with the Marines. That was more the butch side of it, I guess.

Z: Was this a gay corpsman thing?

R: No. It was practiced by straight and gay corpsmen. Some chose not to do it. It was a mixture. It was not the gay side. It was all handled within the corpsman field. There were also a few Marines who wanted to experience it, too. They were the ones who worked closely with us, like our drivers.

Z: Was there some ceremony?

R: Not really a ceremony. A lot of times it would be like a trade-off; whoever was piercing your nipple, you would pierce theirs. Some would just go through basically a line, and one person would do everyone. Anyone who wanted to watch could, and anyone who wanted to have it done, we always took care of them.

Z: How many people were present at your piercing?

R: Actually I have three holes. Two in my left nipple and one in the right. I got one of them done first. There was me and my roommate along with this other corpsman who wanted his nipple pierced. My roommate was just watching. I pierced the other corpsman's nipple and he pierced my nipple. It was very close to the tip. I was always wondering—worrying, I guess—whether it was going to get pulled out or not. So I decided that I was going to have another one put in my left nipple set further back. And then to pierce my right one. That was done over at the medical battalion by a friend of mine.

Z: I'm surprised that you wouldn't demand more experience of your first piercer. This sounds like prisoners giving each other tattoos or something.
R: Well, it's—it was something that you definitely took slowly! You just didn't jab it through. The first one I had, the corpsman who did it for me was very nervous. He had never pierced anyone's nipple before. I think that was part of what the problem was. With the second one, the corpsman had already had both of his done, and he wasn't nervous about it at all. And he did a very good job.

I was a little nervous about the first piercing that I received. I have my ears pierced too and that didn't bother me. But my nipples, I just wasn't sure of. It's kind of a sensitive area.
Z: Sensitive and erogenous.
R: But being corpsmen, we were able not only to get the needles, but also to get Lidocaine. So there wasn't a great deal of pain. But there was still the fact that somebody was sticking a needle through my nipple.
Z: Was there any feeling of sexual excitement?
R: There really wasn't. Most of it just felt like—pressure, because you had Lidocaine which numbed the area. So even when he was sticking the needle through, it felt like a finger being pushed into the nipple. I did not find [the piercing itself] sexual. But now that it's done, once your nipples are pierced, they are even more so an erotic area. You tend to feel them more.

The very first time I pierced somebody else, it went just fine. I'm a lab tech, so I've dealt a lot with needles. He worked at the clinic with me. There were no complications.
Z: Was it fun? Did you enjoy doing it?
R: Yeah. It was interesting. Semi-erotic. Playing with a man's chest.
Z: Was he gay?
R: It was unknown. It was suspected. He seemed to keep to himself.
Z: Were you attracted to him?
R: Not really. But I didn't mind doing it for him.

Z: Tell me about coming out.
R: My very first lover I met while I was in high school. He was a friend of mine in our group. In high school everyone wrote notes that you'd pass between class. One note—and I didn't realize I was doing it at the time—when I signed it, I signed it "love." Later in our relationship I asked him, "Why did you ever decide to ask me out?" He said, "Because of the way you signed one of your letters." It was kind of a coincidence that it happened that way. We dated for little over a year. It was my very first relationship, and the first time I came out.

My mother ended up finding out about it. That was a problem. In fact, after she found out I kind of went back into the closet, because she wasn't handling it well. It was hard for me, because my mother and I have always been really close. She refused to let me go out with him anymore. That's more or less what came between him and me. I had to sneak around just to see him. We started getting into fights after that, and ended up breaking up.

I think that was actually one of the reasons why I did come into the military—because it got me away from my family. I needed to see what I wanted for myself. My mother was very upset that I joined, because she wanted me to go to [a nearby college] and stay at home and be with the family. But that wasn't enough—I don't want to say escape, but I just wanted to be off on my own and find out for myself what I wanted.

Z: Why did you pick the Navy?

R: I was very interested in the medical field. I always have been. I went around to all the different branches, and I think that the Navy has the best medical field. They offer you a greater choice of [job fields within] the medical field.

I went through boot camp and I had no intention of coming back out. Then I went on to corps school and found out that there actually are gays in the military, that it is in fact quite prevalent. You can meet a lot of them. There were even friends of mine in corps school who I knew were gay, but I would never get too close to them. Because I always thought: this is the military, you're not *allowed* to be gay. It was something I was still worried about at that time. I wasn't really ready to come back out yet. I would go and meet people who I did not know. That was the only way I was going to do it. I was not going to bring it back into my life fully.

Z: You would meet people you didn't know? Do you mean that you would have sex with strangers?

R: Yes. There was a gym on base. I met some over there. Just different places around base.

Z: Were these anonymous contacts where you would never speak, or was there sometimes more involvement?

R: No, when I was going through corps school it was all anonymous. They were one time meetings. It wasn't that long that I was in corps school, a couple of months. Even if I wanted to there was no real chance of a relationship. And I didn't try. It wasn't what I wanted.

That sort of carried over to my first duty station. That's really more when I started coming out. I started having friends who were gay, and we did things on occasion, but even then it was limited. I would be very cautious about who I would come out to. The first time that I really started coming out with all of my close friends was when I was over in Okinawa. I had straight friends over there who knew I was gay. That's when I started realizing that there wasn't as much conflict as a lot of people imagine.

The ones who are homophobic—I think some of the problem is that they just don't know any openly gay men. They don't think they could handle being friends with them. When chances are they have one or two friends they're close with who are gay.

The closest straight friend that I've come out to—that happened when I went through lab school in San Antonio. There is one club there I found really interesting because it was a good mixture of both gay and straight. Gays would go there and they would be allowed to be open and no one was persecuting them and everyone got along really well.

Todd was one of my classmates. We got to be really close friends. One night we were out at the bar and I just felt that I had to tell him. I think being in the club helped. He would see other gay men out there, and realize that he could be with them and get along with them and not have to worry whether these gay men were going to come up and attack him. Todd was a little surprised that I was gay, but he took it well. In fact, about a month before we had made plans that within a year or so we would get back together and just take some leave and go someplace for a week or so. That night he said, "Well, I hope you don't think any of this is going to change. You're still a really good friend of mine, and I still want to keep our pact." He was very open about it. I think it actually made our relationship stronger. To this day we still keep in really close touch, even though he's stationed on the other coast.

Z: Was there something special about him that made you such close friends?

R: When you're going through military school, you're with each other all day long in class, you're in the same room together, and you sleep with each other at night. Everyone tends to get really close. I see it the same way as being on the ship. You're constantly around each other. That bond seems to grow. You're very protective of each other, and the friendship just gets very strong.

Z: So was it more just the situation that made you and Todd close? Could he just as well have been one of the other guys?

R: There were other things. He was going through a divorce. He had talked to me about it, things that he was feeling, and I helped him out with that. There were a few things that made our relationship closer than others. We talked more openly. He felt comfortable discussing things with me that he was having a hard time dealing with.

Z: Were you sexually attracted to this man?

R: No.

R: Okinawa is where I really started coming out. I met a lot of people. There were clubs there too that we went to a lot. Because most of the Americans there were in the military, it was still kind of an underground thing, the gay military family. I would see friends of mine there who I saw at work. I think being overseas, especially in Okinawa—it's hard, because if you go off base, they don't speak English. And you don't have that freedom to just go anywhere and be able to get around. You have to rely on each other and you tend to stick together. Some of the Okinawans were not thrilled with the Americans being over there, and that was another thing that you had to watch out for. They would never get violent or anything, but it was something that played with your mind a little bit. So my friendships seemed to be stronger.

One friend I made was James. It was about three months after I got to the island. He was a Marine. He was stationed down at the south end of the island. At the time I was down there too at the naval hospital on temporary duty. We ended up making it a monogamous relationship. I continued to see him for the rest of the time I was there, about six months.

Z: Where exactly did you first meet?

R: [Laughs.] We were in the Exchange [military shopping complex] and we just kept looking at each other. After about ten minutes I walked into the bathroom. He followed me in there and we started talking. He had his own room, so we ended up going back there.

Z: How long were you in Okinawa?

R: A year.

Z: Did you have a lot of contacts in the other six months?

R: Um, I had a few, yes. [Pause.] To break them down, I was with two Air Force, three Navy, and I'm really not sure of the number of Marine Corps. [Laughs.] Probably in the upper thirties, forties.

Z: Were Marines more accessible, or do you just have a special taste for them?

R: I am attracted to Marines. I don't know if I could really say that they're any more attractive than any other branch.

Z: So if it's not that, then what is it?

R: Marines tend to like corpsmen. You always hear of conflict between Navy and Marines; they don't get along. But corpsmen—we're Navy, but we're separate in the fact that we go out there and serve with the Marine Corps. All the medical field does. They know that in time of war, we're going to be the ones out there trying to save their lives. And at the same time a corpsman will realize, while I'm out there trying to fix this guy, this guy over here is going to be protecting me. So there's a special bond there.

Z: You're saying that also shows up sexually?

R: Yes.

Z: These Marines that you were meeting, would they know that you were a corpsman?

R: Most of the time they would, yes.

Z: Where did you meet them?

R: There were a lot of places on the island where you could meet. Just about any one of the bases, especially the Marine bases, you can meet men in every one of the bathrooms. There would be messages on the wall, but one of the primary ways was passing messages back and forth underneath the stall. Another way to meet was just in the Exchange. It was a big area. You could go in there and just walk around. You would see people and make eye contact. Then you would go into the bathroom just to talk and find out more about each other.

Z: Do you have any special attraction to men in uniform?

R: I don't think I'm so much attracted to the uniform itself. I like military men because they take care of themselves. They have nice haircuts, they're clean cut. I like that. I don't like long stringy hair.

Z: Marines are stereotypically very butch. Is that part of your attraction?

R: Myself, it doesn't matter one way or another. That's not something I look at. Whether they're flamboyant or butch, I've been attracted to both. I have gone out with some of them who are butch when you're out, but when they're behind closed doors they aren't so butch. [Laughs.]

Z: There's another stereotype about Marines—I'm sure you know it—

R: That all Marines are bottoms.

Z: What do you have to tell me about that based on your experiences?

R: A lot of them do seem to be bottoms. Not all of them; just because they're a Marine doesn't guarantee they're a bottom. Once in a while you will run across one who's strictly a top, but most times you'll find they're either a bottom, or at least versatile.

Z: The Marines you met in Okinawa—what do you think their sexual identities were?

R: Some of them I think are very confused. Some of the Marines I've come across do not want themselves to be referred to as gay. A lot of them—well, to give you an exact detail, I was with this one; he told me he wasn't gay, he just wanted me to fuck him. That kind of threw me off.

There was another Marine who I met shortly after I arrived on the island. I didn't see him for very long because he was getting ready to leave. But he was married and his wife was over there with him on the island. When his wife was at work we went back to his apartment. He was another one who didn't really want to be considered gay, he didn't like that. He just wanted to get fucked.

Z: How did that make you feel?

R: Um, I try and understand it because there's always a time . . . it varies from man to man, how long they go through, but there's always a time when every gay man is unsure what he wants. I'm over that; I know I don't want to be with a woman. I'm very happy to be a gay man. But when I'm with them—at times it's very frustrating, but I also try and remember what it was like when I was going through it.

Z: Do you think there's a certain kind of masculinity that the Navy expects of its sailors?

R: Again, the medical field is different from the rest of the Navy.

Z: Are all corpsmen fags?

R: [Laughs.] Sometimes I wish they all were. But a good majority are, yes.

Z: If you had to guess, based on your experiences, what percentage would you say have had sex with other men?

R: I would say at least eighty percent have had at least some experience. Just based on the ones I've met. The gay underground in the military is really extensive. Even if you don't know individuals personally, you hear things about them. There are certain areas even within the medical field that seem to attract gays more than others. One of the biggest fields is the OR, operating room technicians, and laboratory technicians. For some reason they seem to be more attracted to these areas.

Z: What is your job?

R: I am a lab tech. [Laughs.]

Z: Gay military people use the word "family" as a code word, but it also has this meaning of a substitute family relationship. Have you had relationships like that, that you think of as brother-brother, sister-sister—

R: Josh [not interviewed]. Josh's and my friendship—we're really close. In fact he's probably my closest friend here. We got here just about the same time. We do just about everything together. If one of us is going out, chances are the other one is right there with him. We don't do many things without each other.

Z: Has there ever been a sexual component to your relationship?

R: When we first met. And it was the only time. There was nothing very deeply involved in it. As far as sex itself—it wasn't taken to the full extent. We did not have sex per se, but there was sexual contact.

Z: How do you define sex?

R: Anal sex.

Z: And anything else—

R: Is foreplay.

Z: Did the experience bring you closer, or was it just sort of incidental?

R: Our meeting—I mean, that's how we met. Our friendship started to build after the encounter.

Z: Where did you meet?

R: [Laughs.] In one of the bathrooms, here in the barracks.

I don't have a lot of sex. If I'm going to go out with somebody and it's just going to be a one night thing, then it would be more oral sex. But as far as to have sex, I don't do that with just anybody I go home with.

Z: Having your own room, are you able to take men back here?

R: Yes, I can.

Z: Do you have to worry about sneaking them in?

R: If they're military, there's not a problem. When you come in the barracks you have to pass the quarterdeck. At night they watch over who comes in and out of the barracks. If they have a military ID they can get past the quarterdeck, but if they were a civilian and didn't have it I would have to sneak them up the stairs. Although you can have guests in your rooms, you can't have them after two o'clock at night.

Z: That sounds like an incentive to meet other ID card holders.

R: It is an incentive, yeah. That way you don't have as much of a problem.

Z: Do you like the Navy?

R: Yes I do. In fact I just reenlisted. So I guess I have to like it. I enjoy my job, and everything I've gone through since I've been in. I'm happy I joined. I have no regrets.

Z: Some men describe having a strong feeling of camaraderie with other sailors.

R: Different places I've gone to, different experiences I've gone through will bring out different relationships, friendships. Whether you're going through school and you're in an open squad bay, or you're out in the field or you're on the ship, they all play different roles in how close you get to people. A lot of times it's because you spend so much time with somebody, you get to know them so well, you start to feel closer than just somebody you would normally work with at a civilian job. A lot of times you're kind of thrown into having friendships with these people. Sometimes you don't end up getting along with somebody and you're stuck with them all day at work and in the barracks. That can be a problem. But for the most part I tend to get along with everyone I work with. I have my own room now, but when I've had roommates or been out at sea—you tend to get close to these people. There's a special friendship, something that you just don't get anywhere else. You keep in touch with them, and a lot of times you are brought back to see them again. So it's a family, all around. Not just the gay family, but all around.

Part Two, Five Months Later

Over the months separating our two taped conversations, Ray and I became part of a circle of friends that met for weekend parties and picnics. The next four interviewees—Gregg, Russell, Sonny, and Kevin—along with Anthony, Ray, a Mexican-American corpsman named Ramon who declined to be interviewed, and me, made up the group's core. Occasional participants included Eddy, a straight corpsman named Aaron, and others. I dubbed our public and private gatherings "love-ins," because of their tendency, especially in the beginning, to dissolve into physically intimate group contact that, while sexually electric, never included what most people would call sex. The love-in group dynamic has been discussed in Part Three of Anthony's interview and will be addressed at greater length in the following conversations, culminating with Kevin's. (This material reveals another dimension to my interviewees' personalities, and offers clues as to how these sailors truly view their own—and each other's—sexualities.)

Ray played a special love-in role.

Z: What was your reaction to the President's "Don't Ask, Don't Tell" policy announced last Monday?
R: A lot of mixed emotions. I'm still happy that the whole subject has been brought in front of the public. What made me unhappy was the fact that he compromised so much. I really don't see a lot of difference between this policy and the old policy.
Z: Do you see any difference?
R: When you come into the service, it's not on the questionnaire anymore. That is one positive thing. And it seems right now that it's going to be more difficult for them to start investigations, which is another good thing. But outside of that, no, it's basically the same.
Z: Do you envision any possible changes in your own life as a result of the change in policy?
R: No. Even if the ban was totally lifted I didn't see myself changing. I would probably feel more relaxed overall, and I wouldn't worry so much that somebody is going to overhear something I say somewhere—I would

no longer have to worry about saying "her" instead of "him"—but as far as coming out at work, or really to anyone else that I haven't come out to, I wouldn't see it happening.

Z: I asked Kevin about how he behaves at work, and he insists that he is fully himself. He talks about George, or whoever he's dating, and doesn't call him his boyfriend, but says, "My friend and I went to the beach and watched the sunset." He also said he thinks he makes you nervous sometimes when you're around him because. . . . He says he thinks of you as being more noticeably gay than him, but he says that you try to act more butch at work—

R: [Coughs violently.]

Z: He sees himself positioned in the middle between the more-butch role you play at work and the not-so-butch way you might act off duty.

R: He really never made me feel uncomfortable. Certain times—it depends on the crowd that we're in, whether we're in the chow hall or we're alone—he might say something and I might turn and look to see who's around to hear. But it never really bothered me.

I really don't know that I act any more butch at work. [Laughs.] I don't see that happening.

Z: But Anthony says that too; they both say that you act differently at work.

R: I think I act different in that I tend to be professional. But I don't really see it as being a big difference. I still do most of the things that I would do off base. I just sort of tone things down a little.

Z: Do you make a conscious effort to walk or talk differently at work?

R: No, everyone tells me that I sashay through the halls of the hospital too, so I don't think I walk any differently. To the average person at work I don't talk about my personal life, so there's really no difference there, either.

Z: It sounds like you think of this difference not so much in terms of femininity/masculinity, but in terms of just being more serious at work. Would that be a fair description?

R: Yes.

Z: Has anyone given you a hard time in connection with the gays in the military debate?

R: There really hasn't been that much talk about it at the hospital. There have been a few [discussions], but it's nothing really bad or good, they're more or less just talking about the policy and what's going on with it. In fact, since the new policy was announced I haven't heard anything. Nobody has said "Now they're gonna let faggots in the military." There was nothing like that.

Z: You told me before that the hospital is sort of a special case. Have you ever even known anyone personally who was investigated and discharged for homosexuality?

R: No.

Z: So you've probably known more than a hundred military queers, and none of them that you know of has ever gone through a witch hunt?

R: No.

Z: We can agree that you've known a hundred?

R: Oh. Definitely. I'm sure we could at least say a hundred. I think that's very kind of you [to make it so few]. [Laughs.]

Z: Since the last time we spoke on tape you and I have been part of a small group of sailors and civilians, mostly gay, that have gotten together for "love-ins." You know my theory that Kevin acted as a sort of sexual pole at the middle—

R: Yes. I think that—I don't know if he was so much the cause of the picnics, but he was definitely the magnetic center. Kevin is very open. He doesn't hide very much, whether it's at work or in his private life. He's a very friendly person. He gets along well with just about everyone; no matter how much they annoy him he always smiles and carries on. And of course he's adorable. Everyone loves Kevin.

Z: What was your own role at the love-ins?

R: [Laughs.] To keep it going. At times I kept tension in the air.

Z: You give yourself over to wild displays of sensuality, and you get this look on your face when you do it that has sometimes made me wonder just how much you really enjoy it. Is this just campy play? Or is there more to it than that?

R: If you're talking about sexually enjoying it, no, I don't sexually enjoy it. I enjoy being with my friends, and the displays that we put on— I just enjoy doing it. It sort of helps the love-ins go on. It tends to get everyone in the mood. When we had Russell and Aaron [Aaron declined to be interviewed] there, I seemed to keep tension going with them. I didn't really treat them any differently than anyone else in our group. I think they were comfortable for the most part being there. I'm sure certain things made each of them uncomfortable. . . . I'm sure I had a good part to do with that!

Z: I think I observed tension in Aaron's face when you simulated going down on him, and he called to Kevin for help.

R: Of course Kevin was nowhere to be found!

Z: Conveniently. Some of the gay guys I think were sort of curious as to what Russell and Aaron were doing there.

R: I wasn't so much curious as to why they were there. I don't think that they're trying to get into the gay life necessarily. Both Russell and Aaron seem to accept us. It does add a little tension at times when somebody does or says something, makes some gesture in one way or another that makes them a little uncomfortable. But that just adds to the whole love-in.

Z: Uncomfortable how? Just being around gay guys talking about and playing at sex? Or uncomfortable with intimations questioning their presence, or suggesting that they themselves might be gay?

R: I'm sure it has at least crossed their minds that we have all thought about at one time or another whether or not they might cross over at least for one of us. [Laughs.] At least one time. I know the thought has crossed my mind.

Z: You say this with a certain weighty significance, which brings me to a question I have about Aaron.

R: Oh.

Z: Kevin said that when you were first getting to know Aaron, that you went out with him one night and spent the night with him, and that Aaron later complained that you had tried to molest him. Is that what happened?

R: We did end up spending the night together. At the time we both lived in the barracks. I lived in staff barracks, which meant it was no problem for me to pass the quarterdeck, but he was in the student barracks, and they tend to get a little irate when they have a student walking past who is trashed. So he really didn't want to go back to his room. I suggested that we go to a motel, and of course I would be ever so gracious and not do anything. It was agreed that it would be nice just for the night—not to do anything necessarily, but just to sleep together. I know I was looking forward to it, and he seemed to be comfortable with the idea, and in a way looked forward to it too. The next morning when I awoke certain things were rising [laughs] and my hand just happened to be there. He laid there for awhile and just seemed to enjoy it, until the point that it no longer was my hand that was caressing. Then he seemed to get a little worried, and it stopped there.

Z: Had he given you some signal that he might be open to the idea of experimenting with another guy? Or did he insist from the beginning that he was just straight and open-minded?

R: A little of both. It always seemed like he was trying to portray that he was completely straight, that he had no thoughts of ever going to bed with another man. But little gestures that he would make seemed to suggest otherwise.

Z: Like what?

R: For a straight man he dances very erotically with other men on the dance floor, and I was one of them who he was dancing with that way. It just was not something that a man who never thought of being with another man would do. He seemed to get very into it. Just little things like that. Even the next morning when we woke up—he was awake but he really wasn't doing anything, he was just laying there. And it was fine with him until I tried to . . .

Z: Why do you think that would make a difference?

R: I never really thought about it. That was just the point where he decided it was enough.

Z: Did that change your relationship with him at all?

R: No, not really. It did to the point where I never tried—except for the love-ins when I had too much to drink, and that was playing, but from then on I decided I was not going to pursue anything more. It changed that, but as far as us really growing apart, no, not really.

Z: Let's say Aaron had done something more with you that one time. Would you still consider him straight? What is your definition of what is gay and what is straight?

R: Actually, I find it hard to believe that there are that many men out there who are totally straight. From my understanding, most guys who consider themselves straight will admit to thinking about it, at least a little. So there's always that line there: they've never crossed it, but they've thought about crossing it.

Z: Some people will think that this is just wishful thinking on your part.

R: I wouldn't say that, because there have been men out there who I would never want to sleep with and they have told me things like this. This was not wishful thinking.

Z: Of course a lot of straight guys who do have sex with other guys will impose certain limitations. Like the Marines who told you they weren't gay, they just wanted you to fuck them. Or the men who say, "Don't kiss me, I'm straight." Or the ones who think that if they just get a blowjob from another guy, it's not gay because they're not actively doing anything.

R: There's not really a hard line there for me. It depends on the individual.

Z: I don't believe in a "hard line" either. I hope you're not just saying that because you think it's what I want to hear.

R: No. Actually you have never really gone into deep discussion with me about that, so I don't know what your views are. You always seem to find out what everyone else's opinions are, but you don't give yours that freely.

Z: Anthony and Kevin have both complained that you called them sluts.

R: [Laughs.]

Z: It does seem sort of funny to see you simulating animal acts in public parks, and hear you tell me about trying to blow a straight guy in a motel room, and then hear you call those guys sluts. Did you really mean what you said?

R: No, I think it's more of a running joke. They call me a slut, I call them sluts, it sort of goes back and forth. Somebody always seems to be outdoing one of the others. That's when they get put in the lead for being the slut. I really don't consider either one of them to be sluts.

Z: They do both have a lot of sex.

R: Just because somebody has a lot of sex, doesn't make them a slut. I think outside of the sex, one's actions and how they carry themselves, I think that plays a part in, to me, of what a slut is.

Z: Another person I have to ask you about is Gregg, who kind of came along and—well, what happened with Gregg?

R: Gregg reminds me of what I think a lot of people out there view gays as being. He's sort of like ACT-UP. That's his attitude towards things. I was talking to my mother; I just came out to her recently. ACT-UP is one of the groups you're always seeing on TV for gay rights, and I told her I don't agree with everything ACT-UP does. They take things too far. I think it tends to give homosexuals a bad name.

Z: ACT-UP campaigns for AIDS awareness. I think you're thinking more of Queer Nation.

R: Them too.

Z: But what you mean is confrontational, in-your-face activism. Blocking traffic, yelling at people. . . . You really haven't seen Gregg engaging in political activities; he's suspended that now. So what did he do in our group that made you think that of him?

R: Well, one comment he made that I always think of when people ask me why I don't care for Gregg that much was . . . it was something along the lines that he wanted to fit all heterosexuals with these collar devices so that at one particular time all he had to do was push this button and they would all jump out into traffic and get hit by cars and die. He said this at the love-in at Kevin's.

All the heterosexuals who seem to be so against us, the sides they take, and the extremes to which they go—he seems to take it the same against heterosexuals as they do against us. And I don't think that's any more right.

Z: So it's just his views that annoy you, not his personality?

R: He does seem to think that everyone is in love with him, and— [Laughs.] He tends to get on everyone's nerves. It's the way he says things, the way he puts them. He will never let anything rest. He will always have a different viewpoint than you unless it's the radical side that

he stands on, which I don't think there are any of us that go to the lengths he does. There's always something he can argue about and he'll never drop a subject. He's never wrong, he's always right, and everyone who doesn't agree with him should just go away. So, we went away! [Laughs.]
Z: So you think Gregg is antistraight, but he is best friends with a straight guy. Russell and he have a very close relationship.
R: [Pause.] Their relationship is close?
Z: Yeah. They sleep in the same bed.
R: I don't see their relationship as being that close. Actually, just from the facial expressions that I have seen come over Russell when Gregg comes around, the attitude that's in the air, it just doesn't seem like they're that close. He seems to annoy Russell.
Z: You've never spent any time alone with Russell, have you?
R: No.
Z: So I think we can safely say the most involved or intense contact you ever had with Russell was at the love-in where he took off his belt and beat you with it. Was that fun?
R: [Laughs.] I enjoyed it.
Z: Do you think he enjoyed it?
R: The more it went on the more he seemed to get into it. He seemed to enjoy the fact that each time he hit me all I would do in response was have him hit me harder. And each time he did hit me harder, all I kept asking for was him to hit me harder again. He seemed to like the fact that he could do this to me, and I was not turning away. I think in a way it sort of shocked him. [Laughs.]
Z: Why would it be pleasurable for him to hit you with a belt?
R: [Laughs.] I don't know Russell that well. I can't say what exactly he enjoys and what he doesn't. He just seemed like he was enjoying it.
Z: He did seem very pleased. Why was it pleasurable for you?
R: [Laughs.] Because I like to be spanked? Well, I do like that, in the first place. I enjoy it, so that part was enjoyable. I have always thought that Russell is very attractive. Actually, that was—I can probably say that was the only time that I can look back at anything that happened during our love-ins that I have thought about in a sexual sense.
Z: Meaning that you fantasized about the experience later?
R: Um, well, I don't know if it was so much later as at that particular moment in time! It was sort of a mixture. At the same time I was looking at it sexual, I realized that he was . . . like I said, I don't know exactly his views, although I have my questions. But yeah, it was pleasurable, and I thought a little about it then, and I've thought a little about it since then.

And when you told me that you interviewed him and it was one of the things you talked about, it made me think about it a little bit more!

Z: Anthony theorizes that corpsmen have a special relationship with pain.

R: [Long pause.] I don't see that as being true. I know a lot of corpsmen who don't enjoy pain.

Z: For you personally, are there any connections that you are aware of—

R: Between me liking pain and me being a corpsman? No, I don't see a connection. Myself, I enjoy pain to a point. There are things that get deep into the S & M side that I would never want to do. Fisting is one. I would not partake in that. That's not something I would find pleasurable. There are some things that cross the line into S & M that I do enjoy, but I really just sort of touch on it lightly.

Z: Do you enjoy administering pain? Would you have enjoyed whipping Russell?

R: Oh, I think I could have found some pleasure in whipping Russell.

Z: Is this something you and Anthony have talked about?

R: We don't go into deep conversations about it. I think I'm as much aware of—the whippings, for example. For both Anthony and I, that's become sort of public knowledge. So we're both aware at least to some of the extent that we enjoy it. As to the role that plays in our sex lives, we haven't talked about that.

Z: Marines remain something of a mystery to me. They tend to stick together. They have an image of themselves as Marines that sailors don't have of themselves as sailors. I have come to see Marines as sort of a cross between Buddhist monks and butch drag queens.

R: [Laughs.]

Z: You said before that a lot of Marines are bottoms. I think what I failed to ask you was, why?

R: A lot of times with the Marines I've run across—Marines are always the butch ones, and I think they like to feel that they can go through anything. A lot of them seem to like to be the bottoms and to get fucked hard. It seems to be more that they can deal with the pain, and they have survived it. It's just sort of an additional thing to be a Marine. It's almost like you need to be a bottom at least a few times in your Marine career.

Z: That's so funny, because a lot of men think just the opposite. They fear that playing the bottom role will feminize them, that being penetrated will make them "like a woman." Which is what a lot of people have theorized is behind this "I don't want no fag lookin' at my butt in the shower" line we hear from so many straight military men. If a man's ass is being admired, he could be made to feel like a powerless woman.

R: That may be true, but there's nothing to say that Marines have ever been that intelligent to look at it any other way than it's a pain thing that they have overcome and it makes them a better Marine.

Z: And you had no problem giving a little bit of pain to the Marines.

R: I was always right there by their side to help them out in any way that I could.

Z: You said that there are very few men out there who you consider to be totally straight because you think that there's some curiosity or some potential for homosexual experimentation in most men. Is that what you said?

R: Yes.

Z: One thing you do have in common with Gregg is that, out of the whole group, you both seem—not only to consider yourselves a hundred percent gay, you both express repulsion at the idea of sex with women. So if all men are supposedly bisexual, how come you aren't?

R: [Laughs.] Oh, you have put me on the spot, haven't you? This is hard to explain. I've never gotten into any serious relationship with a woman. When I was younger and trying to hide the fact that I was gay I would date women. There was some experimentation with it that I would do. I feel no need to go any further; I didn't enjoy what happened. So, I guess in my own sense I have experimented a little with being heterosexual. I know in the group I tend to seem repulsed about it, and when our friends joke about doing certain things with women, it does repulse me. I can't figure out how anyone could receive pleasure from it. But sometimes I carry it further than I need to.

Z: You sometimes sound genuinely misogynistic.

R: No, I don't hate women. In fact my best friend from Michigan is a woman.

Z: [She] does not have a penis?

R: She never had a penis.

Z: And probably never will?

R: Except for her fiancee.

Z: Someone else's penis. What we all need.

R: Yes.

Z: Speaking of which, tell me about your current relationship.

R: [Laughs.] Jeremy [not interviewed] and I have been dating for two months now. He's an FC [fire control technician]; he's stationed on a ship. We get along very well. There are some differences between us, some very distinct differences. He's only been out for a year. He will go to great lengths to deny that he ever acts like a queen, even though he has some characteristics that do definitely put him into that category. I keep telling him that he's a queen and he keeps saying that he's the big butch man. At times he tends to worry too much about what everyone thinks. I guess most of us go through that at one point or another. And I think I've had a little to do with making him feel more comfortable. I think that I tend to help a lot of people feel more comfortable with the gay lifestyle. I like to think that's one of my better qualities. When people go out with me and they see the things that I do—they're actually OK and they're not that awful—I think a lot of people, whether they're gay or straight, they tend to feel more comfortable.

But Jeremy and I are doing very well together.

Z: Any long cruises coming up?

R: In October he'll be gone for three months.

Z: Do you anticipate having a closed relationship?

R: He has left a few times already, once for two weeks, and both of us have agreed to this point to keep this a closed relationship. To the best of my knowledge we both have. And I pray that we will continue to do so. We have talked a little bit about it. We decided that even when he's gone for three months that it will be a closed relationship.

Z: You think you can handle going without sex for that long?

R: I've gone three months before.

Z: But not voluntarily.

R: [Laughs.] That's true. But to know that he's coming back to me, I feel I can do it. And I want to do it. I don't want to see anyone else while he's gone. I'm very happy to be with him. We have talked a little about more long-term goals between us. As far as our careers in the Navy and what we plan on doing, and different things that may change in the future if we're still together. More or less how we can, with the Navy's help, stay together.

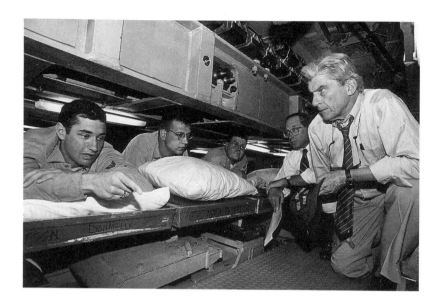

FIGURE 1. (Top) Senators Sam Nunn and John Warner talk with Navy submariners about what would happen if homosexuals were allowed to serve in the U.S. military. (Jose R. Lopez/NYT Pictures). FIGURE 2. (Bottom) An active-duty Marine's tattoo combines the U.S.M.C. eagle, globe, and anchor logo with a gay rainbow triangle. (Zeeland)

FIGURE 3. This *Life* magazine photo was reprinted in U.S. Naval Institute *Proceedings* with this caption: "For most active-duty men the issue boils down to an uneasiness about potentially being regarded as sex objects. How will avowed homosexuals handle close proximity—such as this cold-shower treatment during SEAL training—to men for whom they feel physical attraction?" (D. Gatley)

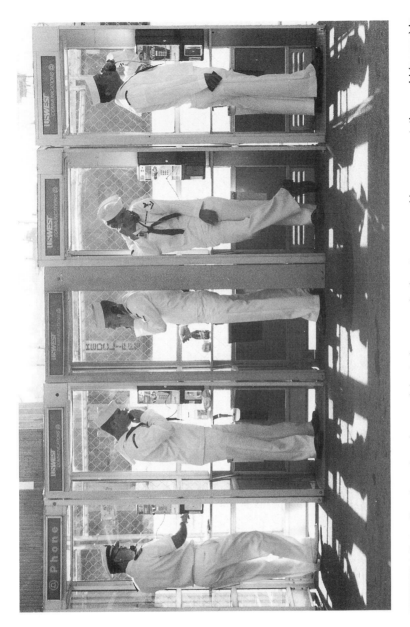

FIGURE 4. But sailors have long been celebrated as sexual adventurers—and have a *reputation:* a girl (or guy) in every port. (Jim Bates/*The Seattle Times*)

FIGURE 5. "It's only queer if you're tied to the pier." Sailors on the flight deck of an aircraft carrier. (National Archives)

FIGURE 6. Sailor in combat, World War II. (National Archives)

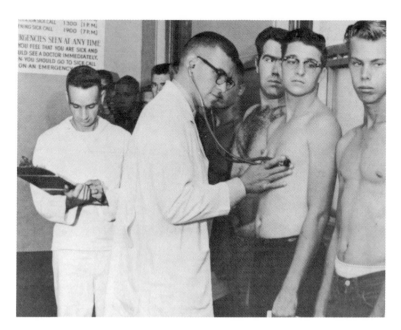

FIGURE 7. (Top) Navy medical personnel have long been stereotyped as "soft." (U.S. Navy). FIGURE 8. (Bottom) Boatswain's mates are expected to be rough and tough. (Zeeland)

FIGURE 9. A Navy hospital corpsman. (Zeeland)

FIGURE 10. Shore leave. (Zeeland)

FIGURE 11. (Top) San Diego sailor. FIGURE 12. (Bottom) Oceanside Marine. (Zeeland)

FIGURE 13. On Sonny's destroyer, the "crossing the line" initiation ceremony included (Top) the application of Crisco to shipmates' anuses, and (Bottom) simulated analingus. Sonny found nothing homosexual or homoerotic about the ritual. (Sonny)

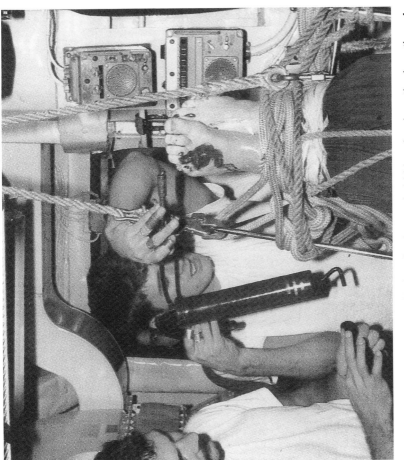

FIGURE 14. Another Navy initiation ritual, now forbidden, involves the insertion of a grease gun into a shipmate's anus. (Sonny)

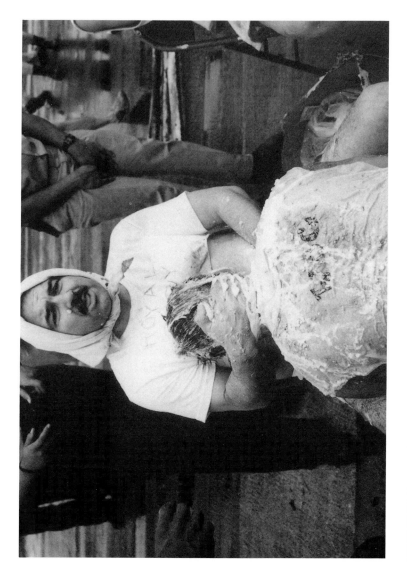

FIGURE 15. No crossing the line ceremony would be complete without "wogs" being made to suck olives out of the belly button of the "royal baby," traditionally the ship's fattest chief petty officer. (Eddy)

FIGURE 16. In the wake of the Tailhook sex harassment scandal, revised Navy guidelines for the crossing the line ceremony prohibited sailors from dressing in drag and spanking each other with firehoses. Instead, as on Eddy's ship, the USS *Ranger*, wogs were squirted with chocolate syrup and ordered to simulate anal intercourse. (Eddy)

FIGURE 17. One of these sailors is the author's ex-lover, Troy. Pick the known queer. (U.S. Navy) (Answer: Figure 18.)

FIGURE 18. *Troy.* (Zeeland)

Gregg: The Unmaking of an Activist

A nuclear machinist's mate and petty officer second class at the time of his discharge, Gregg is the only one of my interviewees to have come out publicly. He did this after becoming the first active duty service member ever to head a gay veterans organization, a distinction that landed the 23-year-old Flagstaff, Arizona native on the cover of the "authorized unofficial" weekly *Navy Times*.

Seeing his face on a magazine rack in Oak Harbor, Washington, I thought I felt a strong presentiment that we would somehow become friends. To this end, I wrote Gregg a letter. As a result of his sudden fame Gregg was the recipient of several hundred letters from supporters and various crackpots. He responded to mine with a stiffly cordial note of thanks and a disconnected pager number.

(I arranged for Gregg to receive a prepublication copy of *Barrack Buddies and Soldier Lovers*. He only recently confided to me that he hated the book and drafted, but never mailed, a vicious poison pen review. Gregg resents comparisons between his own story and anyone else's. And, like a good Dutch-American, he feels sexuality is a private matter inappropriate for public discussion.)

After moving to San Diego I again tried contacting Gregg, who continued to ignore me. Finally I did manage to catch up with him at the Veterans Day parade, where the eminently recognizable figure (he is six foot seven inches tall) led a small contingent of gay vets and me (not media whoring, but representing my absent military friends) down Broadway Street to wary acknowledgment from the parade marshall and public (Clinton had just been elected, and change was in the air. Or so it seemed). But many months passed before I saw him again.

I had frankly given up on the man when one night I ran into him at West Coast, San Diego's premier gay dance club. I succeeded in buttonholing him for his telephone number. Soon after we met for dinner and, in fulfillment of my presentiment, hit it off.

Military gays who come out publicly are expected to say certain things. How they are model service members (as if it will be forever in doubt that gays can perform as well as straights, or that they must actually perform better). How they did not choose to be gay (as if choosing would be sinful). How they are patriotic and clean-cut Americans (and, by implication, sexually monogamous and free of disease). How their "sexual orientation" does not mean they will engage in "sexual misconduct" (although under military law, all homosexual and many heterosexual acts are illegal).

Gregg made all of these requisite pronouncements in his public appearances. But as the President of the San Diego Veterans Association he became something of an activist gadfly, bluntly denouncing what he perceived as the hypocrisy of certain gay community leaders and articulating his sometimes idiosyncratic ideas in tactless violation of the party line.

Gregg has a penchant for shocking people. Once, at his dining room table over spaghetti marinara (thrift is another mark of a good Dutch-American), he told me a story about a friend who had died of AIDS. In his last will, the friend asked that he be cremated, his ashes mixed with paint, and rolled onto the ceiling of his surviving lover's bedroom. But during the final stages of his illness his lover abandoned him and moved on to a new relationship; upon the man's death he could not even be bothered to visit the crematorium. Acting as instruments of justice Gregg and a collaborator collected the ashes, blended them with off-white latex, gained entry to the lover's bedroom, and executed the dead man's last wish—much to the faithless lover's irritation.

"Of course," Gregg chirped brightly, "when you get the remains back from the crematorium, they're not just ashes. There are also some pretty big chunks of bone fragment in there. So we had to sift those out. In fact, we used the same colander I used for the spaghetti I made tonight."

And then there is this story. At the height of his fame after the *Navy Times* piece, a New York City talk radio host telephoned asking if he could interview Gregg the following week. Gregg consented, then promptly forgot about it. On the day of the scheduled interview, when the talk show host called and announced he was ready to patch Gregg into the cars and homes of thousands of listeners, he caught Gregg masturbating. They went on the air, and Gregg continued to masturbate until, while a woman caller was articulating a long question, he came. Gregg says (he has kept the tape, but I have not asked to hear it) that some significant seconds of dead airtime passed before the host inquired whether he was alright. "Oh yes. Much better than before," Gregg said, and then answered the woman's question.

Gregg has since dropped out of activism.

For part one of this interview Gregg drove me on the back of his motorcycle to Julian, California, an old mining town in the mountains some 50 miles east of San Diego now regionally famous for its apple pies. He took me to the ruins of the town jail, which he suggested would make a fun setting for a porno film, and selected as his interview site a tree stump in a hillside cemetery overlooking the town. In this exceedingly peaceful setting we were interrupted only by a fire ant, which Gregg killed, and by a salamander, who skipped by unmolested.

Gregg: I spent a little over two years on the USS *Long Beach*. We had gone on a WESTPAC over to the Persian Gulf in time for the Gulf War. We were over there, and on the ship—there was a lot of tension in the air. We had been out to sea for a long time. A lot of people were really stressed about that. The morale on the ship was very low. People were angry with each other, looking for places to vent that anger. The liberty ports really sucked because they were very expensive, alcohol was in short supply, and there were no women for the guys to go screw, except for the women off the tenders and they tended to have a lot of attitude. So when you got liberty, it wasn't a relaxing release kind of liberty that people had expected.

My division was about sixteen people, and we were short one guy. Nine of them had been on-board as long as I had, or longer. They pretty much accepted me; even if they thought I was gay they pretty much just ignored it. But there were six new guys who had come aboard. For whatever reason they had taken a dislike to me. My being gay—and it was sort of well-known by then that I probably was—especially upset them. There was one guy, his name was Johnson, he used to have a rack right below mine; he'd sit there and tell me, [sing-song voice:] "Don't come down and fuck me tonight. Stay out of my rack or I'll have to kill you."

We pulled into Bahrain. We had been on liberty there for a couple days. One night I had been at the administrative support unit, which is a Navy base there. I was walking out past this dark alley when someone reached out and pulled me into the alley and threw me down and people started kicking me and hitting me. And even though I was screaming out, the shore patrol and the MPs—nobody came around. It was on a base; right on the other side of the building people were in the pool and drinking at the bar. I know people heard me. There's just no way that they could not have. Yet no one saw fit to see what was going on.

This lasted for a little while. Then somebody said something about the MPs and they all ran off and I was left in the alley. I staggered to my feet. My face was bleeding; I had obviously been kicked around, but when I went to get on the bus to go back to the ship everybody just stared at me, like "What happened to you?" But nobody asked it. And when I got back to the ship, the next morning when I reported what had happened, the XO [executive officer] told me that if I pursued it he'd kick me out of the Navy for being gay.

There was a lot of other stuff. Pretty much just those six guys and the few other cohorts they had on the ship would throw their elbows out when I was walking down the hall. Somebody smashed my Walkman to pieces. There were a lot of nasty things being said.

Zeeland: You didn't have friends that were able to counter that at all with support?

G: Not really. Because so many people thought I was gay, the other gay people didn't talk to me. They tried to avoid me as much as possible.

Z: What about straight friends?

G: I didn't really have many straight friends on-board the *Long Beach*. I had sort of a policy, and later I realized how stupid and vain it was, but I didn't party with the people I worked with. Part of that was . . . just by saying "I don't party with the people I work with" no one would ever ask to come over to my home, and that made it easier. So, there was no one I could really turn to for help. And there wasn't really anything that could be done anyway. If the XO decides to ignore it, the only thing you can do is take it to the captain, and chances are he'd just follow the recommendations of the XO.

Shortly after that I was accused of doing something. We had some secrets leaked from the ship and they accused me of forging some signatures and allowing those papers to be released. Everybody knew who had done it, but the accusation fell on me since I was in charge of the division and ultimately responsible for what happened below me. I didn't fight it, just because at the time the pressure on the ship was so great, and I knew that if I didn't fight it I'd be transferred off the ship. And so I got found guilty at captain's mast, which later was overturned by an admiral, but they took me out of the nuclear division. I worked in the A-gang, auxiliary division, working on auxiliary equipment, until we reached the Philippines and I got transferred off the ship.

When I got back to the States I was put on-board the USS *Berkeley*, which is a small destroyer. I was really happy about going to the *Berkeley* because I had met a guy [from the *Berkeley*] named James. He was gay and we had dated for a little while before we both had gone overseas.

I reported on-board. The *Berkeley*'s a real small ship, real tight quarters, and so you're bound to run into somebody. And James walked by and I said hello to him. He turned around and his mouth just dropped open. He looked at me and said, "What are you doing here?" I said, "This is my command now." He walked away, and the rest of the time he was on the ship we only talked once. He avoided me like the plague. A lot of that was due to the fact that shortly after that I became very out, and was involved with the media, so he didn't want to be associated with that. Which is really funny because a lot of other people who were straight, it didn't bother them.

The presidency [of the San Diego Veterans Association] was open for election. I had been a member for a couple of years. I decided I didn't want to come out publicly and say I was gay, but I thought by taking the presidency of SDVA as an active-duty member—the Navy had never said if it was OK to join and participate in a gay organization without declaring your sexuality. It took a couple of months for the Navy to respond; there was a gap, and during that time I was working on the *Berkeley* and becoming good friends with the people I worked with.

When the media first hit, I talked to the guys I worked with and told them I had taken the presidency of a gay group, but I didn't tell them whether I was gay or not. My CO [commanding officer] started to harass me, and called me up to his cabin and called me a faggot. He said he knew that I was gay and that he was going to throw me out. But the Navy soon afterwards issued a statement saying it was alright for me to participate in SDVA because that in itself did not mean I was gay, and they made it an official policy whereby sailors and Marines could on their off-duty time associate with gay organizations. Which I thought was a major step in the right direction. But my CO started an NIS investigation to prove that I was gay, and started really harassing me. NIS was following me around. Finally I just got fed up with it, and I decided to come out to my command and just sort of end it. I knew that they would discharge me after I came out.

The day that it was going to be published in the paper that I was gay I
went in front of quarters . . . everyone was assembled there in the morning
and my division officer asked if anyone had anything to say. I said,
"Yeah, I have something to say. You're going to read it in the papers
today, but I'm going to tell you first." I said, "I'm gay," then I got back in
line. The division officer looked at the chief and they really didn't know
what to say about it. But a lot of the guys started talking to me about it.
Unlike other people, they had no choice, they had to work with me. And it
was such a small division that if they didn't work with me they would end
up carrying more of the workload. So as we would work we would
discuss things. They wanted to know about gay things. Most of them said
that they'd never known someone who was gay before; I corrected them
and said they never knew anyone who was *openly* gay. Over time we all
became very good friends and they just accepted it. By the time I left, the
ten guys I worked with had all gone to a gay bar with me, and many of
them had spent the night at my house. And it was no big thing; I was one
of the group and it didn't matter. Then at the end—a ship's decommissioning party was held two days after I was discharged. My shipmates had
pulled together to buy me my tickets to go, because I couldn't afford them
myself, but the CO refused to let me in because I brought a male date. The
crew was very upset. When I left, out of three hundred and fifty people
aboard ship a hundred and forty-four signed a letter to the commanding
officer saying they wanted me to stay, that my sexuality wasn't an issue. It
was just a matter of them getting to know me and understanding that it
didn't make a difference. In contrast to the *Long Beach*—where it was
just a suggestion that I was gay that drove people crazy—on the *Berkeley*,
once they had a chance to talk about it and express their feelings and learn
about it . . . it was a lot different.

There were only a few people on-board the *Berkeley* who didn't accept
me. It was impossible not to know I was gay because it was published on
the front page of *Navy Times*.

I had a party and there was a yeoman who came over. All the women
who were there were lesbians, most of the guys were gay. When he
realized what was going on he said "You're an asshole!" and ran out the
door. But then there were other guys I'd come out to and it was just cool.
Most of the people who said, "You're an asshole," I think were dealing
with problems of their own or just were afraid. They didn't have the inner
strength to stand up to someone who said, "You're friends with a fag."
That was very difficult for them sometimes.

Z: What led you to join the military?
G: I was from a small town. My parents were very domineering and I

wanted to get away from them. The Navy seemed to be something different. I've always wanted to do things that are sort of eccentric and not tow
the line, so I decided to join the Navy. It had really nothing to do with
sexuality. I knew I was gay when I was in fourth grade. But joining the
Navy really had nothing to do with meeting men.

Z: Why did you pick the Navy?

G: The Army just seemed a little too dumb and I didn't want to crawl
through the mud and eat out of green cans. The Marines were just a little
too tough for my taste, and plus I'm not a bottom. The Air Force recruiter
was really arrogant and never returned my phone calls. And the Navy
recruiter was just a nice guy and he offered me a good program. The
nuclear power program was very challenging, but it offers a lot of bonus
money and rank and promotions very quickly. By the time I had spent five
years in the Navy I was an E-6. There's no other program in the military
that allows an enlisted person to move up that quickly.

Z: Did you have any idea there would be other queers in the military? Or
did you think you would be the only one?

G: I felt like the only one for years. I knew that there were other gay
people, I just didn't know how to reach them or where they were. I was
obviously afraid, being in the military, to reach out and try and go anywhere.

When I was in Orlando there was a place called the Parliament House,
a very notorious gay place. You had to drive by it to get to the big mall, or
to get to the Orange Blossom Trail, which is where all the strip bars are. I
remember out front they had this huge statue of a drunken friar holding a
cup of wine. [Laughs.] And men would be holding hands. We used to go
by and yell "Fag!" out the window.

Z: You would yell with them?

G: Oh yeah. And people . . . I never threw bottles at anybody, but I knew
other sailors who threw bottles out the windows of cars at the gay guys.
So, I knew that that's where they were, but I was always scared to go,
because someone might see me, and it was off-limits, and at that point in
my Navy career I never realized that that was something that could be
challenged. So I avoided it. I mean, I didn't really know anything about it.

Z: What was your first sexual experience with another male?

G: One time when I was in high-school—I was working in McDonald's
and there was this guy named Tim. He was very cute. He was in JROTC
(Junior Reserve Officers Training Corps). One night we went out with the
manager and we got drunk and Tim couldn't go back to his house so he
came back to mine. He passed out on the floor. I thought at the time that
anyone who got drunk and passed out forgot everything that happened to

him, because that's what always happened to me. So I took his pants off and gave him a blowjob. I remember he came in my mouth and I didn't know what that funny taste was and I ran to the bathroom and spit it out. That was the first time that I ever did anything.

There was another friend of mine who came over to my house one time who I tried to do the same thing to, but he sort of realized what was going on and rolled over on his stomach, so it never happened again until I was in the Navy. Then there was a sailor down in Orlando, and for lack of a better explanation I sort of forced him into letting me give him a blowjob. He enjoyed it, and then on the way back to the base he was holding my hand as we were driving in my car, but we never spoke again after that.

It was despicable, but it wasn't rape, by any means. It was just—I convinced him that I had something that he needed, and that was my silence. It's not something I'm proud of doing. I thought that he was gay, and he may have actually been gay. He had gotten really drunk a couple nights before; we had a hotel room and we were sharing it with a third man. There were two beds, so he and I ended up in the same bed. Through the night I had my hand in his shorts, fondling him, and he didn't say anything or stop me.

I didn't have sex with a man again until I was in Idaho. I spent a year in Orlando and a year in Idaho, and the rest of my time in the fleet.

Z: How long were you in the Navy altogether?

G: Six and a half years. Much too long.

Z: You come from a very religious family. Growing up, was sexuality ever even alluded to?

G: Yeah, there was a guy who got excommunicated from our church for masturbation.

Z: Was this a Christian Reformed church?

G: No, we had left the Christian Reformed church and we were at a place called the First Baptist Church. I think they professed to be Southern Baptists, but they were a little weird. In fact they were just wacko. I don't think there's a child that went through that church that escaped unscathed.

This guy had apparently been caught masturbating by his wife. And I remember he was confined to a wheelchair and I don't know why. He was caught and called by the church elders and he refused to stop and so they excommunicated him from the church. . . .

[Deleted: Gregg tells the story of his estrangement from his parents, who, after learning of his homosexuality, decided it must have been caused by incest with his sister, episodes of which she was only able to recall in the presence of a Christian fundamentalist pseudo-therapist, and which Gregg, despite repeated visits to hypnotists, psychiatrists, and other therapists, has no recollection of at all.]

My father told me that gay relationships don't last and so he was worried that I'd always be lonely. He also told me that he was worried I would get AIDS and die. Then they left and my little sister was glancing at me like, "Oh my God I have to spend the night with these people now." My mom didn't say anything, she just cried. They didn't hug me or anything. They just got in the car and drove away.

Z: [Pause.] Lately you've been thinking about going back there and seeing them.

G: I did for a while, and then I realized it was pretty futile. I toss about the notion every now and then. But I don't think there's any point to it right now. Nor any reason. I mean, after all these years it doesn't really matter. They're not part of my life and they haven't been part of my life.

Recently my dad and my brothers all got together and went backpacking. My sister was telling me about it and how they joke around with each other. I just know that even if I went back I wouldn't be included, and that even if I was invited I would be the outsider to the group. I don't think I'll ever be part of the family again.

Z: You told me a few weeks back that you wanted to change your name.

G: I still do. It's just—I don't feel like that person anymore. There are a lot of reasons for it, but I don't feel like that's my—I don't know. I associate that name with a lot of hate.

Z: You picked this cemetery to be interviewed in. Just because it's a pretty and quiet place?

G: I guess so. Lots of places to sit. I don't have a fixation with death!

Z: But the other week you told me—do you remember? You couldn't imagine anything more sickening—

G: I can't imagine anything more sickening than eternal life. People think it's almost morbid to say that you grow tired of life, but life is a chore. There are wonderful things that happen, but I perceive life as a chore. A go-around once was alright, but I can't imagine living forever or being reincarnated again. The idea of just going to sleep and never waking up, just sort of an eternal sleep, is much more appealing to me than walking on streets of gold.

Z: Well, of course it wouldn't necessarily have to be that hokey.

G: I realize that. I just find the idea of existence after this pretty disgusting. I don't believe there is an existence after this, but. Death is not something that—it's a little unsettling, you never know what happens afterwards, but. . . . I don't know. Death is just there.

Z: Do you think the pain you've gone through has made you a stronger person? Or does it just wear you down, ultimately?

G: I don't know. It's definitely changed me. I think that I've always been a strong person. In order to survive where I grew up I think we were encouraged to be strong people by my parents. My father is such a perfectionist that quitting was never really an option. I inherited some of his perfectionism, so I don't like doing things half-assed. I think that's made me a strong person. Sometimes I think people perceive me to be stronger than I am. I don't believe people should display their emotions openly. I think that should be intensely private.

I don't know. I often have this tremendous sense of loss about my life. Sometimes I feel like someone without direction, just sort of . . . there's no real. . . . Most people, if you asked them where home is, they would tell you where their parents are or where they grew up. If you asked me where my home is I really couldn't answer the question because there really is no such place. I'm not saddened about it, it's just the way my life is.

Z: I think it's hard for civilians to picture what life aboard ship is like.

G: The *Long Beach* was a lot different from the *Berkeley*. The *Long Beach* is a cruiser; it's got a lot of space, and there are places to go hide, and a library and a chapel. The *Berkeley* had none of that; it was very small and confined.

Being out at sea is like nothing else in the world and I love it. You can't really describe the feeling. It's hard to describe what it's like to work with the heavy machinery powering that ship through the water. You get to know the engineering plant . . . you can tell everything that's running by the sound, and when something's wrong you can hear it and you fix it. It's quite something to keep a steam plant like that running.

Z: What kind of men did you work with? How are the "nukes" different from men in other job fields?

G: Nukes are different because they have so much training, so much money invested in them that they often get left alone by the officers. They're allowed a great deal more leeway than the other sailors. They can tell an officer to go fuck himself without really having to worry about getting into too much trouble. They tend to be more intelligent and not as good looking as other sailors. Sometimes it breeds problems, because there is a certain lack of discipline among nukes. They always try and press the rules to the limits.

Z: You told me you drank radioactive water with them?

G: Oh yeah, yeah, yeah. That was sort of an initiation thing, you just sort of drank a bottle of radioactive water. What's there to talk about? You take a sample of radioactive coolant when the reactor's operating and you just chug the thing. It tastes like shit and it's got ammonia in it, so it doesn't really do well for your insides.

Z: There's a higher cancer rate for men who work in that job?

G: Oh yeah. Much higher.

Z: What can you tell me about the sexual tensions aboard ship?

G: On the *Long Beach* there were a number of gay people I knew who, for one reason or another, stayed in their closets. A lot of closeted Marines.

There was a sailor named Lonnie; he was in charge of the wardroom. He would sometimes show up for work in a dress. He'd change into his uniform, of course, but he'd be serving the officers in the wardroom wearing Lee press-on nails. Because he did his job very well everyone left him alone.

Z: Was he treated somewhat like a clown?

G: Actually, the crew didn't like him too much because he was such a flaming fag, but he didn't have to work with much of the crew. He worked pretty much with the officers, and since he was in charge of the wardroom the people who worked for him were very junior. So he got away with it.

When I was on-board the *Berkeley*, I had about twenty-two people who came to me at one point or another and said that they were gay, but there were no real flamers like there were on-board the *Long Beach*. One lieutenant called me into his stateroom. He had a locker, and he opened up the door and there were all these pictures of women from magazines and in the middle was a small photograph of a very attractive man, and he said, "That's my lover. All these other pictures are just here for camouflage."

Z: But what can you tell me about the sexual tensions between the *straight* guys? The horseplay, the joking around. [Pause.] You told me about some incident with a thumb. . . .

G: My first boat was the USS *Chicago*, which is a submarine. I was only on there for a couple weeks, and they pinned one guy down on the mess decks and were pretending to screw him. They had him down on a table and someone shoved their thumb up his ass, and the captain was watching and laughing and it was all quite humorous. This guy thought he was getting screwed, and everyone was sitting around laughing at him.

Z: But he *was* getting screwed.

G: By a thumb, but I mean, he thought he was getting screwed by a dick. An awful small dick, if that's the case.

The only person who really ever made sexual overtures on-board the *Long Beach* while we were out at sea was a guy named Pat, and he tried to coerce me into having sex in the radioactive material storage area.

Eventually I did end up going down on him. He was very small, about as small as a pinkie. He kept telling me his girlfriend told him he was small, and I said, "No no, a lot of guys think they're small, but it's just not true." And I got down there to find that it was! But I couldn't tell him. That was really the only time I ever had sex on-board ship. And then there were some Marines that I played around with that were in our MARDET [Marine detachment]. But that was—sex with Marines is sort of a thing by itself.

Marines are trained to be part of a group. They're men, they're fighting machines. I think in the Navy you're not really taught to die for your shipmates. Most guys would, but it's mostly out of friendship, not out of a feeling that "this is my fellow sailor." The Marines have more of a group mentality and they have to be tough. In the Navy you don't. You can sit there with your coffee cup and your big fat belly and do nothing all day. The Marines have to maintain that they're *men*; in the Navy you don't have to maintain anything, really. The appearance you maintain in the Navy is all by your own choosing, where in the Marine Corps it's sort of enforced. The only image sailors have to live up to is drink a lot and stagger down streets.

Z: How would this difference translate into different attitudes toward sexuality? Or is there no difference?

G: My experience with Marines is that they all tend to be bottoms. Although I've met a few that are tops, but not very many. You're going to make me out to be a slut! I once had a little grouping of Marines, four Marines and a sailor, the sailor being me, We were all in the shower at the same time, and—four of the Marines were getting screwed and the sailor wasn't. [Laughs.] It was a chain fuck, and all the people being fucked were Marines.

Z: Where did this happen?

G: In an apartment in Oceanside.

Z: If it really is true that most Marines prefer the passive role in anal intercourse, why do you think that is?

G: I think Marines crave affection. I mean, the Marines have two-man sleeping bags for God's sakes. They teach this camaraderie, and I guess the natural outflow of that is something sexual.

Z: But why would that make them bottoms?

G: [Pause.] I don't know. Maybe they're just so used to being the dominant strong man they like to be dominated. Maybe the Marine Corps attracts people who are naturally bottoms and they just have something to prove.

It's funny. I've had lots of Marines tell me "Don't kiss me, I'm straight" or, "I'm not gay, I'm just having sex." "Sure, whatever, shut up." [Laughs.] Marines are just a different breed. Marines and sailors always try and fight; Marines say they're better than sailors, and sailors say, "Well, Marines are really just a division of the Navy." But I think that's mostly just surface stuff. I know a lot of Marines who are good friends with sailors.

Z: Do you think there might be a special attraction between Marines and sailors?

G: Yeah, I think there is. Well, Marines are rough and tough and generally macho, and they work out, so they usually tend to be more attractive than the average lifetime sailor, who usually tends to have a beergut and coffee and cigarette breath.

Z: But why would a Marine be attracted to that?

G: I'm just comparing the two. I mean, if you had a choice between a bodybuilder and some fat slob—

Z: So you're talking about *your* choice.

G: Yeah, yeah. Maybe it's a conquest thing. I'm not sure. I find myself physically attracted to Marines, but most of them just turn out to be such head cases that you have to run the other way. They're just dealing with so much shit, they can't be free to be themselves. They are Marines.

Z: With a capital "m."

G: Sailors are sailors nine to five, then they go home and they're whoever they are.

Z: But sailors do have their own traditions and rituals that are intended to forge a common identity. What about the shellback initiation?

G: I don't think you're upholding any image when you go through the shellback initiation. . . . It starts out with the wog queen ceremony. We had a doctor on-board who everybody called "Doc Finger." You'd go to him for a nasal drip and he'd put on the glove and check and make sure that you didn't have any hemorrhoids. For anything—an eye infection, crabs—he'd check your ass. Doc Finger won the wog queen contest because he looked the most like a woman. People didn't even realize who it was, which was probably good for him. He was generally considered gay.

The commander of the MARDET was a wog and he got beat really bad by the Marines. We had wog-fucking, where two guys get on top of each other and screw doggie style, or even missionary position sometimes. Officers often got that really bad.

Z: Simulated fucking?

G: Oh yeah, simulated. Simulated fucking, simulated blowjobs, simulated everything. Pretty much every sexual act that can be simulated was. But the last time I did it they made us stop the wog-fucking because apparently someone was complaining.

It's fun. It broke up the monotony. I really don't think it has anything to do with homosexuality. I think it was just fun.

Z: There weren't aspects of the ceremony that you found sexually—

G: Arousing? Um, well, we always had—we called them wog dogs. When you're a shellback you can pick one or two wogs as your personal wogs; you put them on a leash and run them around the ship. And I picked this guy—his name was Craig and he was gorgeous. So I often had him screwing or getting screwed by other wogs, and I sort of fantasized about it and it was sort of funny but I didn't really . . . we never did anything. I think crossing the line is pretty innocent.

Z: You didn't like the article in *Spy* [magazine, March 1993, "The U.S. Navy's Dirty Little Secrets"].

G: No, I didn't. I think it made it out to be some huge terrible thing that the Navy's hiding. The Navy's never hid that we go through crossing the line. It's just a tradition.

Z: You had another drag story that was pretty cool. . . .

G: We were in Thailand. There was some bet. It was between the MARDET and a large number of sailors. I don't remember the exact number or what the bet was, but whoever lost had to dress in drag in the next liberty port, which happened to be Thailand. Well, as it turned out the bet was a tie, and the captain decided that it had to be carried out by both the Marines and the sailors.

Thailand is notorious for its transvestite drag community. We went ashore and went to shops and had these beautiful dresses made. Foam rubber tits were readily available there. Wigs, and shoes, and all sorts of things. We really did it up. Makeup, the whole thing. I had this blue-sequined dress, slit up the side, very tight.

We all went ashore—forty military guys in drag—and we all got drunk and trounced around the city and acted very queer. Most of these guys professed to be straight. We were just laughing and drinking, and I was *drunk*. I was wearing six-inch high heels, which made me seven-foot-one.

The ship was in the harbor. The liberty boat goes back out, and you have to go up a thing called an A-con ladder, which is a stairway up the side of the ship. The bottom of the stairway has a little platform which is made out of wooden slats with gaps in between them, and the liberty boat's bobbing alongside the ship on the waves. Not very big waves, just in the harbor. And I went to step off the boat and my heel caught in one of the gaps in this platform. I fell over backwards into the water, and my tits popped out, and one was floating on either side of my face. The rest of the guys thought this was entirely too funny, and they all jumped in the water. It was quite funny to see this group of sailors and Marines in drag floating in the water with miscellaneous tits and handbags floating around them.

Z: You pointed out before that if any one of these guys had been seen through a window dressing up in women's clothes—

G: There's actually a case right now; a sailor went to prison because he was dressing as a woman in his own house. The man who lived next door saw him through the bedroom window, went to the commanding officer, said this guy was a transvestite, and they sent him to prison. He'll be discharged with an Other Than Honorable discharge.

Z: Tell me about the Greeks.

G: The *Berkeley* was sold to the Greek Navy. It was supposed to be decommissioned, but then the Greeks got a wonderful deal and bought it and four other ships for ten million bucks.

Greeks are a lot different from Americans. Greece allows gays in its service, and if a Greek service member is gay and has a lover, and they declare that, they'll be moved from duty station to duty station together. The Greeks have to serve two years, and they can enlist for an additional sixteen or they can get out. So either you make it a career or you don't; there's no in-between.

When the Greeks came on-board, at first the Americans liked them, but as time went on things deteriorated. The Greeks have very, very poor hygiene by American standards. They didn't shower, or shave, and they smelled quite hideous when they'd been sweating down in the engineering spaces, which are usually around a hundred and twenty degrees. As time went on, the Americans started noticing—they'd run into Greeks kissing or holding hands and even occasionally having sex. On the *Berkeley* there were not many places to hide, so it was pretty easy to run into them if they were having sex.

One of the cooks I worked with, a Greek cook, his lover would come visit him every day on the mess decks for lunch. They sat together and held hands while they ate lunch. Or just sat next to each other. It was actually really neat. Our captain got quite upset and went to their captain, and their captain said, "There's nothing we're going to do about it. This is the way we are."

The Greeks—it doesn't bother them at all. It's just part of life to them. There are a lot of Greeks who just have sex with men because there are no women available at the time, and it's OK. It's not an affront to their sexuality to have sex with a man. But the Americans didn't deal with it. They said real bad things about the Greeks, treated the Greeks very poorly, and I have to admit I didn't particularly care for the Greeks. Mostly because they smelled bad.

Z: In your travels with the Navy, what kinds of sexual experiences did you have with people from other cultures?

G: I never had sex with anyone from a foreign country. Except Australia. I was in Singapore and we were partying at the Hard Rock Cafe. We were getting very drunk and there were two attractive Australian guys. The first night I met them we just partied. The second night we ended up going somewhere, and I didn't remember where we were. We had sex, and it was pretty good sex—the Australians are pretty wild. I do remember I kept hitting my head on something. The next morning when I woke up I found myself in what appeared to be a bunk aboard a ship. I stuck my head outside the curtain and I saw this huge Heineken banner hanging behind this table, and I thought, "Oh no." [The U.S. Navy prohibits its sailors from displaying materials promoting drug or alcohol use.] And the Australian guy I had had sex with, apparently in his bunk, said, "I took you back to my ship because you couldn't remember what ship you were from." I had duty that day and I was just a few minutes away from being late, which would have gotten me into a lot of trouble, so this Australian guy—he was a boatswain's mate—lowered one of their small boats and drove me back to my ship. Sort of the Navy version of driving someone home the next morning.

I don't find Asian guys attractive, and a lot of time we spent in port was in Asia, so I didn't really have sex.

When I was in Bahrain—the Saudis and a lot of the Middle Eastern guys find Americans very attractive, especially blonds, and they would actually offer American men upwards of six hundred dollars to go to bed with them. They would proposition the Marines and the sailors to do it, but it was very dangerous . . . I never did it. Although six hundred dollars was a lot of cash.

Z: I think you would have been a bottom there for sure.

G: They tend to be very violent. And over there—it's not really acceptable to kill someone, but prostitution is illegal and very much frowned upon, so it wasn't really bad to kill a prostitute. They also got very violent and tended to disfigure people and stuff, so.

Z: You watched a public decapitation while you were over there.

G: Yeah, I watched someone get their head cut off for some stupid crime, so I never took them up on that offer.

Z: Sailors have a reputation of being promiscuous.

G: Oh, it's very true. In the Philippines, before you pull in, they have sexual disease lectures on the ship's TV, and they pass out condoms on the quarterdeck. I remember on the *Long Beach*, the doctor told me that they passed out seven gross of condoms in one three-day port visit to the Philippines. That's thousands of condoms.

The rule is, what happens overseas stays overseas. So many guys go over there; they wear their wedding bands out in town, and hire Filipino prostitutes to fuck and whatever. It's expected. And these guys will have pictures of the prostitutes in their locker all the way until they pull back into the States, then the pictures will disappear—get put somewhere where the wife doesn't see 'em. It's just accepted and known. I've seen the COs of ships go ashore and have sex. It's quite common to go get drunk and have sex with lots of women.

Z: How would you know? You haven't physically watched your CO having sex.

G: No, but they have live sex shows in Thailand, and sailors get up on-stage and screw the prostitutes. And I saw the XO of the ship, the same XO who said "I'm gonna throw you out for being gay if you report this"—I saw him pull down his pants and screw a Thai prostitute on a stage. He was quite drunk. But yeah, it's really an accepted thing. The sex industry is alive and well. Not in the Philippines anymore because the fleet doesn't pull in there, but there was a clinic there, set up with American assistance, that gave health cards to the prostitutes. They had to go every six months or whatever to prove that they didn't have any venereal diseases, so when a sailor hired a girl he could ask to see her health card.

Z: Have you ever found love?

G: Oh yeah. New Year's Eve of 1992 I met a Marine by the name of Jim. I love Jim a lot. If I could picture my life with anyone, it would have been Jim.

I met Jim and of course I was attracted to him sexually. It seems that most relationships begin that way. Jim was almost as tall as I am, but was very muscular. Had a really furry chest, which I of course love. Very attractive, and he smiled a lot, and he was very funny. He made anybody feel good to be with him. And was very at ease with himself and with others.

We started dating. The sex was really good, and one of the hardest problems we had is that he felt many times that I only loved him because of the sex, which was the furthest thing from the truth. But that's the way he felt about it. Unfortunately Jim got out of the Marine Corps before I got out of the Navy. He needed to move on with his life, and although he was right for me, I wasn't right for him.

Z: You mentioned he had a hard time with your being a public figure.

G: Yeah. He didn't like it too much. Often I think he felt like he was in

competition with my public life. And the stress I was under a lot of times
. . . I don't think I gave him the emotional support he needed. He's very
much of the opinion that being gay is just part of him and doesn't really
affect his outside life. He doesn't feel the need to be an activist.

Z: What attracts you to a man?
G: Employed. [Laughs.] I like guys that have a little fur on their chest. I
don't like guys who shave their chest. I think bodybuilders who build up
their upper body and ignore their lower body and walk around on these
little twig-legs look ridiculous and stupid. And—I don't know. I can meet
a person who I might not find immediately attractive and, talking to them,
if they're intelligent and appear to be on an even keel, then I will find
myself more attracted to that person than to a pretty boy whose head is
completely helium.
Z: What's good sex?
G: Oh, that's undefinable.
Z: What's bad sex?
G: When you start counting the cracks in the ceiling. I've definitely had
more bad sex than I've had good sex, I think. I tend to find the best sex is
with someone you love. When I was with Jim I had the best sex of my life.
Love seems to take it up a notch. I was very happy being with him, and
having sex made me even happier. Sometimes you just want to meld with
someone. It's almost like when you love someone you can't get close
enough to them. You want your body to melt into theirs. That's the way I
felt about Jim, and when we were having sex, that's the closest I ever
came to that. And so I think that's when good sex begins. Bad sex, there's
lots of that out there to be had. Most of it includes crabs.

G: I had sex with a guy who had full-blown AIDS. We were having sex,
and he came all over my chest. And not anywhere close to any openings
or anything, but I went to put my hand in it, and he screamed "Don't
touch that!" He ran into the bathroom and got a bottle of Windex and
sprayed it on my chest and then wiped it off quickly, screaming, "It's
poison!"

I used to get tested for HIV all the time. Especially being in the Navy,
of course. I always got tested anonymously outside because I didn't trust
the Navy, and I also wanted to know before they did. But I'm becoming
more and more of the opinion that it doesn't matter, because there's really
not many effective treatments, although people tell me there are. AZT is a
poison, and—I'd just rather not know, to tell you the truth. I treat everyone like they're infected, and therefore limit my own risk. I've made up

my mind about which safer sex practices I use, and which ones I don't. And it doesn't really matter to me, whether someone's HIV infected or not. If someone feels they need to tell me that then that's fine, if they don't, they don't.

I've had a number of friends who have passed away from AIDS, and a number who are sick or have various stages of HIV. I often chafe over the thing my father said about "Gay relationships don't last" and "You're gonna die of AIDS," because so far his first prediction has been pretty much true—at least in my life—and as more of my friends become infected—and it seems to be the vogue thing to do—I wonder if the second prediction will come true, too. Which is sort of a morbid way of thinking about things, but, AIDS doesn't scare me. I wouldn't want to die from AIDS, but it doesn't scare me.

Z: It's a sailor tradition to get tattoos, but when I asked you about yours you said you intended to have them removed by laser.
G: Yeah. When I first got one I was very much pro-Navy, and so I got a little anchor and steering wheel on my arm about six months after boot camp. I went by myself. And I liked that one, so I got another one, and then another one, and ended up eventually with five. I still do like a couple of them, they're sort of artwork, but the ones that show when I'm wearing a short-sleeved shirt have got to go. Employers have this preconceived notion that people with tattoos are druggies, mondo bike riders who ride a Harley to work and are going to bash in windows of cars in their parking space or something.
Z: What was the sensation of getting tattooed?
G: It hurt. I don't like needles. I passed out every time I got one. I don't find tattoos a turn-on, I don't find them a turnoff. I've had a couple people who liked to lick my tattoos, and since they're not in any particularly sensitive area of my body it doesn't really do anything for me, except I'm watching this person get excited, and it's like, "Well, if it does it for you." Those usually go in the category of bad sex. I don't think I've ever had any good sex with someone who was attracted to my tattoos. Mostly because they're just into it for themselves.
Z: Do you have any attraction to uniforms?
G: I find the Marine Corps uniform attractive but clothing doesn't really do anything for me. I find the person attractive. There is an attractiveness to some military guys that I like, maybe it's the short hair, maybe it's the idea of innocence. Military guys are usually from small towns and not as jaded as other people. But a lot of that is just myth and legend, because Navy guys are often—I think Navy guys tend to be more promiscuous than Marines. A lot of Marines I know tend to travel in small groups of four or five that know

each other and have sex with each other and not many people outside of the group; when they find someone they tend to stick with them. Sailors on the other hand tend to screw anything that moves.

Z: Tell me about Russell.

G: Russell and I met—The CO of the *Berkeley* didn't like me, and he transferred me from supervising a division to washing dishes in the scullery. I was working late one night and had just finished cleaning all the dishes in the scullery. I was tired, I was hot, and I was sweaty. I was covered with half-eaten food and Russell stuck his head in and grabbed a dish so he could eat something. I yelled at him for doing so and he yelled back. We had a little tiff.

I thought Russell was sort of cute but not worth jumping after. A couple weeks later I was on the fantail talking to a guy about the environment, and Russell of course being from the Northwest stuck his head in and started talking.

I eventually invited him over to my house. He came over for dinner one night, and we were going down to my motorcycle, and he asked me what all the pink triangles were. I told him about the Nazis and gays, but I didn't tell him I was gay. Finally he asked me straight out and I told him, and we've just become very good friends. He was very cool with it. He's straight, but he likes going to gay bars; he likes going to parties and stuff. It's really funny because—we tend to chafe on each other, like brothers, but we care about each other enough to where he confides in me a lot. And he knows I'm not going to make any sexual overtures towards him.

Z: But you did, early on.

G: Um, yeah, yeah, when we were first sleeping together I put my arm around him, rubbed his back, or whatever, just to see how far it would go. He said that he wasn't interested in sex, so I didn't ever push it further than that. He likes cuddling up next to me, and he likes getting a back massage. I think a lot of that is that he's far away from home and he needs affection. I often look at Russell and think if our world is going to be saved it's going to be by people like him who are nonjudgmental about other people. I mean, Russell's got a lot of things to work through, but he's a lot more balanced than other people I know.

Z: How do you think your sexuality might be different today had you gone to college instead of joining the Navy?

G: I don't think I'd be the activist that I am today. I think you really have to experience being in the military to know what it's like to live in constant fear. Civilians can lose their jobs, but they don't go to prison for loving someone. And in the military that's a very real prospect. I think it would have taken me probably longer to come out had I stayed in my hometown, because there is really no gay life of any sort.

I wouldn't trade the military experience for anything. I think that a lot of people who aren't in the military are still very childish years afterwards. A lot of people in the military are still childish, but I think in some aspects it's much better. I wouldn't change a single thing about my life.

Part Two, Three Months Later

Gregg and I remained friends despite the fact that he quit unemployment benefits and got a job working for some defense industry corporation, telling me he wanted to make lots of money and be respectable. Soon, Gregg began to regale me with stories about the people at the office and offered to get me a job there.

I was horrified. And yet I need not have worried that Gregg was losing his edge. He outed himself to a company vice president as the two men were ascending a stairwell, causing the shocked executive to fall and break an arm. And he went to a company picnic, bringing with him a person with AIDS suffering from dementia, who took hours to consume a small plate of chicken wings, enthusing over and over, "This is so good," then, tossing the bones aside, began gesticulating and making loud proclamations about how he hated straight people.

G: "Don't Ask, Don't Tell' " is the same thing we've always had. It's not a change. They even said it, it's the same thing we've always had. They've just changed the wording. It's OK to be gay as long as you don't tell anyone, you don't act upon it, and you live in a closet. Which is where our society wants us.
Z: Are you disappointed with Clinton?
G: I think I'm disappointed with him only because he said he was going to lift the ban and he didn't. But this wasn't a big shock. I knew it was coming. I think most politicians are garbage anyway.
Z: To include Bill Clinton?
G: Sure. I don't know a single elected official I respect. He's on par with the rest of them.

Z: You said at one point that in coming out and taking on a public role that you wanted to become a saint.

G: Did I say that? Well, I don't feel like a saint. [Pause.] I must have had a different train of thought at the time. I don't remember what I was thinking.

Z: In our first [unrecorded] conversation you described what motivated you to want to take the presidency of SDVA, and the good that you thought that you could accomplish. You traveled to Washington, you spoke before large groups, you discovered that by talking about having been beaten you were able to pull certain strings emotionally. As someone who had suffered—

G: I don't remember calling myself a saint.

Z: No, no. You said that you were trying to become one. Or did you mean that you were trying to present yourself as one?

G: Well yeah, for purposes of what I was doing at the time, it was better that people saw me as being saint-like. I mean, nobody's really what they appear to be. People want to see you a certain way, and they will see you a certain way.

When I was in the public spotlight I would have a lot of people come up to me and want to go out with me and give me their phone numbers. And a few I did go out with. But when they realized I wasn't the image that they had thought I was, their interest waned quickly. I was very uncomfortable when people told me, "I'm proud of what you're doing, I really appreciate it," because I didn't see it as being the same thing. I saw the whole picture and they didn't.

Z: You told me before that you resented any comparisons between yourself and other gay military people who had come out publicly.

G: Well, at the time I did, because I saw—the people who had come out, like Keith Meinhold, I saw just as publicity hounds. Where, getting in the media, that's not what I had set out to do. It was a tool, but it was never my goal. I always thought, and still today to some extent think, that that's primarily what several people did. Like Joseph Steffan: He didn't give a fuck about the movement; he wanted to write a book and get rich. He was no one special, he was just some scummy midshipman who did that.

Z: What makes you think that?

G: He's from a rich family, he's never experienced anything but being rich, he goes to the academy, and the first time someone asks him he says, "Yes, I'm gay," not because he wants to stand up for himself, but because he wanted to get out of the service.

Z: That's not entirely true. He was caught and got kicked out, that's what motivated him to—

G: He wasn't really caught. He could have denied it, he could have gotten out of it. At least in my opinion. I just don't see him as any huge hero. I've changed my opinion somewhat of Keith Meinhold. I think his continued court fight has some merit, although I don't really think it's going to go anywhere.

Z: How much might your distaste for these men be personally motivated? You described having met Joseph Steffan and Tracy Thorne and—

G: They're fucking assholes. They're just like every officer I've ever met in the service. If you're not an officer, they want nothing to do with you. Especially in the Navy, with the officers and the enlisted being so separated. The officers often forget that the enlisted are the ones that do the work. And the officers are the ones who parade around and look nice. They live that up to a tee. It's easy when you're an officer and you have a college degree, you get out and say, "OK, now I'm going to go work with my college degree." When you're enlisted and you get kicked out for being gay, it's a lot different. You've got a harder road to go.

Z: You don't have any respect for Tracy Thorne for his efforts in putting forward a positive image of military gays to Americans?

G: No. Gay sailors are people just like everybody else. They're good, they're bad, they do their job, they just have that added pressure to it. Tracy Thorne came out so he could be on the news. His coming out was specifically engineered to be a news item.

Z: You don't think that was motivated by his wanting to effect change?

G: No, I think he wanted to be on the news.

Z: Well, what was it like when you were thrust into the news? It must have been gratifying to your ego to get some attention.

G: No, I really don't think I got excited or enjoyed it. I've saved a total of two news clippings that I was in. The video and audiotapes I had I've all gotten rid of, because it really doesn't mean that much to me.

Z: In San Diego you came to be regarded as politically incorrect; the gay publications would no longer print your letters. Why did you fall from favor with those people? Was it something you actively sought to bring about?

G: I don't believe that what I say should be censored by how I think people are going to take it. I think there is a generally accepted standard of: This is what gays believe. I don't believe a lot of those things, and I'll tell you when I don't believe them.

A lot of the gay organizations have become so politically correct they don't get anything done. They have to have a black, a Jew, a woman, an Indian on the governing board; everyone has to have an equal opinion, an equal time to state it; everyone has to be treated with respect. Nothing gets done that way. They all sit in these committee meetings and do nothing. Some people don't deserve respect. And sometimes you won't have equal representation. The world is not an equal or fair place.

Z: But beyond that, there were certain ideas you had that were unpopular. For example, you said that gays in the military didn't deserve any better, because—

G: Gay people are apathetic, especially in Southern California. They won't get off their barstools and do anything. I've always believed that if the policy banning gays in the military was overturned, if you're not willing to come forward and say, "I'm gay," then you don't deserve any protection. None. If you are going to go around hiding and trying to pretend to be straight—it doesn't work that way. You have to make some sort of decision. You can't have it both ways: you can't cry for gay rights and try and live under straight rules. I've always felt that if you can't stand up for who you are, why should I win protections for you? So many people take their civil rights for granted. The religious right is actively pursuing us to try and take our rights away.

Z: I've heard you say before that you wished that every gay person would suddenly turn green so you could recognize them. Of course my view is that there are many different shades of color, subject to chameleon-like shifts.

G: I don't know about that. People have so many other psychoses, it's hard to tell sometimes what—They have other problems in life, other than trying to figure out what their sexual identity is.

Z: You've since dropped out of SDVA. I told you that I wanted to include a picture of you in the book, and I'd talked about using the photo from *Navy Times*. You answered that you wanted to "disappear" and printing your picture in my book would not facilitate that. Why do you want to disappear?

G: After you spend a year in the public spotlight where everyone recognizes you, it gets old, real fast. I mean, I have friends because I've met them and introduced myself, not because they've seen my picture on the front of a magazine. I don't want to be an image, I want to be a person. And news reporting does not lend itself to creating a person, it creates an image, completely based on the author or editor's picture of who you are. [Pause.] At this point, you have to print in your book that I'm very butch. That way people will get an image of me being very butch. Print it in your book. I am very butch.

Z: This is an abrupt and unexpected turn to the interview.

G: [Laughs.]

Z: But it is something I didn't ask you very much about the first time. Let me continue this tack in confronting you with contradictory statements you have made: Not too long after I met you, in fact right around the time of the first love-in, you were talking about Ray, and said that being around him had made you feel more comfortable about expressing your own femininity.

G: Oh. Ray's fine. I don't have a problem expressing my sides; I think you should put it in there I'm butch, but I'm mostly joking. Mostly it's just a sarcastic comment. But no, I'm not—I think people take feminine with being weak, which is really not true, but it is a stereotype.

Z: Well, how masculine do you consider yourself?

G: Mmm. I've never really taken a very strong masculine role. I've never been feminine either. I've just sort of been like, as always, this indefinable person who exists somewhere between the two groups and belongs to neither.

Z: How would you characterize my masculinity?

G: [Pause.] I wouldn't—You wouldn't really characterize it—You're not fem.

Z: But in relation to how you just described yourself—

G: Um, you probably sort of fall the same way.

Z: How about Anthony?

G: Um. [Pause.] I think Anthony desperately seeks, either consciously or subconsciously, a huge amount of attention and acceptance from those he's with. He can be whatever the group requires, which means if that's fem or butch—I think he probably plays more toward the butch role model. Partially because it fits with who I see him attracted to and wishing to be with, although I'm not sure that that's exactly true. Anthony strikes me as someone who desperately wants to feel comfort, to feel that he's secure, and he doesn't have that, so he keeps looking and looking and looking. I think that when the opportunity presents itself he might let it go, because by that time he won't know how to recognize it anymore.

Z: This brings us to the "love-ins." This group that coalesced for a time, and the gatherings we had—was there anything really special or different about us?

G: It was a very interesting group of people. It started out of course because everyone was sexually attracted to everyone. Not everybody knew each other, and of course everyone's main connection seemed to be that we all had sex with Kevin.

Z: Or wanted to.

G: And the first couple love-ins were very sexually charged, because everybody was thinking about everybody. But after time passed and people started to get to know each other a little better, then you got the tensions and the personality conflicts and things like that. Then it started to fall to pieces. I don't agree with your analysis that Kevin was the core of the group. I think he may have been one of the reasons it started, but I think that the group itself, much like a nuclear reaction, where the pieces of the atom are drawn together at first and then the mass becomes so dense that it explodes and expands outward at a huge rate—I think that is exactly what happened. Everything came together and sort of self-destructed. So.

Z: How would you describe Ray's masculinity and his role at the love-ins?

G: I see Ray as being the kind of person who has been shunned all his life and has come to enjoy the role and so everything he does is to be extreme. Ray is sort of a flamboyant queen who tends to wear clothing which is often open too much or too restrictive. He often takes off this clothing after just a few drinks. He has a well-toned viciousness that when applied in the right manner can be quite funny. He appears to enjoy at least some amount of pain, although it's questionable how much—no, he enjoys it. But as to why, I don't know. If I had to cast him I'd say he's probably a bottom, and I think most of the people he finds to have sex with—he just asks everybody, and like a can with holes in the bottom, he just keeps shaking it until some of the sand inside falls through the holes. [Laughs.] And that's who he ends up with. But he's a likeable fellow, and I think he would probably stand by his friends. Except me after he reads this.

Z: You mentioned personality conflicts. You and Sonny had perhaps the most pronounced one.

G: Sonny falls into the category of people I wouldn't give any protection to under the clause. I think he is a closeted fag. He keeps saying that he'll come out to his parents when he finds someone to fall in love with, and I think that prerequisite is going to keep him from ever coming out to his parents, and possibly knowing their support and acceptance. As in my case it could turn the other way, but I think that he could be pleasantly surprised. And I think his overpatriotic zeal, his blind trust of the government and its authority is sort of sickening. I think his collection of eagle statuettes is nauseating, and that he decorates his house like a straight man. When I first met Sonny, I found him very despicable. I just can't imagine a person who's so—uptight. I guess I would call him an anal retentive queen.

Z: Can you imagine yourself in bed with Sonny?

G: Um, Sonny has some attractive features, but I can't imagine myself having sex with him because I can't imagine getting into bed with the roles already defined. His insistence on being a top is nauseating. I like getting into bed and sort of eventually working my way into who's going to be on top and who's going to be on the bottom. Because I don't see either role as being better or worse in terms of the person on top being controlling or dominant. I think that that isn't really true.

Z: But then you've been attracted to Marines before, and you have stated unequivocally that Marines are invariably bottoms.

G: Well that's true, but—that's a stereotype. I mean, when you meet someone and you go to bed with them, you really don't know where they're going to end up. My lover Jim was a great top and a great bottom and we had fantastic sex.

Z: Sonny, and several other members of the love-in group consider you to be a gay rights radical in the Queer Nation mold. [Quotes comments from Sonny, Kevin, and Ray's interviews.]

G: [Laughs.] I tend to be very sarcastic. I think the majority of the people in the military tend to be fairly conservative, and in some ways I am fairly conservative, but I refuse to accept situations which I feel are wrong. I think the way gay people are treated, especially in the military, is appalling. And if you won't stand up and try and change anything, you really have no right to bitch about it.

Z: Kevin understood that as a personal attack on him, that he should be required to come out and engage in some of the political activities you have in the past.

G: I don't think people should be required to engage in political activity, and coming out doesn't necessarily mean jumping up and down saying I'm gay in public. It's little things. When people are having conversations about girlfriends you don't pretend you have one when you don't. You don't put up pictures of women who have no special meaning to you only to appear to be straight. When you go overseas, you don't pay for female prostitutes and let them go just to appear to have sex with them. And when people are making gay jokes that offend you, you don't just stand there and take it: you walk away. It's little things like that that let people know, and they'll pick up on it eventually. Although I've met a lot of straight people who tend to be sort of thick-skulled about it. But I definitely think you just can't play the straight role. There were thousands of Germans who played along with the Nazis although they felt it was hideous, but they did it instead of standing up for what they felt was right, and I think that it's almost the same thing. It's a life and death situation. It's not a joke. I think that it's easy when you lead sort of a sheltered life, and no one that you care about has ever been hurt by it, to say, "I don't want to be part of it." It's easy to be apathetic. I'm sure Sonny has never held a friend's hand as they've died of AIDS.

Z: Actually, beyond the misfortunes that you've suffered, Sonny is—well, he's more tormented about his sexuality than you ever were, probably, but he's also really made miserable by having to live a double life in the military. So, I think maybe he has experienced a similar pain.

G: But what has he done to remedy the situation? He probably voted for Bush.

Z: No, he voted for Clinton, although he's a Republican.

G: He's a liar.

Z: No, he did, and he's been disappointed in him. Anyway, what attracted you to Kevin?

G: I had this image of Kevin, that he was sort of a recluse, and didn't go out a lot. I soon learned that was the furthest thing from the truth. What attracted me to Kevin? Well, he's a handsome person; he's attractive in his physical features, and he treats people well. He has sort of a boyish charm about him. I don't know. It's his whole being. He has sort of an excitement that he carries with him.

Z: An energy?

G: Yeah.

Z: So you think he's a nice person. Um. . . . The perception among some of the love-in crowd is that you're not always so friendly to people, and that you can sometimes say things that—

G: Oh, I'm not friendly.

Z: Your little barbs really sting people. I'm not saying this as a criticism, just an observation. And this leads me to a pointed and difficult question. You told me that when you were on the *Long Beach* you didn't have very many friends. And when you described the guys who attacked you, you first of all talked about the tensions aboard the ship, and you mentioned the fact that the guys disliked you personally. Then you added, "they especially disliked the fact that I was gay." And—it's easy for me to picture you really pissing people off. I don't want to in any way discount the terrible thing that happened to you, but I guess I want to know: How much of that attack do you think was motivated by homophobia, by other factors, and how much by actual personal dislike for you?

G: I think a lot of it had to do with homophobia. In my experience in the service, people tend to be very competitive, and always trying to one up each other, and the way I act, a lot of the people I worked with were the same way. You had to stand up for yourself and fight back or they'd walk all over you. And sometimes—when I say things, nine times out of ten I mean them. And if someone gets upset, that's life. People have described me as arrogant and mean, and sometimes I'm arrogant, sometimes I'm mean. But . . . I'm sure there was some personal dislike. There's always personality conflicts. You can't live in a berthing, a ten by sixteen room with twenty other people, and not have some problems. I'm sure that was part of it. But, I mean, if you already dislike someone, and then you find out or think that there's something else that makes it worse, it becomes a catalyst for your anger.

Z: It just seems to me, the more I hear about cases of gay bashings, either they seem to involve people who don't know each other, or know each other and have an intense dislike for each other. It's not somebody who's sort of accepted as a good guy then suddenly revealed to be gay.

G: Well no, I think that that's true—With the exception possibly of one person who was involved who was sort of a friend almost, and I stored his motorcycle at my house while we were overseas, I would say that probably holds true.

Z: I haven't interviewed many guys who've been harassed or bashed, but there almost seems to be a pattern. You remarked that on the *Long Beach*, when you were attacked, it was in part because of the *suspicion* that you were gay; you hadn't totally acknowledged it to these people. Whereas on the *Berkeley* you were accepted having done just that. Most of the gay bashing cases I know of usually involve people who are *thought* to be gay, and not ones who come out to a small circle of trusted coworkers. There seems to be a lot more flak given to guys who are suspected of being gay but deny it.

G: Yeah, I think—I think if people suspect you, and you deny it, it becomes something to needle you with. If you just openly say "I'm gay," then it takes their ammunition away. You've admitted it; there's no denial, there's no reason for you to be scared of it anymore. And I think when they just suspect it there are reasons. And I guess beating you is trying to get you to confess to being it. I don't know, because, in my situation, I can't really contrast—the people I worked with on the *Long Beach* were completely different from the people I worked with on the *Berkeley*. There aren't many nuclear power people in San Diego; nuclear power is like a whole different world inside of itself. The people tend to be highly intelligent, highly competitive, and they have very little respect for each other. They stick together only out of protection. On the *Berkeley*, the people there were—I won't say less intelligent, but less educated, and they tended to do things in groups, and had to rely on each other more. So it's just different situations.

I would never be so arrogant to say that perhaps I didn't have something to do with causing those people to want to attack me. But I wouldn't say that would ever condone what happened.

Z: Well certainly not. But it would be interesting to know what transpired in their heads while they did it. You didn't mention whether they shouted "fag" or called you names while they did it.

G: Oh yeah, they did.

Z: Let me move on to another difficult question, and that involves your having worked for NIS. You never made any reference to having done any work that concerned hunting down gays until a few days ago, when you told me about the efforts of your supervisor to check personal ads in a local gay paper.

G: When I was working for NIS—NIS is probably the most disreputable, poorly managed investigative agency in the world. They probably couldn't find the toilet paper next to them while they were sitting on the toilet. Ninety percent of the convictions the Navy gets at court martials are because people confess. And when interviewing someone, [NIS] will use every tactic possible to get that person to admit to something, because when it comes to actual investigative skills, they have none. So when I worked for NIS the majority of what I did was not based on witch hunts or anything. We did do some things that were related to finding gay people. But I never, ever, was involved where a gay person was discharged or court martialed for anything they did. When I was placed in that situation I went out of my way to either warn the person beforehand or skew the evidence. I was very careful about that. I never ever was hypocritical in the way I treated someone. I would twist interviews all the way.

Z: You helped sabotage NIS efforts?

G: Oh, yeah. All the time. We taped all the interviews, and sometimes tapes would be lost, or people would be transferred. There's always ways around things. I was always very careful about that. There were people after I started working with SDVA, before I became the president, who wanted to exploit my ties with NIS, and since then I still have a number of friends who are in very high positions with NIS who have told me about things going on or investigations. I've passed that information on to the appropriate people, but I don't use those ties to help the political organizations. Because I don't think it would be right.

Z: Following your interview will be Russell's. One thing about the love-ins that was special was the participation of straight guys—Russell and Aaron—and the fact that not everybody there fit the same mold. How would you describe the attitudes of the gay guys toward Russell and Aaron?

G: Well, I think of course because both Russell and Aaron are handsome men that there was some sexual attraction there. Everybody there was having a good time, and since Russell and Aaron just merged into the crowd, it worked out well. [Pause.] This makes me think of something you asked earlier. [Sonny and Ray's comments that Gregg is antistraight.] You know, I treat Russell the same way I treat everyone else. And Russell doesn't get upset by things I say. I think a lot of times, things that I say, people become upset because it hits too close to home. It really touches something that bothers them, and *that's* why they get angry—not because I've said something so mean. I've always told people, you should say what you think, and I do. Because if everyone walked around holding back everything they thought, I mean, political correctness in speech—

Z: I didn't mean to put you on the defensive.

G: Anyways, that's just a point about Russell. Russell's a very accepting person.

Z: "Very accepting." What does that mean? It becomes—

G: A cliché?

Z: —Suspect, even to the gay guys. A straight guy is allowed to be accepting to a certain point; that's good, that makes him "open-minded." But if he hangs around gay men a lot, then he's "almost too accepting," and becomes sexually suspect.

G: That's because very few straight people hang around gay people. When you see someone who's attractive and handsome and they're hanging around gays a lot, of course then you want to think that there's a possibility. Since I've been out, I've increased the number of straight friends I have, and I've gone out with them, and once I told them that I'm gay, they never suspect I might be straight. I don't know any straight person that's ever lied and said they're gay, but I know a lot of gay people who have lied and said they're straight.

Z: Which makes anyone's declaration of bisexuality suspect in gay men's eyes.

G: I've already told you I have real difficulties believing there is such a thing as a real bisexual. Meaning someone who can go equally both ways. Not sexually, but in terms of who they can love. I've met a lot of people in my time, and they all seem to fall on one side or the other. It's just like drawing a line down the middle of the field, and you're on one side of the line or you're on the other, but you're not exactly in the middle.

Z: But the line is *drawn*—

G: Oh I agree, it's all silly. Having to define one's self is sort of a silly thing.

Z: In addition to sometimes engaging in verbal straight bashing, you've also said some pretty loathsome things about women before. I suppose you'll tell me you were just being humorous and sarcastic. Or do you hate women?

G: No, I don't hate women. In fact, I work in an office where I'm the only guy. The reason I sometimes say things like that is because the thought of having sex with a woman makes me ill. I mean, I can actually make myself vomit if I think about it too much. And I do work with some femi-nazis who absolutely hate men. But it's mostly joking. I'm not really serious.

Z: What does this mean, that you're so incredibly repulsed by the thought of sex with women? Might it be that you're actually repressing some heterosexual urges—

G: Oh, I'm sure it is, I'm sure that one of these days I'm going to fly out of my heterosexual closet and marry some woman.

Z: But you told me that you thought it was suspicious that Russell went so far out of his way to avoid thinking about sex with men. You said you thought it was unnatural.

G: Well, maybe I said that. That was several months ago.

Z: No, you said that more recently.

G: I don't know. Russell—You probably said these things to him. "Gregg said—" I know you did! I'm going to slap you senseless! [Gregg and I go off the record. I assure him that I have not betrayed any of his confidences.]

I've done a lot of thinking about Russell, and you know, whether or not Russell's straight or gay, or anything else about Russell—Russell's a close friend of mine. And it doesn't really matter. I love him a lot. I love him like a brother. And I would never ever want to lose that.

Z: Is there anything that you want to ask me, about anything?

G: No. I think the only thing that I would want to add, is, even though I've said these things and said, "That's the way it is," that's the way it is at the moment you interview me. I constantly mull things over. I may not have the same opinion two days from now, or two weeks from now, or two years from now.

Z: That's kind of a cheap disclaimer.

G: Well it is a disclaimer! Because you can't . . . . Look at Malcolm X, he said a lot of mean things in his younger days, and when he got older he said "I don't agree with those things."

Z: Ah, so perhaps you're considering some future run for office and you're thinking about how you can distance yourself—

G: I'm not saying that at all. I'm saying you have to give people the room to change. Sonny could change. He could become a likeable person. [Laughs.] People are going to hate me after they read this interview.

Z: Do you care?

G: Of course I care! I do care.

Z: Why?

G: Because if they're going to beat off to my picture I want them to—[Laughs.]

Z: Do you have anything else to add?

G: No. Now I want to hear the tape of Russell's interview!

Russell: Strong Friendship

Thwack!

The belt comes down. Hard. "Oh," the corpsman moans, "again." "Again? You want me to hit you again?" the radioman asks. "Yes."

Thwack!

Nervous titters from the onlookers. The radioman grins, steps back, prepared to quit. But the corpsman, lifting his face from the carpet only slightly, breathes "Harder." The radioman is incredulous but obviously pleased. "Harder? You want it harder?! OK—but it's gonna hurt!" "Yes."

Thwack!!

And again the black leather falls against the kneeling corpsman's diminutive buttocks.

The scene is not from a gay S&M porno; neither is it a journalist's portrayal of the Navy's crossing the line ceremony. But that is the picture in the mind of the radioman as he lashes the corpsman: how he as a wog was whipped by shellbacks crossing that imaginary great line around the planet's surface known as the equator. "Pleeease. Hit me as hard as you can."

"As hard as I can?!" Russell excitedly shouts, jumping about animatedly. "You really want me to hit you as hard as I can?!" I wince, look at the open patio door, and wonder what the neighbors must think. "Please. I need it," Ray whimpers, and returns his face to the carpet.

THWACK!!!

My most sensational picture of Russell is at our "love-in" at Carlsbad near the drunken party's close, when Gregg's best friend, at Anthony and then Ray's request, removed his belt and beat them with it. It is an interesting scene for several reasons: Because Russell is a gentle and kind young man, now plainly enthralled by this act of sadism. Because each of the parties has a differing interpretation of what the whipping means: Anthony dismisses it as theater,

Ray accepts it as genuine and is sexually pleasured, Russell doesn't know what to think but enjoys the turnaround from when his own ass was paddled by the U.S. Navy. So too does each gay member of the love-in crowd place a different interpretation on this straight Navy radioman's presence in the group.

Russell is a boyishly handsome 21 year old. He exudes an easy, natural masculinity; his pretty blue Pacific Northwest eyes are friendly and optimistic. It is true that most of us would have liked to have slept with him. And yet you must not think that we fawned over him. Russell was treated by all of us as an equal, and in this interview he says that was how he felt—but does reveal the limits of his "acceptance."

I was very glad when, just prior to his departure on a WESTPAC cruise, Russell invited me out to lunch. We walked along Sunset Cliffs, I took pictures of him poking around the tidepools. On our way to the restaurant Russell ran over a dove on a sidestreet; this distressed him, but he laughed about it, too. "I feel terrible. I wonder if he's dead. Did you see all those feathers? Oh, man. I thought for sure he would move. God, I feel sick."

Z: You're from Washington state. Tell me a little bit about your background.
R: I'm from a small town, population about four thousand. In the Northwest, in the area I grew up in, it's either logging or mink ranching, so it's not a really high income area. It was kind of a poor town, but my father works for the state. He's a state patrolman.
Z: Do you consider your family middle class?
R: I think so. I can't ever remember not being able to get anything I wanted. Growing up, I didn't have many friends who were too much different from me. Being in the military I've seen a lot wider view and had a lot more contact with people.
Z: Why did you join the Navy instead of going to college?
R: Financially I had no means of going to school. And even if I did have the money I would be very reluctant to go to college, because of my grades in high school.

I've been told by many people that I have a good appearance and that I'm quite intelligent, but I guess I have low self-esteem. But now lately that I'm a little bit more mature—I've turned twenty-one, I've got my own car, and I'm out there in the adult world now—I think that's given me some confidence. And meeting people like you, and Gregg, and all my friends—whether they're gay or not, it doesn't matter: they're adults, they're my friends. You have no idea what my history was like, my background, or who I was as a kid. You don't know if I was the class jock or the class nerd. You just see me for who I am now, a responsible good-looking adult. It's interesting to see what kinds of friends I draw to me as the person that I am now. Then I get to experience all their views, when we go to coffee shops, or out to dinner, or the little love-ins and we all socialize. We come from all walks of life but we're here together now communicating and talking and sharing ideas and growing through each other's knowledge. It's kind of neat.

Z: Tell me about meeting Gregg. You were on the USS *Berkeley*.

R: The way we met was a complete coincidence. I heard that there was "some fag" on-board the ship, and that he was the president of "some fag organization," and that he was creating all sorts of trouble. I didn't hear a whole lot about it, and I had no idea what he looked like. But somehow I found out this guy was on the ship. And I was like, "Our ship? This fag's on *our* ship?!" And they were like, "Yeah!" They were laughing about it. "Well, who the hell is he?" "He's that tall guy." Tall guy? I was trying to think: who is this person? I was really anxious to see who he was.

Z: Why? What were you thinking after being told that?

R: Well, I had never actually met any homosexual person before. It was something that was only a joke in TV sitcoms or conversations. I just had never met anyone. I probably had, I just didn't know it; I'm learning that now. But it was something that was never talked about. Not because it was bad, it was just something that was not even in my world. I think that's probably why I have such an open mind to it; it doesn't seem abnormal, it doesn't seem normal. I can't really explain it. It doesn't even go through my mind. But it just seemed like, to think that this person who's created such a ruckus is here on my ship . . . *my* ship, you know? It was almost like he was a celebrity. So I was looking for this person. Also I was kind of curious, 'cause I guess I was sort of wondering: what does a fag look like?

But it's funny, because I had seen him even before this happened— when his name was still good, when he was an "outstanding sailor" and "a great asset to the ship." I remember I saw him a couple times; he was in coveralls and he was really tall. He was in engineering so he was always going down in the hole. 'Course him being a snipe and me being a top-sider we really didn't see much of each other anyway. That's probably why I had a hard time finding him. And I never did find him when I was actually looking for him. I just kind of gave up. I forgot about it.

One day we were out to sea, but just anchored off the coast of Point Loma doing some sort of drill. I think we had the Greeks on-board. It was a real casual day. I was sitting on the fantail, just skating, basically because I didn't want to work. And I heard these two guys behind me talking. They were talking about all sorts of topics. Politics and the environment. They were talking about the trees being cut in Washington and Oregon. I think that's what got my attention. I heard that, and me being from the area, I kind of turned my head a little bit to listen better. I wasn't looking at them directly. Finally they started talking about the spotted owl, and I had to say something. Then the other guy left and Gregg and I continued to talk and went on and on and on. We talked a lot for the rest of the day.

A couple days later he asked if I wanted to go out sometime, go to dinner or catch a movie or something. I don't think I knew if he was homosexual at that time or not. I just thought it would be good to have another friend. We had dinner and a pretty good conversation. After that, we just talked a lot more on the ship. Eventually he invited me over to his house for the first time.

I think I knew who he was by this time, but I wasn't quite sure if he was still homosexual or not, because he had said in the paper that he could neither confirm nor deny that fact. So I accepted that.

I went to his house, and he—I didn't find this out until later—but he had taken a lot of pictures down and moved things away, so it wasn't quite so obvious. But there were some things that didn't quite . . . I don't know, he had this one card up on his bookshelf of two guys making out. [Laughs.] But that was about it.

Well, he invited me over the next time, and this time everything was up. I found some things a little bizarre. He had a picture of a couple men that were nude and they were holding each other and one of them was erect and had a condom on. That was the whole idea of the poster, promoting condom use. He had that right above his bed. Then he had this calendar with black and white drawings of men with very large penises. I thought that was a little absurd. By this time I pretty much knew that he was homosexual. It didn't even bother me though, because I already knew who he was as a friend and I really liked him. So I didn't let that bother me. [Pause.] I don't know . . . I think—it does seem to bother me a little bit when I see guys kiss.

Z: It bothers you?

R: It doesn't bother me, it—well, I don't know how to explain it. It's just something that seems—it gives me a weird feeling, almost like—not grossed out, but—really a turn-off. Like something says "that's not right."

Z: More so than seeing actual sex acts between guys?

R: Oh no, that would really go beyond me. I don't think I could handle that.

Z: You've never seen a gay porno?

R: No. I don't think I'd want to. See, he took me to a couple gay clubs. That's where I saw guys kiss, right there in the club. That just was kind of, "Whoa!" But, as long as there's no serious physical contact I guess it doesn't bother me. I don't think about it. I think that's why I'm able to have such a good relationship with Gregg: I don't really see a lot of that around him. There's hugging and everything, but that's nothing big. In the family I was brought up in, it was pretty much when the New Age came about, into this self-God and love one's self. So I've been brought up to have a very open mind and to be lightspirited and not so judgmental.

Z: As you were getting to know Gregg, and he took you over to his place and exposed you to all this stuff, were you conscious of him being attracted to you, and his hoping perhaps that you might be interested in having sex with him?

R: No, not really. The first time I spent the night there, I slept in the same bed with him, but it didn't bother me at all. I didn't think anything of it. I've slept in the bed with my friends back home; whenever I'd spend the night, or they spent the night with me, we always slept in each other's bed. There was nothing sexual about it. It's just the bed versus the floor.

Z: But a friend back home is different from a famous Navy homosexual.

R: Yeah, that's true. But I didn't really think of him as that. I just thought of him as another friend. So it didn't bother me. We stayed up at night watching television, talking, and laughing, just sort of being the guys together. So when it came to getting late I just crashed out there in the bed with him. No big deal.

But then later on that night, I can remember he kind of snuggled up next to me. He even put his arm around me. And that woke me up out of a dead sleep. I was wide awake then. It didn't scare me, but it was just like—what am I going to do? I don't want to piss him off; I don't want to insult him; I don't want to hurt his feelings. Because at this point he had still not come out and said if he was gay or not. Even though he had all these pictures up and it was pretty obvious, he still hadn't said it. And I didn't want to upset him in any way.

This all went through my mind like that [snaps finger]. I just took his hand and placed it off me. He let out this deep sigh and rolled over the other way. I rolled over and was thinking: I wonder what he's thinking. Should I say anything or just keep quiet? Because it seemed the way his heavy breathing had increased now, and his tossing and turning, it seemed like he was really frustrated or nervous—like he was thinking about what I was thinking. I didn't know if I should say something to comfort him; to tell him like, "Hey, it's no problem, that's just not what I'm into." But I didn't say anything; I waited until that morning. We woke up and we kind of talked about it and made it clear.

Z: You did talk about it?

R: We didn't talk about it a lot. I just said, "OK, look. I don't want you to think that I'm any certain way, but I'm not the way you might think I am." That's kind of the terms we used. No one still had said the word. He goes, "Well, how do you think I am?" And I said, "I think you're a little not like me." [Laughs.] So it was beating around the bush a lot. But we understood each other. Then he said, "Well, I am." I said, "Yeah, I thought so. I guess you know I'm not." He goes, "Well, how much not? On a scale of one to ten—" This is what he made up; he has some name for this scale, ten being a total homosexual, and one being the exact opposite. And he says "I don't think anybody is a ten or a one. I think they're either at the most a two or a three or a nine or an eight." And I was like, "Well, I'm a one! I don't care what you think. I'm a one." But he was determined.

Z: Do you think he really believes that? Or do you think it was just an attempt by him to get you to do what he was maybe fantasizing about?

R: Yeah, I think it was an attempt to get me to fulfill whatever fantasy he had. To this day, I still think that he thinks that I don't know what I am. 'Cause I'm very open-minded. I think it's even a little too much at times for Gregg to handle. I think he may misinterpret some things. I think he thinks that I could probably go both ways or would like to experiment. I have a feeling he thinks I'm in some sort of denial because he still says things and kind of jokes about it.

Z: Maybe he thinks you would try it with some other guy, but not necessarily him.

R: That's a good possibility.

Z: It's not something you have ever fantasized about, in any way?

R: No.

Z: You told our whole group that you had some experience when you were a kid.

R: In second grade. His name was Larry. All it was—it wasn't touching or anything. It was "I'll show you mine if you show me yours." But we didn't do it. Something came up. It blew over fast and we said, "Let's go out and ride bikes!"

Z: You never had any other experiences with boys, say, when you were around thirteen and just starting puberty?

R: No. Like I said, the whole thing, within my whole town as far as I know, was never even thought of. [Pause.] I'd be kind of curious to know. Gregg says he wishes he could see everyone who is homosexual turn green for a day. It would be kind of interesting to go back to school and see just how many there were.

Z: I think Gregg pretty much believes that people are either gay or straight—green or white—and that they're born that way. Unless of course he's trying to convince someone that they should have sex with him, in which case the whole world takes on a pastel celadon shade. I've learned that men come in every possible sexual variation, and that they can change color very quickly. Not that I'm trying to sell you on it; of course you should only do whatever you're comfortable with. But anyway, you told me that Gregg was trying to convince you before that you should just let him blow you, because it would be the same as a woman doing it.

R: Oh. Yeah. Well, I don't know if he was trying necessarily to convince me so he could do it to me, but just saying that if anyone did it to me, male or female, the sensation is the same. That was the question— whether or not I would become erect. I was like, "No, I really don't think I could or would." He said, "Oh yes you would. It's the same feeling. Don't tell me that you wouldn't get erect if I was to go down on your knob!"

There is an attraction—there's two different kinds of attractions. I find the male body . . . not attractive in a sexual sense, but I can really admire it. I look at some of these models; to think that a body can be that huge and that strong—even though it's pretty weak compared to the animal kingdom—but to put that much work into something really takes a lot. I have pictures of guys in my locker that I've cut out, but when I look at those pictures I look at the beauty of the body as being art. My favorite magazines are *GQ* and *Vogue* and *Cosmopolitan*. I love the advertisements. My favorite advertisements are usually for some sort of cologne or Levi 501s—that's my favorite. It's an ocean scene, three men that are pretty well built. The other one I got is from a cologne ad. This guy, he's pretty built too. He's got this hose and he's all wet and everything.

Z: [Laughs.] These of course are the kinds of images that a lot of gay men respond to, and it's one of the ironies of your and Gregg's friendship that you are much more fashion conscious, and fit certain stereotypes of a gay man more than he does. He just throws on a T-shirt, and sometimes he has some pretty bad haircuts, and—You know what I'm trying to say?

R: You're saying that Gregg should be more like me and I should be more like Gregg?

Z: No. I'm saying that you've kind of reversed the stereotypes. He's like the straight guy who doesn't know how to dress, you're like the gay guy who clips out pictures of hot men from fashion magazines.

R: Yeah. I have a couple pictures that are just guys. There's something about it that just—it seems sexy, although I don't find it sexually attractive, like I would want to be all over his body. It just seems—it's got style.

Z: But that could be sexual, too. Sexuality doesn't necessarily only mean getting it hard and sticking it in and getting off. What does excite you sexually, when you masturbate and fantasize? What do you picture in your mind?

R: Certain positions of the woman. A lot has to do with her face. Her looks. Just sort of the image that she creates. Her eyes, her hair. Just the way she carries herself. Everything about her. Just being feminine seems to be a turnon. I love the body itself, but most of all it's the sharing, I think. Her giving herself up. Whatever position she's in, it's almost like she's saying, "Take me. This is me. Experience me. Feel me."

Z: Do you prefer women in a submissive posture?

R: Sort of. But at the same time I don't want them to be submissive, I want it to be equal. I like at times where she takes and I give, and I like at other times where she can feel open enough to where she would want to give to me. Be on top of me. And just to watch the expression on her face as I'm in her. I know that as much as I'm enjoying being in her and feeling her and just experiencing her total self, whatever she's offering me, she's also doing the same thing with me. She's wanting me and feeling me. It's a mutual sharing thing.

Z: There's one aspect of heterosexual sex that is different from male/male sex or female/female sex. With gay sex, you know pretty much what a certain touch to a certain spot will feel like because you're capable of the same sensations. With you and a woman, I guess you can't ever really know what a woman's orgasm is like. There's a certain mystery there.

R: Right. I've thought about that, and that also excites me. To think that we're so different. I've sort of fantasized what it would be like for a woman to feel a man—for her to take him in. Her laying on her back or whatever.

Z: You've fantasized that while you were having sex?

R: Oh, no. I've just thought about it. What turns a woman on? Just to think what's going on in their minds. Because I know there's a lot more going on than what they say. They play the dumb role that women aren't supposed to enjoy sex, let the man make the first move, let the man stay in control. I know that's not the case, even though they play along with it a lot.

Z: Growing up, did you think of yourself as being as typically masculine as other boys?

R: No, not really. I was never involved in sports or anything. I was more artistic. I liked to draw.

Z: Did anybody ever give you a hard time about not being masculine enough?

R: Oh, no. I never gave it a second thought. The group of guys that I hung out with in high school, most of them weren't into any sports either. In fact they were probably more like druggies instead. They smoked pot and skateboarded or made pipe bombs. They were probably the misfits, but that's who I hung out with for the most part. Just because they were creative and artistic. And the jocks, I didn't really talk to them a whole lot. There were a couple that I hung out with. In my senior year I did go into wrestling. I just felt I should do something. I kind of thought of it as pretraining for the military, because by that time I had kind of decided that the military was the only option. I had very poor grades. C's, D's, and F's. Many F's. I was happy to get a C.

Because of my grades my father and I had a pretty bitter relationship. At one time I can even remember—I think it was my junior year—he suggested that I just drop out of school. "If you're just going to be like this, why the hell even stay in school? You might as well get out. Quit wasting your time, quit wasting my time." I was sort of shocked that he said that. I knew what that would lead up to. So I stayed in. I eventually did graduate from high school, though I think the faculty helped me out a lot. Pushed me through.

I came real close to joining the Army. I talked to the recruiter, and because I wasn't eighteen yet he wanted to talk to my father to get permission. So he stopped by the house, and my dad was pretty excited about that. It was a total surprise. The recruiter threw the same pitch to my dad about the benefits, all the career opportunities. My dad was glad to hear that I had made somewhat of an adult decision to take such a big step. It kind of put me in the limelight there for a while.

Not too long after that I got a call from a Navy recruiter. I said, "I've already talked to the Army recruiter. I'm going to go into the Army. You're wasting your time." He said, "It's not too late. You haven't signed anything. Why don't you give me a chance? Let me tell you what I got to offer you." So I said, what the hell. I went in there with the attitude I was just going to get it over with so he'd stop calling me. But actually I listened to him and it seemed a little more appealing. Just little things kind of tilted the scales. They said the food was better; you get to do the traveling and the overseas thing. So I decided to go with the Navy.

After that, things took a drastic turn. All of a sudden my dad and I became buddies, I guess. He had spent four years in the military himself; he was a Marine. He always told me stories about it, but I never really listened to him. But I could feel a stronger bond created just because of this simple move.

Z: That wasn't something you expected or hoped to accomplish by joining?

R: No, I was thinking of my own interests. I just knew that when I graduated I had to get my ass together and get out of the house. I knew Dad was not going to be supporting me much longer. Having the grades that I did, I didn't see myself getting a good job.

Z: Did any part of joining the Navy have to do with fulfilling an image of yourself as a man?

R: Hell, no! Fuck, no. I just wanted the money, the education, and the benefits, and I'm outta here. I've got better things to do and better places to go.

Z: What kind of a ship are you on now?

R: It's a fast frigate.

Z: How many men?

R: I'd say approximately two hundred and thirty. It's fairly small.

Z: Some of the guys tell me that there's a lot of sexual tension at sea. I've heard there's even a tradition that a new guy is called "the sea bitch," and they joke that he'll have to take care of the other guys.

R: I haven't been aware of anything like that.

Z: No? What about just joking that some guy's gonna fuck some other guy because you've been at sea too long and he's starting to look too good?

R: Oh. That's sort of—I wouldn't consider that a routine thing, but it's something we do to humiliate the guy that we're talking about. The only guy that we do it to in radio is RM1. It's just because he's such a nerdy little guy. You probably would understand if you saw him. He's got these little ears that stick out, he wears glasses, and he's got a tight little butt and a tight little body. But he's a first class; he's supposed to be our fearless leader. It's so ironic. We call him our little bitch. We joke about his ass. "Look at RM1's ass! He's got a tight little ass, doesn't he?" [Laughs.]

I guess to be able to talk like that we're all pretty comfortable with each other. No one seems to suspect anything. And even though there was someone in our group that I work with—I don't think he's gay, but I think there are some people in the shack who probably thought that he was. But that didn't stop them from being his friend either. We got along pretty well with him.

Z: What do you think you would have said before you knew Gregg if some reporter had come aboard your ship and asked you, in front of everyone else, what you thought about gays in the military?

R: Probably the same answer that I've heard a lot of guys say: "It doesn't bother me as long as they don't touch me." And I guess I'd still give 'em the same answer. It doesn't matter to me if you're gay or not.

Z: There must have been a lot of talk among the guys you work with after Clinton got elected about his plans to lift the gay ban. What were they saying, and what have they been saying since them?

R: Like I said, our shack is pretty cool about the homosexual thing. I don't know if it's because they find it acceptable, or if they just think that everyone is so heterosexual that they don't actually question if it's real or just a joke. But no one seems to question anyone's sexuality. And no one seems to be disturbed by it. I don't think anyone seems to care about the ban on gays, other than—well, our LPO [leading petty officer]—he's one step below our RM1—he says that he doesn't want to have any fags in his Navy and he thinks it's sick. When he sees us messing around and kidding around about it, he goes, "You guys are warped! I don't want any more guys like you in *my* Navy!" It's always his Navy. And Logan, who's an ET, he just says, "It's sick." It's almost like he's so scared of it he doesn't even want to talk about it.

Z: Don't guys like that usually say "I don't want no fag looking at me in the shower"?

R: Yeah, I've heard that.

Z: How do you feel about the idea of some gay guy looking at you naked in the shower?

R: Doesn't bother me. In a way I guess I would feel flattered, to think that someone finds me attractive. Don't want to disappoint 'em, but [laughs] it doesn't bother me.

Z: And these other guys? Why do you think that would scare them?

R: It's hard to say. Maybe they're just afraid to challenge their own sexualness. Or they feel that if they didn't care if someone gay was looking at them, someone might think that they're also gay.

Z: When you became friends with Gregg, did anybody give you a hard time about it?

R: Oh yes. Eric, a friend of mine, he definitely thought I was gay. And in fact—he was with me when I met Marcella in TJ [Tijuana], and even then, after her and I slept together he still had it in his mind that if I wasn't gay then I must be bi. No matter what I said, I couldn't convince him. Because like you said, if you didn't know me, I do fit into what's considered to be the gay stereotype as far as my looks and my liking of fashion or whatever.

Z: Did it bother you that he thought that?

R: Yeah, it did. Because—that's just not the way I was, and I didn't wanna be thought of that way. I thought he should trust me or understand at least, if I told him I'm not, I'm not. But at the same time it bothered me that it bothered me. I thought, why do I care? It shouldn't bother me.

Z: Did you consider not hanging around Gregg so much, or at least not as publicly?

R: No, not really. I still continued to see him. But even now sometimes it bothers me if I'm around him too much. I find it's not too healthy for me to be around it too long. It becomes irritating and sort of uncomfortable.

Z: Gregg took you to some drag show that you didn't especially enjoy.

R: I didn't like that at all. I just wanted to leave. I found it repulsive and sick, almost. It just seemed really disgusting.

Z: What about it?

R: It's hard to explain. A sense of—I don't want to be rude when I say this, but, so faggy. So fucking gay and homosexual. I guess it's things like that, or when I seriously try to think of myself with a guy or anything, I just get—no. It doesn't click at all.

Z: But most gay guys aren't like drag queens, are they?

R: Well no. But I was like, repulsed at the crowd even. Some of the guys together holding their hands. I just didn't like it. And Gregg was whistling and clapping his hands. It just seemed like a sick joke. These are gay guys, in a gay bar, pretending to be women—it's like they were trying to play some sort of reversed role. The gay guys act like they like the women, feeling their legs . . . it was almost like they were making fun of heterosexuals and women. If they had known that I was straight, it would have been really weird. They probably would have looked at me like—I don't know. I felt sort of like that guy in that French movie you showed us [*Europa, Europa*], that Jewish guy amongst a bunch of Nazis.

Z: For a while you were hanging out with our love-in crowd of mostly gay friends. Did you ever feel that those guys gave you a hard time about being straight?

R: Oh no. I felt really comfortable with them.

Z: But they did sometimes joke about your being straight.

R: Sort of. I guess they did. It doesn't make me mad or upset, or want to say "Stop it, I don't like that." If anything, I'm intruding on them. This is their home, I'm a guest here. It's not my place to say anything. But I didn't want to say anything. The thought never even crossed my mind.

Z: Kevin took my camcorder and asked you why you would want to hang out with a bunch of fags. What did you answer him?

R: I just don't think of it that way, I guess. Until they start playing around with each other, and hugging and kissing and feeling each other, I don't even think of them as gays. As long as they keep it somewhat clean it doesn't bother me. They never really displayed a strong physical sexualness.

Z: But sometimes they did!

R: Yeah, sometimes. But there wasn't a lot of heavy kissing, or going down the pants or anything. Sometimes it did cross my line, but I would sort of look away or just ignore it. They weren't too gross about it. I have a bunch of friends, we do the exact same thing, it's just that—I think that we're all straight guys. It just felt like the same thing. And until I see anything going on that's different, it doesn't feel any different. It's just a bunch of friends having a good time.

Z: Are there any differences?

R: Only when they start playing around and grabbing each other.

Z: But that's only play. And straight guys do that, too.

R: As a joke.

Z: Well, what about the crossing the line ceremony? You had men dressed in drag there, you had flagellation with firehoses, and on some ships I guess there's even simulated oral sex and fucking, where they pretend to be doing things to each other just like our love-in crowd did at these gatherings. Did they do that on your ship?

R: Yeah, they did. And I was involved in that. [Laughs.]

Z: What would you do exactly?

R: It's all just to humiliate you. It's got to be tough, it's got to be embarrassing, just so you can say, "Yeah, I did it, I went through it," to become part of the group they call the shellbacks.

They woke us up at like, two in the morning. They come in fucking banging the garbage cans and turning on all the lights, and we're all sleeping. They're yelling, "Get up you fucking slimy wogs! Get out of your racks! Don't look at me wog! Keep your eyes on the ground!" We'd just be going around on our hands and knees in circles, and they'd be smacking us. Some of them, for whatever reason—just by chance; no one really concentrated on anyone, they didn't want to cause any hurt feelings or think that anyone was being picked on—they would pull you off out of the assembly line, and they would say, "Get up there and fuck him, wog! I wanna see you fuck him! Fuck him *hard*, wog! Fuck him like the bitch he is!" [Laughs.] And if you didn't do it hard enough they'd slap you on the ass.

Z: So one wog would have to fuck another?

R: Yeah.

Z: Did you have to do that?

R: Yup. Yup. I was up there.

Z: You were the fucker, or the—

R: I was the fucker. I was going on like a dog from hell!

Z: Did you fuck hard enough, or did you have to be spanked?

R: I had to be spanked a couple times. [Laughs.]

Z: Was that fun?

R: It was humiliating, but it seemed OK, because everyone else was going through it.

Z: You didn't see any sexual meanings to this?

R: Oh no. There wasn't any sexual meanings. I don't think there was any. It was just embarrassing.

Z: You didn't try out for wog queen?

R: I was supposed to. But I was mess cranking at the time, and during the wog queen contest I was in the scullery, so I missed out on it. I had to do the dishes.

Z: You said that you found the simulated sex humiliating. Which is more humiliating, to be the fucker or to be the fucked?

R: Probably the fucker, I think.

Z: That's more humiliating?

R: I would think so, because if you do it too well, or if you do it too hard, it seems like you're enjoying it.

Z: See, I would have said the one who's on the bottom. Like with your wimpy first class, with everyone joking about wanting his tight little butt, there's almost this meaning that he's like a woman, not completely male. "Fuck him like the *bitch* he is."

R: No. In most cases maybe, but in this case I think it's reversed, because the guy who's getting fucked doesn't have any choice. If he says anything then he gets his ass beat. And he doesn't want that, because it starts to hurt. Your ass is black and blue for the next two days. So he's not going to say anything, he's just going to take it, because he doesn't want any attention focused on him. He has no choice; he can't help it. It's being done to him. Whereas the other guy, he's the one in control. He's doing it. He's the dude who's fucking the guy, pumping away on his ass! [Laughs.]

Z: And I guess we already know that didn't get you excited.

R: Right. I was more concentrated on the dude beating my ass. I was gritting my teeth.

Z: You told me that you enjoyed the ceremony, that it was a lot of fun.

R: Yeah. In the Navy, to be able to say that you're a shellback is an honorable thing. I guess my attitude has sort of changed now, just because I'm so sick of the military and I feel it's holding me back. But at the time, yeah, I guess I liked it.

Z: What do you think the crossing the line ceremony means? I know it's an old tradition, but do you think it serves any purpose?

R: I don't know. They say it goes back to the pirate days. But how it got started beats the shit out of me. I never thought about it.

Z: So now of course when you go on this next cruise you'll be a shellback.

R: I'm looking forward to it! In fact I have one of the shillelaghs in my locker that was used upon my ass, and I intend to use it on someone else and pass that down.

Z: This is a perfect transition back to my questions about the love-in crowd, because there was that one time up in Carlsbad. . . .

R: [Falls over laughing, clapping his hands.]

Z: What happened there?

R: I don't know! That was pretty fun though.

Z: How did you get started doing that?

R: I think it had something to do with the shellback thing. I remember feeling what it was like to get smacked on the ass with a hose or a belt. And I remember specifically asking Anthony, "I'm going to do this hard. I'm going to do this as hard as I want!" And he said, "Do it. Do it." But I was afraid to, because I don't think he realized how much it was going to hurt. I said, "I'm going to do this with my full force. Do you really want me to do this?" But he said yeah, so. And I've never hit anyone with full force in my life. It's just something I've never had the opportunity to do. So maybe it was just kinda cool. I started hitting him pretty hard. [Laughs.]

Z: You were really into it, shouting out and making all kinds of noise.

R: [Laughs.] Were you turned on by that?

Z: I wasn't turned on. I don't know about Anthony.

R: You seemed like you were a little turned on. You had this grin on your face.

Z: Maybe I was wondering why it would be so enjoyable for you.

R: Just to be able to totally let go and not hold anything back, just to beat the shit out of him. He seemed to like it, though. I don't think I could have taken it. And then Ray of course wanted to jump up there. I think with Ray, he probably would have gone on. I said, "Do you want another?" "Yeah." And I hit him again. But I stopped, because I'm sure that had to sting.

Z: Suppose you were told that that was giving those guys sexual pleasure; how would you feel?

R: Shit, I don't know. [Pause.] I probably would have kept on doing it, I guess. Not any more or any less than what I did. Just the same amount.

Z: Anthony enjoys a certain amount of pain in his sexual encounters. Have you ever had any experience with that?

R: No. All the women I've been with have been pretty submissive, if you want to call it that. I guess that's something I'm looking for. A woman that won't be afraid to tell me what she wants, or to be able to do something to me, or to touch me in some way. 'Cause I know they want to. Why else would they be there? They're obviously attracted to me. But they just don't want to free themselves to be able to touch me in any way they feel like they want to.

Z: You get tired of having to be the aggressor in sexual situations?

R: Not tired, just bored.

Z: Tell me about your SOUTHPAC [Southern Pacific] cruise and a little bit about what it's like to be at sea.

R: It sucks! On a SOUTHPAC, you're out to sea a lot, and the ports that you do pull into are very minimal. Mostly all of Central America they pretty much don't even like America anyway. Liberty was really restricted. You couldn't go to certain places; you couldn't do certain things.

Z: You did have some fun, you told me.

R: Oh yeah. I did have some very good times. The times that we pulled in, we had fun. The guys, we would go out. The first stop was in Panama. We went to this bathhouse, where we got a massage, and if you wanted to you could take advantage of your masseuse, and do whatever you want with her.

Z: And you wanted to do that?

R: Oh definitely! It was great. They wanted sixty but we talked 'em down a whole ten dollars to fifty. [Laughs.] That included the massage. That was the most expensive there. That's because we've got a military base in Panama and there's a lot of military that goes there.

I had a pretty good experience in Guatemala. There was this place that all the sailors were going to. Just shacks, sometimes with sheets for the wall. There was this guy, his name was Jesus. [Laughs.] He hooked us up. I did two chicks that night. I did one who was nineteen years old. She wasn't too good, though; she wouldn't let me put her legs up in the air. The other one, who was fourteen years old, she was very good. She really got into it.

Z: Was this just fucking, or would you do other things with them too?

R: Like what?

Z: I don't know. Oral, anal sex—

R: Oh no. Just fucking. I wouldn't want to trust anything else with them.

Z: Did you get gonorrhea or anything from these women?

R: Nope. I was kind of nervous about it, 'cause the rubbers broke.

Z: Why did the rubbers break?

R: 'Cause I do it like a bunny! [Laughs.] I don't know. They were cheap. There were the ones that the ship passed out. They had a big box on the quarterdeck for the guys to take as you leave the ship.

Z: Did you put the condoms on for your own protection or did the prostitutes demand that you put them on?

R: The only place that the prostitutes had them was in Panama. The rest of the time I remember supplying them myself. Yeah, simply for my own protection.

Z: What is your attitude toward AIDS? Do you worry about it? Or do you think that because you're straight and the female to male transmission rate is comparatively low that you don't have to worry?

R: No, I don't have that view at all. I know that it doesn't matter what you are, you can get AIDS. But I just don't worry about it, because before I would have any kind of unprotected sex with any woman, I'm definitely going to know her pretty well. [Pause.] I guess I have had unprotected sex with two women. And one time I was worried about it, because I really didn't know her that well. Luckily, she's an OK girl, and I've gotten to know her a lot better since then.

Z: Do you have any tattoos?

R: No, but I sort of wanted to get one. I'm so glad I didn't, but when I first came in I wanted to get the Navy surface warfare tattoo on my shoulder.

Z: Why are you glad you didn't get it?

R: Just for what it represents. I don't like the military anymore. The military totally contradicts everything that we're fighting for. All your rights as a human being—gone. All your dignity—gone. It's just fascist bullshit. The military is so hard on everything, trying to frame everyone, fuck 'em here and fuck 'em there. I hate it.

Z: Did you, or do you still feel any sense of camaraderie with other sailors?

R: Yeah, I guess so. Sometimes more than others. Sometimes I get pissed off at the military and I don't want to talk to any of 'em, and I don't really find anything in common with them because most of them still have the gung ho attitude. That's just not me anymore. But then other times I feel like—I think I have more of a camaraderie feeling when we're out to sea. Because it's only us, there's no one else around, it's just us guys. We've got to pull together if we want to live through this, because if we don't work together, the ship's gonna run down. If the ship runs down, we fucking die. There's no one else out there. So you have a feeling of togetherness, because you're all sharing the same feelings. Everyone's missing their family, everyone's missing their girlfriend—or boyfriend, I guess—we all gotta eat the same fucking crappy food, we all gotta work long-ass hours, so we all have a lot in common when we're out to sea. Whereas when we're in port we kind of separate from each other because we have our own private lives to take care of, and our families and friends and interests.

Z: Are you aware of differences, not just personal differences, but differences in the sexualities of some of the gay guys you've met in our group?
R: [Pause.] No, not really. Except for Ray. I'd say Ray's the only one that stands out from the rest. Because he seems like such a queen, I guess. A flamer. But the rest of 'em—I think if I met the rest of them on my own, anywhere else in the outside world, including yourself, I would probably not even guess that these were homosexuals.
Z: Are you aware of men in the group, apart from Gregg, finding you attractive?
R: No. Not until Sonny mentioned that Kevin found me attractive.
Z: Sonny finds you attractive himself.
R: Oh does he.
Z: The two of you went out drinking one night. I would guess that, at least in the back of his mind, there was probably some hope that. . . . You didn't think about that at all?
R: No, because the way the ground rules were laid out—he said he wanted to become straight. He said he was very unhappy in the gay community. He said it was sick and he didn't like it. And he said that he found women very attractive. But at the last love-in, at that same party when I was beating Anthony and Ray, Sonny sort of showed me that might not be the case, the way he was hanging on that other guy and kissing him. I was like—I don't know. I can't say for sure, but to me—I'm heterosexual, I know it, I feel it. It doesn't matter who I'm with, I know my sexuality, so I'm not put off by anything. I definitely know what I like and what I don't like. Whereas he said he doesn't want to be part of this, he likes women. I gave him the benefit of the doubt, but now I really don't think he does. I think he just feels that it's wrong, but I don't think he can help it.

Z: How would you describe your relationship with Gregg today?
R: Good friendship, I guess. We're able to talk a lot to each other. [Pause.] Sometimes it's hard, because he doesn't seem to understand the problems I have with Marcella. When I tell him the problems that her and I have it's easy for him to say, "Fuck her, she's just a bitch. She's no good for you.

Drop her. She's just a dumb cunt." "That's easy for you to say! You have no attraction to the female species at all anyway." Now if I was having some problems with some guy, and he found him attractive, he might say, "Oh, give him another chance. He's really a good guy." So there's some things we can talk about and get along with; other things, mostly things like that, we just can't. There's no concept of each other's desires. They're totally different.

Z: You called him your good friend. You didn't say that he's your best friend.

R: I find it sort of silly to say "best friends."

Z: Do you think sometimes you take advantage of him just because of the fact that he has an apartment and someplace for you to go, knowing that he does find you attractive? That is probably at least an element of how your friendship started.

R: Yes, I think that's how it started. Now, I don't know. He says that he doesn't feel that way anymore. He says now he looks at me as a brother, or strong male friendship. But I think he still has some sort of sexual attraction to me. Yeah, sometimes I do feel guilty that I'm taking advantage of him. He doesn't say anything about it, but I come over a lot. I almost always have dinner with him. Sometimes I feel like he might think that that's the only reason I come over is just to hang out there, watch television, relax at his place because he does have an apartment, and eat his food. Because what do I offer to him, other than if he is attracted to me? That's why I try to go out and do other things with him, because I don't want him to think that. Once I came over with a bunch of groceries and I made dinner for a change, instead of him. I should probably say something or ask him about that.

Z: Do you still sleep in the same bed with him some nights?

R: Oh, every night, if I ever spend the night there I always sleep with him.

Z: Do you ever touch at all? [Pause.] Do you sleep close together, or do you sleep at opposite ends of the bed?

R: [Pause.] Usually at opposite ends of the bed. It's nothing intended, but it's just normal touching like your knees bump into each other or your feet hit each other's feet because you toss and turn. But there's nothing intended by it. I don't feel any different knowing that he's gay sleeping with him. I feel confident that he's not going to jeopardize the friendship we've created.

Z: You didn't say you thought of him as being like a brother.

R: I've never had a brother, so I don't have anything to compare it to. But I feel pretty close to him. I know I could tell him just about anything, and I think he tells me most anything.

Z: Would you say that you love him?

R: Love him? How—If he was to die or something, how would I react, maybe? I don't . . . no, I don't see how I could say I love him. I just find that term hard to use with another male. It's just a strong friendship.

Sonny: Navy Tradition

Perhaps the most malignant form of gay misbehavior is public sex. . . . Despite . . . attempts by authorities to squelch them . . . a coterie of gay men continues, daily and nightly, to perform . . . in the public lavatories, parks, and alleyways of every major city in the United States. Theirs is the wretchedest of all gay excesses.

These are not the words of any antigay demagogue, but of two gay men, Marshall Kirk and Hunter Madsen. They are the authors of *After the Ball*, a 1989 manual for gay people on how to—and how not to—ingratiate ourselves with straight America. I quote from a chapter titled "How Gays Misbehave":

. . . When they ejaculate—and they do—on the seats, walls, or floors, they leave it there to congeal into a nasty, highly identifiable puddle. One can imagine the effect such a charming tableau has upon a young, sheltered, or uptight straight man, when he comes upon it suddenly and unexpectedly in a place in which he is accustomed to do his embarrassing but necessary business in peace and quiet. . . .

Kirk and Madsen speculate that the gay press must itself be composed of tearoom queens,

. . . for it is quick to condemn any question that such public frolics are a bad idea, and readily labels police efforts to put a stop to these activities as "antigay" harassment. In fact, we don't consider this antigay at all—merely antinuisance. If a woman came into a public men's room, disrobed, and began masturbating before a mirror, she also would, no doubt, be carted away. . . .[1]

Kirk and Madsen need to be apprised of certain facts.

It is a mistake to assume that all men who engage in semi-public sex are "gay." As Kirk and Madsen correctly note elsewhere in their book (but not on the dust jacket, which speaks of "America's 25 million gays and 225 million straights"), "sexual orientation isn't an either/or situation."[2] Arrest reports from police sting operations at highway rest stops reveal that a large percentage of those caught are married family men. Of all men involved in homosexual contacts anywhere, men who seek sex in bathrooms are probably least likely to call themselves gay.

Gay men are also not the only ones to ejaculate on restroom floors. My soldier friends in Germany complained of often finding come-splattered pages torn from girlie magazines littering their barracks latrines. And my own Peeping Tom observations confirm without question that straight servicemen are just as likely as gay servicemen to autograph "Kilroy Was Here" in spunk. If anything, gay men might, like Kirk and Madsen, tend to be more fastidiously Kleenex conscientious. (Spooge, by the way, does not "congeal," it liquefies and thins.)

No one likes to brush up unawares against someone else's cold semen. And certainly there are only too many ill-mannered tearoom trolls (I use the term to describe men both young and old) defiling the men's rooms of America with their militantly obtrusive desperation. I in fact recall once applying the toe of my shoe to a man who, without invitation or any warning, thrust his face beneath the partition of a university library men's room stall. There is such a thing as tearoom etiquette.

But cruising toilets is not a preferred method of making contact for very many men, and in my observation tends to diminish in inverse proportion to the accessibility of less malodorous venues. In Frankfurt, with its myriad sexual marketplaces, few cruisy tearooms existed, and none of them were very busy. But in Hanau, Germany, a town with a huge soldier population and no sex shops or gay bars, the men's rooms in on-base libraries and snack bars were festive, the stalls bountiful with tidings of hope and apertures of glory.

Bathroom cruising is a viable avenue of sexual exploration for many young military men who are otherwise without means of connecting sexually with other men. For some, it remains a furtive and secret pleasure, but for others, it is an exciting first step toward establishing a gay identity that will take them away from the men's room.

In this interview, Sonny, a blond 26-year-old Navy cryptologic technician of middle-class background from Maine, tells of his journey over the stations of gay Navy San Diego—from a glory hole at the 32nd Street Naval Station to the servicemen's lounge at the Armed Forces YMCA to the "Queen's Green" at Balboa Park and finally to the Hillcrest gay bar Flicks, where he met his first lover.

Sonny: I have been out for—I have been going to the bars for only a year and a couple months now.

Zeeland: You're twenty-six. How old were you when you first had sex?

S: Twenty-four. And then some months.

Z: What did you do all those years?

S: Fantasized and played with Rosie! When I first started having fantasies—probably when I was thirteen—it was about women. And it was about women all the way up until I was twenty-one. And—I will be totally honest, I am still attracted to women. I still fantasize sometimes about sex with women.

Z: And males? How far can you date that back to?

S: When I was five years old I talked another guy into dropping his drawers and letting me look at him. And for years after that I would do the play wrestling type stuff. You know, your hands fall where they may. But as far as fantasizing about having sex with men, it didn't happen until well into the Navy.

Z: Why did you join the Navy?

S: Because I wanted to ever since the sixth grade, so I did.

Z: What attracted you to the Navy in sixth grade?

S: I really don't know.

Z: There must have been some image, some picture of Navy life that you had.

S: Not really. Maybe it was because my father and most of my uncles were Army. A couple of 'em were Air Force and one of them had been a Marine. I was the first Navy. I still am the only Navy in my family. Rebellion against my father probably is another thing. Army-Navy rivalry. That might be it.

When I was growing up we didn't get along. He cared more for his first son than he did for me. Because of that I became a mama's boy. Spoiled rotten type of kid. And I had no love for him. I joined the Navy with my mind set on doing better than he did in the Army. Which I have achieved.

I have achieved the same rank in eight and a half years—actually I did it in six years—that he achieved in twenty. So I have accomplished my goal, and I know I'm going to surpass it. He's very proud of me now. He brags about me to everybody. So now there is a mutual love between us.

Z: You're a first class petty officer. And I think for your age you're the highest ranking enlisted man I've met.

S: I was a twenty-four-year-old E-6. I haven't met anybody else recently that made it as fast as I did. I hope to make chief this year.

Z: When you joined, did you think of yourself as straight? Was that your sexual identity?

S: Yes.

Z: How did that start to change?

S: Like I said, always that play wrestling thing. Always interested, always looking, checking out guys in the locker room. But I always also wanted a wife and kids. Still do as a matter of fact. I don't know at what point I decided to try, because I didn't even see any gay pornography until I was twenty-three. That's basically the turning point. I started going out to the bookstores and buying solely gay pornography.

Z: How did your fantasies progress to an experience with another person?

S: On Thirty-second Street Naval Base here in San Diego—the "wet side," which is where the ships are—at the Exchange there was a bathroom with two toilet stalls. I went in there to use the toilet, and there was a big glory hole and a lot of graffiti. And my curiosity was aroused to the state that I was ready to try it, so I went back another day when it was safe, later in the day. Someone came into the other stall, and I proceeded from there. They would perform on me, but I was not at the level that I would want to perform on them.

In Yokosuka, Japan, I went to the old Navy lodge. Again there was a glory hole, and there was graffiti; this guy said what he wanted to do, and to meet him at a certain time. I came back at that certain time, and I guess he must have come in right behind me. He motioned for me to put my dick through the hole and he proceeded to give me a blowjob. Then after he was satisfied by doing that he pushed a rubber through the hole. I put it on, and he wanted me to put my dick through there and he pushed himself back on it. That was the first time I had any experience with anal sex. It wasn't very gratifying because—through a glory hole you're worried about cutting your dick off. It was metal! [Laughs.]

After Japan, I went celibate for about three months, and then I ended up following graffiti again. I didn't know anything about clubs. To be totally honest, I didn't know that gay clubs existed. So I went to the USO. There was graffiti on the wall that said "Go to the YMCA." I went to the

Armed Forces YMCA. I walked into the common area, where people sit around and watch TV, and I saw an attractive guy sitting in a chair watching an Oriental laying on a couch. The Oriental was sound asleep. I sat down on a chair that this guy could look at also. He started looking at me and I looked at him, and the eye contact led to shifting positions in the chair, until you had full crotch view and lo and behold you could see the outline of his erection and that got me erect. We looked at each other. Then he got up and went into the movie room. I followed him, he waved for me to sit beside him, and we started groping each other right there in the movie room. Didn't pull anything out.

We went back to my apartment and had sex. He was an HT [hull technician]. Nineteen years old. I spent one night with him, then that morning we got up, had breakfast, then we went to Balboa Park. He introduced me to a couple of his friends. We proceeded from there to Soho, the coffee house, where I met more people, then he said "Do you want to go to a gay bar?" He took me to Flicks. That was really my first time in a gay bar. I was afraid to go back for a couple weeks, but then I did go back and I saw the people that he had introduced me to. I talked to them. We exchanged phone numbers. One of them called me up and invited me and several other people he knew to a party. And so I met more people. I left with somebody, and we had sex sex sex. But yeah, because of meeting that one HT at the Armed Forces YMCA, I am now basically in the gay lifestyle.

Z: "The gay lifestyle"? I usually hear this phrase from antigay people. It's sort of a catchword for homophobes, and gay people say that there is no such thing, that there are many divergent gay lifestyles.

S: I just use the term to mean the way gays live.

Z: Do you think of yourself as gay?

S: [Pause.] Confused.

Z: You think of yourself as confused?

S: Uh, nothing leaves this room, right? Except in the book.

About a month after my ex dumped me I came to totally accept that I was gay. If I had been in a relationship at that point in time, I would have been willing to walk down any street in this city holding hands with that person. But lately, because of all the games that are played in this life-style—the soap operas, the backstabbing—it's just so totally ridiculous. That and the stress and the worry caused by leading a double life. And the fact that I am still attracted to women and have never had sex with a woman, so I don't know whether I'll enjoy it or not, leads me to the desire to try it. I may just be bi, I may prefer women more than men but still want men. I may not be able to make the switch. But until I do I guess you'd have to say I'm confused.

Z: Have you not had opportunities to have sex with women? I would think, being a sailor . . .

S: I'm just extremely shy. I'm from the backwoods, and I was brought up with beliefs, which may be self-instilled, this wasn't the way my parents brought me up; it was my own morals, my own beliefs—wait until you get married to have sex. And so, I did not have sex with women.

Z: Tell me about your ex. Where did you meet?

S: Flicks. From there we went back to his house and spent the night like you would expect. Then in the morning, and for the next several weeks, the subject of going our separate ways never came up. I mean, it was just—from that first day together on it was just natural for us to go everywhere together.

I met Della [not interviewed] after being in the scene for only two months. I had just been told that day that I was going out to sea. I went to the bar that night, and I told my best friend, "Now that I know I'm leaving in two and a half weeks, I'll probably meet someone tonight that I want to stay with." And that's exactly what happened.

I went out to sea and by the end of the first day I knew I was hooked. I was in love. I just couldn't stop thinking about him. Always. Constantly. No matter where I was at or what I was doing, I would think about him. When I got to Panama I ran up a serious phone bill! Called him and told him I loved him. And Della said the same thing, that he felt that way since the first week.

While I was out at sea we made plans to get a place together, which was a stupid move in the end. I think that led to the downfall of the relationship. Because—for me it was fine. The type of relationship that I want is one where the partners do things together. They don't have to get away from each other, "I need my own space" type of thing, they enjoy being with each other. He needed to have his space. I wanted to stay together day and night. I forced him to tell me over the phone while I was in Hawaii that he had lost the feeling of being in love with me.

I tried at friendship. I bent over backwards to be nice. And I just got shit on. In the beginning he treated me alright, but as time progressed he said, "I don't think we should go out to the same bars anymore."

Z: How long were you together with him?

S: It was a day after our six-month anniversary that he dumped me. That was after I gave him this ring. [Shows Zeeland.] Thirty two hundred dollars. So, I mean, I'm a romantic sonofagun. That's one thing he would not deny. Every week: flowers, cards, clothes, thirty-two-hundred-dollar rings. I spoiled him rotten and I loved doing it. I do not regret a minute of it. Romance is my middle name. I love it.

Z: You mentioned that Della has tested HIV positive. When did you find that out?

S: The first night I met him. That was one of the first things out of his mouth.

Z: You didn't have any problem with that?

S: I was worried. When he took bathroom breaks, I would go to one of my friends that had dealt with that before and talk to him about it. I just tried to get educated as much as I could, so I could determine whether or not I would want to progress with that. Which I did. I mean, your feelings for someone can override your worries about that, and if you practice—you can't practice totally safe sex, but if you practice safer sex, then you really don't have to worry too much about contracting it. And he would not let me do anything but practice safer sex.

Z: Safer sex defined how?

S: Condoms.

Z: For?

S: Well, considering the roles we played, I would wear the condom. As far as oral sex, no ejaculating in the mouth. After he ejaculated there was no way I was allowed to put my mouth down in that area, even though he could on me if he wanted to.

Z: Della was in the Navy, too. Is that just a coincidence?

S: For me it's just coincidence. I have no type, really. Other than you have to be fit and attractive.

Z: You were saying that when you met Frank [a Navy ensign, present during part of this interview] at work and knew that he was gay, it was a big help to you.

S: Yeah. Because at work I didn't know anybody gay. There's a lot of stress in leading a double life. Every day you hear the gay jokes. You have to worry about getting caught. If you plan on making it a career, like I do, you have to play the games. Nobody knows anything about my private life. I leave work, I leave everybody behind. And because of that, they have to make stuff up. They tease me about being gay, but little do they know that I am! Knowing someone at work that is the same as you are, you can talk to them. You've got to be careful about who's around, but we have talked at work. So it's just helpful at relieving the stress. It has been for me since I met him.

I really like meeting and having friends in the military that are gay because you can associate as both a gay person and as a military person; you can talk about anything in your life, and you're going to understand each other. Whereas a military person talking to a civilian, you just can't talk about everything.

Z: Have you experienced the crossing the line ceremony?
S: Yes. [Makes grunting sound to Frank, who has not yet gone through the initiation.] Shellback! Shellback! Dirty wog, slimy wog! I missed the beginning, thank God. That's the worst part, where they get woken up at three in the morning and have a mixture of nastiness shoved down their throats. After eating the breakfast you have to put your clothes on backwards and inside out. You put your pants on, then your underwear. You have to crawl everywhere you go, so the night before I had made up these awesome kneepads. My knees were safe. But my boots got torn all to hell.

You crawl up to the forward part of the ship, the fo'c'sle, in front of the superstructure, and you work your way back aft. You get the "truth serum"—a syringe without the needle, full of Kool-Aid and Tabasco sauce. They squirt it in your mouth. The guy who's doing it has two vials. If he likes you, you might get something that's not so bad. But if he hates you, you'll get the nasty stuff.

From there you start crawling across the deck. And that's where they pulled my drawers down and shoved Crisco up my ass!
Z: Someone you knew?
S: Oh yeah. Well, on that class of ship, you basically know everybody. It's a great ship to be on. And I was proud of being on it. But from there you crawl to this toilet. There's cherries floating in it. They tell you to go down with just your face and bring out a cherry. So you get down there and they push a button and the water—salt water—shoots you in the face.

You keep on crawling, and you get over to ol' King Neptune and his friend Davy Jones, and they tell you your crimes against the ocean and what your punishment is. I had to go over to the fat man. In this case it was the master chief, a Guamanian. Fat. Belly full of Crisco. And he stuck an olive right in his bellybutton. You're on your knees between his legs, and you go down to get it. You don't want to get your teeth too close, you want to just bite the top of that olive, and he grabs your head and shoves your face down in there and you come out with Crisco between your teeth.

You get to stand up and walk down the ladder to the very back part of the ship, the fantail. There you have to crawl through this cloth tube that is enclosed and full of nastiness. People's puke, noodles, leftover food, eggs—you name it, it's in there. When you're halfway through it they sit on the damn thing and tell you to roll around in it.

You get through that, then you go over and they try to teach you something. "Shellbacks can't swim." Until you understand what they're saying they hit you with a shillelagh. You get into this makeshift swimming pool, and the guy standing there tells you, "OK, swim over to that corner and tell the master chief you're a shellback." So obviously he said swim, and all along you've been doing what everybody tells you so you swim. He tells you "You did something wrong! Swim back and figure out what you did wrong!" And this water's nasty, it's had people swimming through it all day. With people's puke and hot dogs and everything. So you swim back, and they try to teach you again. "Shellbacks don't swim. Shellbacks don't swim." Ahhh! That's right, I'm supposed to be a shellback now! So you *walk* over.

You're still wearing your clothes while you're going through the initiation, even if they are pulled down around your knees and stuff is dangling. But at the end they don't want you carrying that through the ship, so there's a guy there up one level above you with a firehose squirting everybody down. Your clothes are trashed, your boots are trashed—you just throw everything overboard. So everybody's standing there outside the skin of the ship, totally naked, being shot down by this guy with the firehose. I was one of the last people to go through so I didn't get to see the bodies I wanted to see. But I walked all the way through the ship naked, and I saw other guys walking naked, and when I got to my berthing compartment there were guys waiting to get into the shower. And I finally got to see some I wanted to see! Then you get into the shower and you have to scrape all this stuff out of crevices where it doesn't belong. [Laughs.] So, the shellback initiation is fun. It's something to be proud of.

Z: You didn't mention the wog queen competition.

S: I know why I didn't mention that too. I was one of 'em! [Frank and Anthony, who has since joined us, laugh.] I was one of the candidates. I've got a picture of it, as a matter of fact. I should have brought my cruise book. As a matter of fact I have some good pictures of the ceremonies. They've got some nice butts in there! I'll have to find those.

But—the wog queen ceremony. I was—what was my name? "Alotta Carlotta." We blew up some rubbers, and I put on this T-shirt and they tied it in a knot. I was a slut. But wait until I tell you about the guy that won! We put the rubbers up there, and I had tits that stuck out to here—a straight man's dream. I wore this skimpy skirt that just hid. I was one of the few that had it hid. And I wore a wig and makeup and everything.

That was the only time I guess you could say I was in drag and I'll never do it again. The only people allowed to watch it are shellbacks. I was the first one down there, and all these other guys start walking in in panties. One guy couldn't hide it at all. He was wearing such skimpy panties that his balls kept dropping out. It was funny. But some of 'em—

the guy that won knew how to hide what he had. He dressed in black lace panties, black lace bra, and he had a cat-o'-nine-tails with a long handle. He put on the music and started swishing and stuff. You've got to put on a show. He was dancing, and he got up to the captain. The captain's sitting in his chair, and he just sits on the captain's lap, right on his cock, and starts scrunching. Then he stands up and he goes over to the XO, this big musclebound dude. Sticks that cat-o'-nine-tails right on his crank and starts acting like he's giving him a blowjob. We're all going crazy over this, we couldn't believe it—all of a sudden white stuff just spooges out of his mouth. Don't know where it came from or how it got there, but white stuff [makes sound effect]. And he won. I didn't even come close.

Z: So how do the other guys watching react to this?

S: They all get into it. I mean, it's funny.

Z: What do you think the ceremony means?

S: It's a tradition. It's just basically a brotherhood type deal. And if you refuse to go through the ceremony, people think less of you.

Z: How long ago did you do this?

S: Three and a half years ago.

Z: Did you have any feeling about the homosexual overtones of this?

S: No, because it's all tradition that's been done for, shoot, generations. And it's just—there were no homosexual overtones, that I saw.

Z: You don't see any homosexual overtones to getting Crisco shoved up your ass?

S: No! Because it was part of the initiation. It wasn't something that these people do because they want to do it, it's something that's been handed down from generation to generation.

Z: White stuff spooging out of a cat-o'-nine-tails, you can't tell me—

S: Now that's the one I'm curious about. That FC [fire control technician], I betcha he's gay.

Z: Why do you think that?

S: Because what straight man would go to that extent just to win a stupid contest?

Z: So you're just speculating?

S: Oh yeah. I don't know. I just can't see going that far.

Z: Were there any other times when you observed homosexual overtones to Navy life at sea? Even just horseplay or joking around?

S: I never saw any horseplay on my ship that would be of the homosexual type. One time one of my guys, one of my seamen, told a second class to suck him. The second class said, "Pull it out." So the seaman pulled it out. The second class just happened to have a nice old dry paintbrush in his hand. WHACK! Smacked him hard! Needless to say I don't think that seaman's ever gonna pull his dick out for another guy again.

Z: Do you feel a camaraderie with other Navy men?
S: As far as straight men or gay men?
Z: All men in the Navy.
S: I've never thought about it.
Z: Marines are famous for their—
S: Teamwork. Uh, no. I'd have to say no. The Navy is so—there's so much backstabbing in the Navy, that no, it's not a brotherhood like the Marine Corps is. On a ship, more so than anywhere else, it is a brotherhood, because when you're in a situation where your life depends on everybody else, yes, there is going to be more camaraderie. I was happy to wear my ship's name on my arm. I was proud of that. Anyone puts down that ship—even though being on that ship, I can say anything bad and derogatory I wanted to—if anyone else from anywhere else put down that ship I'd get mad at 'em. But that's basically the only camaraderie in the Navy.
Z: What about with gay sailors? Gay people in the military use the term "family."
S: Yes. It is like a little family. You can be anything or anybody you want to in the gay lifestyle. The overall lifestyle is not accepted by the majority of society anyway, so the little subcultures inside the gay lifestyle are accepted by everybody in the lifestyle. You should be able to be like that with your real family. Most of us cannot or will not. I can basically tell you guys anything. And with my own family I cannot do that.

Part Two

I met with Sonny for a follow-up interview four months later. I asked him about the group we had both belonged to in the interim.

Z: Was there anything special about these love-ins that distinguished them from just ordinary parties or picnics that people have?
S: Well, they were definitely more sexual than most parties.
Z: Sexual how? None of us had sex at these parties.
S: People were thinking about it, though. I'll admit it—I was one of them.
Z: Who were you thinking about?
S: Kevin. Of course. I'd had him in the past before we started the love-ins. And I would have liked to have had him again.
Z: Kevin was the only one?

S: Russell. [Laughs.] Everybody wants Russell. The straight boy!

Z: What attracted you to him?

S: He's intelligent. We had a lot of good conversations. Just a very nice person. And he's got beautiful eyes.

Z: Was there any element of it that had to do with his being straight and unavailable?

S: No. That doesn't affect me at all.

Z: You and Russell went out one night together.

S: Yeah. To a straight bar.

Z: What was the idea behind that?

S: For me to see the straight life. And see if I could convert.

Z: That was your stated purpose, but was it something you really pursued, or was this more just an opportunity to go out with Russell?

S: No, it was something I was going to pursue. Because I have to try it. Because I'm not totally happy as a gay person. So sooner or later I've got to take the step and pursue that. But I didn't totally enjoy [that night]. Because I didn't know anybody there except for Russell. And I wasn't very active in getting to know people.

Z: It seems sort of funny, though, your going to a straight bar ostensibly to pursue women, and here you are with—

S: A man I want to go to bed with. But that wasn't my motive, to try to get him to convert.

Z: No? It wasn't in the back of your mind that, who knows, maybe you would go out and try to find some chicks, but if you didn't then maybe you'd have each other?

S: No, because I knew where he stood. That's one of the things we talked about when we first met.

Z: Do you think of Russell as completely straight?

S: Well from his explanation he likes to learn about new things. But my opinion is, he's curious, but he'll never step over the boundaries. I don't think he'll ever take the chance, even out of curiosity.

Z: What attracted you to Kevin?

S: That's a good question! I don't know what attracted me to him. I guess because I wanted a one-night stand. And I don't know what got us into bed. Probably just because he was horny that night. We were at West Coast, and when we did a round of kissing, both he and I, as soon as we touched lips, got raging hard-ons. And I guess it was a given from that moment on that we were going home with each other.

He was really nice. He told me to call him, so I did. We arranged to meet, and he called and cancelled, and arranged for another night, and cancelled again. That's how it continued until I finally gave up and threw away his phone number. And then I just saw him at the love-ins.

Z: Do you agree with my assessment that he was the center person of the love-ins?

S: Oh, definitely. Without a doubt. Something about him attracts everybody. I don't know what it is. He must put out a strange man-scent or something! [Laughs.] That's something that could be studied for years.

Z: You and Gregg got into it at one of our love-ins. Something he said offended you.

S: There was a thing on CNN on gay people. One of the segments was about gay people trying to convert themselves to straight. Gregg was just totally against that, totally didn't believe it could happen. And some of the things he said—in my opinion he thinks about straight people the same way a lot of straight people think about gay people. He's totally against straight people. He's the Strom Thurmond of the gay world. That's the best way I can put it.

Z: You think he thinks straight people are sick and perverted?

S: Yes. That's what I got from him that night. And ever since that night I haven't cared for him much.

Z: I told you that I disapproved of that CNN segment for another reason. Unlike you, the people profiled weren't trying to establish what was sexually natural and right for them; they were trying to "convert" because society tells them that homosexuality is a sin.

S: You don't know that, though.

Z: They were operating under some Christian fundamentalist organization.

S: True, they should probably try to find another avenue. If they truly want to convert not because it's what society wants, but because it's what they want—

Z: Why is it such a big deal? Why is it such a concern whether you're gay or straight?

S: To me it's not really a *concern*, I'm just indecisive because I haven't tried the straight lifestyle. So I don't know whether I would fit in there or not. I've got to find out for myself, and until I do, I can't say that I don't fit into it.

Z: Why do you have to "fit in" to one of two choices? Why does it have to be "the gay lifestyle" or "the straight lifestyle"? Why can't you just pursue the Sonny lifestyle and do whatever feels natural at the time?

S: Because I'm not totally happy at it. I have got to find out whether or not I would work as a straight person. And if not, then I will know that I am meant to be totally gay and I can be happy that way. Until I know one way or another I will not be happy either way. It's just like the straight guys that tried gay sex and finally gave up their wives because they finally realized they were meant to be gay all along. Until I know for a fact that I wouldn't work with a woman, then I can't be totally satisfied in the gay life.

Z: Let me ask you about Ray—
S: My "sister"? [Laughs.] I hate it when gay men say that.
Z: Tell me about his role at the love-ins.
S: He's the festive one. He's the one that really gets 'em pumpin'. The one that starts the sexual activity.
Z: Is it really sexual activity?
S: It's sex with clothes on. It's erotic. It's fun. It gets energy going.
Z: Is there anything really sexual between him and you?
S: No. We know we will never have sex. We're too close. I don't have sex with really close friends. When we first met, the possibility of sex was there. Definitely. From both sides. But then we became and are really close friends.
Z: How would you describe Ray's masculinity?
S: Not! He's a queen.
Z: You told me before that you are attracted to more masculine men, but now you say that you could have had sex with Ray, and of course the guy you're dating now—
S: He's a queen. I admit it. And I never thought I could be attracted to someone that queeny. When he and I are together alone, he will tone it down. His voice won't sound so feminine. But whenever we're around his friends he starts acting more so. Like every attraction, it was physical attraction at first. He's a classy dresser, and I just find him very good looking. Then when we finally talked, I really enjoyed talking with him. Because of that I overlooked the effeminate side.

I really think I can love anybody. I can fall for anybody. That's what I've determined. If you believe in the Zodiac, I'm a Scorpio, and that's what they say about Scorpios. One of the things we do is overlook things like that. And I've always been like that. I can overlook flaws or differences.
Z: Well, maybe it really isn't so important whether your lover has a penis or not.
S: True. Oh, I know I could fall in love with a woman if she has the right personality. The question when it comes down to me going the straight route or staying on the gay route is the sex. The only difference between being straight and being gay is the sex. Because you're going to get the same thing out of a straight relationship that you get out of a gay relationship.

Z: Somebody famous said the reverse. The only thing that's the same about gay people and straight people is the sex.

S: Oh right! Tell me what man has to suck a dick on a woman?

Z: But they say that the clitoris is like a small penis.

S: That's true.

Z: So what's the difference?

S: Because you can't stick it down your throat and gag!

Z: Is gagging so important?

S: What straight man is going to have to take a penis anally?

Z: I think that a lot of straight men secretly crave it, or at least wonder what it would be like.

S: True. A lot of them take fingers.

Z: I think the flip side of being dominant and aggressive is wanting somebody to—flip you. I'm just suggesting that maybe you should just do whatever feels natural to you, and quit worrying so much about whether you're "totally gay" or not, and leave yourself open to whatever sexual possibilities might present themselves.

S: I want to see whether or not I would enjoy it with a woman. And if I do, then maybe I can go that avenue. If I enjoy it, I would have to enjoy it more than I do with men. It would have to be an overriding pleasure. It would have to be more emotional and more erotic than it is with a man. Otherwise I would still always want to have sex with men. And that's not conducive to a good relationship with a woman.

But if I could go straight, I would. In a heartbeat.

You've been very hard on me today!

Kevin: The Network

Kevin is not a heavy drinker but during his final weekend in San Diego he was drunk for 72 hours. The blond, blue-eyed, 24-year-old Pennsylvanian was trashed on Friday night when all of us did "cocksuckers" (Kahlua mixed with liqueurs in shot glasses one goes down on, lifts, and drains with one's mouth, not using one's hands). He was buzzing at brunch the next morning, when I plied him with mimosas—and during this interview with Red Hook—just for fun. He was guzzling Bud that afternoon at Fiesta Island while I chatted with Alex (see David, "'Hard' Not 'Tough'"). But he was most celebratory that night, at West Coast, when we all took turns buying him rounds, and, at his civilian boyfriend George's insistence, he stripped down to his white Calvin Klein briefs. The popular corpsman pretended to be bashful about wearing only his skivvies in the dance club, but the real cause of his embarrassment was that he could not lose his very noticeable hard-on. All night.

Despite the considerable time we spent together with the love-in group, this interview constitutes the only time Kevin and I spent alone together before his departure for an overseas assignment.

Kevin: I've known you for about six months. Why have you waited so long to interview me?
Zeeland: The longer I know people the more I know about them. When I first meet someone it's hard to know what questions to ask. Also, at first I wasn't sure how your interview would fit in. You're different from the other guys, you're not—
K: Gung ho military?
Z: Exactly. You've been in the Navy for almost five years but you've never once been on a boat. You don't talk like a sailor. You subscribe to the *New Yorker*. I don't know, do you see yourself as—
K: Yeah, I really don't see myself as a military person. I never wear my uniform unless I have to. I know that I'm not going to be in the military for the rest of my life. This is just a stepping stone for me.

Z: You've told me before that you're not especially attracted to military men.

K: I prefer civilians over the military, for the most part. Military people leave. They're unstable. Every time you turn around either you're leaving or they're leaving. And that makes it difficult. Civilians just seem to have a little more stability in them, and I like that. They're not going anywhere.

Z: That's a practical reason. Some of our friends have an attraction to other military men rooted in image; the haircut, the idea that men in the military are—

K: More butch.

Z: That's a big part of it, I think. You don't feel any of that?

K: Not really. Military men just don't turn me on. For the most part. Granted, at work there are a lot of men that are nineteen years old and really cute. But for some reason or other it just doesn't—I really prefer civilians. Not to stereotype, not to say that I like them because they're a civilian, but as a civilian I'm more apt to allow myself to feel more for them.

Z: Was there any part of your joining the military that had to do with some image of yourself as a man? For a lot of guys that seems to be sort of a secret reason.

K: No. I joined because I needed to get away from where I was. I'd been going to college for a year. I was laying in bed one day and I was thinking, God, I've got to do something with my life. Things aren't going the way I want them to. I've got all this stuff going on and I'm just not happy. I'm not doing as well in school as I should be because of all this stuff. I need to get away. I just decided: I'll join the military. The next day I called the recruiter and said, "I need to talk to you. I'm going to join the military, but I don't want anybody else to know, because I don't want them to influence my decision." I was eighteen. It was the first decision I made completely and totally by myself for myself.

Z: Why did you pick the Navy?

K: I went to the Air Force recruiter first, and I didn't like his attitude. Then I walked across the hall to the Navy people, and they were eager to have me.

Z: Did you know that you were gay when you joined?

K: Yes. I can look back to my childhood and know that I was gay. I remember the week I thought about it and realized: OK, I'm gay. It took me a week. I started to think about it on a Monday when I went to school. "I wonder if all this stuff that's going on means I'm gay." By Thursday of that week I was like, "Well, I guess I am."

Z: How old were you?

K: Twelve.

Z: What exactly was going on? How did you even know about being gay at that age?

K: Through a teacher of mine who I befriended. In retrospect it was a pretty bad experience.

My father and mother were having marital problems. My father left and joined the Army. This guy was my sister's art teacher. He was thirty. I went up to him and introduced myself, and we got to be friends. He was a person I looked up to; a father figure, since my father was gone. Then one day I was riding my bike around after school and I went to his house. He took me out to dinner. And it just developed into this friendship that eventually turned into a sexual relationship. At the time I thought it was cool.

Z: How exactly did it turn into a sexual relationship?

K: We went camping. We used to go to his parents' trailer up in the mountains. He talked to me about the things boys need to know growing up, like jacking off and things like that. We slept in the same bed as friends; it was no big deal. Then one morning we were there and we just started jacking off or whatever. That's how it started. It just went from there and got more and more intense.

Z: To where you eventually had anal sex?

K: A little bit of everything. And, you know, I was a little too young to be doing this.

Z: That's how you feel now, but you said at the time—

K: At the time it seemed like it was right, because this was a man that I respected. A teacher, someone I looked up to. So of course I thought it was the right thing to do. And of course I thought that I was the one who instigated everything. That's the way I was made to feel. But now I look back on it and I don't think that.

Z: You feel he betrayed your friendship by making it into a sexual relationship. How old were you when you began to look at it that way?

K: I guess I was fourteen when I started to realize that.

I didn't know what to do. I mean, I was a kid. I didn't know how to deal with it. So I told him anything he needed to hear, anything that was the right thing for me to say. [I] tried to please him. I was always left feeling like I had to do what was right to make him happy. Because if I didn't my life was just hell. 'Cause he was the most possessive—he would just get so upset.

Z: So did you finally just cut it off at some point?

K: Well, I joined the military. And left. And I still dealt with two years of hell after that.

Z: You'd been seeing him all that time?

K: All that time. He like, controlled me—

Z: Even after you were in the Navy?

K: He was there at my graduation from boot camp. One of the main reasons for me joining the Navy was to get away from him. It was horrible. I was twenty when I finally got him out of my life. So, I knew from the time I was thirteen that I was gay. And I knew how to have sex, and that seemed to go over well with a lot of people.

Z: So you did meet other people along the way. Mostly adults?

K: Yeah.

Z: Males and females?

K: Well, when I was in high school— [Laughs.] It all actually started because my best friend, who joined the Navy right out of high school, told everybody we worked with at this grocery store that I was a nymphomaniac. [Laughs.] I didn't find this out until after all these girls had been approaching me. I was wondering why things were going so well for me!

The first girl I ever had sex with was thirty-three at the time. It was pretty wild. I thought she looked really hot. It was intense. I went over to her place, we were looking at pictures and laying on the dining room floor, and the next thing you know we're going at it. And five hours later we're still going at it. I enjoyed it, but I couldn't get off. It took me hours and hours.

Z: That wasn't a problem you had with men?

K: No. Not at all. Then there were others. . . . See, this is why I think that guy just totally screwed me up. Because the first girl I ever had sex with was thirty-three, and I'm sixteen, and the next girl I had sex with was married. Obviously something is not right in my head for me to think that this is normal. I told her, "So what if you're married?" Because all this time I was having sex with a married man.

Z: What can you tell me about sex with women?

K: I definitely enjoyed it. I will admit that some of the best sex I ever had was with women. I think that first time ranks in the top ten.

Z: So why do you say then that you're gay and not bisexual?

K: Because I don't feel the same—I mean, just because I had sex with them doesn't mean I felt for them. I was having sex with a lot of people then that I didn't feel anything for. Sex then was *sex*; I didn't think of it as something that was a part of love or part of any feeling. It was just something you did. It was just fun. And now I don't look at it that way.

Z: You must have had some emotional feeling for the teacher.

K: Yeah. But then it became hatred. It wasn't until I got to San Diego here that I met someone that I cared for, and in conjunction had sex with.

Z: Did you think going into the Navy that there would be other gay men in it?

K: I honestly didn't think so. I thought I was going to have to spend the next six years living a closeted miserable life.

Z: It didn't turn out that way, though.

K: No!

Z: When did it start to get festive?

K: Two months out of boot camp, when I was in Chicago.

Z: In my notes on you here I have written "Corpsman 'A' school—'Like a Brothel.'"

K: [Laughs.] Corpsman "A" school was pretty wild. To say the least.

I met some guy in the gym on base, and he said, "You feel so tense from this workout. . . ." The whole classic "Let's go back to my place for a massage." That's how it started. Then I met one of the guys in "A" school with me. We kind of clocked each other. He started talking to me in the lounge, and we started queening out, having a good time. He invited me back to a friend's room in the barracks. And it was just queer heaven. All the fags hung out there. His room was the social center. And there were just sooooo many gay men who went in that room! Any time anyone would find anyone else, they would invite them into our little crowd. There was this one guy walking down the hall, we saw him and he had this cute little butt, and we knew he had to be gay, he had to be family. So of course we invited him into the room. We had a good network of friends. It wasn't anything seedy like bathrooms or hiding out in corners. It was all pretty open.

Z: How open are you in your job now? How gay can you be as a corpsman in the U.S. Navy?

K: I am myself. I go to work and I am no different than I am outside of work. The only thing that might be different is, if I queen out at work for the sake of entertainment, I look around first. And depending on who's around I still do it. I'm really not a different person at work.

Z: Do you see yourself as queeny?

K: No. I know I'm not the most masculine person, but I know I'm not a queen. I think I view myself as—I don't think it would be difficult for someone to figure out that I'm gay. Now at work I don't say anything about my boyfriend, but I do talk about, "Last night I went to the beach with my friend George. We watched the sunset. It was really nice." I don't go calling my friend Georgette instead of George.

Z: So you're not a queen, but you do sometimes queen out. Explain that.

K: Well, like if I'm talking with Ray and I just decide I'm going to go, "Oh honey! Stop!" then I just do it. Or if we're hanging out in the smoking area and there's some guy over on the other side that we're all talking about, I'll say, "Look at his cute butt!" Or snap. Just camping it up.

Z: How would you describe Ray at work?

K: Ray tries really hard not to look like a queen at work. I feel that he's uncomfortable with me, because we'll go down to the smoking area and I'll just go off. I'll be laughing and carrying on and talking about anything in the world, and he just kind of sits there and doesn't really say anything. Not at all like outside of work.

Z: So you think of yourself as being somewhere in between hypermasculine and effeminate, and you're comfortable being yourself at work, whereas you think that Ray is a queen but tries hard to butch it up, and so moves back and forth of either side of where you are in the middle?

K: Pretty much so.

Z: Has anyone ever given you any trouble about being gay in the Navy?

K: One guy gave me a hard time when I first started in patient administration in the hospital. He instantly clocked me as being gay, and was talking to all these other people in the department about me. One day after a couple weeks of dealing with him and his little games I just finally walked into the office, shut the door behind me, and threw down this article in front of him that I had cut out of a magazine saying how the most homophobic people are probably having problems with their own sexuality. I said, "Obviously there's a problem here. There's something inside you that you need to deal with, and until you deal with that I don't want to hear anything more from you. If you have any questions about anything you come and ask me; I don't want to hear any more of this stuff going around the department of you asking other people. Come right to me and I will tell you anything you need to know." So basically I told him that he was a faggot and he needed to figure this out and leave me alone. He was very pissed off at me and floored by all that. He told me later that he just wanted to pick me up and throw me through the window. And then he came to me a couple of days later and asked me all these questions about being gay.

Z: Like what?

K: Like "Are all gay men real effeminate? Do you have to be effeminate to be gay?"

Z: Did he ask you any questions about what you do in bed?

K: No. He didn't ask me anything like that. Then finally one day he was like, "What are you doing tonight?" "Nothing." "Well, why don't you come over? We can order pizza and watch movies." And I thought: The last thing in the world I want to do is spend time with you outside of work because I know you're an arrogant asshole. But I said, "OK."

I went over and we were talking, and we got a little closer. Of course we had lots of beer and pizza. And the next thing I know we're in the bedroom and I'm on top of him going at it.

Z: Wait a minute! How did you get in the bedroom?

K: I don't know exactly how it happened. We were just sitting around. He was being goofy. He wasn't being an asshole, like he was at work. We got closer, and closer, and then we started kissing. It turned out that he had been involved with a guy before, but the only time they ever had sex it would end with "Get away from me, don't touch me." So I just basically got him to relax. Eventually he got out of the Navy for being gay.

Z: He was the only person who ever gave you a hard time?

K: Yeah. Except one time at work when I got in an argument with somebody about gays in the military.

Z: Was there a lot of discussion on the issue after Clinton's election?

K: There were discussions, but the hospital is kind of different. Most people just kind of joke about it as something that's going to happen eventually anyway. Everyone at the hospital knows that there are a lot of gay people there.

Z: One time Gregg became very annoyed with you over your political apathy. You said that you didn't particularly care about Defense Department policy one way or the other. You said that you didn't feel any need to get involved.

K: It's never been a problem for me. I've never been discriminated against because of my sexuality. And I think a lot of people bring it on themselves. Like for Gregg, I think a lot of his problems as far as his sexuality in the military he brought upon himself, by saying that other people have to feel the way he feels. Which to me is just as wrong.

Z: How does Gregg feel that other people should feel?

K: I think he feels that homosexuality should be an issue. For me it's not an issue. It's obvious that people should not be discriminated against, but I don't like the whole idea of, let's make this an issue: we are being discriminated against, we need to fight, we need to be against everyone else.

Z: Of course you might feel differently if you'd been beaten by your shipmates or thrown in the brig for consensual sodomy.

K: Yeah, but I just honestly feel—Like my friend Dan, he's black, and he just feels [his race] has to be an issue. Everywhere he goes he sees this discrimination going on. It's like, we go into a restroom, we walk out, and he says, "Those two urinals next to me were empty. If it was a white man standing there anyone would have stood next to him. But because it was a black man standing there they all went to the other side." I'm like, why do you even see this? To me, it didn't look like anybody was being discriminated against by anybody else.

Z: I hope you recognize that as a blond, blue-eyed male you do enjoy certain privileges in American society.

K: Y-yeah. But as a homosexual I'm a minority, too.

Z: But no one necessarily knows about that, especially since you don't make an issue of it. You haven't relinquished those privileges.

K: [Pause.] I don't know. I don't think I hide it. Like I said before, I am me. People can like me for me, or not. I have a lot of straight friends that I'm sure know I'm gay but it's not an issue. They never bring it up.

Z: People who oppose allowing gays into the military usually admit that they don't know anyone gay. You say these people know, but there's often a gap between what people know and what they want to know. Have you come out to any straight Navy friends?

K: Yeah, I have.

Z: Well—tell me about Aaron [see Ray's interview]. How did you get to know him?

K: Through Ray and Josh one night at Cafe Roma. I thought he was cute. Ray just assumed that we were going to go home together because we started talking and everything, but I knew that Aaron was straight and I'm not going to violate that. I just don't think that's right. If he wants something to happen he's gonna make it happen. I'm not gonna force something on him. Unlike Ray and Josh.

Z: They did that with Aaron?

K: Well, Ray did. One night that we all went out to West Coast everyone was all over Aaron. He got really drunk and went back with Ray to some hotel. And of course they wake up the next morning and Ray's deciding that he's gonna have his way. I heard that nothing really happened; Ray just kind of tried to give him a blowjob.

Z: Aaron's straight—Is Aaron straight?

K: Aaron likes women, Aaron sleeps with women, Aaron has a good time with women, and he's married and everything else. That's what makes him happy. But I think if the right man came along he would also be willing to have a relationship with him. And I think the reason for that is he's comfortable with himself. If he were to have a relationship with a man it would be because that's what he wanted. It wouldn't be because he's a homosexual. It would be because it was the right person. It would be for the person, not the sex.

Z: Do you think he's special in that regard?

K: I don't think he's special. I know quite a few people that are like that. Different friends of mine have mentioned that it isn't the act of sex that's important, it's the person.

With Aaron I just think that—when I say he's comfortable with himself, I mean he knows what he likes, and if he likes a man then he's going to like that man. *For that man*, for the person. Not because—There are a lot of gay people who sleep with another man because, "Well I'm gay and he's another man and if we're going to have a friendship, or get to know each other, we're going to have to sleep together." You meet somebody, you sleep with them, and then the friendship starts.

With Aaron and I, we developed a friendship. We got to know each other, we hung out together, we would drink together and sit around and listen to music and talk. And one time we kissed. And one time we sat around and watched pornos and something a little more than that happened.

Z: What?

K: [Pause.]

Z: You just jacked off together? Or—

K: No. I gave him a blowjob. But I think that—

Z: Was it a straight porno?

K: Yeah. I think the reason that happened was because—The relationship that Aaron and I established was as friends. But I think that he felt a little more for me than just friends, and I felt a little bit more for him than just friends. But I knew nothing would ever come of a relationship with him. Just as I know or I feel that he knew that.

Z: So why was it OK for you to blow him and not Ray?

K: Because this was something that took a long time before it happened. It wasn't something I had forced on him. It was quite apparent to me that this was what he wanted.

Z: What signal did he give you?

K: It was just obvious. We were sitting there watching this movie and we started jacking off.

Z: Were there certain things he did to make it clear that he still thought of himself as straight? Did he make some excuses or impose some limitations?

K: No. That's why I say that he was comfortable with himself, because he didn't do that. This was something that he consciously decided was an OK thing to do. There were never any excuses afterward like "We were drunk and this just happened."

Z: Aaron came along to one of the love-ins, and there he seemed at times quite uncomfortable. He definitely wanted it made clear that he was straight. Do you still think of him as straight?

K: Yeah.

Z: Do you think what you did together was homosexual? Or not?

K: Well of course it was a homosexual act because it was two men. After it happened, it didn't happen again. There were a couple of other times that I slept with him, and we were close, but nothing happened. But it wasn't an issue. He never made excuses as to why not to do something with me. He still called me and wanted to get together and do things and just be the friends that we were. It didn't change.

Z: What do you think about Russell?

K: I really don't know that much about Russell. I think that, from what I've heard, he would probably be willing to do something. Once again I think he needs to—if he finds the right person. He's not going to be like a lot of gay men who just go out and sleep with someone because "We're two men and we're horny and we're gay so we're gonna do this."

Z: He sleeps in the same bed with Gregg, but makes it clear to him that he doesn't want to do anything sexual with him.

K: Just like Aaron made it very clear to Ray that he didn't want to do anything with him. Yet he was willing to allow that guard to be lowered for me. That's why I say it's the person.

Z: Ray, of course, is wont to call both you and Anthony sluts. Why do you think he says that? Do you think he means that?

K: Well, I think he means it. [Laughs.] Do I think of myself as a slut? Not really. But it depends. I know that throughout my life I've had a lot of sexual encounters. And throughout the last couple months I've had quite a few sexual encounters. I've used the excuse that I'm leaving. But I still don't think of it as all that many, in comparison to some people.

Z: Is it bad to be a slut?

K: It depends on how you view a slut. If you're talking about somebody that's going out every single night and sleeping with somebody different, that's pretty bad. Because there's got to be meaning behind the sex.

Z: Does there?

K: I think. Because I've gone through enough sex without meaning to know that I don't like that. Then it's just an act. It's just—there.

Z: What kinds of meaning have you found in your recent short-term sex relationships? Like, say, with Anthony?

K: Well, I really like Anthony. Our relationship—We got along well and everything, but I mean, I just—I pushed him away because I began to feel—It's like everything was going along well, then all of a sudden I just didn't feel the same way for some reason. I could tell that this wasn't something that was going to be a lifelong thing. So what's the sense? I'm a relationship-oriented person. I really think that when I am with some-one, the reason I am with them is because I want to pursue some sort of relationship. Granted, there are people that I quickly find out that this is just not a possibility, and henceforth I just—

Z: For example, Gregg and Sonny?

K: Yeah! [Laughs.]

Z: What attracted you to Gregg?

K: I really wasn't even attracted to Gregg that much. He'd been talking to me about going out to dinner, and we'd run into each other all over the place. Finally one day I said, "Yeah, let's go out to dinner." He invited me over. We talked, it was really nice, the conversation went well. But then after the third time we got together I just realized: this man has some whacked out points of view.

Z: Why did you have sex with him?

K: It was something that just happened. We were sitting there watching television, we were talking, we'd had—not a lot to drink, but we had a couple drinks. We were very relaxed and very comfortable. It had been a while since I had had anything.

Z: You were horny, you'd been drinking . . .

K: Well, yeah, all these excuses, but also I thought, "He's a nice guy." I thought I'd give him a chance. Then after we went out a couple times, I just realized: this guy is not in line with the way I think.

Z: Then there was Sonny . . .

K: God. I don't remember how long ago I met Sonny. We were at West Coast and someone decided that everyone was going to give everyone else a kiss. So we did. And Sonny and I, for some reason . . . when we kissed it ended up being more passionate and longer. I'll be honest, I was not planning on going home with him. But all of a sudden Ray arranges it so conveniently that Sonny would take me home. So we ended up back at my place, and the polite thing to say was, "Well, why don't you come up for a drink." The next thing I know, he's still there, and we're talking, and something happened.

Z: It's tempting to offer a cheap instant pop psychology analysis explain-ing your submission to Gregg and Sonny as the inevitable result of your twisted relationship with the controlling pedophile schoolteacher.

K: But it really does all fall back on that! There are so many people I had sex with when I was younger, not because I wanted to, but because it was the expected thing to do. That's something I have seriously been working to get away from, and I think I'm doing a pretty good job. Doing things that I want to do for *me*, not because somebody else wants me to do them.

But I still find like in that instance, I'm sitting with Sonny and it's getting late, and of course any time I drink a lot my hormones go up and my resistance goes down, and I say, "Oh well, let's do it."

Z: Get it over with.

K: Pretty much!

Z: But for whatever reason, you have this effect on people. Both those two were quite taken with you, and I guess there have been many others. And you know my theory that the reason our first couple of parties were so much fun was that you functioned as a kind of sexual magnetic pole. Gregg and Sonny were still lusting after you, Anthony of course wanted you, and—well, I find you attractive, too. I admit it.

K: Well, let me ask you a question: why? Why do you think all these people are finding me attractive?

Z: Um. I'd rather ask you first.

K: I don't understand why! I really don't, but I know that for some reason or other [stutters in exasperation] people find me attractive. And I don't know what it is. I know—I don't know. I just don't understand—

Z: You don't have any ideas?

K: I mean, I know I'm a nice person, but why? Why does that make me any different?

Z: Well, of course there are also physical attributes that they appreciate about you.

K: Well why? [Laughs.] I don't think—I mean—But I know that people do find me sexually attractive, and I know that for some reason or other they tend to fall for me. I know this from years of experience.

Z: And hours of frustrated messages on your answering machine.

K: Yeah! People fall for me. And I don't understand why. [Pause.] So why? I ask you.

Z: Well, I haven't "fallen" for you, so I can't say for sure. But you do have a very definite sexual energy about you; a mischievous little-boyish quality, a certain arresting . . . naughtiness. I in fact felt a little left out, because I was the only person in the crowd who didn't sleep with you.

K: [Laughs.] Wait a second! There were a couple others!

Z: Who? Ramon.

K: Ramon! And Ray!

Z: You slept with Ray before.

K: No I didn't. Well, the two of us have fallen asleep together. And there was one time when he tried to—See, that's why I fall back on Aaron. I say that Ray forced himself on Aaron more than I did, because I never forced myself on him, and I know that Ray did.

Z: Why did you find Anthony attractive, and not Ray?

K: Ray's just not my type. Not that I have a type.

Z: What attracts you to a man?

K: For me to be attracted to a man they need to be masculine. They need to be a man. I don't like men that are very effeminate, because if I wanted a woman I'd be with a woman. I like men, and the characteristics of men. Nice chest, nice arms. Masculine personality.

Z: You never answered my question as to why Ray calls you a slut when here he was trying to blow Aaron and you.

K: I guess because I'm a little bit more successful. [Laughs.]

Z: What do you hope for yourself now as you prepare to go overseas?

K: When I get over there I want to do a lot to improve myself. I want to go to school, I want to start working out more. I don't want to be as social as I am here. One of the things that I'm worried about going overseas, I know that it's a temporary situation. I know that I'm only going to be there for two years. What's the sense of me developing all sorts of friendships that I know are going to be forced to end?

Z: That's part of military life, isn't it? These transitory relationships.

K: Which is one of the things that I don't like. I've established friendships with people who have left the area that I've maintained contact with—in Washington and Orlando and the Bay Area and Bolivia and Okinawa. If I consider someone a friend, the distance isn't going to stop me from being a friend. One of the things that's going to be difficult for me is, I have so many friends here in San Diego, and I'm going to be so distant from them . . . and I don't think that just because I move that it should end. Because friendship to me is very important.

Jack: "Don't Kiss Me, I'm Straight"

Down the street from the Naval Training Center in San Diego are several strip joints and peep show arcades frequented by sailors and an often larger number of gay civilian "military chasers." One arcade is particularly cruisy despite capricious intermittent crackdowns by the staff, who bark at, threaten, eject, or otherwise tyrannize cruisers who fail to spend the requisite tokens or scurry cockroach-like from the view of the video surveillance cameras, or are simply unlucky enough to cross one of the clerks on a day when his power trip wants exercising. The cruisers sometimes have an even harder time with each other, as they are a fiercely competitive lot. All such places have a corrupt and undemocratic etiquette, and persons laying despotic territorial claims. Undisputed queen of the peep show down the street from the Naval Training Center is Boris. It is a title he works to retain through sheer unmitigated gall.

Boris is quite beautiful. At 26 he is younger than the other queens who fear him. He stalks the arcade with the grace and stealth of an alley tom with pedigree. A Russian blue, I decide. After my first few visits I dare to approach him. Our mutual Friend from the Park had introduced us, I remind him and—

Boris' cat eyes burn, his military-chaser mane flares. He arches his back and hisses "I don't know who you are, but I do not like your style. If you're going to cruise here—and it appears that you intend to—then you had better learn how to keep quiet and stay out of the way. I don't know where you've been before, but this is a very straight place. I've been coming here for five years. Everyone who works here knows me and they'll kick out anyone I tell them to. I don't tell anyone else how to run their backroom. This one is mine. Do you understand?" I answer Boris in a serene and deferential way, successfully resisting an impulse to "key" his classic American luxury sedan on the street outside (which is exactly what I learned someone else did a few weeks subsequent.)

Later I run into Boris at a gay bar. He buys me a drink and calls me his "cruising sister." He explains that he prefers to work "The Library," but admits it does get lonely. "Once in a while I just need to go back to the bar scene to remind myself who I am." We sit near the door and he makes loud expert pronouncements on the men's endowments as they enter. I joke that he could form a new gay activist group, Size Queen Nation. Similar to me, Boris does not demand that his men be buff and perfectly coifed and attired, and allows for what he calls "straight appeal"—masculine scruffy edges—with the reluctant guilty air of someone who understands that this is not gay community p.c.

At The Library, Boris only gives blowjobs and only to straight men. He says he prefers sailors because Marines too often want to get fucked, and Boris does not do that. I ask him how he reacts if the sailor wants to blow him. "If they're bad at it I don't mind. If their teeth scrape. But if they're too good at it you know they've done it before." Which means the subject is a fag and a different set of rules applies. (Boris is familiar with the concept of internalized homophobia. A certain kind of bookstore queen eroticizes the self-abasement of "straight worship." But it is also true that bar scene gays have their own flavors of self-loathing and are more likely to be infected with attitude and HIV than the straight men Boris services, and less likely to possess the masculine attributes they typically place the same worth on as he.)

Boris is masterfully smooth in his verbal approaches, but his preferred method is to toss little Post-it notes into the arcade booths of men he finds attractive. The notes begin with an apology for disturbing, followed by instructions on how to signal if they would like a blowjob. I observe several men mutter curses or exclaim "Fuckin' fag!" and once in a while someone takes the note to the staff and gets Boris in trouble. But many more either offer the signal or at least stick their heads out of their booths in a curious and inquiring manner.

The key to success for Boris and the other cruisers is to convince the sailors (or civilians; a premium is placed on military men but others will do) that getting blown by another man is not "gay." Boris gets a sailor in a booth and flicks to a channel that shows a woman fellating a man. He points to the woman and says, "That's me," indicates the man and says, "That's you." The sailor protests, "But that's gay!" Boris shakes his head with the stern intransigence of a teacher who has given this lesson a thousand times. "No no. *That*'s me. I'm gay. *That*'s you. You're straight. Do you understand?" Often, he says, they do.

Our Friend from the Park tells me a story, too, about how he has saved a drunken Marine from arrest for indecent exposure. He had stopped his car earlier to flirt with the Marine, who was on his way to a strip club. Later, the boy was standing on Rosecrans Street beside a female prostitute who he had permitted to open his fly, inviting the attentions of "America's finest," the San Diego Police Department. Our Friend happens by with his newly acquired bogus officer's windshield decal and manages to convince the cops that he is the Marine's commanding officer. The cops release the Marine into our Friend's custody. He lectures the Marine on the evils of prostitutes and tells him that there are other ways to find sexual release, that sometimes "buddies have to take care of each other." The Marine is doubtful, saying his buddies would never do that. But after learning that this kind of thing is "not gay," he accompanies our Friend to his motel room and, at his behest, happily takes out all of his pent-up aggression against officers on our Friend, who enjoys being fucked hard by straight men.

For the skeptics among my readers I shift my research into first person. One night I arrive at the arcade early, and so am there as other familiar cruisers began to punch in for the late shift. A Manila-born ex-Navy dental technician I recognize sees me and smiles; I wave hello. Ducking the cameras, he approaches. "Who else is here?" George asks warily, "Boris?" He appears supremely pleased when I tell him that he will not have to compete with the Russian blue.

Other cruisers drift in and out. We shift, mill about, exchange grimaces at the appearance of undesirable subjects, but an hour passes and The Library remains bereft of quarry.

Out of nowhere, or more probably the strip joint next door, four drunken sailors in uniform come tumbling in and jam into one booth loudly shouting and falling about. All cruisers immediately converge to file by and throw appraising glances. A man in his forties smiles at the sailors and says, "Boy you guys are cheap to have to share a quarter movie!" "That's us," one squid (there is no other word for him) answers happily, "just cheap drunk sailors!" "Drunken *horny* sailors, I'll bet," the man answers, leering.

I swear I'm not making this up.

But George seizes the moment. "Hey, there's a free one here!" the Filipino calls out from the door of a large private booth with a locking door. "A free one?!" a tall sailor with glasses echoes and in an instant the door behind them clicks shut and locks. Muffled sounds of conversation from behind the door, more tokens dropping in, then quiet.

Other cruisers disperse. But I—you—*we* need to know what is happening in there. The neighboring booth opens and I step inside. As Boris, my teacher, has shown me to do, I climb up on the bench and gingerly lift the plastic grate that covers the top of the stall. Thinking of Laud Humphries, and reminding myself of my title Research Assistant at the Center for Research and Education in Sexuality at San Francisco State University—but not denying the thrill I feel in playing voyeur—I peer over the top of the partition down into the next stall.

The Filipino ex-dental technician and the squid sit on opposite sides of the spacious, six foot square "mini-theater" booth. Because of the volume of the video and the distance between them all dialogue is shouted. (From my notes after returning home:)

"How long has it been since you had pussy?"

"Too long! Not since I was with my girlfriend back in Norfolk."

"Oh, so you haven't had it in a while then. You must be very horny! What do you like to do for sex?"

"Everything!"

The video booth has dual controls. George uses his to flip to a gay video. "You like to do *every*thing?"

"Well, maybe not everything." The sailor hits the channel changer. George hits it again.

"Can your girlfriend give you a blowjob as good as that?"

"Yeah, I guess."

"I'm sure you noticed this is a weird place. There's a lot of weird people around here. I bet some of these faggots around here have asked you if you want a blowjob before. Has anybody asked you that?"

"No, uh-uh."

"You ever get a blowjob from a guy before?"

"No. Uh-uh."

"No? A guy can give you a better blowjob than a girl can. It's better, I'm serious. What would you say if somebody asked you?"

"What?"

"What would you say if some guy asked you if you wanted a blowjob?"

"I don't know."

"Well, you want one?"

"What?"

"Do you want a blowjob?"

"I don't know." The squid asks: "What's in it for me?"

George laughs. "What do you want to be in it for you?"

"I don't know. Money."

"Money! Hey, you'll be getting a free blowjob!"

"Yeah. But you'll be getting something, too."

"But I'm already paying for the tokens." More wavering, some pauses. George isn't begging—yet. "Why don't you come back later without your friends."

"Fuck my friends!"

I anticipate George's success. So does he. "You're pretty drunk." The squid agrees. "You think you can even handle it? Can you even get it up?" Very good, I think to myself, hanging like a monkey from the top of the booth: offer him an excuse and present him a means to affirm his masculine virility.

"You better have a lot of tokens." The deal is clinched. The squid waits as George runs out and returns with a five-dollar roll.

The sailor begins to undo his fly. The ex-dental tech tries to help him with it but gets his hand swatted away. The sailor takes out his large erect penis and George goes down on it. He tries to rub the sailor's thigh with his free left hand, and is again pushed off. Affection would be queer. George's head is bobbing. He pauses to take out and hold the sailor's penis and admire it. The sailor complains, "Don't stop." After a few minutes the sailor's head rolls about, and then the Filipino, with elegance and dignity, is spitting semen out into the ashtray. The sailor seems very pleased with himself. He shouts, "Hey, thanks a lot man!" and leaves to find his friends.

Approximately one hour later he returns. George, of course, is still there. The sailor finds him and says, "I'm back! You better hurry, though. I'm almost not drunk anymore!"

On my next visit I watch the same scene play out with the ex-dental tech and another sailor. This sailor tries to politely decline. He has a broken leg. George becomes insistent and aggressive, won't take no for an answer. He makes a grab for it. The sailor becomes indignant and hobbles away. This time, I identify with the sailor, and feel he should have bastinadoed George with his crutch.

The subject of this interview, Jack, is a 28-year-old gay Navy mess cook of mixed European ancestry from Alabama and California. He recently was promoted to the rank of chief petty officer. Anthony introduced us, having gone home with Jack one night after responding to his Marine-style "high and tight" haircut. Jack's story is remarkable for the degree of his sexual involvement with men who call themselves straight.

Jack: I was working at a fast food restaurant my senior year in high school. I met this girl, Jan. She sat behind me in my economics class. Then she started working at the restaurant. We got really close. I guess she knew from the start that I was gay, but I didn't tell her for the longest time.

One night she said, "We're going to meet one of my friends; her name is Dawn." We went to the drive-in. They were sitting in the front seat, I was in back. The window was fogged up. Jan wrote something on the windshield. I was like, what does that say? And then I realized it said "Jan loves Dawn." I was like, oh no, I can't believe they're gay! Then Jan erased it with her hand. I played stupid like I didn't know what was going on. We were driving home, then Jan says, "Jack, there's something we have to tell you." "What?" "We're gay." "Oh, really." "Is there any problem with that?" "No, whatever." They both knew at the time that I was. They were trying to fish it out of me, and I wouldn't come out and tell them.

Finally we went—it was almost the end of our senior year. We started going to the beach a lot. There was a gay beach right next to it, but you had to go over these rocks. A couple weeks went by, and finally they said, "Jack, why don't you come down here with us." We went for a walk, and I was like in shock that I was at a gay beach. That night I ended up telling them. We'd been drinking, and on the way home I said, "Jan and Dawn, there's something I've got to tell you." "What?" "I'm gay." "We knew."

To backtrack a little, back in January I had already decided to go in the Navy. Jan said she was interested, so I got her to come in, and Dawn said, "I'll do it too." The three of us joined the Navy the same day. I didn't actually go to boot camp until August. Jan went in September, and Dawn went a couple weeks later. We sort of lost contact with each other, because we were all stationed in different places.

I went to boot camp and it was really hard. It was scary enough as it was—your company commander, the way he used to talk. Then you were paranoid about being gay and sleeping and showering with eighty men.

The way they did things in boot camp, the guy that you were bunkmates with, you helped make each other's racks; you took care of him, he took care of you. My bunkmate's name was Michael. He and I got to be really good friends. We went all the way through boot camp, graduated, then we were together in school after basic training, still in San Diego. He was from Idaho. He'd come home with me to Orange County for the weekend all the time. One of us would sleep on the floor, one would sleep on the bed.

One time my sister was there, and all the other rooms were taken. She was drunk, so she wanted to sleep on the floor. I told Michael, "Hell, where am I going to sleep? Scoot on over, I'm going to sleep on the bed!" I had a king-sized bed, and he didn't mind. We were both drinking, and hands got to getting frisky, and before we knew it it was happening.

He was straight. Afterwards he said, "I can't believe I did that. I don't want you to say anything." I said, "God, why would I want to say anything? I'd be in just as much trouble as you."

Zeeland: What exactly did you do?

J: He was a top and he would let me blow him. That was it. Well, after that we both got orders, and then we got transferred. I went to Florida. Got to my first ship and I met this guy Craig. We worked together. After a couple weeks he asked me, "Hey, you wanna go have a beer?" "Sure." We got to know each other. For my nineteenth birthday he took me out. We got a hotel room together. It was a Friday night.

He was straight. Supposedly. We went to the bar and we got drunk and we went back to the hotel room. He was in the shower and I was brushing my teeth. I opened the curtain and I got my toothbrush holder and I poked him in the butt with it. Well, he had to get revenge on me so he got a handful of shampoo and threw it in my face. And I think this was done on purpose. I'm like, "Get out of there, I've got to get in the shower! My eyes are burning!" "Well hurry up and get in here then. I'm not done."

He started it. I was in the shower washing my eyes, and he kept on putting his dick up to me and rubbing my butt with it. We had sex, and afterwards he was very paranoid. "I just can't believe I did that." "Are you gay?" "No." Then he asked me if I was, and I was afraid to tell him yes, so I told him no. "Well, why did you do that?" "Why did *you* do that?" And we messed around a lot for a couple years.

Z: For years?

J: Yeah. Until I did the crazy thing and decided to get married. I married this girl that I had grown up with. She got pregnant. I went overseas on my cruise, and Craig and I still messed around overseas.

Z: Was he having sex with women at the same time, too?

J: Yeah. He had a girlfriend. And every port we went to we'd always go out together and party, get a hotel room, and go mess around. But he always—he never—he said he was straight. I didn't question him because if I did then he wouldn't want to mess around no more. So I just left it as it was. He said he wasn't gay, but he would suck dick. But he would not let me fuck him, he never did, not once. He was always the top in this situation. And he would not kiss. Not one time. That's really strange. If you're gonna suck dick but you won't kiss . . . and the only time we messed around was when we were drunk. One night we did it four times. "What the hell? He's got to be gay!" But I didn't want to scare him. I figured he was just coming out. But to this day—

Matter of fact, he called me one night last summer. I was watching TV. He was drunk. We started talking, and he started beating around the bush about, "Yeah, we've had some good times." "What are you saying, Craig?" He wouldn't come out and say it. So finally I said, "There's something I want to tell you that I never have. I just want to know how you feel about this. I hope it doesn't cause any heartache in our friendship, 'cause we've known each other for nine years. But I'm gonna tell you flat out right now. I'm not gonna bullshit with you no more. I'm gay." He said, "Yeah, I knew you were." I asked him, "Are you?" He said, "No. You are the only man that I've ever been to bed with. You're the only man that I ever will." I said, "Craig, that just seems really odd. You say you're not gay, and yet you go to bed with me and you have sex with me. It's just not—it doesn't make sense. Either you're bi or—" And he didn't want to claim that he was bi, he just wanted to claim that he was straight, that I was the only guy that he would ever go to bed with because he loved having sex with me. "Whatever." I think he's very confused. He just doesn't want to admit to himself that he's gay.

Z: You don't think he enjoyed being with this woman and his other girlfriends?

J: Y-yeah. Yeah. But I don't know, it just—it's really weird. I don't know how to explain it. Honestly.

Z: Did you guys ever have sex aboard ship?

J: Yeah. Where I worked at, it was pretty private. So Craig and I used to mess around in there.

Z: Behind a door that you could lock?

J: Oh yeah. In the galley. Especially overseas—if we didn't feel like staying in a hotel we'd come back and mess around on the ship.

When I was on the ship, I knew guys that—I didn't know for sure, but I had ideas of guys that were gay. There was a guy in our division, he was such a queen. Another cook. Black guy. His name was Gary. And everybody in the division knew he was gay. I mean, the whole ship just about knew. He was pretty popular. He used to run the ice cream parlor. He would put these ice cream cones in his mouth and act like he was sucking a dick. Guys used to get a kick out of it. He had these massive hot dogs and he would sit there and deepthroat them in front of all these guys. Hot sauce bottles—he didn't care what it was, as long as it had the shape of a dick or close to it. Some guys sort of got offended by it, but most would laugh. We were out to sea one time, and Gary was walking around the berthing in this pink lingerie. [Laughs.] I used to sleep not too far from him, and I was laying in my rack, and he came by. I was like, "What the fuck are you doing?" I shut my curtains and he just walked on by. The guys were all laughing and carrying on with him. Some guys would call him a faggot, and he'd just laugh at 'em. As long as he didn't say he was gay they couldn't prove anything.

Z: Do you know if he had sex with any of them?

J: Well, he's the one who went up to this one kid when he came back drunk and was sucking his dick while the kid was asleep. That was it. The next day he was gone.

But all my close friends—I never really heard 'em doggin' out "faggots." I don't remember any negative comments. Of course me trying to hide it, we'd go to all these straight bars, we'd dance with girls and whistle at 'em and carry on, and I was like, "Ugh." But I had to play along with it 'cause I didn't want them to know.

The main reason I got married was the fear of people knowing that I was gay. It was hard for me, having sex with a woman. I would do it because I had to. We were married for four years. The average straight man loves to go down and eat a woman out. I tried that one time and it made me sick. It stunk. And she wanted me to do that. I told her, "I don't do that." It didn't do anything for me. And there just wasn't that love. She still doesn't know I'm gay.

It took her a couple months to get pregnant. We had our first kid while I was overseas. When I got back he was three months old. The whole time

I was overseas I messed around with Craig. I came back, we'd been married a year already. Of course we probably spent at most two months together because I was gone so much. When I got back I saw my first child, and our marriage was sort of—I think she felt that I wasn't happy being married to her. I cared for her, I just didn't want to be married to a woman.

We left Florida and we got transferred up to Washington, D.C. She got pregnant again. It was an accident. I was pretty pissed, because I wasn't ready. "Oh well, here we go again. This is it, you're gettin' fixed, because I'm not having any more kids." So she did after she had my second one.

While we were stationed in Florida I had a good friend. I met him when I was on my ship. His name was Alex and he was a really good-looking guy. He had an awesome body. He was an engineer and used to work down in the engine spaces, and he'd wear these coveralls. When I'd talk to him on the ship he would unzip his coveralls all the way down to his crotch and be playing with himself right there in the passageway. I was like, oh my God, somebody's gonna walk by and think that we're gay! So I would try to ignore him and walk off. Even though I didn't want to. I was trying to figure out if he was gay or not.

When I got transferred up to D.C., the ship I had been on, they were up in Virginia. So I got ahold of Alex and I invited him to come on up. I picked him up at the bus station and he spent three days with my wife and me. Well, my wife was working part time at night. She went and bought me and him a case of beer. We put the kids to bed, she went to work, and he and I were gonna sit and talk about old times. We hadn't seen each other in about eight months.

Alex and I are sitting on the couch, and we're getting pretty loaded by this time. I'm in the kitchen, and he comes in and grabs my butt. I'm like, "Whoa. No way. You didn't just do what I think you did." So he puts his arm around me and grabs me and puts his mouth on me and kisses me. We start making out. "Alex, are you gay?" "Yeah." And he was married also, before.

Z: So he had been teasing you on the ship with his zipper?

J: I asked him later on that evening what that was all about. He said, "I thought I would get your attention. I could just read you that you were gay." I said, "How? I'm not a queen." "I just had a feeling you were." He said when he was growing up he never had any ideas that he was gay. He got married to this really pretty girl. In fact, we were both on the cruise together and got married about the same time. Well, when he came back, he found out that his wife had turned into a prostitute—fucked him over really bad. And he said, "Fuck this. I'll never go to bed with another woman again. I'm gonna try to be gay."

I didn't question him. The weekend that he was up in Virginia with me—my wife worked the whole weekend at night, so we had a lot of time together to ourselves when she put the kids to bed and it was just him and me. We had sex. It was really weird, because I used to drool over this guy. It was like a dream.

For a while he used to come up all the time. Then all of a sudden he stopped. I never found out what his reasons were. Another friend of mine told me that Alex let some guy blow him on the ship, and I guess this guy wrote on the bathroom wall that "Alex has a big dick" or something. Alex found out that this was on a stall wall and he was like, "Fuck this." I think that's why he stopped coming up. I think he got scared.

My ex-wife and I started having a lot of problems. She never complained about sex; she just said that she felt I didn't love her enough. Then we got into some really evil battles. It just got ugly. So I said, "Well maybe we need to go our separate ways for a while. I'll move out and maybe things will heal and it'll work out." The next day I came in from work and she was gone. She had packed up and took the kids. I didn't know where she was. I was pretty pissed, and then I heard she had flown back to California. We got our divorce.

I was still pretty closeted. I had two roommates who moved in, because I had a three-bedroom apartment. They were straight. I used to go out to all the straight bars with them. Then this guy started working with me in the Pentagon. Steve. He was in the Army. Really good-looking guy. And from day one I had a crush on this guy. He was married. I was like, "Oh well, this will never happen."

I was going through my divorce and I was having some rough times, and Steve and his wife, they used to invite me over to his house a lot. Then his wife got pregnant, and he used to always complain how he wasn't getting sex, and here I had a crush on him. Three or four nights a week I was at their house. Weekends we used to get drunk together. We got to be really good friends.

Finally after a while Steve's wife told him that she thought I was gay. His wife had ideas I was, because when I would spend the night I would do laundry and iron his uniforms when I'd iron mine, and shit like that. Finally Steve said, "There's something I've got to talk to you about." He acted like he was really pissed. He said, "Jack, I'm gonna ask you one question and I want the fuckin' truth. Are you gay? I'm not gonna say anything to nobody if you are, just tell me the truth." "Yeah." "My brother's gay, I have nothing against it. If that's what you want, that's your prerogative, but just keep it to yourself. I'm gonna tell you something. I'm married, I'm straight, I have no ideas of ever having a homosexual relationship. So you might as well get that out of your mind. It's not gonna happen. My second question is: Are you in love with me?" That was another hard one to swallow. I said, "Yeah, I am." "Get it out of your mind. If I ever get interested I'll let you know, trust me I will. But as for the time being: no. Just forget it." And we stayed friends after that. We still stay in contact.

We've talked about the gay issue in the military and Steve says, "I don't know what the big fucking problem is. I don't know why these people are so paranoid. I'm sure there's all kinds of gay people in the Army. If they're gay they're gay, that's what they want. If they want to look and admire if I have a nice butt, hey, I take it as a compliment, if they say I got a nice dick or whatever. As long as they don't touch me."

My feeling on the whole situation is, a lot of us just want—if Clinton issues an executive order lifting the ban, I don't foresee myself coming out. If somebody asks if I'm gay, I'm gonna say no, because it's too early right now to say yes. I wanna see how things go, and maybe I will, maybe I won't. I talk to a lot of guys I know that are in the Navy and are gay, and I think what a lot of us want is just the security of—that I can go to a gay bar, and I can sit there and relax and not have to worry about the Naval Investigative Service coming in and snatching me and saying, "You're gay, you're gone." Because it's not right. What I do on the outside is my business. It's just like heterosexuals. They don't bring it to work. That's the issue. You leave sex and all that outside. If that happens, of course I believe you should be punished.

Z: Do you think you should have been punished for having sex with Craig on-board ship?

J: If anybody found out, sure. If somebody walked in, of course. Because I mean—it was wrong, we shouldn't have been doing that.

Z: Why was it wrong? Who did it hurt?

J: Who did it hurt? It didn't hurt nobody, because nobody knew. But I mean if somebody had walked in and caught us, of course we should have been punished. I knew it was wrong. You don't bring sex to work, and that's at work, it's on the ship. It's not the "Love Boat."

J: On my second ship, during Desert Storm, there was a guy who used to work for me named Bruce. He was such a queen, and I knew from day one that he was gay. He was just so obvious. And the guys used to tease him and call him a girl.

After being on the ship for about a month—Bruce used to hang out at the galley next door. I was like, what's he doing over there all the time?

So one night I went over and there was like ten guys there. Bruce was with them, and it was obvious that they were all gay. As soon as I walked in everybody got all paranoid. I played stupid and borrowed a cookbook. Then I came back and I made it a habit to go over there once a week and see. A month went by and by that time there were twenty guys there.

So this went on for half the cruise, then one of the guys that used to hang out there got stupid one night. He was in the shower and he made the move on this boy, grabbed his butt. Then they started terrorizing, wanting to do one of these witch-hunts. "Who else do you know on the ship who's gay? You better tell us." And he said, "Fuck you. I'm not telling you shit. I don't know anybody else on this ship who's gay." But he got an honorable discharge out of it.

After we left Desert Storm we went to the Philippines. I went out with a couple of my friends to these bars. Oh God, it was so gross. These women were grabbing you as soon as you walked in the door, grabbing your crotch, grabbing your butt, telling you "Let's go to the room and fuck." "No thanks." All these married guys, it didn't matter. They just go in there, get a girl and leave, come back, go get another girl. I guess it was ten dollars to get laid. These guys had been out to sea for four months so all of them were horny as hell. But every port is like that. As soon as you get to the port all the guys just go crazy.

Z: What can you tell me about the shellback initiation that I may not have already heard?

J: I don't know. It was different. Of course when I went through it they were more open-minded about it. Now with sexual harassment and all this other crap going on they're cracking down on all those initiations. It's not as fun as it used to be. They'd whip you with firehoses. And just torment you the whole day. Making you eat all kinds of crazy wild stuff, throwing stuff on you, hitting you.

Z: Were there any aspects that were ever erotic to you at all?

J: No.

Z: Not even at the end? Being on a carrier with all those naked men?

J: Well, I guess that, sort of. After you go through, everybody has to strip down on the flight deck and you're down to your underwear. Some guys would even take their underwear off and throw them away because they were so trashed out with junk and crap and stink. Matter of fact, there were a bunch of Marines right ahead of us and of course my eyes were focused up there! I was trying to hurry up and get through so I could get up there.

Z: You have a Marine Corps haircut, not a Navy haircut. Why?

J: I don't know. Just a habit.

One of my really good friends is a Marine. He was on my first ship. A lot of my friends on the ship were Marines. This guy Jason was like my best friend. We used to party together a lot. And there was a time when I thought he was gay.

We were in Italy, we were in port, and him and I decided to take the weekend off and go to this island and get a hotel together. Of course the hotel was full; the only room they had was one with a double bed. So we shared a bed. And he said, "I don't wanna wake up in the middle of the night and you be sucking my dick, Jack." So I just blew it off. Then the next morning he woke up and said, "Will you do me a favor? Will you massage my back?" Both of us [were] in our underwear. "Are you sure?" "Yeah." So I'm sitting on his butt and massaging his back. Of course I'm hard as a rock. He's like, "Oh man this feels so good, don't stop." So I'm going and going and going. "Well, it's my turn." So he gave me a massage. I was waiting for something to happen. I wasn't going to make the first move. But nothing happened. He got married and then after my divorce—

I just recently told him that I'm gay. And he's got no problem with it. He's pretty open-minded. "Just be careful and don't let the military find out." He said, "Yeah, I had my suspicions after you got your divorce that you were. But I was never gonna ask you." I asked him if he knew anybody that was gay, and he said, "No. I'm sure there's plenty of Marines that are gay, but they don't come out." Because the Marines are the roughest of the services about that.

Z: There's a famous rivalry between sailors and Marines, and I'm finding that there often seems to be a sexual charge to it.

J: Yeah. I don't know what it is. And I was that way for a while, and sometimes I still find myself attracted to Marines. I don't know if it's because of the butch thing, the rough and tough image of Marines, or the bodies. Most Marines are built and buff. There's a lot of Navy guys that get their hair cut like Marines, but they're actually sailors. Like Anthony, me. There's a lot.

We went to Wolf's [a San Diego leather bar] a couple weeks ago and there was this kid there, twenty-two or twenty-three years old. He was just infatuated with Marines. He thought I was in the Marine Corps. Of course I told him right away, "I'm not in the Marine Corps. I'm in the Navy." And as soon as I told him that he didn't want anything to do with me. I was like, get over it! But I guess, being that most of my friends before I came out were Marines, I was more attracted to Marines than sailors. Marines have got nice uniforms, of course. The nicest of them all.

Z: Every sailor tells me that.

J: They do. They've got nice uniforms. We've got the ugliest.

Z: You don't like Navy uniforms?

J: God no!

Z: Tell me about your first "gay" relationship.

J: Sam and I started talking when I was on cruise. I found out that he was from Alabama. I told him I was originally from there. From the first day I met him there was something about him that I really liked.

We got back from Desert Storm and I knew he didn't have a car, so I used to always invite him to go to Orange County to visit friends of mine. We'd go up every weekend; we'd get drunk and have a lot of fun and party. We used to always sleep in the living room, but one time Robert, my friend, said, "Hey you guys can sleep in the guest room, but you're gonna have to sleep together." And of course he joked about it. He said, "I don't wanna hear no strange noises comin' out of there." Robert was like my best friend, him and his wife. He was straight. Of course him and I messed around once before also.

Sam and I were laying in bed. We were pretty trashed, and I made the move on him. So it happened. We didn't ask each other if we were gay. Then a couple months went by and we were seeing each other.

Z: Had he had sex with men before?

J: No. Never. I was the first. But he knew he was gay. So we decided to move off base and get an apartment together. It worked out really nice. We had a two-bedroom apartment. We used to sleep in my room, but we had his room made up so when we had our straight friends over from work, they would think that he was sleeping in his bed. I used to hate that. I used to tell him I didn't want anybody from work coming to spend the night over, because I didn't want to sleep separate. The thing was, Sam was more paranoid than I was. We always had to go to straight bars. It just got to the point—

We'd been living together for a year already. Well, it was December of last year. I really hadn't come out, just to him. And my best friend David that I work with, he sort of had an idea that I was gay, and I had an idea that he was.

I used to come to work and I'd have bruises and stuff. David was like, "God Jack, what's wrong with you? Is he hitting you?" "No, we just wrestle around." Then finally I told him. He said, "You've gotta stop that." I told him I was gay and he told me he was and I invited him over. Sam was in Alabama on Christmas vacation.

David asked me to go out to a gay bar. I was pretty paranoid. "No, I can't. Sam would kill me." "Come on. He's not gonna know. Nobody's gonna tell." So he took me to The Loft. That was the first gay bar I'd been to. I walked in, and this guy that I used to work with was there with his lover. He was so shocked when I saw him. He was like, "Oh my God! What are you doing in here?" He knew David was gay but he didn't know I was. I started going there, and David took me to a lot of gay bars in San Diego and I had a really good time until Sam came back. I told David, "I'm gonna tell him."

Well, of course he beat the shit out of me. He was so scared that the military was going to find out and that they were gonna get him. I finally told him, "Sam, we need to get something straight. I'm tired of you hitting me for one, and I'm tired of hiding. I just want to be myself. It's not like I'm going to let the Navy know I'm gay. I just want to go to a gay bar with my friends." He said he didn't want to do it.

We broke up. I moved back in the barracks. That was it.

We see each other every day at work. We're good friends. He's getting ready to get out of the Navy here in a month. I'm gonna miss him a lot. I care for him a lot. I really do. I miss being with him. But it was such a rough relationship.

Z: No, it's good that you got out.

J: Him being so closeted. Me wanting to be out.

Z: Has he changed at all since then?

J: No. Well, there were rumors going around that he was gay, that him and I were gay. I don't give a fuck what people say; let 'em talk; they don't know the truth. But Sam got scared. So what does he do? He's starting to date girls. I told David, "He's sort of doing what I did." I can see where he's coming from. He doesn't want the military to know.

J: I've had no regrets. I mean, I've had a pretty fortunate ten years in the military. It's been pretty easy for me. It gets hard at times, especially when you go to sea. You're always having to control your frustrations. But it's really not that hard. You've just got to set your mind to it and realize, hey, this is the way it is. You leave that at home, and when you're on the ship you do your job.

Z: Are you going to do your twenty years in the Navy?

J: Yeah.

Z: Do you like your job?

J: Oh, I love my job. I really enjoy what I do. I like the people that I work with, and some of the people I work for. My boss is probably the best person I've ever worked for. We have a very good working relationship. He likes me a lot. I like working for him a lot.

Z: The admiral?

J: I won't say his name, but he's—I've never heard negative comments out of his mouth about gays. He was asked about sexual harassment in the military, and then he was asked about the gay issue. His comment was, "This is the nineties."

One time I told him I was going on a date. He asked me if he would approve of her. And then he goes, "Or him." Which threw me for a loop! I think he does have ideas, but I don't think he would ever ask. Of course I would never tell him, I don't think. I don't know how he would react. I would not want to risk my job. It's his decision who he wants working for him. He could say, "I'm just not happy with your performance." I'd rather not tell him. I have a lot of respect for him as my boss, as a person, as a leader in the military. I'd just rather leave it that way.

Chaplain Phil: Gay, Straight, Whatever

Phil just barely has time for me. The former chaplain candidate, now a naval reserve lieutenant, has allocated me exactly two 45-minute audiotape sides.

He is East Coast, aggressively middle class, Italian/other European, 24. We sit at an outside table at a Hillcrest coffee house. On the table are two lattes, both mine, and a bottle of mineral water for Phil. He has brought his cellular phone and his chihuahua. She looks at me with large nervous eyes in some aspects not dissimilar to Phil's. But infinitely less calculating.

I am careful not to put Phil on the defensive. I have already caught the former part-time police officer and future priest at an adult bookstore (his first visit, he says, calling me "a mess," and escorting me back to Hillcrest). But I think this only makes it easier for us to level with each other.

Phil: It was in high school that I felt callings toward the priesthood. And also felt a similar calling or desire to be in the military. It wasn't until college that I discovered I could do both.

One of the hardest problems of me becoming a priest was seeing myself rotting in a parish as a young person. In the military you have to go where the troops go, so you learn to parachute, and all these other things. It's a very dynamic ministry dealing with very young people—people who are seeking something. And it's fun to help them find God and tie that into that search.

I got out of college in 1990 and was commissioned upon entering the seminary as a chaplain candidate program officer, CCPO, with the rank of ensign in the United States Navy. I entered active duty for the purposes of training, and then was retained on active duty throughout Desert Storm. I was assigned to Marine Corps Recruit Depot [MCRD] San Diego in the capacity of a chaplain candidate, but for all intents and purposes, due to the shortage of chaplains, I functioned as a chaplain with the exception of liturgical rites. I didn't perform any of those. At the time I was working on my master's in clinical psychology, so I had a heavy counseling background, and I spent a lot of time counseling recruits.

I did the job of a chaplain, and actually my counseling schedule was more booked than about half the chaplains there. Some of that being that I had more time and less duties and could fulfill the needs more. And I think especially in the gay counseling, if you've got fourteen chaplains to pick from, you're going to pick the one that you feel is going to accept you for your problem. You're not going to go to the Baptist who's standing there on Sunday saying "Faggots are going to hell." And obviously as a gay chaplain I was secure enough in myself that—I didn't come out and say "I'm gay," but I was very loving and caring and came across that way. I think many of the gay people gravitated with their problems toward myself and the chaplains who were gay there.

Zeeland: You're a stockbroker now. You're in the reserves?

P: At the present time I retain my commission in the reserves of the United States Navy apart from the chaplain program. I'll probably, when I hit [my] mid-thirties or so, return to the seminary. I have two more years of work to complete. I would like to get ordained and serve with the chaplain corps.

Z: How old are you now?

P: Twenty-four. I've done a lot for twenty-four years of age. I grew up young.

Z: Going to Marine Corps Recruit Depot—was that an assignment you chose for yourself?

P: Actually, it was offered to me, and at the time I wasn't very thrilled with it. I had entered the Navy and liked serving with the Navy. Marines seemed to me to be just morons. It wasn't until after serving with them for a few weeks that I began to develop a deep respect for them and what they go through. I ended up with a love of Marines and would spend as much time as I could with them. They're far more excellent than the Army, the Navy, and the Air Force. Marine Corps training is more demanding. They play more mind games with them; they strip them of their identity far more from the very beginning. The Navy kids arrive at Lindbergh field here and are picked up by some nice guy in a van who has nothing to do with Navy training. The Marines are all herded to the airport and left sitting for hours, and—I've had the privilege of actually having this done to me; in order for me to fully understand recruits I was put through what a recruit would go through.

I was put on the bus with the recruits and the door closes and the biggest, blackest DI [drill instructor] in the world comes down the bus at you screaming that you're a no-good motherfucker and you're on your ride to hell! Say goodbye! The door is closed there's no getting off! They intimidate the living shit out of these kids the entire way to the base. They're rushed off the bus running, and are read the four general articles dealing with discipline and not hitting a superior officer and what happens to you if you do, which is kind of telltale of what they're getting into. They're rushed in, their heads are shaved, they're stripped naked, and taught how to put on a uniform. By this time they're quaking. They're kept up seventy-two hours for the purpose of sleep deprivation and asked a series of questions. "Are you a homosexual? Have you ever had a homosexual experience? Do you do drugs? Did you bring any contraband here? Did you lie to your recruiter?" Overall, almost half the hands in the crowd would go up. Because they're so intimidated that they're all paranoid and they think they've done something wrong. I mean, if they've wet the bed they're going to raise their hand and tell the drill instructor. It's very effective. And at that point they would meet with the chaplains and the other line officers and the DIs to determine if they needed to be sent back home. Ninety-nine percent of them were not sent home but were just advised that these things do not go on in the Marine Corps.

Z: You were put through the same treatment?

P: I was put through the same treatment with the exception of getting my head shaved.

Z: So you were naked and quaking with the rest of them?

P: Yeah. And no one knew I was an officer at the time. It was an interesting experience, and it intimidated me. There was another person there who was getting put through that for the purposes of training. He had been a prior enlisted Marine. He had a flashback and just locked and cocked and came to attention and started shaking; he was so intimidated. It just brought back so many horrors of boot camp ten years earlier.

I chose to go through it only because I knew that counseling Marine Corps recruits was going to be my sole responsibility. So whenever I could find time in my schedule I would go out with them and rappel and everything else, just like most officers there will do. If they're involved with recruits at all, they'll do anything a recruit will do. Just to show them they can do it and to set an example. And the chaplains are expected to do it, too.

I didn't have it as grueling as the recruits did by any means, because I had duties that I had to attend to, so I was forced to leave from time to time and would just step out of the back of the room. The DIs knew who I was. They're funny; give them the chance to demonstrate that it is a skill to be able to yell in someone's face and to intimidate them, and they really—not with any kind of vengeance toward an officer, but—they go to great lengths to show you what they can do. Just out of professional pride. And they are very effective and very intimidating.

Z: The differences that you've observed between Marines and sailors—do you see them as being primarily the result of the boot camp experience? Or are you also aware of differences in the kinds of men who choose the different service branches?

P: I think from the beginning that there's a different temperament for someone who becomes a Marine. They know what they're getting into. Very often the Marines that come in our doors are among the most insecure people, and they are seeking the security they have not found in their families. Very often Marines get the worst of the worst. After other service branches started demanding that you be a high school graduate the Marine Corps for years went on accepting people who were not. The Marines in one sense have lower standards on that end of it; they are willing to take someone who is perhaps a little bit more of a derelict, but who wants the sense of pride and wants the title United States Marine.

Recruits are never addressed as "Marine" until they graduate; they're addressed as "Recruit" until the third phase of training; they're not called by their last name until the second phase, and with the exception of the chaplains and the medical personnel no one ever calls them by their first name. Sometimes because of the way that the training program is set up, we would see them when they came in and then not again for three weeks, and at that point when you set them down in your office and you use their first name, they're in shock. They very often won't even respond to it. Counseling a Marine who's got a problem of any kind, you spend about the first ten minutes breaking down what the DIs have built up, in order to get him to be able to talk to you on a human level.

Z: They're brainwashed.

P: I hate that term. They're broken down and rebuilt to be somebody different than they are. Very much broken down and changed. A Marine is trained to develop a pride in himself, in his country, and in his Corps. And he leaves training with that pride intact.

P: It's funny—I have a lot of friends who are completely straight in the Marine Corps, and some of the things they do, from the perspective of someone gay like myself, are completely gay.

One of the things that threw me for a loop when I first saw field training is how they're taught to field clean. Many of the DIs make them stand naked and shave each other's faces. Their reasoning is you can't shave your own face in the mirror in the field. And if there's anything more homoerotic than that, I don't know what it is—two hundred naked

Marines standing face to face shaving each other. Some of them will be beginning to get hard-ons or get hard-ons, much to their embarrassment.

Sometimes Marines leave recruit training with some stupid ideas of what is masculine. Marines are forever doing stupid things just to prove that they're a real man or a real Marine. I have friends who are on the Presidential detail at Camp David, and, oddly enough, they were up there one night jerking off into a styrofoam cup to see if they could fill it, passing it around while they were on guard duty because they were bored. And then tried to con somebody into drinking it. Marines are always ingesting the weirdest substances for dollars or on a dare. I've seen Marines drink urine, all kinds of odd shit.

Z: How many Marines ejaculated into the cup?

P: That one I didn't get to personally witness, unfortunately. It would have been fun. But from what I heard talking to the whole group all the day after, at least twenty.

Z: Did they do this in front of each other?

P: Marines are all the time jerking off in front of each other. They'll just stand there and do it. And jerk each other off, too. That's very very common from what I have seen. Either on a dare, on a bet, or while they're drunk.

There's a saying: for three beers you can have any Marine. I would end up with some permanent personnel in my office from time to time and that was one of the subjects that would come up. "Well I was drunk and I had sex with so and so, but I really like women and I'm married, but it was kind of fun. What do I do?"

I was at a party not long ago with a whole slew of straight young enlisted Marines, and about ten of them ended up in a Jacuzzi. I'm sure there were a few gay ones in there, but a couple of them had wives, and they were all playing around at the end of it. Straight, gay, I don't know.

Z: So what does that mean? How did you interpret their readiness to engage in sex play with each other?

P: I personally am one who believes that we all come from the perspective of desiring and loving people, and that, although you're predominately geared toward the opposite sex or the same sex, you can play both sides. In other words I think the world's bisexual. And I think Marine Corps training teaches men so much security that very often they can do it with each other and get away with it, although they would never have sex with somebody that wasn't a Marine.

It was amazing to me the number of times—and granted these are eighteen and nineteen-year-old boys, but the number of recruits for who that was the question on their minds. The Marine Corps breakdown of training has got them thinking so much. I saw so many Marines dealing with the fact that they're in with all these guys, and they're attracted to them, or there's somebody that they become real close to. They'll bond with one or two people to get them through recruit training, and they'll end up with sexual feelings toward them. That was always a topic coming up in my office behind closed doors. And of my cohorts in arms, the other chaplains, I know from ones that I was close to and would talk about these things with that that was a topic that they had coming up, too.

The other thing is, I saw many Marines turning to God. They're broken down, they can depend on nothing else. There are no atheists in canoes, and I don't think there are any atheists at Marine Corps training. Twice during my time there I had people who were professed satanists—rotten kids with criminal records that had been waivered into the Corps, and literally had devil tattoos on their arms—find God in the Corps, and decide to become religious.

Z: What would you tell recruits in response to their question about what their attraction to other men meant?

P: First of all, without telling them that I was gay or without sounding negative, I let them know the current policy in the military and/or the policies of recruit training if they got caught playing around. And getting over the official end of it, what was important to me was that they learned that, just because you have sex with a man, or sex with a woman, it does not make you straight or gay. These are artificial labels that society has applied to people. Simply be who you are, love who you are, and develop a sense of security and don't worry about it.

The next question out of their mouths always would be—especially the ones who were coming to me because of their particular Catholic background, "What about the Church?" The Church condemns homosexuality. And I always used to pull out the Bible and start looking at John the Beloved. If there was anybody who was gay in the Bible it was John. During that time period in the Middle East men did not go around laying their heads on the breasts of other men, and, while I'm not saying Jesus got laid, there was clear evidence that He loved this man more than anybody else in the world. In the four Gospels, John was always referred to as "the one who Christ loved." The Gospel of John ends with Peter jealous of John, asking "What's going to happen to John?" and Jesus says "What business is it of yours that the one whom I love should be here until I come again?" Legend has it that John the Beloved is still seen walking around the Earth, waiting. Whether that's true or not, it still shows that Jesus had a compelling reason to show that He did love these people. And homosexuals are, in my opinion, people created and loved by God in a very special way.

That usually shocked the Marines. "Well, I've never heard that before." They left, and it wasn't as much of an issue. And that was my goal. Not to try to make someone gay who wasn't, or to make someone straight who wasn't, but just to get them to not care because it's an irrelevant issue; just simply to be who they are.

Z: A study released last week claimed to prove that only one percent of American men in their twenties and thirties are exclusively homosexual, and only two percent have ever had sex with other men.

P: That study, I believe, is way off. I would put the Marines closer to—by the time the Marine gets out of the Corps at seventy percent, if not higher.

Z: Do you think these Marines would answer truthfully if someone were to ask them about that?

P: I would hazard to guess that most, if not all of them, would not. I would not. And I'm a gay male.

Z: You would lie?

P: Serving in the military in the current situation? Sure.

Z: What did you tell Marines about masturbation?

P: I've done a lot of work with youth on the parish level, as a seminarian, and one of the things that amazed me was the number of people who had had sex with another person of the same sex and were just emotionally fucked for it because of society, and particularly the churches and what they'd done to them.

There's a reason for everything. There's a mandate for love throughout the Old and New Testament. To love someone monogamously and singularly. And clearly, because you find greater enjoyment in that than you will your right hand. Masturbation only becomes a problem if you become dependent on it as a replacement for seeking a healthy monogamous relationship with someone. Whether it's a sin or not I wouldn't say. But you do have a problem if you don't love yourself enough to give of yourself. I would get into a very mature discussion about it with anyone coming to me with that question. In fact I've talked on that subject in forum before, and know enough, have studied enough, that I'm very good at getting the message across without ever getting hung for not teaching church teachings.

Z: During this debate on gays in the military there were several high-ranking chaplains who made very public statements against lifting the ban.

P: I was aware of that, and I was very disappointed for one of the people who spoke out against lifting the ban. I know him to be gay and I know he has a lover. I find that abhorrent. But there are always going to be people living in their own closets. I hold from everything I've ever learned about humanity that the people who scream the loudest against something are usually suffering from that problem themselves. Actually I would say there have been a far greater number of chaplains who have been in favor of lifting the ban and have spoken out for it. A mixture of gay and straight chaplains.

I know very few straight chaplains. Most of the chaplains I know are Catholic. I also know of many Protestant ones that are gay and have got wives for whatever reasons.

Z: What would incline gay men to want to be chaplains in the military?

P: For the same reason that many corpsmen and many doctors are gay. Simply because of the temperament of the person, stereotypically more sensitive and more caring and more compassionate. You find more of these qualities in a gay male. So I think you're going to find that the national averages are way out of kilter when it comes to the clergy, and they're either gay or bisexual or accepting of it, for the most part. Unless they're some hardcore church. A lot of the Protestant chaplains who were straight knew who those of us were who were gay, and really had no problem with it.

Z: How did they know? Did you tell them?

P: It was never, "I'm gay," but they simply saw who hung together and where we went.

Within the confines of the military, you have the greatest group of ministers that I have seen anywhere. There was a great spirit there that I experienced with them. Why does someone become a chaplain? Belief in serving their country I think is a lot of it. Belief in serving the people who are defending the country. Belief that this country is founded on God-like principles.

Z: You told me that a chaplain friend of yours is planning on coming out publicly after the ban is lifted. Have you considered doing that?

P: My problem with coming out would be the fact that I'm going to pursue the possibility of becoming a priest and a chaplain. Even after the ban is lifted in the military, it's not going to be lifted in my church. And as long as there are the conservative crusty old men with dried-up sex drives governing the laws of my church, they gun for people like me. One of my closest friends, who is now an ordained priest, was just mentally brutalized by bishops who wanted to sleep with him and literally threatened to not ordain him if he didn't do this and that. That's actually very common;

a number of my friends have had experiences like that. So no, I won't be coming out. I feel if I decide to pursue priesthood down the road, I will be far more advantaged being able to serve the people I need to serve than to not be ordained because I took a stand on the soap box. My sexuality is not something that has been an issue for me in the last few years. I think a lot of people know I'm gay. I've never ever been harassed about it. I've never felt discriminated against. I just kind of carry on with my life and it's just never been an issue for me.

Z: What attracted you to the Navy of the four service branches?
P: I'm a coastal/ocean kind of guy. Your chances of being in San Diego, Hawaii, Guam—somewhere near water with a beautiful coast—is definitely greater with the Navy.
Z: What was your picture of homosexuality in the Navy going in?
P: Speaking of gay sailors, look across the street. [Pause.] [Laughs.] What a queen. Um, my perception of it in the Navy was knowing it would be there, but pleasantly surprised at the degree that it was there.   ♪
Z: How old were you when you came out?
P: Twenty when I began accepting. I started experimenting with gay sex when I was thirteen and had the same male for eight years. My neighbor across the street. In fact we took two girls to the prom, got them drunk and passed out, then we had sex together. So that was kind of my start. I didn't come out and accept who I was though until my final year of college. "OK, give it up, you're not straight, this isn't a phase." Society had convinced me it was a phase I was going through, and it was easier to accept that at the time.

And I look back, and especially with the rugby and lacrosse teams in college, who were supposedly straight, but the things that went on in the showers there. . . . You know what? I was innocent enough back then to think if someone got an erection in the shower it was the wind blowing. I only wish I knew then what I know now.
Z: You say that masturbation is harmful if it becomes a substitute for a loving monogamous relationship. A rugby player waving a hard-on around in the shower doesn't necessarily offer you that. What is your attitude toward casual sex for yourself?
P: It's something that I avoid. Granted I'm not perfect at it. I've had the occasional encounter. And again, it's not because I think I'm going to go to hell for having sex with somebody, it's because, from my studies of scriptures, everything that's in the Bible is something that you should do. There's a reason behind it. And I believe that fundamentally people are happier in a relationship. . . .

My first real boyfriend was when I came on active duty, about three weeks into it. It was an enlisted guy, same age I was, at the next base over, and for five months he lived in my BOQ [bachelor officers' quarters] room.

A lot of us who were gay officers in the Navy lived in the BOQ on base and knew each other—we were always joking around about how many of us there were. I think we outnumbered the straight ones. And in fact the swimming pool at NTC [Naval Training Center], at the BOQ, was hysterically cruisy. The BOQ in the summertime housed the chaplain candidates, the dental candidates, the doctor candidates, the lawyer candidates, so you got all these recent college graduates who are ensigns and lieutenant JGs flouncing around the pool. And there were a number of people who had lovers who frequently stayed in the BOQ. My maid in fact caught my friend and me in bed all the time. It didn't particularly faze her, I didn't particularly care. I knew she wasn't going to say anything.

While I was in training, just after being commissioned and reporting to San Diego, one of the chaplain candidates, another Catholic seminarian, was investigated by NIS and offered a chance to either resign or be thrown out. He had met a kid at a bar who turned out to be seventeen. Didn't do anything with the kid but told him too much about where he was from. And then refused to go out with the kid. The kid subsequently wrote a letter to the CO of NTC. And it caused quite a mess. So he had a very short-lived military career. It was very sad. He had been out of the closet maybe three weeks. He was just beginning to deal with who he was and trying to reconcile that with what he had been taught by the Church, and had that happen. We were there when NIS came in and raided his room. It was a very frightening Gestapo-like experience to see that happen. And one of the humorous sides to it, it was amazing to see in a BOQ, which houses maybe five hundred officers, how many gay porno magazines and copies of the *Gay and Lesbian Times* were in the trash can the next morning. Trash cans were literally overflowing with porno tapes and magazines.

Chaplains are human too. Definitely.

Z: This man that you were dating, what was his rank?

P: Third class and then second class.

Z: So of course that's a violation of another taboo, fraternization.

P: I had a lance corporal that was in my chain of command that worked for me who was nineteen and gorgeous. We would end up out in the field together, and as he drove me around he was always trying to get me to sleep with him. I wouldn't simply because he was in my chain of command. But as far as the fraternization thing, I always thought that was pure unmitigated bullshit. I figured I was going to get hung for being gay and sleeping with a guy a lot quicker than I was going to get hung for fraternizing.

P: One of the biggest fears that I had—and I met chaplains who succumbed to it—is, when you're dealing with somebody who's very upset about any kind of issue—it's a Florence Nightingale effect. Chaplains have an extraordinary power over people. Literally, anybody who comes to a chaplain with a problem, you have the power to seduce them into doing whatever you want. And we've seen evidence of that among Catholic priests and Protestant ministers in this country. So I was always very cautious never to let anything like that get out of hand in any kind of counseling situation.

I had one Marine who was showing me his tattoos, and the next thing I know the pants and underwear were around his ankles, showing me the tattoo next to his dick. I mean. "Pull your pants up, Marine! For God's sake, you're in my office."

The military chaplain corps itself would deal with the discipline in a situation like that. There are chaplains who have taken advantage of people that way and they are very swiftly pushed right out by the chaplain corps. I was very cognizant of that. Image and impressions are everything. And very often you might not even do anything, but if it looked like it . . . it's just not something you need.

It's a very delicate balance. I never ever crossed the line with the exception of one private that was my age, who went through recruit training, and when he got out had ten days leave. He called me from his home and flew back and spent the last couple days with me. He had never been with a guy, but wanted to be. We'd never talked about that in the counseling, but inside an hour of landing in San Diego we were at dinner, and he said—with a colonel and a major sitting at the next table—"Have you ever thought about having sex with a guy?" He said it loud enough— it mortified me, sitting there in my uniform. But things led to things, and we got very close. At that point it really wasn't a counseling situation; however, he had stemmed from my job. That was the closest I'd come— and the most uncomfortable I'd ever been with what I did for a living.

Z: The first documented Navy witch-hunt of homosexuals occurred in Newport, Rhode Island in 1919. One of the men implicated was a civilian chaplain. Some of the evidence was just that he was "soft" and enjoyed the company of young men. A lot of other ministers rallied to his defense, angered at the idea that it was homosexual for a minister to comfort other men. The question came to be the distinction between Christian brotherhood and homosexuality. Is there a point where they cross over, and is that a part of your own sexuality in your job? What is the dividing line there?

P: It's a dilemma. As tough as Marines are, and as tough as they're forced to be, there are chaplains who serve with them who practice what pop psychologists call hug therapy. A hug is better than a thousand counseling words to a Marine who has just been stripped of who he was. And so I hugged a lot of Marines in my time. Including permanent personnel. Gunnery sergeants who, because I was a chaplain, were just completely accepting of that male-to-male contact. And granted, from my perspective, you've got a young, cute, hard-bodied little Marine in your arms. That is in the back of your mind. I would be lying if I said it wasn't. But to take it any further would be where the line would be crossed. To make a date, or dinner, or [do] something unprofessional. That would betray the oath and the job which you've agreed to do. So there is a dividing line.

Z: I guess what I'm asking is more theoretical. The close buddy relationships that these Marines form, and the love and caring you feel for them—whether or not there is ever penetration and ejaculation—what is the difference between homosexuality and this sense of brotherhood? How is the line defined there?

P: Militarily by regulations. Personally, I would say that there is no line. And I would fall back again to believing that everyone is bisexual. And that the military and especially the Marine Corps just allows them to come out and be more who they are.

Z: The more men I talk to, the more I understand how fluid sexuality really is; that people have a lot of unrealized potential for sexual expression. At the same time I've never been sexually excited by women. Have you had sex with women?

P: Oral sex, yes, never intercourse. Was I attracted to them? [Pause.] Not in the sense that I looked and went, "Oh wow, look at that body" like I would a guy. However, there have been women that I've loved a lot and were close friends with, and from time to time did feel something sexual there. As is the case I think with Marines who lean toward women and occasionally feel something for men. And sometimes a few beers removes the inhibitions. And/or the beer is simply an excuse the next morning.

Z: In the gay community we are expected to say that we were born this way; there's this idea gayness is something innate and immutable. And that seems to me to conflict with the idea that the Marine Corps could foster a homoeroticism that—

P: I don't know that the Marine Corps fostering homoeroticism could make someone gay. I simply think that Marine Corps training makes them more secure in who they are, and that little bit of homoerotic behavior in the Corps stimulates who they are, and those who were born that way, it comes bouncing out. And those who have a few feelings that way it gets heightened.

Z: You told me before that you find enlisted men more attractive; you find them fresher and less pretentious.

P: That definitely is part of it. Part of my problem is that I'm always attracted to men my own age, and men my own age that are officers tend to be assholes: people who have been given rank and lord it over people instead of exercising it properly. I actually get along much better with the O-5s and 6s. I have never met a lieutenant to this day that I would date. And I'm not attracted to the captains, they're too old.

Z: Does this have anything to do with class differences?

P: Actually the particular guy that I dated had two and a half years of college under his belt. We related very much on the same level. The makeup of the military has changed so much; so many people go to college in this country that in that sense the classes seem to be disappearing. And I knew enlisted kids who were far wealthier than many officers.

The majority of the guys I've dated have been military. Military guys for one thing—I perceive them as cleaner, safer. [Pause.] I don't see where HIV has been more educated than in the Navy and in the Marine Corps. It's just beaten into their heads. They have yearly HIV tests. So military people are much more cognizant about it.

Z: So you think that by dating someone in the military there's less chance for you to become infected with HIV?

P: That and, I mean—I have yet to encounter anyone in the military who would practice unsafe sex.

Z: Really.

P: As opposed to the first guy I ever tricked with outside of the military, who swallowed. I was shocked. I couldn't believe he had done it. It completely turned me off. And I was glad that there was no unsafe contact from my end. I wouldn't have anything to do with him after that. I mean, clearly if he had swallowed me, God knows who he had swallowed all around town. Life's too good to die that way.

Z: What would you hope for yourself at age fifty?

P: That I'm married. And have been married happily for twenty-five years. To a guy. I have a gay bishop and a whole bunch of gay priest friends who all want to celebrate some kind of wedding between me and the guy that I finally marry. They drive me crazy telling me I need to find a husband just so they can perform this wedding. And I've got to love them for it.

I know very much what I want, and what kind of person would fit into my life. I have not yet found him. And I've been honest enough with myself, especially as I've gotten older, the great age of twenty-four—I don't see a need to be with someone who isn't right just for the sake of filling the void temporarily. So I'll very quickly move on, "OK, this person isn't what I'm looking for; let's go to the next person." As a consequence I really haven't had a relationship for the last year. I'm just kind of waiting.

Z: Are you as attracted to men who are not stereotypically masculine as to men who are?

P: No. If I wanted to date a woman I'd date a woman. I'm not attracted to queens. One of the biggest irritants to me personally in gay society is the transgenders and transvestites. I'm not attracted to men who wear dresses and who are effeminate. At all.

Z: The Marines are probably more butch than Navy guys by and large. That probably makes them more attractive to you.

P: Yeah. The Marines have a higher standard of masculinity which they adhere to. And they're always ragging on the corpsmen because the corpsmen are so flighty.

Z: How masculine do you consider yourself?

P: [Pause.] I would say that it's something—I don't know that it's something I'd measure. If you're around a bunch of friends and they're all gay, yeah, you tend to get a little more flamboyant. [Pause.] Is that something that bothers me? Not necessarily. Do I go around with dresses snapping my finger? No.

Z: Were you conventionally masculine growing up?

P: Yeah.

Z: You mentioned you were a part-time cop in college. Then you joined the military. That makes me kind of wonder—

P: I have a uniform fetish. One of my asshole friends said I'm the Village People rolled into one. Cop, priest, officer.

Z: You find uniforms attractive?

P: Yeah, I guess I do. And the funny part is, growing up I was always someone who kind of rebelled against conformity. I went to Catholic school all my life. I was always in a uniform and I hated it. But as much as I used to try to rebel against the uniform, I find that I've been in one uniform or another ever since kindergarten. All my Catholic years at school up to college, then in college I was a cop. In a uniform. Then into the military. In a uniform. And now I'm a businessman. I wear a dark suit because it's my uniform. So I am a conformist, I guess.

Z: Have you eroticized these uniforms?

P: To some extent.

Z: Do you have a favorite?

P: Marine Corps dress blues or camis without underwear.

If you're in any kind of a sweaty [tropical] area they teach you not to wear underwear because you get crotchrot if you do. So it's very common to "freeball," especially in places like Panama. And when you freeball in fatigues you're a walking hard-on anyway, just because of the feeling of that coarse material against you all day long. I mean, you can tell when someone doesn't have underwear on. And with dress blues, when they're tailored right on a Marine—the Marine Corps spends an inordinate amount of money tailoring the uniform even for recruits, where the Navy just throws on basic uniforms. And a Marine Corps uniform is tailored to perfectly hug their ass and hug their balls. And . . . it's funny to me that every base I've ever been on, either the provost marshall—the head guy of the MPs—is gay, or he's definitely got a lot of . . . feelings. Because the cutest little boys are always the general's driver and always guarding the gates.

Z: I did an interview with an RP [see David] who told me that he worked with the Navy for a number of years, and now he's at Pendleton. And he said that the Marines are a lot more accepting of him as a queen; that because he goes on their marches, and cuts his hair like them they don't mind so much that he has a high voice and kind of a swishy walk. Would that be unusual?

P: I would say that would be standard. From my experience with Marines, if you can hang with them and have proven yourself able to do what they can do, they're accepting of you. I know of instances where Marines have bashed people who were trying to bash gay Marines or sailors. They go to great lengths to protect those secrets. Once you've achieved acceptance with them, these other little things are simply minor issues to them.

For the most part, the generals seem to be having a far bigger problem with sexuality than anyone. And I wonder sometimes if that isn't because—if the military, when they lift the ban, will fundamentally change, and a lot of straight men who get to play around with guys all the time and fulfill that side of their needs aren't going to be able to as freely. And some of the rituals that go on within the military, which are very homoerotic, and almost homosexual, aren't going to be able to be done.

If you have all the gay people out being gay, the things that are more homosexual are going to be labeled as homosexual. And I think that it will greatly change. In fact, a lot of the free sex environment, or the fantasies and the occasions for a quick whatever in the military will fundamentally change. Some of the things they claim are time-honored traditions are just amazing in how far they cross the lines of what would be proper.

Joey: I'll Aways Be a Sailor

It is a Saturday morning in July and, like almost every day in San Diego, sunny and warm as Anthony and I arrive by bus at Naval Air Station North Island in Coronado to witness the decommissioning ceremony for the USS *Ranger*. I am not a morning person. It is a few minutes before ten, the time Eddy has told Anthony we need to be here.

Walking toward the waterfront we unexpectedly encounter Fred, another radioman from the *Ranger*. Both Anthony and Eddy have described him to me as a duplicitous two-faced straight guy with "tendencies," possibly a "closet queen" (it was he who opened and circulated Eddy's gay love letter). Fred is goofy and swaggering, not at all how I had pictured him. Anthony seems discomfited and oddly disadvantaged by his presence. The two exchange sailor talk.

Fred says, "So what are you guys doing here? The ceremony's not 'til one." I mutter a curse at Anthony, who tells Fred, "Steve is like an uncle to me." I snort, "Yes, and my nephew needs discipline." Fred makes as though he would swat Anthony's butt, but holds off, saying, "No, you would like it too much." I raise an eyebrow and comment, "I would not have guessed that you knew that about him." "He doesn't," Anthony says wryly, smiling. "Well, if it's any consolation I haven't done it with any guy, huh huh huh," says Fred. I think sarcastically "What a loss," but cannot help but eye the seductive bulging crotch of the straight sailor's dress whites—just as he is smiling downward obviously ogling me from behind his stupid sunglasses.

To my disappointment, Fred leaves to find his father. Anthony and I are left to mill about and kill three hours in the sun. We laugh at and take pictures of what appears to be a huge frosted cake in the shape of the carrier, but is only a crude plaster model, and an ice sculpture of the ship's hull number, CV-61, that is wheeled, rapidly melting, beneath a canopy. Crusty veterans from all over the country

263

file in and purchase souvenir caps and memorabilia. I content myself with a free program and learn that over its 36-year history
96,000 men have served aboard the *Ranger*, surpassing by far any
mass sailor fantasy of mine. Present day *Ranger* sailors stride by
with rolling gaits (sailors don't march, they strike attitudes), stuffed
like sausages into their tight polyester dress whites, some threatening to burst at the midriff from too much galley food. But others are
quite flattered by the uniform. Because of the white pants' lining it
looks like they all wear boxer shorts. The vision is blinding in the
San Diego sun. Somewhat feverish, I study them half-hard enter-
taining the idea of simulated wog sex. But wouldn't the synthetic
fabric chafe? Guiltily, I think how disgusted Lieutenant Tim would
be with me. But this doesn't keep me from walking over to the base
of the ladder and videotaping the ship's decommissioning crew as
they ascend to the brow.

Suddenly, our friends are there: Eddy appears somewhat dishev-
eled. He has lost his uniform and borrowed an ill-fitting one from
someone only minutes before. A Nicaraguan, Gabriel, is, like I
always see him in the clubs, smiling radiantly. Ed, a short sailor with
attitude I hope to interview but never get the chance to, is character-
istically cute but remote. And Joey, a Navy storekeeper from inner-
city Chicago, is there, too, with his shy self-effacing smile. I take a
group snapshot of the four before they climb the stairs to the gang-
plank, my videocamera taping their butts, too.

The ceremony is long. I cling to the shade of a eucalyptus sapling
and try not to snicker at the commanding officer's similes. Sailors
". . . are like blood coursing through the ship. . . . are like notes on
sheet music. . . are like—" Paper dolls at parade rest, I remember
from my introduction to Anthony's interview, squinting up at the
men, a skeleton crew manning the rails much farther apart than
when the ship pulled in six months ago. I wonder which ones are
our friends and hope they will not notice and disapprove of my
wandering attention. From this distance, the men are utterly indistin-
guishable. Each could fit my sailor fantasy. I feel distance—they are
so far away up there; I will always be outside this ship—and closeness: I have come to know sailors.

I know this because their sea stories have started to loop. Just
days before I interviewed a sailor and found myself able to complete

his sentences with him. But now I cannot even remember his name. Overload. What more do I need to do for this book? Sleep with X more sailors, adopt "The Connie," collect how many more stories? I think, as so often these last few days, about the young Marine I have just met, Alex. I like him. I don't want to interview him, don't want our personal relationship sullied by professional interest. I want to leave some mystery. . . . Last night I met some nameless sailor in the video booths. We had sex, started to talk, but I wanted to clap my hand over his mouth: DON'T TELL ME YOUR STORY. I've got enough material. "I have come to know sailors." But I will be forever on this shore . . .

I am startled by silence. The captain has stopped speaking, stands unmoving. I realize that he is choked up. The stillness is powerful. This is a kind of funeral. With careful control he concludes: "And always remember to take care of yourself and take care of your shipmates. Captain, out." I look at Anthony. He wipes back a tear. Somewhere up there, Eddy, as always, is happy. And Joey—maybe I can interview him before he goes? Yes. He will be the last one.

In a few days Clinton will issue an executive order. Lifting the gay ban? We hardly think so.

In the decommissioning program there is a letter from the President on White House stationery. "Every *Ranger* crewmember who has walked her decks should take great pride in his contribution to our Navy and our nation."

My head throbs. I realize that my face has been badly sunburned. I need to get out of here.

Zeeland: Saturday was kind of a sad day for you.
Joey: There was a lot of sadness. Saying goodbye to the ship. Then getting discharged the same day, right after the ceremony. It was saying goodbye to a big chunk of my life.
Z: Because of the ship being decommissioned you were given the option of getting out early. Why did you decide to do it?
J: Well, my objective in coming into the military was to get money for school. Not many people in my family have gone to college. The other part was, I wanted to serve my country. But this early out gave me the opportunity to start school a year earlier. So it was just: get on with life. The signs were right. Take it, get it accepted, go.

Z: Tell me a little more about your decision to first join the military. Were there any other reasons apart from patriotism and going to college?

J: I've always kind of liked the military, even when I was little. I thought that was neat, how everything is so organized. Just to say I'm in the military, and to serve my country. And—the uniform. Not only from the neatness, but also for the men. I didn't do it so I could meet men; I don't want to give that impression. I've just always liked it. I've always liked military programs, like *Hogan's Heroes* and *Private Benjamin*. All that stuff.

I thought about being in the Army, but I didn't want to be on the ground and get blown away. Then again I was kind of afraid of water, being on the ship. I can swim, but once that ship goes down it goes down! [Laughs.] I wanted to join the Air Force, but they wouldn't take me because I had a traffic ticket. I blew a stop sign. They said, "Come back and see us in six months after this clears." I really didn't want to wait that long. And the Marines—forget it. That's too hard-core. Or it seemed to be. Maybe now, I could probably handle it, but back then I thought, no, that's too stepfather-like. The Navy seems more relaxed. A lot of my family was in there. My grandfather and uncles, and they all said the Navy was great for them.

Z: Did you think there would be other gay men in the Navy?

J: Oh yeah. I figured there would be.

Z: You'd heard the Village People song?

J. [Laughs.] The way I look at it there's gays everywhere. So, I knew there would be some gays there, but that wasn't what I was looking for. I wasn't looking for sex.

Z: What was your first awareness of being gay, growing up?

J: I always knew, even when I was real young. For the first four or five years of my life my mom raised me. We always had our special time together. Then my step-father came along and he just ruined everything. He took over, and I didn't like that. He was always too masculine. "We're gonna do this *this* way." He was always hard, played sports. I never liked sports. I never liked being around boys when I was little, I always liked being around the girls. Playing jump rope. [Laughs.] Even dressing like them sometimes. Wearing their hair pins, or spraying perfume on. I just liked being with girls.

I remember, when I was little, I had experiences with boyfriends, schoolmates—little innocent-type things. But then when I got older, ten or eleven, I started lusting after grown men. I would never look at anybody in my class; from junior high all through high school I never looked at my classmates in a sexual way. Some of 'em were good looking, but a lot of them were assholes; they were jocks, and always saying "faggot" to me, so that turned me off. But I always liked full-grown men. Ten, eleven, twelve—right in the beginning of puberty is when I really started lusting.

Z: What exactly would you picture?

J: [Laughs.]

Z: What could you know about sex at that age?

J: I knew a lot of things. I had a city life. I grew up fast, because a lot of times my parents were both working. I learned quick. But when I had those thoughts I would just. . . I'd see a man walking down the street and see the hair on his chest. He just looked sexy by the way he walked. And his body, a man's body—I would picture taking his clothes off, and just—The main thing would be to suck his dick. And have him hold me. I never thought of anything past that. Just kiss him. Rub each other. But I'd always think that. I had a dirty mind!

Z: When was the first time you acted on that—beyond the little innocent experiences you spoke of?

J: Past puberty? [Pause.] I would have to say between my sophomore and junior year in high school. A guy that was a year older than me, we went out driving with some friends. It was me and him in the back, and my buddy and another friend. I was only sixteen, seventeen and didn't really do anything yet. I wasn't into drugs. Not yet. I was in marching band, blah blah blah. Anyway, we went to an arcade. He and I went to get cigarettes and left the other two in there. After we went to the store he said, "Why don't we go for a walk?" The sun was setting. He kind of rubbed himself against me and was lookin' at me and sending me signals. Made my throat lumpy and my stomach was mushy and my dick was hard. I kind of had an idea what was gonna happen, but I followed him anyway. And that was the first time I ever seriously sucked a guy off. It was great; just the innocence broken there. Then the next morning I woke up kind of feeling guilty. "Uh-oh. What'd I do?" I felt kind of scummy in a way. Still thinking that it was wrong. But it felt right. I only had one more experience after that. I continued to date girls through high school.

Z: Did you have sex with them?

J: Yeah. Not frequently. I had two steady girlfriends, one in my freshman and one in my senior year. I had sex with both of them. My freshman year, I knew that I was gay, but I was still fighting it off. "No, maybe I'm not; let me try this." That's when I lost my virginity. I was fourteen. I just wanted to try it. It wasn't all that bad. I prefer men, greatly, but it's not bad. Everyone's like, "Ewww!" I don't think it's "ewww," it's a woman.

Z: Some guys tell me they have to think of a guy to keep it up.

J: Oh no. I didn't think of a guy at all. I just thought of it as what it was.

Pussy. I don't need to think of a man when I have sex with a woman. I can think of her. . . . But that was it. And then I went to boot camp.

Z: You told me that when you drive past [Great Lakes Naval Training Center, outside of Chicago] now, you get—

J: I get the chills! It was such a mind trip. A lot of sailors I've talked to say "It was nothing." I think it was something. I think it was very intense for everybody. They want to play it off that it didn't bother them, but I think it did. Just the way—I can't even describe it. I pulled up as a civilian, the door opened, and then my whole life changed. Got off the bus, and they were just screaming from the first second. It was like they owned me from that minute. And they did.

It was strange . . . you know how you are when you're somewhere you're not used to? You notice everything around you. New smells, the crisp uniforms. You can just smell the authority: "We're here and we're taking you over!" Sometimes I wonder, why did I even go into the military? Especially with my childhood and my stepfather. But there was something that drove me to discipline. Maybe I needed it. I'm not very self-confident even now. I'm working at it, but I grew up not liking myself. I hated myself, because no matter where I went I was always made fun of. At school, and at home by my stepdad. Then when I got to boot camp . . . no one really fucked with me, but it was still like I was being treated like a piece of shit. But I dealt with it. Because you have to. I'm not a quitter. And it makes you stronger. Just like you go to the gym to work on your body, you go through this bullshit to strengthen your mind. So yeah, I still get the creeps when I go past it, but I have good memories of boot camp too. My CCs [company commanders], they were pretty nice for the most part.

Z: What happened to your sexuality while you were in boot camp?

J: I would say I repressed everything. I didn't see any sign of anyone being gay. But then again I was very naive, I didn't know how to read people like I can now. I wasn't aware of anything.

Throughout my whole life I've been alone. Even though I have a great mother—she's my best friend—and I have other friends now, too, I always look at myself as a loner. So I wasn't going to really pay attention to anybody else. I looked at their bodies, and there were some fine guys that I went to boot camp with, but. Another reason I didn't pay attention to it was because I was a section leader, and I was so nervous about doing my job that I didn't really have time to look around or be flirtatious. I never masturbated at boot camp. I really didn't get horny either. Because I was just too goddamn tired. You just want to go to sleep. And they wake you up so fucking early, three thirty, four o'clock. I was too exhausted, too worried about my people passing inspection. It was too many changes at once to even think about sexuality.

There was one guy [in boot camp] who acted rather effeminate. And everybody singled him out and picked on him. They made fun of him a lot, and finally they wrote "faggot" on his pillow in pen. And that upset him. He got really disturbed about it. He was crying and he punched a wall, and he broke his wrist. So for the remaining time in boot camp he had a cast. Our CCs were pissed off to find out what happened. "What made you do this?" And he told them what happened. But what I thought was cool was, our CCs never harassed him. Even though he was different, the chief and the first class never singled him out and made him feel bad. And I respect that. Instead they got mad at the company. "One of you motherfuckers had better admit to it, otherwise you're all gonna get set back a couple weeks." And that started scaring everybody. Well, it turns out they never did set us back, they just punished us. They MASHed us. "MASHing"—that means "Making A Sailor Hurt." Just tons of push-ups and sit-ups and all that shit. They lied to medical, they said, "He tripped and fell." Because if [the Navy] had known the truth about him hitting himself, he might have got set back, and it would have made the company look bad. . . .

J: It was like a totally different world getting on the *Ranger*. I kind of noticed one guy that was in my sister division, he was really nelly. I always knew he was, even though I never brought it up to him, because at that point he was a third class and I was still an airman apprentice. I abided by military rule and treated everybody above me in rank with respect, so I could never come out and ask him.

How I started meeting people was, my second weekend here I decided to go out and see San Diego by myself. Everyone's like, "You're gonna get mugged!" I'm like, "I'm from Chicago. This is a hick town compared to where I come from." I went downtown, and I asked this one guy where all the gay people were at.
Z: You asked who?
J: This one guy that was collecting money for a church. "Where are all the gays at?" He just looked at me. "Ennh!" He was through with me. He said, "You need to come to church." [Laughs.]
Z: Why did you pick him?
J: I didn't know it was a church right away. He just said, "Can you spare a donation for the homeless?" And I said, "Yeah, sure, I'll give a couple bucks." 'Cause I feel bad for that shit. So I gave it to him, and I said, "Well hey, where's the homosexual people at?" He finally told me, "It's

called Hillcrest, but I really don't think a young man like you should be going over there. You need to be saved."

So I found the gay community. I went [to Hillcrest] numerous times, and I kind of turned into a little whore. I just started being very promiscuous. I was nineteen, too young for clubs. So I'd go to the park. Or I'd walk up and down University [Avenue] and look for people. It's kinda fucking disgraceful now, when I look at it.

Z: There's nothing disgraceful about it. You do what you have to do to meet people. Would you go down into the bushes?

J: No, I'd just wait for people riding by in cars and then usually get picked up. Well, one time I met this guy, Ned. He had a nice older sports car, a classic Chevy. He said, "You wanna go for a ride?" He was cute. He had a Marine haircut. Marines turn me on for some reason. He was an older man, but I figured, maybe he's like a staff sergeant or an officer. So we went for a ride. We got to talking, and he found out I was on the *Ranger*. We went back and messed around in his hotel room. When it was all over, he said he wanted to take my picture. I said, "With clothes on, right?" He said yeah. So I stood up against the wall and he took my picture. He said, "Would you be interested in meeting other people off your ship? Because I know one or two." He asked me if I knew the person. I was right out of boot camp, I didn't know anybody. "I write this guy letters. Is it alright if I send him a copy of your picture and have him look for you? Would you mind?" I said no. He wrote the guy's name down for me and said, "This guy's gonna be looking for you in a couple weeks."

Well, I never heard anything. I went on the WESTPAC and I hung around with my straight friends. I was working really hard, because I wanted to make a good impression. And then for a lot of the cruise I was in the galley, too. I did my ninety days, like everybody has to do on a ship. So I was always working. It was real tough, plus the [Persian Gulf] war. So I wasn't thinking about it. Then the very last part of that cruise, right when we were about to go into Hawaii, I found him. We were standing on the mess decks one day, and he was sitting there. He goes, "Hey!" I looked at him, and I didn't know who he was. "Do you know Ned?" I'm like, "Oh shit!" "He gave me your picture five months ago and here it is the end of cruise. You could have had so much fun if I would have found you earlier. But at least now I found you." And that's where it began, me knowing people on the *Ranger*. I met him, then a few others. Eddy checked on-board a couple months after we got back from cruise; we saw him walking down the street. "Oh, he's cute."

I was twenty. Still too young to get into the clubs. I'd go out with them every now and then, but then I'd go out with straight people too a lot.

Z: How long were you on land between WESTPACs?

J: A year and two months.

Z: How was the second WESTPAC different?

J: It was a lot different. From the military aspect, I'd been advanced two ranks, so now I was a third class. I was in kind of a position of authority, I had people below me. I felt different, felt like I'd "been there, done that" already, and I felt good about it. I said, "This is my turn. I know what's going on." I discovered the holes in the walls in the heads and met people through there and all that type of thing. I was learning.

You see all these guys, and there are so many of 'em, and they're so hot, you know? Everyone has a different appeal about them. It's one thing or another. It's eyes, body, package; you can see their dick just bulging out of their pants. I mean, you can't stand it. It gets so bad that you just feel like you're gonna explode. I've never been this way before. I was not like this. I didn't even think about sex all that much before I came in the Navy.

Z: So that's where you would go for release at sea? The heads? Would you just reach under the stall partitions, or would there be someplace else you would go with the guys?

J: It would really be too dangerous to go anywhere else. There's five thousand men on the ship, there's always somebody wandering somewhere. So your best bet would be to stay in the head and just jerk each other off. Or watch each other. Some guys, you meet them once, and they want to talk to you. Other guys are real nervous about it: the closets. They're like, let's jerk off together, let's feel each other—and then they don't want to talk to you; they don't want you to look at 'em, they don't want to know you. They go there to fuckin' bust a nut and that's it. And then there's the guys that don't know they're being watched—I think that's pretty kinky, too. They got the girlie magazine out, there's pussy and tits everywhere, and you think that they're so butch.

Z: Did you ever encounter any exhibitionists who wanted to be watched?

J: Yeah. Some of 'em I honestly think didn't know, but then some I think, maybe they did, but maybe they didn't, but maybe they don't care? I've run across quite a few of those. I'd see wedding rings on 'em, and they'd be jerkin' off, and they'd look over. They wouldn't care. It was kind of erotic. I reached around and touched one one time, and he pushed my hand away, but he didn't like slap it away or nothing. He didn't want me to touch him, but he wanted to watch me, and have me watch him, and he got off that way. And it was funny, because when he was ready to come he stood up and shot it towards me.

Z: So you could appreciate the full effect.

J: I guess that's what he was thinking.

Z: If a married straight guy jerks off with you, do you then consider him a closet gay? Or what's your way of categorizing straight and gay?

J: Well, maybe I shouldn't call them closets. I don't know. Because everybody's different. My personal way of looking at everybody, and myself, is, if it happens, it happens. Whatever. Some people are just straightforward up straight, don't even want to think about it. And then there's those people that are like, "Fucking faggots!" but they're curious. It just depends on the person. One minute they're totally straight, but I think the majority of men have a curiosity. And women. The majority of humans, I think, are curious about their same sex. They just don't wanna admit it, because society looks at it wrong.

Another thing about being at sea—there's also the hidden question mark of the looks that guys give you. Those signs. I used to work a night-check position. We'd have a drill during the day—like a man overboard drill, where you've got to go muster—and a lot of guys would just wear shorts. And a couple times I would just wear shorts and boots. And guys would just stare; they would be like in my crotch with their eyes. So aside from the actual touch or whatever, there's also a lot of guys whose heads turn and eyes wander. They look at you a little too deep, a little too long in your eyes, or they smile a little too much. There's a lot of that going on.

Z: Eddy told me that the fantail was very festive on dark moonless nights, and that some of his friends would go back there and have anonymous sex with people they couldn't even see.

J: I have no knowledge of that. I've heard of stuff like that, but I would never dare to do that. It's too dark. I was too scared. And you could trip over things. When I went out to the fantail it was my time with myself. I'd go out there to get fresh air and to meditate. Because it's so beautiful being at sea. Our fantail wraps around the entire back part of the ship, the stern. I'd always hang out on the side, right where the door is. No one's gonna do anything there.

Z: On your second WESTPAC, after you'd gotten to know some other gay sailors, were you part of a clique or a "family" with them?

J: I knew quite a few people, but I didn't really hang out with them. We'd always talk on the ship, but then when it came to going out, we wouldn't really go out together. Toward the end we did, like when we hit Australia, and everybody knew about everybody. Gabriel. Him and I worked together. We went to "A" school together, and we went to the *Ranger* together. We were in the same division; we worked side by side all this time. I figured he was gay, because of the way he walked, and he was always,

"Oooooooo" [makes sashay movement]. But he's from Nicaragua, so everybody tends to classify him as, "Oh, he's strange because he's foreign. Don't worry about it. He's not gay, he's just from another land." So that's kind of the way I looked at it, too. "Maybe that's just the way they are in Nicaragua." Me and Gabriel were close in a way, but not really. He knew I was, because of the people on the ship he'd seen me talking to that were notoriously gay. We never admitted it to each other. Me and Gabriel were just shipmates and that was it. Then we had this guy named Jonny come along. He was sent to our division to work, and he was put right in my work center. Now Gabriel and me are best friends; Jonny brought us together. Jonny was very outgoing. He could read people very well. He was very bold. And he kind of got us all together. And then we went to the gay clubs, both in Perth and then in Sydney. We spent a lot of time together in Australia. We had a good time.

Z: Did you guys actually call yourself "Rangerettes"?

J: [Laughs.] Yeah. We call ourself Rangerettes. A lot of us do. Of course the Connie Girls are, from what I've heard, more infamous. But that was five, six years ago, when [the USS *Constellation*] was in San Diego. But now it's coming back here. It's taking the *Ranger*'s place, so I'm kind of like [makes disapproving sound]. I have kind of a grudge against it, even though I don't know it, because it's filling my ship's place. But I mean, I wish all those guys luck, too. Go, Connie Girls. But yeah, that's another reason why I'm sad to see the *Ranger* go, because of the Rangerettes. My friends.

Z: For some reason, I've met more guys off the *Ranger* than any other ship. In fact, probably more than all of the other ships put together.

J: [Laughs.] It's a big command.

Z: But then there's also the *Kitty Hawk*, which is just as big, and I've only met one guy from there.

J: Well, they're in a similar predicament to what the *Constellation* is in right now. Because they don't know the area. They were in Philly with the "Connie." They just got here, and then they went on WESTPAC two or three months later. And now they're back here again. So they're really not familiar with San Diego yet. I think all the people that were on the "Kitty" and "Connie" that knew about Hillcrest are obviously gone from when they were first here. I imagine there's a lot of people on the *Kitty Hawk*, they just haven't found it yet. It'll probably take a couple more years.

Z: You said you think of yourself as a loner. Did you ever really develop a strong sense of camaraderie with your shipmates, straight as well as gay?

J: [Pause.] Well, I used to be very close friends with this straight guy. I knew him from day one that I got on the ship. We kind of clicked right away. We were very tight throughout the first WESTPAC especially. Throughout Desert Storm. That's another reason why I didn't work nothing, because he was straight, and we were always in my storeroom listening to music, talking, and having other straight guys come down. We would just talk and have a good time. So I felt camaraderie there with my fellow shipmates. And you know, it's not like I spent one hundred percent of my time drooling over these guys. 'Cause I cared about a lot of other people in a different way where I wouldn't even want to touch 'em. I cared about 'em like a brother. But this guy that I was close with, Mark, wound up fucking me over in the end.

I shared an apartment with him and his wife. He found out that I was gay before then, but he said he didn't care, because he's from L.A. He said, "Everybody who's a native Californian knows that gays are here to stay and they just accept it. That's the way I am. I don't care." But it turns out I guess he did care. It bothered him.

I went on leave back home to Chicago in April of last year. Well, while I was away he just went crazy telling everybody that I work with. He didn't tell the higher-ups; he didn't go up to my division officer or my master chief and say "So and so's gay." But he might as well have done it. Well, not really, 'cause I never had any of the higher-ups look down on me in that way. Even if they did know, they kept it professional.

Z: But how did your shipmates react?

J: [Pause.] Well, even for a while after I got back I didn't know. Because they never brought it up to my face. I think they liked me better than they liked him, to be honest with you. Finally, this older guy—he's ten years older than me, he's more mature than everybody else, shipmates my age—and I really respect this guy for this. He's another person I'm really gonna miss. Kind of like an older brother. He said, "There's something you should know. Are you close with [Mark's last name]? You guys are really close friends, aren't you? Well, I think you should know that while you've been gone he's been telling everyone '[Joey's] in Chicago suckin' dick.' He told everyone you're gay. He said you came right out and said it." He goes, "I don't know if you are or if you're not, but it really doesn't matter. I just think you should be aware of what's going on."

I didn't even confront Mark for a long time. I didn't even talk to him. I wanted to beat the shit out of him, and I still do today because of that, when I really think about it. But I went home and just packed my shit and left. I was very cold toward him. I could sense he was that way toward me, too. And I couldn't figure out what I had done. I have no idea.

Z: So you never really did discuss it?

J: Yeah, we did. It was later on during the second WESTPAC. We kind of talked a little bit. But then in Saudi Arabia—Oh, you'll like this. [Chuckles.] [Sighs.]

Mark invited me to go out with him. We were in the United Arab Emirates. It's a totally Arab country and there's nothing to do. It's just fucking desert. The bus ride to the main city was like, forty minutes. There's a place called Leisureland. I guess it's kind of like Magic Mountain but not quite, more like a kiddie park. There's no serious rides, but there's ice skating and bars. So we were getting drunk at the bar. We were talking and talking and talking. We were hittin' it off like we used to. We felt something again. So I brought it up to him. I said, "Why did you do that to me?" And all he could say is, "I don't know." And—it didn't really make me all that mad, but I felt—like I loved him. Because we were talking about everything, and I always—I do love him, a lot. I kind of think I did fall in love with him—even though I didn't want to? But he said, "I don't know why I did that." He never really apologized for it. Kind of he did, but kind of he didn't, but he didn't really have no reason for it.

Z: Were you in love with Mark while you were living with him and his wife?

J: No. I always loved him, but I never came on to him. I never looked at him in that way.

Z: You didn't fantasize about him?

J: No. But secretly maybe I was falling in love with him? I don't know. It's weird.

Z: Well, maybe he had some complicated feelings for you that he was trying to deny by—

J: Well, yeah, I'm about to lead up to that. That night, later on, we kept drinkin' and talkin', and I forgot about it after he said he didn't know. I was like, "Shit happens. Don't worry about it." We bought some more drinks, kept drinking. We ran around the park together, drove go-carts, went ice skating. We went upstairs to watch this live band. And then he started hittin' on me up there. He started rubbin' my leg and lookin' at me.

It blew my mind. That this guy was runnin' his mouth about me and all this other bullshit, and here he is comin' on to me. And he's so straight, too! He's like—you know? He loved his wife! And he always talked about pussy. I couldn't figure it out, I was really confused. He goes, "Let's go for a walk." So of course I went.

We went through the desert. We were walking past the grounds, somewhere past where the park was. There happened to be this ticket stand,

this shack. We just opened it up and it was carpeted. It was too perfect!
[Laughs.] And then we got undressed. We started sucking each other off,
and—he wanted me to stick my dick up his ass. I was like "What the
fuck! You're supposed to be straight, aren't you?" He was like, "Just do
it." I kind of started to, and he was like, "Yeah . . ." He kind of enjoyed it
a little, but he took it out because I guess it hurt or whatever. Then I was
sucking his dick, and he was like, "Yeah, faggot, suck my dick!" He
wasn't doing it in a mean way, he was enjoying himself. [Pause.] But then
after that—it was weird seeing him the next day after we sobered up and
everything. We kind of looked at each other with a distance, like "Oh
fuck." But now I was thinking about it, fantasizing about it. Because
that's how I like it to be. I like that type of—when you don't know what's
gonna happen? It adds to it. You know?

Z: [Nodding.] Mmmm.

J: Then I asked him later on, a few months later, after we got back from
WESTPAC, "So why did you do that?" And he didn't have an answer for
me for that either. "I don't know." He's a very free-spirited person. But
strange.

I thought you might enjoy that.

Z: I did.

Z: What was the reaction of the guys on the *Ranger* to Clinton's plans to
lift the gay ban?

J: Oh, I can't describe it to you, Steve. It was a strange time to be at sea on
a WESTPAC and have that go on. Emotionally I felt tormented, because
I'd have to listen to people throughout the campaign, the election, the day
he was inaugurated . . . I found out about Al Schindler's death. Then
people started opening their mouths, and I realized how fucking ignorant—

Z: What kinds of things did they say?

J: "If faggots come in here, I'm leaving!" "This is a *man's* Navy!" You
get so tired of hearing it day after day and it really makes you feel like
shit. Just for being who you are. It fucking hurts. They don't even know
what I've been through or how painful it is. You think if I really had a
fucking choice I'd be gay?

Being in the military, it's like a double life. And then my childhood, I
wouldn't take a million dollars to go through that again, having everybody fucking hate me, call me a fag when I was six, seven years old, and
I didn't even know what it was. I just wanna live my life and be happy. I
don't do anything to anybody. And here these people are gonna fuckin'—

Z: Were there any that would stand up and express another view?

J: There's a few, yeah. They would say, "I don't think it really matters."

And people would be like, "Yeah it does! I don't wanna be taking showers and some guy's gonna be starin' at my dick!" Well guess what? They
do already anyway. [Laughs.]

Z: But why should that bother them? What does that do to them?

J: I have no idea. I don't know why it would upset them. It might make
them a little nervous, because I'm nervous when people look at me, too.
But if they don't want anybody lookin' at 'em all they have to do is just
wear their towel until they're in the shower.

Z: You have private showers on the *Ranger*?

J: Yeah, private stalls. So it's not all that big of a deal. But they'd say, "I
don't want some guy drooling over me. I'd kill the motherfucker." And
all this other shit. "I wouldn't take orders from somebody higher up that
was gay, I wouldn't listen to 'em." Then you got these religious freaks
that are like, "Oh, you're going to hell." That irritates me beyond belief.

Z: So you found that most of these guys were pretty homophobic?

J: Yeah. For the most part. When I was on the ship, at sea, listening to that,
right when the Clinton election was going on, yeah. But—I think it was an
act, too. I think it's all the things that typical men—they have to be *men*,
they have to be manly, and they have to say [lowers voice an octave] "I
don't agree with it." They have to agree with each other just to be sure of
themselves.

Z: Mark took it upon himself to inform everyone you worked with of your
homosexuality. Did any of those men treat you any differently during this
discussion of gays in the military?

J: No. You know, even though Mark did that it really had no impact
because I've always been well-liked on the ship. And they really didn't
like him all that much because he was very pushy; he was moody. But a
lot of people respect me. So they don't say anything to me. And I've
helped them out before. I listen to their problems—I feel like brothers
with a lot of them.

Z: Did you tell stories about women and play at being straight?

J: No. I don't like to lie. I might say, "She's pretty; that girl's fine," when
we'd be watching TV or whatever. But I wouldn't take it past that.

Z: We were walking down the street today and you pointed out—

J: Oh yeah, she was beautiful. She had a beautiful body. I can say that, but
I'm not gonna sit there and tell pussy stories, because it's not true. And I
don't like liars.

Z: Talking about sex in the heads, of course even a lot of gay people in the
military would say that it's wrong, that when you're at sea you're on duty
twenty-four hours a day. What would your response to that be?

J: What would I say to people who told me that it's wrong to do that on a

Naval vessel? Go fuck themselves! [Laughs.] No. I don't think it's wrong. I think it's just something that needs to be relieved. People get grouchy if they don't get sex. Being out at sea, once you get out there for a long time—and I'm talking past the thirty-day point and past the sixty-day point—I've been at sea for almost ninety days at the longest, and you were ready to fucking kill anybody. You're like, "*Fuck* you!" And there's near fights. I've seen circles gathering of people ready to hit each other so many times. You see a lot of that. I've jumped in a lot of people's faces. Me and these other guys would always get in it together. We'd make up later, but you get so on edge. So in a way, maybe it might help a little, if you think of it as that. It's kind of like a secret meeting, no one has to know. It's not like we're advertising it. And in a way it might be a morale booster. [Laughs.] 'Cause you can get off together, and feel better, and maybe do your job better.

Z: What should the policy toward shipboard sex be?

J: If I was writing the policy? I would let it happen. I wouldn't care. As long as this person wasn't sitting in the head all day long, not even coming to work, spending hours of time there. Then there's a problem. But busting a nut here and there at night after your job is over with and done, there's nothing wrong with that.

Z: Sailors have a reputation of going wild on liberty. What can you tell me about that?

J: It's true. [Laughs.] I've seen a lot of wild things overseas. Bloody fights. Massive drunkenness where everybody's fucked up staggering up and down the streets in Thailand, or the Philippines.

Somebody would always come up to me. "Are you gonna hang out with me?" I didn't really want to hang out by myself, so I'd wind up going out with a bunch of straight guys, and we'd get all fucking smashed. And girls just throw themselves at you. It's nothing like the United States. Nothing. You just walk in and [makes sound effect] they're just in your lap. "What's up, handsome?" And they'd throw their arms around you, kiss you, and say "Buy me a drink!" You gotta pay for them, but it's cheap. It's a straight man's paradise. You just pay for 'em and go and fuck and not have to worry about it. I had a woman in Thailand, and in the Philippines too. . . .

I just wanted to have [the Filipino prostitute] around me just because she was a woman. I wanted to hold her and talk to her and stuff. And I did get a chance to do that, even though I fucked her too. But I mean, that wasn't the whole reason I felt good about it. I knew her for four days. She knew pretty good English, up to a point. It was fun. But she said something the first night that kind of hurt me. I was laughing about something,

I was drunk. She said, "The way you laugh make me think of *bakla*."
And *bakla* means gay. I was like, "Oh shit, my guard is down because I'm
drunk. Stuff myself back in that closet!"

Z: How did you decide that you're gay and not bi?
J: I still don't even know which one I am, really. I guess I am more gay,
because I am attracted to men beyond belief, and women are like, "Oh,
she's pretty, but." But my intentions, when I started discovering Hillcrest
and first got to the *Ranger* . . . I just wanted to find one man and have a
relationship, have each other. But it never worked out that way. And I
don't think it's ever going to, for me.
Z: Why?
J: I don't know. It's never right. Something's always wrong. Then when I
look at it, I think, maybe I should just start over with women. And put it in
the back of my mind about guys.
Z: Don't be so pessimistic. Sometimes when you're too anxious and you
want something too badly, you don't get it. Then when you finally decide
that it's never going to happen, it comes true.
J: [Sounding doubtful.] Yeah.

Z: Were you effeminate as a boy?
J: Yeah.
Z: But you strike me as being, you know, pretty masculine.
J: Who? Me?
Z: You.
J: Now? [Laughs.] I like to be more masculine than feminine. I guess I got
the feminine out of me when I was younger. And I don't really like that
nelly type of thing. I mean, it's funny, and I do it, I'm like, "Oh girrrl." I
can do it real good. I can do it as good as anybody else can. Because it's
funny to do. You laugh, you say all these little sarcastic things, and
[makes cat sound] little catfights, but, that's not me. I'm not like that.
Z: So when did you change?
J: Junior high, high school. It's taken practice to cover myself up, but
there's still things that come out.
Z: Do you think there's a certain Navy standard of masculinity?
J: Kind of, but I think the Marines are more toward that. The Navy is kind
of, not so, because I've seen some pretty queeny sailors, and no one says
anything to them. I always liked [Navy men in] butch rates, like HTs and
engineers and [growls] Marines. Marines are my favorite. [Laughs.]
Z: What do you know about Marines?
J: Not much except they turn me on, a lot. The *Ranger* always had a
MARDET, Marine detachment. There was just something about them.

They were different. Butch. They wear those green camis and we wear tired dungarees. But Marines were elite. And their bodies, and the way that they're just so—manly. They'd always be [makes roaring sound] in each other's faces.

I got to know a few Marines, and they always treated me with respect. Partly because I outranked them. I was an E-4, they were E-2s and E-3s, and they'd always look up to me. Their corporals treat them like shit. I'm equivalent to a corporal, but I'm a petty officer, I'm Navy, and I love my Marines! No. [Laughs.] I always babied them, I gave them cigarettes. I'd always talk to them and feel the back of their heads.

Z: Marines like that.

J: Yeah. I'd always rub their bristle heads and pat 'em on the back, and they were telling me about their problems, their corporal being an asshole and all this stuff. I said, "I wish you worked for me, I'd treat you right." And I would. It wouldn't have to be sexual either.

People always say, if a really good-looking guy works for you you're going to give him special treatment. That's a tough one. Maybe I would, maybe I wouldn't, but when it came down to it I'd treat everybody fairly. I would be looking at him, but I'd make sure he would never know. I'm that type of person. I don't let my feelings out, unless he would to me first. But I wouldn't go after somebody if he was working for me. I'd admire him for his beauty, but I would never make direct approaches. I treat my job and my people professionally.

Z: Have you ever had sex with a Marine?

J: No. Well, kind of. There was a sergeant, he was an E-5, I was still an E-3 at the time. I caught him in the head jerkin' off. One of the main ones, the hole [in the partition between toilet stalls] was fuckin' huge, and there was all these other ones; it looked like somebody just took an Uzi to it [makes sound effect]. I mean. [Laughs.] But he was in there. He had a hairy chest, hairy legs. I love that on a man. And he was a Marine, and that turned me on even more. He noticed me too, and he reached around right away. I was like damn. OK!

Z: Do you find Marine uniforms erotic?

J: Mmm-hmm.

Z: What about the Navy uniforms?

J: Mmm-hmm.

Z: Which ones?

J: The crackerjacks. Whites or blues. Some dungarees, too. Just the ass and their cock when it's on tight. Mmm.

Z: The first time I saw those dungarees—

J: You thought they were so ugly.

Z: Yeah. But the more I studied them—because I was making a transition. When I first found myself attracted to military guys it was overseas, and it was to soldiers and airmen. Then when I came to California, I started to see sailors, and at first I wasn't sure how erotic I found their uniforms. The dungarees especially I had a hard time with. Because on a lot of guys they just sort of loosely hang. But then I began to see some men whose bodies they filled out beautifully, so that the sailors looked kind of like those bulgy Tom of Finland drawings. And I thought: this will work.

J: [Laughs.] They're comfortable. That's about the only thing I can say about the dungarees.

Z: How would you describe the sexual turn-on of the crackerjacks?

J: The anticipation: all those buttons that you have to go through! And then the tie. You can pull them by their neck and kiss them.

I have fantasies about Marines. And police officers, too. With handcuffs and everything. Just authority. A man in charge.

Z: What about officers' uniforms?

J: Yeah. Especially dress whites. Blues are alright, it looks kind of like a business suit, but I think the dress choker whites—that's a big turn-on.

Z: You don't have any tattoos. Did you ever think about getting one? It's a—

J: Navy thing. I think a lot of Marines get them too. But no, I never did it. I just thought, I might like it now, but what if I don't like it later? It is kind of a turn-on, a man with a tattoo. But I never felt it was necessary. And I wouldn't want people to look at me and say, "What's that supposed to mean?" Just leave me alone. I got inner tattoos. You know?

Z: Inner tattoos?

J: Scars or whatever. I think they make their own shape. If somebody wants to know me, I'd rather they know the inside, too. I've got lots of inner tattoos. But nothing on the outside.

Z: Tell me about the shellback initiation. I showed you the pictures I have for this book and you said, "I can still smell it."

J: It was disgusting. It was so fucking gross. I would never ever wanna go through it—well, certain things about it I'd want to go through again.

It was kind of funny. I love to have fun. I love getting silly, I don't care how childish it might seem. We had to put our uniforms on backwards, then we had to put our skivvies on backwards, and we had to wear a T-shirt with "WOG" on it. We had to put knee pads on, because we had to be on our hands and knees all day. Which was kind of kinky, too. Then there's all these men with—oh! A lot of [the shellbacks] had just boots on and short shorts or frayed cut-off shorts, and no shirt at all. And then they had like a pirate's handkerchief. They were just screaming at us like [makes pirate sound]. It was so awesome! God. I was sitting there smiling. I was getting off. I was hard a lot of the time, because these guys, they'd fucking pick you up, and get in your face, and go "You think it's funny, wog?" And you can see their—I was looking up, and I seen three guys' dicks just dangling out of their shorts. A lot of 'em didn't wear underwear. I noticed some hard-ons on some guys. And they were spanking us with these shillelaghs. The first couple times it hurt 'cause that shit would be wet, and the hose—they say you're supposed to take the rubber out but nobody did. But after a fucking few smacks my ass got numb, so I just got used to it. That, for me, was a turn-on. Not like I'm into being beat or anything, but it was just kinky getting spanked. And then just rubbing against everybody else. In the hangar bay they made us fuck each other. They said, "Get on him and fuck him and suck his dick!" They would fuckin' shove your head in some guy's crotch.

Z: Into another wog's crotch?

J: Yeah. "Act like you're sucking his dick!" And they'd rub your face in his crotch. That was such a turn-on, especially if the guy was really cute.

Z: Is the simulated fucking just between the wogs? Or do the shellbacks sometimes mount the wogs?

J: I've never seen no shellbacks jump in. They're there ordering you to do it with other wogs. They'd make you roll around with them and stuff. I'd be like, ohhhhhh! [Laughs.] I liked that part. And they'd have a whole train of guys fucking—[Laughs.] It was so funny! I mean, you'd sit there and be pounded on by somebody. And here the Navy says, no you [can't be gay]. I'm like, oh, this is really funny.

Then at the end, when we jumped in the shit—it's a big-ass vat and it's disgusting. You're supposed to be underneath the water, so I just swam and pulled up out, and they go, "What are you?" And if you say you're a shellback, you're done, but if you fuck up and say "I'm a wog," then you gotta go back. [Laughs.] I knew what was coming so of course I had the right response. Then you take off all your clothes and you get hosed off. Everybody's naked and undressing and they're throwing their clothes overboard, and everyone's just walking back, dicks swinging and everything, muscles and—mmm. [Nodding excitedly.] That was fun. That was fun.

Z: What about the wog queen competition? You didn't take part in that?

J: [Laughs.] I wanted to. I think I would've won. Because this guy that won was really tired. I was like, oh, this is through! He had a mop on his head. I was like, oh bitch! 'Cause I dressed like a woman for Halloween in high school, and I looked fine. I think I'd be a very pretty woman.

I should've went for wog queen, but fuck it. It would have raised questions. That's another thing I was scared about. "What would my division think about me?"

Z: What about the second time you went through the ceremony, just a few months ago: did you take advantage of being a shellback to order guys around?

J: [Pause.] I wanted to, but see, with Tailhook and with gays in the military and Clinton and all that other stuff—we didn't even have a lot of the same things. They could stand up. They weren't on their hands and knees at all. They could walk through it. All you could do was yell at 'em and pour food on 'em. You couldn't hit 'em. It sucked. It was not the same.

Z: How did the ceremony strike you the first time you went through it? Apart from being turned on, did you think about what the whole thing is supposed to mean?

J: The honest truth? When I thought about it, I thought: every tradition has some meaning behind it. They said, "This is centuries old," right? Well, when you think about sailors—I've had dreams about this, too. Maybe in one of my past lives . . . I think I was a sailor, long ago. Modern society downs homosexuality, outlaws it, bans it, but way long ago I don't think it was that big of an issue. I think it was a hush-hush thing, but I think that people still did it. Especially sailors at sea, like in the 1500s and 1600s? Even though they'd hit ports and they'd go with women, it was probably something new to them. Or they were attracted to women, too, but while they were at sea they always had their buddy.

Z: What do you base this on? Is this something that you've read about?

J: I don't know how I figured that out. Something inside me tells me that's how it was.

Z: So you thought of the shellback initiation as—what? A reference back to that?

J: Yeah. Long ago I think it was an excuse to, "We're crossing the line. Let's have a party." To those men who liked dick, it was a chance to get it on with somebody. And those of 'em that were kind of straight but curious, it was a time to party and get serious no matter what. But yeah, I think a lot of it represents what went on between men on ships back then. Maybe the whole thing wasn't totally homosexual, but I definitely find a strong homosexual background to parts of it. I bet the higher-ups that had been in for a while wanted to observe what the fresh meat was like. "Who's that? Let's study how he reacts to this." I think it was an initiation to see how far they could push somebody. And to humiliate those people that were assholes. And to maybe kind of hit on the guys they thought were cute.

Z: You said that when you first started coming out in Hillcrest that you were pretty promiscuous. What has your policy toward AIDS been? Do you always practice safer sex? Or sometimes not?

J: Well, to begin with, I don't let anybody fuck me at all. I've tried, but every time I've been safe. Except for one time at a bathhouse, just after this last WESTPAC. This guy, I thought he was cute, he had a real nice body and everything. So we had it going on. And I was like, "You can try it," because I was thinking about it more and more. It always crosses my mind. Everybody tells me, "It feels so good. You've just got to try it." And it's never felt good to me, ever. It always hurts. And I let this guy try. It was only for a couple seconds. I couldn't take it. But he didn't use a condom.

I found out later on that he was HIV positive. He didn't tell me. I was sitting there on the ship. I had duty, and I was watching the news, and he was on it. I said, "That guy looks a lot like" so and so. And then his story came on, how he'd been HIV positive for ten years. I know I turned pale. I was ready to pass out. I was by myself, and I was like—I wanted to scream. The sonofabitch! And he didn't say anything to me. Here he is on TV all happy that he's alive. I wanted to get a gun and fucking find him and assassinate him. Because that's horrible to do to somebody. Anybody who does that and doesn't tell anybody deserves to fucking die.

Z: But hopefully you learned your lesson, that you should assume that everybody you meet—

J: Is positive. That's how I look at it now. I know better now. Now I don't even think about anything anal. Some guys since then have asked me to fuck them, but I always wear a rubber. I don't even like doing it, but I will. Even more recently I haven't sucked as much dick. I used to, a lot. Because I love to do that. It's my favorite thing, to give a guy head. And have him come. But that's dangerous, too. So now, I try to stay away from it.

Z: You know that if you stop before they shoot you reduce your risk.

J: Yeah, but still. Lately a couple of times I've just jerked off with guys together. Because I'm too scared now. I found out another one of my close friends is HIV positive.

Z: So you were pretty choked up at the decommissioning ceremony Saturday?

J: Yeah, I was. I was. I'll always be a sailor at heart. It'll always be there with me until I die.

Z: How do you think the Navy ultimately affected your sexuality?

J: [Pause.] It brought it out. Hard. Uncle Sam just opened up that closet door! [Makes sound effect.] Grabbed me by my ear and dragged me out and said, "Stop being so fucking naive!" But some days I would get so depressed and drunk and everything that I would want to leave. I couldn't stand it. I hated myself. I didn't want to be here anymore. I said, look what this fuckin' shit did to me; it almost got me HIV positive. I'm not; I got tested. But the Navy exposed me to a lot of shit. I'm not gonna blame the Navy on it. It's not fair to say that the Navy did it to me. It was just the situations that I encountered through the Navy. The Navy didn't say, "Go down to Hillcrest, faggot." The Navy didn't say, "Suck his dick." It told me not to. I chose to do it. So it's not fair of me to say the Navy made me jump out of my closet. But it did. And I'm glad it happened.

I wish that some things could have been different. I wish I would have met that one special guy.

Preferably a Marine. No! [Laughs.]

Anthony (Coda)

This is the conclusion of my final interview with Anthony who soon afterward left San Diego for an overseas assignment.

Zeeland: Two weeks ago you drove me to my reading at A Different Light bookstore in West Hollywood. My audience was pretty friendly, and no one gave me a hard time, except you. You practically accused me of giving gays in the military a black eye by talking about sex so much, and thereby providing ammunition to those on the religious right who say that gays are shameless degenerates who would corrupt the moral fabric of our nation's youth. Why did you ask me that?

Anthony: Because it will cross people's minds. Here we are trying to fight a battle saying that homosexuals belong in the military and it's our civil right and we're just asking to be treated as equal, and that having homosexuals in the military is not going to damage morale or break up the cohesion of a unit. Congress' reply is that gay people are going to want to have sex with straight people. And in *Barrack Buddies and Soldier Lovers* there's lots of sex. Sex in the barracks and sex in the field, sex on top of—Where was it that mess cook had sex?

Z: But what about *this* book and *your* sex life? I'd like you to reconcile your remarks with how you think you should be perceived.

A: How should I be perceived? As a normal everyday gay sailor. I don't—and never have and never will—have sex at a duty station or on a ship. I think that that is dead wrong, and I think that anyone who does doesn't belong in the Navy.

Z: But you've had sex in your barracks room, and you've had it in a military building with an "A" school student who I later had the same pleasures with.

A: [Pause.] He wasn't on duty.

Z: He wasn't in his uniform?

A: He was in his uniform. He'd just gotten off duty.

Z: I'm sure the religious right will appreciate the distinction.

A: [Laughs.]

Z: In any event, you've told some sex stories that will be in this book. How do you think people should understand those stories?

A: They should just see it as filler.

Z: You don't attach any meaning to sex?

A: My sex life really has nothing to do with my professional life. So if you're going to look at me in a professional way as a sailor on duty at work, then sex has nothing to do with it. But if you're going to look at me as a sailor off duty on liberty, sex is a big part of my life.

Z: But your sex life is shaped by your military life: you're haunted by dreams that take place in boot camp. And you've talked about retraining as a corpsman so that you can be closer to Marines. You can't convince me that these are two utterly separate aspects of your life. They interpenetrate. That's why your sex stories are significant. [Pause.] Say "Yes, Uncle Steve."

A: [Laughs.]

Z: You have these different nicknames for me. If I call you at work I'm "Corporal Zeeland." Lately you've taken to calling me "Uncle Steve." And of course sometimes I'm "Superauthor." It's been kind of hard for me, sometimes, to be both your friend and your biographer. I've gotten closer to you than to any of the other people I've interviewed for either of my books, with the exception of Troy, and my reason for not including him is that I was too close to him. Your friendship with me has made your interviews less spontaneous than the others. I cue you and you recite rehearsed bits. And, to be frank, it's also become increasingly difficult for me to chronicle your sexual escapades. . . . To a degree I am able, as some readers will be able, to take a certain vicarious pleasure in—

A: [Looks at watch.] [Laughs.]

Z: I guess what I'm saying is that I'd like to quit playing Superauthor to you. I'd like to go on being your friend, but this book is done. I'm tired of playing the observer.

A: Well then you should go out more often and have fun.

Z: I hate going out to clubs—

A: Because you go and you observe! You should go out and not work, and just talk to people, and not be interested in interviewing them, just talk to them. And work your way into their bedroom.

Z: [Laughs.] We do have a special relationship. When I tell people about my work, you always chime in and say, "This book is entirely about me!"

A: I'm just joking. I'll be extremely flattered if my interview even makes it in the book. I mean, I think it's too sexual.

Z: You think your interview is too sexual?

A: There's just too much sex in there.

Z: Why?

A: I think that people reading this book are not going to be looking for sex stories. They're going to be looking for some deep psychological explanations as to why sailors have this reputation of being rowdy and rambunctious sex-starved squids.

Z: Your stories validate that reputation.

A: True, but I don't think people are going to be interested in reading about me in a hot tub with four Marines, or me having versatile sex with a Marine Corps officer. They're gonna be interested in knowing why.

Z: So why?

A: You're the superauthor. You tell them.

Z: One last question. I've spent a lot of time with you over this last year. And you're right, whenever I go out to a club I invariably end up listening to somebody's story. I've expended a lot of energy trying to figure out sailors and Marines. What things might I have gotten wrong after all this time? What misconceptions do you secretly think I might have formed from my necessarily somewhat removed viewpoint?

A: [Pause.] [Sighs.] That we want to be written about. I think that the majority of us would just prefer to go on with our lives quietly and not have books written about us. It's fun and everything, but. I don't like the whole "military chaser" notion. I hate it when people come to me and the first question they ask me is, "Are you in the Navy?" I invariably, time and time again, say "No, I'm from L.A. I'm not in the military, I just have this haircut." Then they go away, because I'm not in the military, therefore I don't fulfill a fantasy for them. It annoys me and it bothers me that people have this fantasy—I don't even understand what it is about the military that people respond to. True, the majority of the men I've been with lately are in the military, but I think I'm just looking for my own kind.

Z: There will be people reading your words who have purchased this book for just that reason. What do you say to people who you have purposely teased with titillating little details of your sex life?

A: I haven't teased anyone.

Z: Yes, you have.

A: I was asked questions and I answered them honestly. You wanted dirt, I gave it to you.

Z: So the answer to this question is:

A: I think these people should get a life.

Z: Do you have anything else to add, before I shut off the tape recorder for the last time?

A: I was going to talk about President Clinton and this whole gays in the military thing. But, I mean, it's pointless.

Reference Notes

Prologue

1. Anne Briscoe Pye and Nancy Shea, *The Navy Wife*, (New York: Harper, 1942), p. 133.

Introduction

1. Melissa Healy and Karen Tumulty, "Aides Say Clinton to End Prosecution of Military's Gays"; David Lauter, "Clash with Nunn Becomes Test of Power for Clinton"; and Art Pine, "Issue Explodes Into an All-Out Lobbying War," *Los Angeles Times*, January 28, 1993, all p. 1.

2. Colonel Ronald D. Ray, USMCR, *Military Necessity & Homosexuality*, (Louisville, KY: First Principles, 1993), p. 77. According to its back cover, this book ". . . Reveals the truth about the deception, disinformation and the motives behind the larger agenda of the homosexual movement: to force acceptance of their 'lifestyle' through the military and subvert or overturn the principles on which America was founded and which have made America the most prosperous nation on earth." Colonel Ray's book is a wacky catalog of homo and erotophobia. "Almost all homosexuals engage in sexual practices which are inherently degrading or humiliating and are rarely practiced by heterosexuals." As examples, Colonel Ray cites anal sex, fellatio, and cunnilingus. Ray seems genuinely unaware that heterosexuals might ever know these pleasures, and unwittingly provides the book's most humorous moment when he tells us about mutual masturbation, "Alone or with a friend it is considered very 'hot.'" (p. 34.)

3. "Our abhorrence of assault and murder, regardless of the circumstance, is consonant with abhorrence of a lifestyle that condones aberrant physical behavior." Commander John M. Yunker, U.S. Navy (Retired), *Proceedings*, April 1993, p. 98.

4. On October 27, 1992, U.S. Navy Seaman Allen R. Schindler, 22, was beaten to death in Sasebo, Japan. Airman Apprentice Terry M. Helvey was convicted of murdering his shipmate and sentenced to life in

prison. Airman Charles A. Vins was convicted on lesser charges and served only four months in the brig.

"Schindler . . . died after being battered and mutilated in a public park rest-room in Sasebo, Japan; the beating left his penis slashed, every major organ damaged, his ribs cracked, and his face unrecognizable. His mother, Dorothy Hajdys of Chicago Heights, Ill., said she was able to identify him only by tattoos on his arms. . . . The Navy has denied activists' claims that it tried to camouflage the possibility that the killing was a hate crime. Some activists also have said the case underscores pervasive hostility toward gays and lesbians in the military. . . . " "Charges Filed in Gay Sailor's Death," *The Advocate*, March 9, 1993, p. 33.

"Some reports have quoted [Schindler] . . . as telling friends and his mother that harassment and threats had made the *Belleau Wood* into 'Helleau Wood' for him. But those reports appeared to surprise some of the ship's crew, who had not seen American TV or newspapers since the vessel put out to sea. . . . 'It's not the problem of a ship. It's just a problem of two rednecks who beat up a gay,' said a medical corpsman. . . . Sailors from the *Belleau Wood* as well as other 7th Fleet ships in port here all said they are aware that homosexuals are aboard their ships and said that, for the most part, they cause little trouble. . . . Dave Lippman, 30, of Hoboken, N.J., a sailor stationed at Sasebo with an administrative job who asked that his rank be withheld said . . . many in the Navy are prepared to accept gays, as long as they uphold the Navy's standards of conduct at work. But 'many youths enter the Navy from small towns where they've never met blacks, gays or any ethnic group. The only thing most of them know about gays is from some gag they've heard on a TV comedy show. . . . I knew gays in New York, and my last roommate here was gay. I had no problem with them.'" Sam Jameson, "Crew Calls Gay Sailor's Killing Isolated Incident," *Los Angeles Times*, February 16, 1993, p. A18.

5. "While gays who have been thrown out of the military will testify along with advocacy groups, one group of witnesses that almost certainly will not appear before Nunn's committee will be the gay men and lesbians who now serve in the armed forces. . . . Few of what gay activists believe to be thousands of homosexuals serving in the military have been willing to reveal themselves. They neither will be able to champion their own causes nor show viewers of the hearings the faces of gay men and women serving in uniform." "Nunn to Set Debate Terms," *Los Angeles Times*, March 29, 1993, p. A25-A26.

"When facing the microphones and television lights of reporters who accompanied the senators, most sailors and officers voiced the popular military view that allowing declared homosexuals would harm the services. . . . [But] in conversations away from the senators' spotlight, sailors said that in the end they would obey President Clinton's [proposed] policy perhaps grudgingly, and not leave in droves. . . . Petty Officer Gilberry and other heterosexual sailors said that the false stereotype of gay people as promiscuous fans the fears of many service members, particularly men. 'A lot of the problem is that many people have never met any gays.' " Eric Schmitt, "Gay Shipmates? Senators Listen as Sailors Talk," *The New York Times*, May 11, 1993, p. 1. This article appeared beneath the Jose R. Lopez photo (Figure 1) captioned "Senators John Warner, right, and Sam Nunn interviewed, from left, Chad Gillman, William Peters and Paul Gilberry aboard the *Montpelier*."

"There, with one photo opportunity, supporters of the ban had pushed all the emotional buttons they could. 'Protect us from these perverts,' is the way David M. Smith, the [Campaign for Military Service's] media director, sums up the image. 'We felt overwhelmed,' recalled Thomas Stoddard, who directed the campaign, a coalition of groups that banded together last winter to lobby for an end to the gay ban. . . . 'We were peddling our little bicycle up the mountainside and the big bus of the federal government ran us off the road.' " Bettina Boxall, "Gay, Lesbian Leaders See Silver Lining in Military Defeat," *Los Angeles Times*, July 21, 1993, p. A8.

Eric Schmitt, "Compromise on Military Gay Ban Gaining Support Among Senators," *The New York Times*, May 12, 1993, p.1.

6. "What is clear is that the military is far less concerned with having no homosexuals in the service than with having people think there are no homosexuals in the service." Randy Shilts, *Conduct Unbecoming: Gays & Lesbians in the U.S. Military,* (New York: St. Martin's Press), 1993, p. 6.

7. Thomas L. Friedman, "Chiefs Back Clinton on Gay-Troop Plan," *The New York Times*, July 20, 1993, p. 1., and Richard L. Berke, "Clinton in Crossfire: Compromise on the Military's Gay Ban Comes Under Attack From Both Sides," p. 14.

" '[The new policy] removes an element of uncertainty, an element of friction, an element of tension that has, frankly, reduced some of the readiness of the force in recent months,' said Gen. Colin L. Powell, chairman of the Joint Chiefs." Karen Tumulty, "Joint Chiefs Defend Clinton's New Policy," *Los Angeles Times*, July 21, 1993, p. 1.

"Mr. Clinton's compromise, allowing homosexuals to serve but only if they keep their sexual orientation private, differs only marginally from existing policy, and bows to the chiefs' insistence that open homosexuality could never be tolerated. . . . The chiefs say open homosexuality would undermine discipline and combat readiness, and simply could not fit the military culture. [An alternate proposal by the Rand Corporation], a conservatively oriented group with longstanding ties to the military, suggested that the obstacle might have been neither the lack of a practical option nor the universal opposition of those familiar with military life, but rather the resistance of the six Joint Chiefs." Eric Schmitt, "Pentagon Keeps Silent on Rejected Gay Troop Plan," *The New York Times*, July 23, 1993, p. 7.

8. David Gelman, "Homoeroticism in the Ranks. Gays: The Clinton Administration's Compromise Covers Up an Uncomfortable Truth," *Newsweek*, July 26, 1993, p. 28.

9. Photo by D. Gatley, *Proceedings*, April 1993, p. 96.

10. Naval Military Personnel Manual (Article 3630400), quoted by Captain Philip Adams, USMCR, in "We Are Here to Stay," *Proceedings*, April 1993, p. 92.

11. Ruth Hubbard, "False Genetic Markers," *The New York Times*, August 2, 1993, p. 11. See also John P. De Cecco, PhD and John P. Elia, MA, PhD (cand.), "A Critique and Synthesis of Biological Essentialism and Social Constructionist Views of Sexuality and Gender," *If You Seduce a Straight Person Can You Make Them Gay?* (Binghamton, NY: The Haworth Press, 1993), pp. 1-25.

12. Shilts, *Conduct Unbecoming*, p. 44.

13. Ibid., p. 401, 402, 406.

Two statements of fact in *Conduct Unbecoming* are contradicted by my findings:

"For males as well as for females, going to sea was usually the prime reason for joining the Navy" (p. 268). This was a reason for only three of the 30 sailors I interviewed, most of whom came from economic backgrounds that did not afford them the luxury of such a romantic consideration.

"Homosexual men and women in the military . . . generally avoided the separatism so common among their civilian counterparts. The Family was co-sexual on bases throughout the world" (p. 536). Unfortunately, the gay military communities of both Frankfurt, Germany and San Diego mirror the rigid separation between gays and lesbians found in urban civilian communities. While some of them were married to lesbians, only a few of the men interviewed for this book said they had close friendships with lesbians.

14. George Chauncey, Jr., "Christian Brotherhood or Sexual Perversion? Homosexual Identities and the Construction of Sexual Boundaries in the World War I Era," in *Hidden from History*, ed. Martin Duberman, Martha Vicinus, and George Chauncey, Jr., (New York: Dutton, 1989),

pp. 297,305. See also Lawrence R. Murphy, *Perverts by Official Order: The Campaign Against Homosexuals by the U.S. Navy,* (Binghamton, NY: The Haworth Press, 1988).

15. Ibid, p. 295,307,308.

16. "There seems to be several sources for the traditional connection between men of the sea and homosexuality. Sea voyages frequently used to last a year or more, and a crew's freedom in distant ports was highly restricted. This led to the popular idea that men were thus more or less forced toward homosexual practices. But modern data from prison populations indicate that even where homosexuality is very high (71 percent of long-term inmates) it is 'new' for only 4 percent of the participants; the rest had it in their histories before becoming isolated. Thus there is some indication that many men who chose a life at sea did not mind isolation from women. Furthermore, lost in the censored pages of history is a long tradition of homosexuality at sea. The Spanish galleons, for instance, had a spelled-out code of *matelotage* which specified the amount of sexual freedom and fidelity of all men who 'belonged' to each other during a voyage; it was an attempt to control fierce jealousies and maintain better order aboard ship." C. A. Tripp, *The Homosexual Matrix,* (New York: McGraw-Hill, 1975), p. 222-223.

17. Crisp also describes the appeal of sailor's uniforms: "The fabulous generosity in their natures was an irresistible lure—especially when combined with the tightness of their uniforms, whose crowning aphrodisiac feature was the fly-flap of their trousers. More than one of my friends has swayed about in ecstasy describing the pleasures of undoing this quaint sartorial device." He might just as easily have been talking about the 13-button fly on American sailors' dress blues. Quentin Crisp, *The Naked Civil Servant,* (New York: Holt, Rinehart, Winston, 1968), pp. 90-91.

18. Allan Bérubé, *Coming Out Under Fire: The History of Gay Men and Women in World War Two,* (New York: Plume, 1991), pp. 110-111.

19. See "Can Clinton Make the Navy Any *More* Gay?" *Spy,* March 1993, p. 46-55; "For Abusive Rituals, the Party May Be Over," *Navy Times,* December 21, 1992, p. 19. From a letter to the author from a Navy chief petty officer charged with consensual sodomy after being caught kissing another man aboard ship: "What I don't understand is, why? If you've ever heard of shellbacks and wogs you'll know that prior to the ceremony the ship has various men dress in drag trying to win the title of 'Queen Wog' and they kiss a panel of judges on the cheek. What's the difference?"

20. The stereotype that "all Marines are bottoms" is a staple in military-themed gay porn. "Marines, like dogs, need to know who is master

before they can be really happy." Rick Jackson, "Body Search," *Horndog Squids and Cherry Marines*, (Teaneck, NJ: First Hand Books, 1992), p. 117.

21. Lilian Faderman, *Odd Girls and Twilight Lovers: A History of Lesbian Life in Twentieth-Century America*, (New York: Columbia University Press, 1991), p. 116.

22. "Heterosexuals are uncomfortable around homosexuals because they do create a threat. A former shipmate of mine was approached in the shower aboard ship by a homosexual. Eight guys were caught by the Marine sentry engaged in a daisy chain on the 0-8 level bridge. Two sailors were caught in a stall in the head after taps. This all happened on one six-month cruise to the Persian Gulf. I know: I assisted with the discharge/brig physicals. . . . I would like to see more heterosexual service members speak out to create a gay impermeable military." Michael Stafford, HM2 (SW), USN, letter to *Navy Times*, November 9, 1992, p. 34. Compare the punishment apparently meted out to the daisy chain gang with that given to two heterosexuals caught flagrente delicto aboard ship: "Two sailors have been reprimanded for videotaping their sexual acts while serving on the *Samuel Gompers*. The repair ship was at sea when a male sailor set up a video camera in a secured area Jan. 23 and performed sexual acts with a female crew member. . . . The woman, unaware she was being videotaped, told the captain about the incident. The sailors, whose identities were being withheld, received nonjudicial punishment. . . . Both are still serving on the ship." "Filming Sex on Ship Nets Reprimand," *Navy Times*, March 8, 1992, p. 2.

23. Kevin M. McCrane, "A Proposal," *Proceedings*, April 1993, p. 100.

24. John Waters, *Crackpot*, (New York:Macmillan, 1986), p. 67.

Sonny

1. Marshall Kirk and Hunter Madsen, *After the Ball: How America Will Conquer Its Fear and Hatred of Homosexuals in the 90s,* (New York: Doubleday, 1989), p. 309-311.

2. Ibid., p. 14.

Anthony

1. Edmund White, *States of Desire: Travels in Gay America*, (New York: Dutton, 1980) p.14.